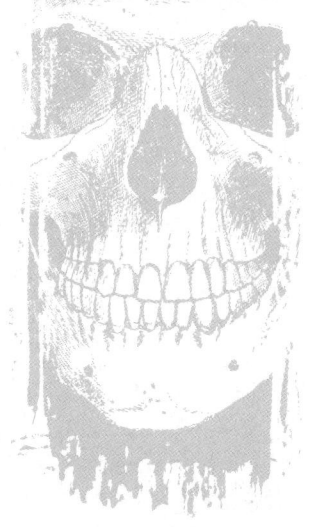

THE ESSENTIAL HORROR OF JOE R. LANSDALE

T0400693

"Prepare to be disturbed, grossed out, and laugh all at the same time. Joe R. Lansdale pulls you through the meat-grinder time after time with these stories, and his hand is always steady on that crank. I'm pretty sure he's smiling with each turn, too."
— Stephen Graham Jones, author of *The Buffalo Hunter Hunter*

"Lansdale is a genre unto himself and has left an indelible mark on American literature. He has deservedly earned a place in the halls alongside Twain, Poe, Faulkner, Hemingway, Steinbeck, King, and the other greats."
— Brian Keene, bestselling author and World Horror Society's Grand Master Award winner

"Lansdale is a legend, and this collection is proof positive of that."
— Chuck Wendig, bestselling author of *The Staircase in the Woods*

"Joe R. Lansdale's storytelling combines unflinching brutality, two-fisted weirdness, and sarcastic humor, while delivering it to the reader with a distinctly Texas twang."
— Nancy A. Collins, author of *Sunglasses After Dark*

"If he'd only written a single horror story, Joe Lansdale would be remembered for it. Instead, he created a body of work almost unmatched in horror fiction, all in a voice so distinctive, you recognize it immediately."
— Derek Austin Johnson, author of *The Faith*

"This collection of [Lansdale's] most terrifying stories is a must-have for anyone who loves well-wrought nightmares. The tales range from the brutal to the surreal to the tragic. . . . Grab a copy, but leave the lights on when you're finished."
— Richard Kadrey, author of the *Sandman Slim* series

"Legendary storyteller Joe R. Lansdale showcases his relentless versatility, raw and fearless imagination, and signature craftsmanship in this quintessential gateway into the dark heart of Lansdale's horror."
— Sadie Hartmann, Bram Stoker Award–winning author of *101 Horror Books to Read Before You're Murdered*

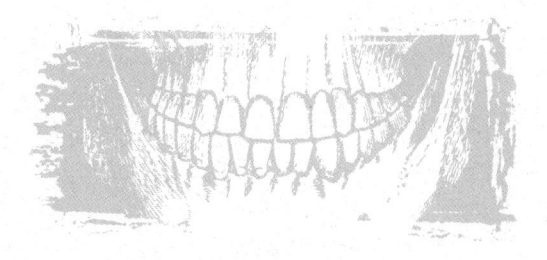

To my readers, in appreciation.

THE ESSENTIAL HORROR OF

JOE R. LANSDALE

TACHYON

Cover art by Dave McKean
Cover design by Elizabeth Story
Interior layout by John Coulthart

Tachyon Publications
1459 18th Street #139
San Francisco, CA 94107
415.285.5615
www.tachyonpublications.com
tachyon@tachyonpublications.com

Series Editor: Jacob Weisman
Editor: Richard Klaw

Print ISBN: 978-1-61696-446-7
Digital ISBN: 978-1-61696-447-4

Printed in the United States by Versa Press, Inc.

First Edition: 2025
9 8 7 6 5 4 3 2 1

SELECTED WORKS BY JOE R. LANSDALE

HAP AND LEONARD

Savage Season (1990)
Mucho Mojo (1994)
The Two-Bear Mambo (1995)
Bad Chili (1997)
Rumble Tumble (1998)
Veil's Visit: A Taste of Hap and Leonard
    (with Andrew Vachss, 1999)
Captains Outrageous (2001)
Vanilla Ride (2009)
Hyenas (2011)
Devil Red (2011)
Dead Aim (2013)
Honky Tonk Samurai (2016)
Hap and Leonard (2016)
Rusty Puppy (2017)
Blood and Lemonade (2017)
The Big Book of Hap and Leonard (2018)
Jack Rabbit Smile (2018)
The Elephant of Surprise (2019)
Of Mice and Minestrone (2020)
Born for Trouble (2021)
Sugar in the Bones (2024)
Hatchet Girls (2025)

OTHER NOVELS

Act of Love (1981)
Dead in the West (1986)
The Magic Wagon (1986)
The Nightrunners (1987)
The Drive-In (1988)
Cold in July (1989)
Batman: Captured by the Engines (1991)
Tarzan: The Lost Adventure
    (with Edgar Rice Burroughs, 1995)
The Boar (1998)
Freezer Burn (1999)
Waltz of Shadows (1999)
The Big Blow (2000)

The Bottoms (2000)
A Fine Dark Line (2002)
Sunset and Sawdust (2004)
Lost Echoes (2007)
Leather Maiden (2008)
Flaming Zeppelins (2010)
All the Earth, Thrown to Sky (2011)
Edge of Dark Water (2012)
The Thicket (2013)
Paradise Sky (2015)
Fender Lizards (2015)
Bubba and the Cosmic Bloodsuckers (2017)
Jane Goes North (2020)
More Better Deals (2020)
Moon Lake (2021)
Donut Legion (2022)

COLLECTIONS

By Bizarre Hands (1989)
Electric Gumbo (1994)
Writer of the Purple Rage (1994)
High Cotton (2000)
Bumper Crop (2004)
Mad Dog Summer and Other Stories (2004)
The Shadows, Kith and Kin (2007)
Sanctified and Chicken Fried (2009)
The Best of Joe R. Lansdale (2010)
Bleeding Shadows (2013)
Miracles Ain't What They Used to Be (2016)
Terror Is Our Business
    (with Kasey Lansdale, 2018)
Driving to Geronimo's Grave
    and Other Stories (2018)
Things Get Ugly (2023)
The Senior Girls Bayonet Drill Team
    and Other Stories (2024)
In the Mad Mountains: Stories Inspired by
    H. P. Lovecraft (2025)

CONTENTS

ICE WATER IN HELL:
An Introduction to the
Essential Horror of Joe Lansdale
by JOE HILL

T IS COMMON enough, in these sorts of introductions, to begin with the comparisons, placing the subject among the ranks of other literary stars. "Franklin F. Fring works in the bare-knuckled, sweaty-balled tradition of Mickey Spillane and Richard Prather." "With his latest goblin-packed epic, Sven R. R. Hørstbörg joins such legends of fantasy as George R. R. Martin and J. R. R. Tolkien in having far too many *R*s in the middle of his name."

We'll have to bypass that kind of thing here. It ain't gonna work.

I was only thirteen when I read my first Lansdale. Was that too young? Maybe for some kids, but not for *this* kid. *Nightmare on Elm Street* was my idea of comfort viewing, and I had a vampire bat in a Lucite block on my desk (no one would sell a thing like that now, and no one would buy it either). I had already worked my way through all of Lovecraft and everything Clive Barker had published. One afternoon, my dad said, "Check this one out," and tossed me a slim paperback copy of *The Drive-In*. I pounded it down in a single day, one sitting, something I have only done with three other books: Peter Benchley's *Jaws*, John D. MacDonald's *A Nightmare in Pink*, and Rex Miller's *Slob*. When I was done, I couldn't have told you what the fuck just hit me. *The Drive-In* was both shocking and ridiculous, like being run down by the clowns in their tiny neon-bright clown car: You're laughing right up until the tires go over you. Then, when you're screaming in the road, all the clowns pile out to finish the job by kicking you to death with their big silly clown shoes.

I had to read another one right away, and I did: *The Nightrunners*. That one got me even harder. No clowns here, but it still felt like a hit-and-run. *The Nightrunners* appalled and gripped in equal measure. It was as fascinating as watching a drop of blood slide down the edge of a mirror-bright straight razor.

What struck me then—and what is even clearer to me now—is that Lansdale's stories were so radically unlike anything else anyone was doing in the genre, it was like he was a painter deploying an entirely new palette. Other painters were working with blues, with yellows, with reds. Joe was painting with leaded gasoline, shitty beer, ruptured organs, mothers' tears. He was painting in shades of fury and scorn. The stories in this book here ring with laughter, but it's a sickened, angry laughter, the disgusted laughter of the man who has watched someone from the Ku Klux Klan light his spotless white robes on fire with his own tiki torch.

In so many stories of terror, a Joe Normal of some sort—a bland everyman with a bland blond wife and bland blond children who say blandly adorable things—encounters a life-threatening species of derangement. His car breaks down, he walks to a nearby house to ask for help, and the man who answers the door is wearing a mask of human skin. The unnatural pierces the flesh of the everyday world like a needle full of rabies.

But in Joe Lansdale's work, where the hero is just as likely to be a geriatric Elvis with a pus-filled lesion on his dick, derangement is the world's natural state. The patient already has rabies and hardly cares if you inject him with more. A bland everyman isn't driving the car—the man behind the wheel is a bounty hunter off to collect a bad man from a strip club where the naked ladies are moldering reanimated corpses. The bland blond wife is a horny evangelical about to leave her husband for a manipulative sociopath. The bland blond little kids are taking a dead dog for a walk (or is that a drag?). Joe Lansdale don't do Joe Normal. Maybe he can't. Maybe he's never met Joe Normal and so lacks the capacity to write about him. I think probably Lansdale is on to something there—come to think of it, I've never met Joe Normal either. I'm not sure he exists. Which raises the question of why so many authors keep writing about him. Well, put it aside.

I am trying and failing to express something about the thrilling freshness of Joe Lansdale's voice and the bracing, sometimes punishing intensity of feeling in these stories. And I have not even mentioned the way they seem to leap from zero to a hundred-and-twenty mph in just a couple of paragraphs, often right on the first page. *The Essential Horror of Joe R. Lansdale* opens with a road race in "The Folding Man," and the narrative is pedal-to-the-floor from the first line to the final sentence. When was the last time a short story moved so fast it made you feel short of breath?

"On the Far Side of the Cadillac Desert with Dead Folk" is a mini-novel that plays like an insane mash-up of *Escape from New York* and *28 Days Later*, and its gonzo reimagining of a certain theme park very much anticipates the work of George Saunders. The sprawling cast of characters includes an army of zombies dressed in black caps with big round mouse ears on them. It's impossible not to see in that image a commentary about the American impulse to gorge ourselves on the canned, overpriced entertainments offered by our various destination adventure parks. (It makes me think of the bit in *Dawn of the Dead* when the two SWAT agents are looking down at the zombies roaming the shopping mall. "Why do they come here?" asks one. "This place was important to them," the other tells him, ruefully.)

The best work here, by my lights, is "Mister Weed-Eater," a story that should've won an O. Henry prize, and maybe would've, if it had been published in the right market—*Harper's* or *The New Yorker*. A blind man has been hired to mow the lawn behind a church, and the guy living across the street is badgered into helping him, and it turns out that no good deed goes unpunished. The abuse heaped upon our narrator—one shovelful of shit after another—is a masterclass in piling comic incident atop comic incident.

"Mister Weed-Eater" is comedy so acidic, you could use it like lye to disintegrate a corpse. That sort of humor is a Lansdale specialty, which makes his occasional turn toward tenderness all the more unexpected and jolting. "Not from Detroit" would've made one hell of an *Amazing Stories* episode (and almost was one) and has a sorrow about it, and a sweetness, that brings to mind the melancholy of Depression-era big-band blues. And then there's "Fish Night," which is like nothing else Lansdale has ever written and feels so luminous, so lovely and surreal, it almost had to be animated—and was, for a memorable episode of *Love, Death & Robots*.

But don't go expecting to find much gentleness here. The language is raw and rawer ("the old diddlebopper was no longer a flesh cannon loaded for bare ass," Elvis reflects mournfully, looking under his hospital johnny at his ancient prick). Writers are often admonished to write what they know. What Joe Lansdale knew when he wrote these stories was a violent, clueless, reckless, racist Southwest. It was shocking to read about the people in these stories then and has become even more shocking to read about them now. (But people in East Texas and the Southern Bottoms really did talk this way. And, yes, here I am referring to the *N*-word. These stories are full of wild leaps into fantasy, but when Joe depicts the casual, nasty, commonplace bigotry of the West, I know that he is simply telling us the truth about what he saw and heard and grew up with. Is it better to know or not to know? It was so much worse than you might imagine, and that past was not very long ago at all. It was the violent racism, and it was the violent sexism too. I went to Fenway Park in the early 1980s, and in the late innings, they'd blow up a nudie doll out in the bleachers and bat it around. Sometimes, a man would snatch the doll out of the air and punch her in the face a bunch of times, and people would *ROAR* with approval. Because it was funny, see? Pretending to beat up a naked woman in front of a crowd of thirty thousand people? Hilarious, right? This is the country that was and maybe not-so-secretly still is, and Joe Lansdale has always depicted its spirit unflinchingly.)

The most unsparing of these stories have in them a darkness as deep as anything one will find in Cormac McCarthy's *Blood Meridian*, but with none of McCarthy's high-flying Faulknerian language to pretty it up for readers. I found myself actively distressed while reading the last tale, a story that offers no kindness or relief at all (it won the Bram Stoker Award for short fiction in 1988 and is the only story here that I almost can't quite manage—and that's not criticism or praise, just an acknowledgment that it goes as dark as a story can go). I will only circle back to where I began: Joe Lansdale wrote a lot of these stories in anger. He was angry that the country boys he knew didn't want to see a movie where a Black man was a tragic hero. Lansdale seems to be saying that if they can't find it in themselves to appreciate a Black man risking his skin for theirs, then they can hurry up and die right next him. It's still a hard one for me.

Some writers of horror fiction will take you to the edge, but Joe Lansdale usually leaves the edge behind by page 2. He runs right over it, like the

Roadrunner leaving Wile E. Coyote behind, and somehow sprints across thin air to the far side of the chasm. Here are his darkest, funniest, and most savage stories: his refreshments from hell. (When I hear that phrase, I think of that old aphorism, "People in hell want ice water." Joe Lansdale opens the door on a variety of hells in this book, but he's much better company than Old Scratch. There's definitely beer where we're going: Texas longnecks.)

I've given you sixteen hundred words, doing my damnedest to describe Joe Lansdale's work to you—trying to capture the fierceness, the originality, and the blunt emotional force of these tales. But I didn't really need sixteen hundred words to tell you about his work. One will do:

Incomparable.

Joe Hill
Exeter, New Hampshire
January 2025

INTRODUCTION by JOE R. LANSDALE

THIS BOOK, *The Essential Horror of Joe R. Lansdale*, is focused on horror. And even then, certain stories might fit into a crime collection or a Southern Gothic collection, fantasy, science fiction, you name it. Fact is, a few have the furniture of horror, but not necessarily the same intent. Some have the furniture from many forms of storytelling, but in the end, I think of them as Lansdale stories. I really prefer that to pure genre labels. I work in all forms, but at the same time, they are all my stories and have my imprint on them.

But to simplify this, these are stories I'm proud of and eager to put in front of you. They vary, a lot. And that's why I'm proud of them. One story is not necessarily supposed to remind you of another, though my tone of voice is present in all of them.

All I can really say is, come on in. The table is set. We have a chair with your name on it, and the table is all set with refreshments from hell.

Enjoy.

There was an old folk tale about the Dark Man who came around on certain nights of the year, Halloween being a prime one, and stole away children or teenagers. Sometimes, the Dark Man didn't kidnap them, he killed them.

Considering where the Dark Man might be taking them, some lost place grim and beyond our understanding, maybe that was best.

I was asked by Ellen Datlow, an active anthologist and old friend, to contribute a story for her anthology *Haunted Legends*. The idea was to find some sort of legend, a piece of folklore, and turn it into a modern story.

This appealed to me in a big way. I grew up with storytellers, many of them like my grandmother, who had tales from way back. She was born in the late 1800s and was nearly a hundred years old when she died.

Unlike a lot of her grandchildren, I wanted to hear those stories. I was a kind of magpie when it came to collecting stories. She had actually seen Buffalo Bill in some form of his Wild West Show when she was a child, and had come to Texas in a covered wagon, and told of seeing Indians camped along creeks and rivers while traveling.

She also told me stories about mysterious miniature creatures that lived in the dark. Pesky little leprechauns, perhaps, or sprites. They stole things, and like the Dark Man, sometimes they stole children.

She told me a tale about a water witch that I barely remember, and she also told me a story that fit in with the Dark Man who came around on those certain spooky nights.

In her story, he rode in a black buggy, or sometimes he rode a black horse. Perhaps his buggy was in the shop.

As time went on, I heard this story from other sources, or read about it, and in some he was a walker, in others a horse rider, and in some he drove a black car. The thing was not to engage with him if he should drive up beside you and call your name.

I wanted to use that basic idea, but I wanted to take it in a new direction. I wanted a dark car full of nuns, although their religion was of a different nature than the nuns we are familiar with.

They ride the roads and backways on Halloween night, and it is certainly best to avoid them. They have a strange assistant that helps them do their evil deeds; its existence was inspired by my time working at a folding lawn chair company in my youth, as you will see.

This is in many ways a campfire story. It has the same feel as those kinds of stories about the Dark Man—though this time it isn't a man, and it's more than one, and they are Dark Side Nuns with a unique approach to terminal mischief.

A tip: Do not, I repeat, do *not* moon nuns on a dark Halloween Night. The humor you seek may turn sour on you.

The Folding Man
(Based on the
Black Car Legend)

THEY HAD COME from a Halloween party, having long shed the masks they'd worn. No one but Harold had been drinking, and he wasn't driving, and he wasn't so drunk he was blind. Just drunk enough he couldn't sit up straight and was lying on the backseat, trying, for some unknown reason, to recite the Pledge of Allegiance, which he didn't accurately recall. He was mixing in verses from "The Star-Spangled Banner" and the Boy Scout oath, which he vaguely remembered from his time in the organization before they drove him out for setting fires.

Even though William, who was driving, and Jim, who was riding shotgun, were sober as Baptists claimed to be, they were fired up and happy and yelling and hooting, and Jim pulled down his pants and literally mooned a black bug of a car carrying a load of nuns.

The car wasn't something that looked as if it had come off the lot. Didn't have the look of any carmaker Jim could identify. It had a cobbled look. It reminded him of something in old movies, the ones with gangsters who were always squealing their tires around corners. Only it seemed bigger, with broader windows through which he could see the nuns, or at least glimpse them in their habits; it was a regular penguin convention inside that car.

Way it happened, when they came up on the nuns, Jim said to William at the wheel, "Man, move over close, I'm gonna show them some butt."

"They're nuns, man."

"That's what makes it funny," Jim said.

William eased the wheel to the right, and Harold in the back said, "Grand Canyon. Grand Canyon. Show them the Grand Canyon. . . . Oh, say can you see. . . ."

Jim got his pants down, swiveled on his knees in the seat, twisted so that his ass was against the glass, and just as they passed the nuns, William hit the electric window switch and slid the glass down. Jim's ass jumped out at the night, like a vibrating moon.

"They lookin'?" Jim asked.

"Oh, yeah," William said, "and they are not amused."

Jim jerked his pants up, shifted in the seat, and turned for a look, and sure enough, they were not amused. Then a funny thing happened, one of the nuns shot him the finger, and then others followed. Jim said, "Man, those nuns are rowdy."

And now he got a good look at them, even though it was night, because there was enough light from the headlights as they passed for him to see faces hard as wardens and ugly as death warmed over. The driver was especially homely, face like that could stop a clock and run it backwards or make shit crawl uphill.

"Did you see that, they shot me the finger?" Jim said.

"I did see it," William said.

Harold had finally gotten "The Star-Spangled Banner" straight, and he kept singing it over and over.

"For Chrissake," William said. "Shut up, Harold."

"You know what," Jim said, studying the rearview mirror, "I think they're speeding up. They're trying to catch us. Oh, hell. What if they get the license plate? Maybe they already have. They call the law, my dad will have my mooning ass."

"Well, if they haven't got the plate," William said, "they won't. This baby can get on up and get on out."

He put his foot on the gas. The car hummed as if it had just had an orgasm, and seemed to leap. Harold was flung off the backseat, onto the floorboard. "Hey, goddamnit," he said. "Put on your seat belt, jackass," Jim said.

William's car was eating up the road. It jumped over a hill and dove down the other side like a porpoise negotiating a wave, and Jim thought, *Goodbye, penguins,* and then he looked back. At the top of the hill were the lights from the nuns' car, and the car was gaining speed and it moved in a jerky manner, as if it were stealing space between blinks of the eye.

"Damn," William said. "They got some juice in that thing, and the driver has her foot down."

"What kind of car is that?" Jim said.

"Black," William said.

"Ha! Mr. Detroit."

"Then you name it."

Jim couldn't. He turned to look back. The nuns' car had already caught up; the big automotive beast was cruising in tight as a coat of varnish, the headlights making the interior of William's machine bright as a Vegas act.

"What the hell they got under the hood?" William said. "Hyperdrive?"

"These nuns," Jim said, "they mean business."

"I can't believe it, they're riding my bumper."

"Slam on your brakes. That'll show them."

"Not this close," William said. "Do that, what it'll show them is the inside of our butts."

"Do nuns do this?"

"These do."

"Oh," Jim said. "I get it. Halloween. They aren't real nuns."

"Then we give them hell," Harold said, and just as the nuns were passing on the right, he crawled out of the floorboard and onto his seat and rolled the window down. The back window of the nuns' car went down and Jim turned to get a look, and the nun, well, she was ugly all right, but uglier than he had first imagined. She looked like something dead, and the nun's outfit she wore was not actually black and white, but purple and white, or so it appeared in the light from head beams and moonlight. The nun's lips pulled back from her teeth and the teeth were long and brown, as if tobacco-stained. One of her eyes looked like a spoiled meatball, and her nostrils flared like a pig's.

Jim said, "That ain't no mask."

Harold leaned way out of the window and flailed his hands and said, "You are so goddamn ugly you have to creep up on your underwear."

Harold kept on with this kind of thing, some of it almost making sense, and then one of the nuns in the back, one closest to the window, bent over in the seat and came up and leaned out of the window, a two-by-four in her hands. Jim noted that her arms, where the nun outfit had fallen back to the elbows, were as thin as sticks and white as the underbelly of a fish, and the elbows were knotty, and bent in the wrong direction.

"Get back in," Jim said to Harold.

Harold waved his arms and made another crack, and then the nun swung the two-by-four, the oddness of her elbows causing it to arrive at a weird angle, and the board made a crack of its own, or rather Harold's skull did, and he fell forward, the lower half of his body hanging from the window, bouncing against the door, his knuckles losing meat on the highway, his ass hanging inside, one foot on the floorboard, the other waggling in the air.

"The nun hit him," Jim said. "With a board."

"What?" William said.

"You deaf, she hit him."

Jim snapped loose his seat belt and leaned over and grabbed Harold by the back of the shirt and yanked him inside. Harold's head looked like it had been in a vise. There was blood everywhere. Jim said, "Oh, man, I think he's dead."

BLAM!

The noise made Jim jump. He slid back in his seat and looked toward the nuns. They were riding close enough to slam the two-by-four into William's car; the driver was pressing that black monster toward them.

Another swing of the board and the side mirror shattered. William tried to gun forward, but the nuns' car was even with him, pushing him to the left. They went across the highway and into a ditch and the car did an acrobatic twist and tumbled down an embankment and rolled into the woods, tossing up mud and leaves and pine straw.

Jim found himself outside the car, and when he moved, everything seemed to whirl for a moment, then gathered up slowly and became solid. He had been thrown free, and so had William, who was lying nearby. The car was a wreck, lying on its roof, spinning still, steam easing out from under the hood in little cotton-white clouds. Gradually, the car quit spinning, like an old-time watch that had wound down. The windshield was gone and three of the four doors lay scattered about.

The nuns were parked up on the road, and the car doors opened and the nuns got out. Four of them. They were unusually tall, and when they walked, like their elbows, their knees bent in the wrong direction. It was impossible to tell this for sure, because of the robes they wore, but it certainly looked that way, and considering the elbows, it fit. There in the moonlight, they were as white and pasty as potstickers, their jaws seeming to have grown longer than when Jim had last looked at them, their noses witchlike, except for those pig flared nostrils, their backs bent like longbows. One of them still held the two-by-four.

Jim slid over to William, who was trying to sit up. "You okay?" Jim asked.

"I think so," William said, patting his fingers at a blood spot on his forehead. "Just before they hit, I stupidly unsnapped my seat belt. I don't know why. I just wanted out I guess. Brain not working right."

"Look up there," Jim said.

They both looked up the hill. One of the nuns was moving down from the highway, toward the wrecked car.

"If you can move," Jim said, "I think we oughta."

William worked himself to his feet. Jim grabbed his arm and half pulled him into the woods, where they leaned against a tree. William said, "Everything's spinning."

"It stops soon enough," Jim said.

"I got to chill, I'm about to faint."

"A moment," Jim said.

The nun who had gone down by herself bent down out of sight behind William's car, then they saw her going back up the hill, dragging Harold by his ankle, his body flopping all over as if all the bones in his body had been broken.

"My God, see that?" William said. "We got to help."

"He's dead," Jim said. "They crushed his head with a board."

"Oh, hell, man. That can't be. They're nuns."

"I don't think they are," Jim said. "Least not the kind of nuns you're thinking."

The nun dragged Harold up the hill and dropped his leg when she reached the big black car. Another of the nuns opened the trunk and reached in and got hold of something. It looked like some kind of folded-up lawn chair, only more awkward in shape. The nun jerked it out and dropped it on the ground and gave it a swift kick. The folded-up thing began to unfold with a clatter and a squeak. A perfectly round head rose up from it, and the head spun on what appeared to be a silver hinge. When it quit whirling, it was upright and in place, though cocked slightly to the left. The eyes and mouth and nostrils were merely holes. Moonlight could be seen through them. The head rose as coatrack-style shoulders pushed it up and a cage of a chest rose under that. The chest looked almost like an old frame on which dresses were placed to be sewn, or perhaps a cage designed to contain something you wouldn't want to get out. With more squeaks and clatters, skeletal hips appeared, and beneath that, long, bony legs with bent-back knees and big metal-framed feet. Stick-like arms swung below its knees, clattering against its legs like tree limbs bumping against a windowpane. It stood at least seven feet tall. Like the nuns, its knees and elbows fit backward.

The nun by the car trunk reached inside and pulled out something fairly large that beat its wings against the night air. She held it in one hand by its clawed feet, and its beak snapped wildly, looking for something to peck. Using her free hand, she opened up the folding man's chest by use of a hinge, and when the cage flung open, she put the black, winged thing inside. It fluttered about like a heart shot full of adrenaline. The holes that were the folding man's eyes filled with a red glow, and the mouth hole grew wormy lips, and a tongue, long as a garden snake, dark as dirt, licked out at the night, and there was a loud sniff as its nostrils sucked air. One of the nuns reached down and grabbed up a handful of clay, and pressed it against the folding man's arms; the clay spread fast as a lie, went all over, filling the thing with flesh of the earth until the entire folding man's body was covered. The nun who had taken the folding man out of the car picked Harold up by the ankle, and as if he were nothing more than a blow-up doll, swung him over her head and slammed him into the darkness of the trunk, shut the lid, and looked out where Jim and William stood recovering by the tree.

The nun said something, a noise between a word and a cough, and the folding man began to move down the hill at a stumble. As he moved, his joints made an un-oiled hinge sound, and the rest of him made a clatter like lug bolts being knocked together, accompanied by a noise akin to wire hangers being twisted by strong hands.

"Run," Jim said.

Jim began to feel pain, knew he was more banged up than he thought. His neck hurt. His back hurt. One of his legs really hurt. He must have jammed his knee against something. William, who ran alongside him, dodging trees, said, "My ribs. I think they're cracked."

Jim looked back. In the distance, just entering the trees, framed in the moonlight behind him, was the folding man. He moved in strange leaps, as if there were springs inside him, and he was making good time.

Jim said, "We can't stop. It's coming."

It was low down in the woods and water had gathered there and the leaves had mucked up with it, and as they ran, they sloshed and splashed, and behind them, they could hear it, the folding man, coming, cracking limbs, squeaking hinges, splashing his way after them. When they had the nerve to look back, they could see him darting between the trees like a bit of the forest itself, and he, or it, was coming quite briskly for a thing its size until it reached the lower-down parts of the bottom land. There its big feet slowed it some as they buried deep in the mud and were pulled free again with a sound like the universe sucking wind. Within moments, however, the thing got its stride, its movements becoming more fluid and its pace faster.

Finally Jim and William came to a tree-thickened rise in the land and were able to get out of the muck, scramble upward and move more freely, even though there was something of a climb ahead, and they had to use trees growing out from the side of the rise to pull themselves upward. When they reached the top of the climb, they were surprised when they looked back to see they had actually gained some space on the thing. It was some distance away, speckled by the moonlight, negotiating its way through the ever-thickening trees and undergrowth.

But still it came, ever onward, never tiring. Jim and William bent over and put their hands on their knees and took some deep breaths.

"There's an old graveyard on the far side of this stretch," Jim said. "Near the wrecking yard."

"Where you worked last summer."

"Yeah, that's the one. It gets clearer in the graveyard, and we can make good time. Get to the wrecking yard, Old Man Gordon lives there. He always has a gun and he has that dog, Chomps. It knows me. It will eat that thing up."

"What about me?"

"You'll be all right. You're with me. Come on. I kinda know where we are now. Used to play in the graveyard, and in this end of the woods. Got to move."

They moved along more swiftly as Jim became more and more familiar with the terrain. It was close to where he had lived when he was a kid, and he had spent a lot of time out here. They came to a place where there was a clearing in the woods, a place where lightning had made a fire. The ground was black, and there were no trees, and in that spot silver moonlight was falling down into it, like mercury filling a cup.

In the center of the clearing they stopped and got their breath again, and William said, "My head feels like it's going to explode. . . . Hey, I don't hear it now."

"It's there. Whatever it is, I don't think it gives up."

"Oh, Jesus," William said, and gasped deep once. "I don't know how much I got left in me."

"You got plenty. We got to have plenty."

"What can it be, Jimbo? What in the hell can it be?"

Jim shook his head. "You know that old story about the black car?"

William shook his head.

"My grandmother used to tell me about a black car that roams the highways and the back roads of the South. It isn't in one area all the time, but it's out there somewhere all the time. Halloween is its peak night. It's always after somebody for whatever reason."

"Bullshit."

Jim, hands still on his knees, lifted his head. "You go down there and tell that clatter-clap thing it's all bullshit. See where that gets you."

"It just doesn't make sense."

"Grandma said before it was a black car, it was a black buggy, and before that a figure dressed in black on a black horse, and that before that, it was just a shadow that clicked and clacked and squeaked. There's people go missing, she said, and it's the black car, the black buggy, the thing on the horse, or the walkin' shadow that gets them. But it's all the same thing, just a different appearance."

"The nuns? What about them?"

Jim shook his head, stood up, tested his ability to breathe. "Those weren't nuns. They were like . . . I don't know . . . anti-nuns. This thing, if Grandma was right, can take a lot of different forms. Come on. We can't stay here anymore."

"Just another moment, I'm so tired. And I think we've lost it. I don't hear it anymore."

As if on cue, there came a clanking and a squeaking and cracking of limbs. William glanced at Jim, and without a word, they moved across the lightning-made clearing and into the trees. Jim looked back, and there it was, crossing the clearing, silver-flooded in the moonlight, still coming, not tiring.

They ran. White stones rose up in front of them. Most of the stones were heaved to the side, or completely pushed out of the ground by growing trees and expanding roots. It was the old graveyard, and Jim knew that meant the wrecking yard was nearby, and so was Gordon's shotgun, and so was one mean dog.

Again the land sloped upward, and this time William fell forward on his hands and knees, throwing up a mess of blackness. "Oh, God. Don't leave me, Jim. . . . I'm tuckered . . . can hardly . . . breathe."

Jim had moved slightly ahead of William. He turned back to help. As he grabbed William's arm to pull him up, the folding man squeaked and clattered forward and grabbed William's ankle, jerked him back, out of Jim's grasp.

The folding man swung William around easily, slammed his body against a tree, then the thing whirled and, as if William were a bullwhip, snapped him so hard his neck popped and an eyeball flew out of his skull. The folding man brought William whipping down across a standing gravestone. There was a cracking sound, like someone had dropped a glass coffee cup, then the folding man whirled and slung William from one tree to another, hitting the trees so hard bark flew off them and clothes and meat flew off William.

Jim bolted. He ran faster than he had ever run, and finally he broke free of the woods and came to a stretch of ground that was rough with gravel. Behind him, breaking free of the woods, was the folding man, making good time with great strides, dragging William's much-abused body behind it by the ankle.

—

Jim could dimly see the wrecking yard from where he was, and he thought he could make it. Still, there was the aluminum fence all the way around the yard, seven feet high. No little barrier. Then he remembered the sycamore tree on the edge of the fence, on the right side. Old Man Gordon was always talking about cutting it because he thought someone could use it to climb over and into the yard, steal one of his precious car parts, though if they did, they had Gordon's shotgun waiting, along with the sizable teeth of his dog. It had been six months since he had seen the old man, and he hoped he hadn't gotten ambitious, that the tree was still there.

Running closer, Jim could see the sycamore tree remained, tight against the long run of shiny wrecking yard fence. Looking over his shoulder, Jim saw the folding man was springing forward, like some kind of electronic rabbit, William's body being pulled along by the ankle, bouncing on the ground as the thing came ever onward. At this rate, it would be only a few seconds before the thing caught up with him.

Jim felt a pain like a knife in his side, and it seemed as if his heart was going to explode. He reached down deep for everything he had, hoping like hell he didn't stumble.

He made the fence and the tree, went up it like a squirrel, dropped over on the roof of an old car, sprang off of that and ran toward a dim light shining in the small window of a wood and aluminum shack nestled in the midst of old cars and piles of junk.

As he neared the shack, Chomps, part pit bull, part just plain big ole dog, came loping out toward him, growling. It was a hard thing to do, but Jim forced himself to stop, bent down, stuck out his hand, and called the dog's name.

"Chomps. Hey, buddy. It's me."

The dog slowed and lowered its head and wagged its tail. "That's right. Your pal, Jim."

The dog came close and Jim gave it a pat. "Good, boy." Jim looked over his shoulder. Nothing.

"Come on, Chomps."

Jim moved quickly toward the shack and hammered on the door. A moment later the door flew open, and standing there in overalls, one strap dangling from a naked arm, was Mr. Gordon. He was old and near toothless, squat and greasy as the insides of the cars in the yard.

"Jim? What the hell you doing in here? You look like hell."

"Something's after me."

"Something?"

"It's outside the fence. It killed two of my friends. . . ."

"What?"

"It killed two of my friends."

"'It'? Some kind of animal?"

"No . . . It."

"We'll call some law."

Jim shook his head. "No use calling the law now, time they arrive it'll be too late."

Gordon leaned inside the shack and pulled a twelve gauge into view, pumped it once. He stepped outside and looked around. "You sure?"

"Oh, yeah. Yes, sir. I'm sure."

"Then I guess you and me and Pump Twelve will check it out." Gordon moved out into the yard, looking left and right. Jim stayed close to Gordon's left elbow. Chomps trotted nearby. They walked about a bit. They stopped between a row of wrecked cars, looked around. Other than the moon-shimmering fence at either end of the row where they stood, there was nothing to see.

"Maybe whatever, or whoever, it is, is gone," Gordon said. "Otherwise, Chomps would be all over it."

"I don't think it smells like humans or animals."

"Are you joshin' an old man? Is this a Halloween prank?"

"No, sir. Two of my friends are dead. This thing killed them. It's real."

"What the hell is it then?"

As if in answer, there was the sound like a huge can opener going to work, and then the long, thin arm of the folding man poked through the fence and there was more ripping as the arm slid upward, tearing at the metal. A big chunk of the fence was torn away, revealing the thing, bathed in moonlight, still holding what was left of William's ragged body by the ankle.

Jim and Gordon both stood locked in amazement. "Sonofabitch," Gordon said.

Chomps growled, ran toward it. "Chomps will fix him," Gordon said.

The folding man dropped William's ankle and bent forward and, just as the dog leaped, caught it and twisted it and ran its long arm down the snapping dog's throat, and began to pull its insides out. It flung the dog's parts in all directions, like someone pulling confetti from a sack. Then it turned the dog inside out.

When the sack was empty, the folding man bent down and fastened the dead, deflated dog to a hook on the back of what passed for its ankle.

"My God," Gordon said.

The thing picked up William by the ankle, stepped forward a step, and paused.

Gordon lifted the shotgun. "Come and get you some, asshole." The thing cocked its head as if to consider the suggestion, and then it began to lope toward them, bringing along its clanks and squeaks, the dead dog flopping at the folding man's heel. For the first time, its mouth, which had been nothing but a hole with wormy lips, twisted into the shape of a smile.

Gordon said, "You run, boy. I got this."

Jim didn't hesitate. He turned and darted between a row of cars and found a gap between a couple of Fords with grass grown up around their flattened tires, ducked down behind one, and hid. He lay down on his belly to see if he could see anything. There was a little bit of space down there, and he could look under the car, and under several others, and he could see Gordon's feet. They had shifted into a firm stance, and Jim could imagine the old man pulling the shotgun to his shoulder.

And even as he imagined, the gun boomed, and then it boomed again. Silence, followed by a noise like someone ripping a piece of thick cardboard in half, and then there were screams and more rips. Jim felt lightheaded, realized he hadn't been breathing. He gasped for air, feared that he had gasped too loudly.

Oh, my God, he thought. *I ran and left it to Mr. Gordon, and now. . . .* He was uncertain. Maybe the screams had come from . . . *It,* the folding man? But so far it hadn't so much as made breathing sounds, let alone anything that might be thought of as a vocalization.

Crawling like a soldier under fire, Jim worked his way to the edge of the car, and took a look. Stalking down the row between the cars was the folding man, and he was dragging behind him by one ankle what was left of William's body. In his other hand, if you could call it a hand, he had Mr. Gordon, who looked thin now because so much had been pulled out of him. Chomps's body was still fastened to the wire hook at the back of the thing's foot. As the folding man came forward, Chomps dragged in the dirt.

Jim pushed back between the cars, and kept pushing, crawling backward. When he was far enough back, he raised to a squat and started between narrower rows that he thought would be harder for the folding man to navigate; they were just spaces really, not rows, and if he could go where it couldn't go, then—

There was a large creaking sound, and Jim, still at a squat, turned to discover its source. The folding man was looking at him. It had grabbed an old car and lifted it up by the front and was holding it so that the back end rested on the ground. Being as close as he was now, Jim realized the folding man was bigger than he had thought, and he saw, too, that just below where the monster's thick torso ended, there were springs, huge springs, silver in the moonlight, vibrating. He had stretched to accommodate the lifting of the car, and where his knees bent backward, springs could be seen as well; he was a garage sale collection of parts and pieces.

For a moment, Jim froze. The folding man opened his mouth wide, wider than Jim had seen before, and inside he could glimpse a turning of gears and a smattering of sparks. Jim broke suddenly, running between cars, leaping on hoods, scrambling across roofs, and behind him came the folding man, picking up cars and flipping them aside as easily as if they had been toys.

Jim could see the fence at the back, and he made for that, and when he got close to it, he thought he had it figured. He could see a Chevy parked next to the fence, and he felt certain he could climb onto the roof, spring off of it, grab the top of the fence, and scramble over. That wouldn't stop the thing behind him, but it would perhaps give him a few moments to gain ground.

The squeaking and clanking behind him was growing louder.

There was a row of cars ahead, he had to leap onto the hood of the first, then spring from hood to hood, drop off, turn slightly right, and go for the Chevy by the fence.

He was knocked forward, hard, and his breath leaped out of him.

He was hit again, painfully in the chest.

It took a moment to process, but he was lying between two cars, and there, standing above him, was the folding man, snapping at him with the two dead bodies like they were wet towels. That's what had hit him: the bodies, used like whips.

Jim found strength he didn't know he had, made it to his feet as Mr. Gordon's body slammed the ground near him. Then, as William's body snapped by his ear, just missing him, he was once more at a run.

The Chevy loomed before him. He made its hood by scrambling up on hands and knees, and then he jumped to the roof. He felt something tug at him, but he jerked loose, didn't stop moving. He sprang off the car top, grabbed at the fence, latching his arms over it. The fence cut into the undersides of his arms, but he couldn't let that stop him, so he kept pulling himself forward, and the next thing he knew, he was over the fence, dropping to the ground.

It seemed as if a bullet had gone up through his right foot, which he now realized was bare, and that the tug he had felt was the folding man grabbing at his foot, only to come away with a shoe. But of more immediate concern was his foot, the pain. There hadn't been any bullet. He had landed crooked coming over the fence, and his foot had broken. It felt like hell, but he moved on it anyway, and within a few steps he had a limp, a bad limp.

He could see the highway ahead, and he could hear the fence coming down behind him, and he knew it was over, all over, because he was out of gas and had blown a tire and his engine was about to blow too. His breath came in chops and blood was pounding in his skull like a thug wanting out.

He saw lights. They were moving very quickly down the highway. A big truck, a Mack, was balling the jack in his direction. If he could get it to stop, maybe there would be help, maybe.

Jim stumbled to the middle of the highway, directly into the lights, waved his arms, glanced to his left—

—and there it was. The folding man. It was only six feet away. The truck was only a little farther away, but moving faster, and then the folding man was reaching for him, and the truck was a sure hit, and Jim, pushing off his good foot, leaped sideways and there was a sound like a box of dishes falling downstairs.

Jim felt the wind from the truck, but he had moved just in time. The folding man had not. As Jim had leaped aside, his body turned, through no plan of his own, and he saw the folding man take the hit. Wood and springs and hinges went everywhere.

The truck bumped right over the folding man and started sliding as the driver tried to put on brakes that weren't designed for fast stops. Tires smoked, brakes squealed, the truck fishtailed.

Jim fell to the side of the highway, got up and limped into the brush there, and tripped on something and went down. He rolled on his back. His butt was in a ditch and his back was against one side of it, and he could see above it on the other side, and through some little bushes that grew there. The highway had a few lights on either side of it, so it was lit up good, and Jim could see the folding man lying in the highway, or rather he could see parts of it everywhere. It looked like a dirty hardware store had come to pieces. William, Gordon, and Chomps lay in the middle of the highway.

The folding man's big torso, which had somehow survived the impact of the truck, vibrated and burst open, and Jim saw the birdlike thing rise up with a squawk. It snatched up the body of Mr. Gordon and William, one in either claw, used its beak to nab the dog, and ignoring the fact that its size was not enough to lift all that weight, it did just that, took hold of them and went up into the night sky, abruptly became one with the dark. Jim turned his head. He could see down the highway, could see the driver of the truck getting out, walking briskly toward the scene of the accident. He walked faster as he got closer, and when he arrived, he bent over the pieces of the folding man. He picked up a spring, examined it, tossed it aside. He looked out where Jim lay in the ditch, but Jim figured, lying as he was, brush in front of him, he couldn't be seen.

He was about to call out to the driver when the truck driver yelled, "You nearly got me killed. You nearly got you killed. Maybe you are killed. I catch you, might as well be, you stupid shit. I'll beat the hell out of you."

Jim didn't move.

"Come on out so I can finish you off."

Great, Jim thought, *first the folding man, and now a truck driver wants to kill me. To hell with him, to hell with everything,* and he laid his head back against the ditch and closed his eyes and went to sleep.

The truck driver didn't come out and find him, and when he awoke the truck was gone and the sky was starting to lighten. His ankle hurt like hell. He bent over and looked at it. He couldn't tell much in the dark, but it looked as big as a sewer pipe. He thought when he got some strength back, he might be able to limp, or crawl out to the edge of the highway, flag down some help. Surely, someone would stop. But for the moment, he was too weak. He laid back again, and was about to close his eyes, when he heard a humming sound.

Looking out at the highway, he saw lights coming from the direction the trucker had come from. Fear crawled up his back like a spider. It was the black car.

The car pulled to the side of the road and stopped. The nuns got out. They sniffed and extended long tongues and licked at the fading night. With speed and agility that seemed impossible, they gathered up the parts of the folding man and put them in a sack they placed in the middle of the highway.

When the sack was full of parts, one nun stuck a long leg into the sack and stomped about, then jerked her leg out, pulled the sack together at the top and swung it over her head and slammed it on the road a few times, then she dropped the sack and moved back and one of the nuns kicked it. Another nun opened up and reached inside the sack and took out the folding man. Jim lost a breath. It appeared to be put back together. The nun didn't unfold the folding man. She opened the trunk of the car and flung it inside.

And then she turned and looked in his direction, held out one arm and waited. The bird-thing came flapping out of the last of the dark and landed on her arm. The bodies of William and Gordon were still in its talons, the dog in its beak, the three of them hanging as if they were nothing heavier than rags. The nun took hold of the bird's legs and tossed it and what it held into the trunk as well. She closed the lid of the trunk. She looked directly where Jim lay. She looked up at the sky, turned to face the rising sun. She turned quickly back in Jim's direction and stuck out her long arm, the robe folding back from it. She pointed a stick-like finger right at him, leaned slightly forward. She held that pose until the others joined her and pointed in Jim's direction.

My God, Jim thought, *they know I'm here. They see me. Or smell me. Or sense me. But they know I'm here.*

The sky brightened and outlined them like that for a moment and they stopped pointing.

They got quickly in the car. The last of the darkness seemed to seep into the ground and give way to a rising pink; Halloween night had ended. The car gunned and went away fast. Jim watched it go a few feet, and then it wasn't there anymore. It faded like fog. All that was left now was the sunrise and the day turning bright.

I had pretty much decided I was through with stories with weird Western content. This happens to me a lot, feeling I've done a certain thing and have nothing more to say in that arena, and then suddenly an idea comes to me, and I'm off to the races.

It was being asked to write for a weird Western anthology that inspired this. The editor was David Boop, and it was for an anthology titled *Straight Outta Dodge City*. I was going to turn it down. I had had my say when it came to weird Westerns.

Or had I?

I wrote this one thinking, and even saying to David via email, that this was my last weird Western.

I enjoyed the story so much, I immediately wrote another, "The Hungry Snow."

Never say never.

I like the tone of this one immensely. It gave me the creeps while writing it, all those spirits lurking about. And then, of course, there's the creepy midnight train and the gunslinger who comes with it.

Now I'm thinking I'd like to write about the Hoodoo Man again.

Will I?

I never know, but I do know this—

My muse, meaning me, is unpredictable.

The Hoodoo Man and the Midnight Train

THERE'S PEOPLE DON'T believe in booger stories, as my grandma used to call them, but that don't mean there isn't strange stuff out there in them dark woods, or for that matter on the streets in town, out there on a buggy ride down to the river for a picnic, or coming through the woods spitting black smoke and carrying hell and damnation with it.

Thing is, once you know the world has a sliced sky from which things leak, well, you can't never lay down at night without your protections.

I work in a gun shop and I live there, too, but it isn't just any gun shop. Zachary, who prefers to be called Zach, repairs and even makes guns, but he's got another kind of job that don't always pay and sometimes does, depending. But it's a job he will take on either way in the end. If he tries to bicker and fails to get some money out of the deal, he just sighs and goes on with it.

Zach had owed a hundred good deeds on account of a bad thing he did, and on the day the old man came in, his black skin graying, his black suit graying as well, thinning, too, a wide-brimmed black hat on his head with a white feather in it, I seen Zach perk up. Zach had done ninety-nine good deeds and still owed one more. That was the only way he could get rid of the baggage. He thought that old man might be the last deed needed for him to get shed of his little problem.

Now, when I say good deeds, I don't mean help an old lady across the street so she don't get run over by wild horses. A thing like that is damn sure a nice thing to do, but it don't go on the ledger, so to speak. It's got to be bigger than that. Something real special.

I guess Zach's around fifty or so, though I have heard people comment on how he seems to stay at an age and not move away from it. Zach is a stout man with a gleam in his eye, and his skin is dark as the bottom of a well, and always shiny, like he just ran a race in the hot sunshine. He's always bent forward a little, like he's considering tying his shoe. If he wore shoes.

Zach not only makes and repairs guns, he can shoot them right smart as well, has a fast draw. And then, of course, there are all the magic books and talismans. He knows that stuff. That's his side business, and all the business he does, he does well.

I was sold to him when I was young by my folks who didn't want me. They were going through town with a traveling medicine wagon. They sold a few bottles of this and that. All of which my mama made, and nearly all of them a mixture of water and whiskey and berry juice, but nothing that would do anything for you but make you slightly drunk and loosen your bowels.

Cure-all, my folks called it, but it didn't cure much. I didn't miss them any. My pa beat me, and Mama didn't love me enough to even hit me. I don't know it for a fact, but I heard they was hung from an oak tree for selling something that made a child get sick and die. Mama probably put the wrong berry juice in a bottle or some such when she was drunk. She could be a bad drunk. It was the parents of that child and some townsfolks that did them in. It wasn't the law, but it was justice, no doubt.

Zach had been good to me. He was teaching me a trade, two trades, like he had. I got three meals a day and I had a bed in the back of the shop. It was set on top of a pentagram, surrounded by all the protections Zach had made for me. Blue bottles full of dead flies and horny-toad guts, crosses, silver doodads, and a salt circle around the inner circle of chalk that made up the outside part of the pentagram.

Early on, I wondered if there was any sense to all that stuff, until I woke up and seen sitting there in the dark, all around that chalk and salt circle, a series of squatting toadlike things. It was frightening, but I knew then that it was the circle and all that other stuff that kept them out. During the day I didn't have to worry, Zach told me, but at night, I wanted something like water or a good book to read, a fresh candle for my night table, I needed to bring it in before the dark got deep and the clock beat twelve. Straight-up midnight was the time the demon door opened and the things came out in search of those that were involved in the hoodoo.

I told Zach I didn't never have to do that before he took me in, and he said, "I know, but them demons want me, and now they want you, or anything to do with me and you. You want a girlfriend, have your fun, but don't never fall in love, 'cause you can't have it, not really. You love someone, you're bringing them into something slimy and dangerous, and once in the life, it takes something really special and goddamn biblical to get out of it." He said there were days when he hated having pulled me into all these dark shenanigans.

I told him I was glad to have been rescued, and that Mama and Pa were a lot worse than the demons, because wasn't no spells and diagrams that could keep them out, and besides, he had educated me some. I could read and write and do my ciphers, and I was learning the gunsmith trade as well as that other trade of his.

I know I'm wandering, but I think for you to understand it better, you got to know Zach's circumstances, about them good deeds. You see, I was good deed number fourteen of the one hundred he owed. I've seen him do all the others up to where he is now. I helped him do quite a few.

He told me once that he had gotten as far as ninety-eight good deeds once, then messed up by doing something bad, and had to start over, and when he did, the baggage got heavier. When I say baggage, I ain't talking about no grip, or a tow sack full of possibles.

In the back of the shop there's a long hallway, and off the hallway are two rooms, one on the left, one on the right. I'm off to the left, and Zach is off to the right. But at the end of the hallway hanging on the wall is a big old mirror made of silver and it's shiny as a baby's ass all greased with lotion. The mirror is framed in hawthorn wood painted red with hog's blood and grave clay, and the painted wood is treated with hoss apple juice.

When Zach enters the hall, even if the light is bad, you can see him and me in the mirror, but you can also see the baggage, and no matter how many times I see it, even expecting it, it gets to me, makes my bones tremble inside of me like an old house rotting its lumber.

It looks a little like an old woman, and she's got her arms around Zach's neck, and her legs wrapped around his middle, and her head rises just above Zach's. Her face is long and she has a possum jaw, with a lot of jagged teeth in it, and once a month she smells so bad Zach can hardly stand it. Just once a month, and on that day he doesn't work, just rides off in the country and lives with the stink, which when the morning breaks and the sun gets warm, goes away, like a visiting in-law you don't care for.

He can do whatever he would do without her on his back, but she's there, in dark spirit he says, and he can feel her arms around his neck and her legs and feet around his waist, and he can always feel her hot breath on the back of his neck, and on that stink day, he says it's the breath that nearly kills him, cause it reeks like a feed lot for cattle. She's his baggage for killing a child to save his own. Both children died, his and the one he sacrificed to the dark ones. I don't know much more than that, but let me ask you, would you kill a child to save your own? You can bet my folks wouldn't have done a thing to save me or any other child either. They sold me for thirty dollars and was glad to get shed of me.

I was telling you about the man that came in, all dressed in fading black, and the first thing he sees is me, working on some leather, designing a holster for a pistol, using the pattern laid out for me by Zach.

I didn't really need the pattern anymore, but I liked to keep it near, just as a way of feeling like I always had it in case I needed it. Working on the guns, well, that's a different story, especially some of the guns Zach worked on, and certainly the ones he made to his own design. I liked him nearby to make sure I was doing that kind of business right.

"Boy," the old man says, "maybe you ought to leave the room. I got to talk to this man here."

"He doesn't leave the room," Zach said, his hands on the glass-top counter that held a number of Colts and Remington pistols. "He's my apprentice. Name is James."

"What is he? A high yella?"

"I suppose you could call him that. I call him James."

The man nodded. "All right then, but I got the kind of business to talk about that you pull out of a deep dark sack."

"I understand that kind of business, and so does the boy."

The old man nodded again.

"I been trying to find someone for years to help me do what I got to do, 'cause there's someone stolen and riding a kind of train that don't never let a passenger off. They say you're the man I need. A hoodoo man."

"Go on," Zach said.

"I heard rumor of you from an old man out in West Texas. Thing is, the whole thing that happened to me happened here in this very town, and now I'm back in it. I find that strange, that I didn't know you were here all along."

"Fate makes circles," Zach said. "I keep a low profile on the hoodoo business, and you got to be in the hoodoo to know who I am and where I am. In the hoodoo like you. But, I don't work for free."

The man came closer to the counter and opened his coat and took out a small bag and set it on the counter in front of Zach, said, "That there is silver dust. It's what I can pay you. It's worth a lot."

Zach pulled the drawstring loose and pinched some of the dust and worked it with his thumb and forefinger, and let it fall back in the bag.

"All right," Zach said. "Tell me about it."

Zach locked the door and turned the sign to closed, and we went into the back room and sat at the table where me and him eat. I got out the bottle and poured them both little glasses full of a dark whiskey.

They took their sips and I sat silent, and then the wrecked old man said, "Some years ago, right here in this town, I made a mistake. I wanted to be rich and powerful, and, well, there was a woman, and she was a fine-looking woman, dark, dark skin, with a heart like a lump of coal. Name was Consuela. Skin like black velvet, long-legged and high-breasted, but she had a gleam in her eye that made you weak."

"I know who Consuela was," Zach said. "We had what you might call a rivalry. Before her house burned down with her in it."

"Again, I had no idea there were two hoodoo masters in town."

"You don't really master the hoodoo. It masters you."

"True enough. Consuela had me do things for her, bad things. I stole and killed for her. She had spells, you see, and she needed certain things and certain events to make those spells happen. Items and sacrifice. She used them spells to help me along with money and for a long time magnificent health. She owned my pecker, owned my soul. I dressed nice, had money in my wallet and fine clothes, of which these I'm wearing are remnants, but there were restrictions and prices to pay. One was, she kept me in her sight. Didn't want me to let on what I knew, I suppose, but mostly she kept me like a pet. All that I was missing was a collar and a bowl on the floor.

"Got so the only time I could get away from her was when I was on one of her errands. It's hard for me to talk about those errands, because sometimes they were bad errands. Really bad. I really don't want to talk about that.

"Then come a day I'm on my own at night, and I'd done a thing so bad I was sick, and I couldn't make myself go back to Consuela, not right then. I went to the café just to have some place to go where the light was bright and the voices in the room weren't demonic whispers.

"There was this young woman worked at the café. She was petite, soft-looking as a puppy, skin the color of coffee with a splash of cream. Not as wildly beautiful as Consuela, but she was certainly pretty. I went there every chance I got, just to be in the warmth and the light, to smell fresh coffee and frying eggs and bacon. But mostly, I went there for her.

"When things were slow in the café, she would pause and talk to me. I learned she lost her parents to a fever, lost everyone she ever loved in one way or another, and yet she was cheerful, positive, and I could feel the meanness I had in me, that Consuela had encouraged, easing out of me, like a snake going away from the chicken house.

"Her name was Jenny. She liked a simple life, and I decided I could like one too. I had to get rid of Consuela. I figured best way to break her hold on me was to kill her. I thought I was most likely able to do that when she slept. You see, at night we slept in a bed inside a circle drawn on the floor, with diagrams—"

"We know all about that," Zach said.

"Why I come to you. You got a reputation for knowing your business. When Consuela was asleep, and I was lying in the bed next to her, I eased over to the side of the bed and pulled the hammer out from under it, where I had placed it earlier in the day, and hit her in the head. She could keep those demons out, but she couldn't keep me out. I hit her and hit her until her skull and wicked brain were nothing but a splash on the sheets. And these demons that were all around us, they cackled.

"I waited until morning, when the cock crowed and the demons around the bed became mist and wafted away. I got out of bed and fell to my knees, weak from fear and guilt and excitement. I'd broken the hold she had on me. I cleaned myself up and waited until Jenny was at work. I was thinking me and her could go away together. It might take some time to convince her, but I was determined. That's how much I loved her. You seem perturbed."

The old man had noticed that Zach's expression had changed and that he had cupped his hands together and let them rest on his chest. He seemed to be holding something inside of himself.

"You're blaming Consuela for the very things you wanted," Zach said. "She didn't make you do nothing. You did bad things on your own to get money and power, and now you want to lay it at her feet, justify what you done. You weren't under any kind of spell, because if you were, you wouldn't have been able to plan killing her, or even want to."

The old man nodded slowly, the feather on his hat bobbing like a big white finger. "Yeah. I can't disagree with that. That doesn't change the fact that she was evil and killing her was a good thing. Shall I go on with my story?"

Zach nodded.

"When morning came, I felt weak. It wasn't like I had slept. I ended up going into the front room to lay down on a pallet. Woke up and it was near dark, checked the big clock in the hall. It wasn't long before midnight. That's how much what I had done had taken out of me. I had slept the entire day and part of the night away.

"I realized, of course, that the demons would soon be out. I had to get back in that bed with Consuela's corpse so I could be protected by the charms and the pentagram. I was in the hoodoo life, a minor hoodoo man, but minor or major, the results would have been the same. These days I make my own pentagram and lay out the protection. It's second nature now. But right then, I didn't have the time. Not that I slept that much with her body in the bed, and after me sleeping all day, I was wide awake. The sheets were bloodstained, her brains splattered about, all of it beginning to stink. And I swear, her dead body twitched in the bed all of the night.

"Still, next morning, I felt happy, just as free and happy as I could be. I cleaned up, fixed me some food, and then I began to feel like I was carrying something heavy on my back."

"You're toting the baggage," Zach said.

The old man nodded.

"I can see its reflection in pools of clear water, and in things that are silver. It looks a little like Consuela. In one way it's heavy, and in another it's not."

"Your baggage is different from mine, but it's still baggage," Zach said. "And it's soul weight, not weight by the pound."

"I know that now, but that day and that night, I was figuring it out, consulting the tomes Consuela had, the books she never let me look in, only allowing me to read the pages she chose, teaching me little spells and having me run her errands, but never teaching me the big things.

"I boarded up the room where Consuela lay, took all the protections into the front room and drew a new pentagram and set myself a fresh pallet inside of it. Next night I could hear a lot of pounding and ripping in that other room. The demons were having their way with her body. Doing whatever they do. That night I started going back to the café to see Jenny."

"You had killed a woman with a hammer, and you went to courting?"

"Consuela was a monster. I had rid the world of her. I wanted a new life, a better one. One without murder and spells. Is that so bad?"

Zach didn't reply, but he sighed heavily.

"After a couple weeks and a lot of sweet talk, I convinced her to walk with me down by the river. She brought a blanket, and we sat on it and looked out at the water. Soon we were kissing, and then we did what men and women do. We hadn't no more than made love, than I felt that baggage on my back grow heavy. I had a moment of joy, and that seemed to make the baggage grow heavy.

"We hadn't no more than gotten dressed than I heard it. A little toot at first, then a long low whistle coming from the north, heading in our direction. Jenny heard it, too, said, 'There aren't any trains near here.'

"But there was. We could hear it, and then we could see its smoke rising up above the forest, floating into the moonlight. It was coming closer. The whistle grew louder, the smoke grew thicker, and my courage grew smaller. I didn't know it right then, but I know it now. It was the Midnight Train."

I saw Zach stiffen.

"Then we saw the tracks. One moment they weren't there, then they were. Not on any bridge, mind you, they lay right on the water, and ended at our feet. There was a split in the woods and the split was shiny like a polished coin, and then we could see the train. It had one big ole red light in front and the smoke it was puffing had turned thick and dark. We were frozen to the spot. It looked as if that train was going to run right over us, and wasn't a thing we could do about it.

"Jenny took my arm and squeezed it. Instinctively we knew there wasn't any reason to run. It would catch us. The train stopped. No metal screeching, no sliding. The engine stopped right where the tracks ended. There was a hiss of stinking steam and the cool air crackled against the hot engine.

"Then a door on the side of the train opened up, and some steps was rolled out. A little creature so white you'd have thought it was made of snow bounced down the steps and landed on the ground and looked at me and Jenny. It looked like a huge white frog, but kind of human too. Its mouth cracked wide, and it was toothless, all pink gums, showing bright in the moonlight.

"Then another one of them toads hopped down. This one was black as a raven's wing, and it had a mouthful of shiny teeth, pointed and long. It looked like it could have chewed its way through an angle of iron.

"Then both them things turned their heads and looked up at the open doorway, like they were scared. First there was a boot, hanging in mid-air. Blood-red, and tipped at the toes with shadow. Then there was a leg stick in the boot, clothed in white pants with thin black stripes. As the boot put a heel on the top step, another boot and leg appeared, and the owner of the boots and pants stepped into view, ducking his head to come out of that door on the train. He wore a big white hat with a thin black band around it. He was eight foot tall if he was an inch. I could feel that burden on my back swell and grow heavy on my soul.

"This tall man, pale of face with the corners of his mouth upturned, like he might break into a smile, came to stand on the ground by the train, the toad-things on either side of him. He looked at us. His eyes were dead-looking. You could barely see his moonlit pupils through the milky covering over them, but now and then in that rich moonlight, you could see red shadows move in the whites of those big, dead eyes. He had on a long white duster and his hands were big and his fingers long and many-knuckled. He lifted one hand, extended a finger and pointed right at Jenny. Then he turned his hand over and wiggled his finger for her to come to him. Jenny clutched my arm harder, and the tall man smiled. It was a smile where the edges of his lips slid up to touch his earlobes, widening so that I could see some blocky white teeth like tombstones and a thin, forked pink tongue that licked at the air like a snake.

"The train had come for Jenny, but the taking of her was to punish me for what I had done to Consuela. Her hex reached out beyond her death to make sure I stayed unhappy.

"Jenny says, 'Pray. Pray to Jesus.' But I knew there wasn't any Jesus that could help us. That's when the tall, white man pushed that duster back with his long-fingered hands and I could see on his hips, in snow-white holsters, two big ole pistols. He kept that horrible smile on his face, linked his fingers, flexed, popped them so loud, both me and Jenny jumped. He pointed at Jenny again and nodded toward the train.

"Now the windows, which had been foggy, cleared, and what I saw through them windows I can't explain. It was full of passengers and they were screaming and howling, had their faces pressed against the windows. They looked as if they had been boiled, fried, and generally shit on. I looked at the tall man and he cocked his hands above his guns, and though I was wearing a pistol, and wasn't a bad hand with a gun, I knew right then I couldn't beat him, and if I could, my bullets wouldn't do a thing to him. It was obvious to me that I either had to draw and lose, or give up Jenny.

"I can't tell you how ashamed I am, which is why I have come to you, to repair as best I can what I did. I put my hand on Jenny's back and pushed her toward him, said, 'Take her.'

"Jenny stumbled forward, looked back at me. I can still see her face, the expression of betrayal. Not long before I had held her in my arms and we had made love, and now I was passing her on to an eternity of torment. She didn't say anything. Not a word, didn't make a sound. Don't think she could. The hopping men came and grabbed her arms, lifted her and carried her onto that horrible train. And then I heard her scream. It was a scream that made the short hairs on my neck stand up, made the goose bumps on my arms ripple and my stomach rumble with fear.

"That tall man, he got on the train, too, and the steps went up with a snap. He leaned out from the door, and he cackled at me, and the sound of it was like having your flesh cut open with a crosscut saw. The train coughed smoke, and when it did, an open space near the engine lit up with a white light. I could see inside that gap, and the Engineer was there with his oversized engineer hat and baggy coveralls. He was little more than bones stretched over wet, dark flesh, and he and the Fireman, I suppose the other man would be called that, were feeding screaming, struggling bodies bound up in guts and skin and long weaves of hair, straight into the blazing fire box. When they went in, you could hear them scream, and then their screams became as one and turned into the sound of the train's whistle. The train coughed and it began to back up, and then in no way I can explain, I was no longer looking at the engine, but at the caboose. Away that train went along those tracks, and as it went the tracks disappeared behind it. The woods swallowed the train, but for a moment I could hear it toot its whistle and I could see smoke above the tree line. Then the whistle stopped screaming and the smoke was gone. There was only the moonlight tipping the trees with hats of silver.

"Everything outside that bubble we had been in set itself free. You could feel it in the wind and in the way the trees weaved a bit in the breeze. Where before the world was silent, you could now hear night birds sing, frogs bleat and crickets chirp.

"The train was gone and Jenny was gone, and there I stood, the weight on my back heavier than even moments before. A coward in moonlight and shadow.

"I ran away quick, didn't go back down there, next day or the day after. Didn't want the train to come back. I had Consuela's books of magic, some she had written herself in her own crabbed handwriting. Heavy of heart, and heavier of soul, I began to read them carefully. I started thinking maybe I could get Jenny off that train, get that burden off my back. But if the answer was in those books, I didn't find it.

"I decided I had to search out someone who could help me, not knowing the very person who could was right here in this town, near where it all happened. I packed up my goods and Consuela's books and all her money, which was considerable, loaded it all in a wagon drawn by two strong horses. I quested for years, looking for help, and now, here I am, looking at you, asking you to help me for a bag of silver. I'm getting old now, and if I die with this thing on my back, well, no telling where I'll end up, but I know this much, it isn't good. And Jenny's on that train, and it's all my fault."

When the story was finished, we all sat there quietly.

It was the old man that broke the ice.

"Will you assist me? Help me rescue Jenny?"

Zach pooched his lips the way he does when he's thinking hard on something. He let the old man's question hang in the air awhile. Finally, he spoke.

"Go back to wherever you're staying, and let me marinate on this thing. Come see me tomorrow when the sun's dying, and I'll tell you what I will or will not do. But let me explain to you what you're up against. It's not just the Midnight Train, but the Dueling Man and his minions you got to deal with. And let me tell you, the Dueling Man is made up of more bad deeds than either of us have seen. He works for the Engineer. He could go bear hunting with harsh language and wipe his ass with an angry badger, and that doesn't even begin to explain what he is and how he is. Go away for now."

That old man got up slow, like he had to build himself bone by bone to stand up, and then he dragged out of there like there was a ball and chain on his foot.

I looked at Zach. "Well?"

"I don't know. He's blaming this Consuela for everything he's ever done, and he mentioned murder as some of the things he done. I'm thinking he did it for himself as well, that he earned his burden more than Consuela gave it to him. Her death was just the final act that put that weight on his soul."

"But what about Jenny?" I said.

Zach didn't answer.

That day I did all the work that was to be done, except some fine touch-ups on a gun being made for a gambling man. It was going to have some etchings on the hilt, and Zach had to do that. He had the talent and he had the steady hand.

Zach sat in the hallway in a padded chair in front of the long mirror and looked at himself and that baggage on his back. He had a stand by his chair, and had a lamp on it and some hoodoo books. I looked in on him a couple times, brought him a cup of coffee and a piece of ham and bread about noon. He took it from me without comment, continued to look at himself and his baggage in the mirror. The thing in the mirror looked at me, and when it did, it made me feel cold from the top of my head all the way down to the heels of my feet. I got out of there pretty quick, left Zach to his considerations.

It was late afternoon of the next day when the bell over the door clanked and the old man came in and walked over to me.

I got up and told Zach he had arrived. Zach sighed deep, rose, and followed me into the main part of the shop.

"Your decision?" said the old man.

"I've studied on it. I have to build you a gun, a special gun to use against the Dueling Man. I'll have to make some special ammunition for you too. Come back in a week's time, and I'll have it ready."

The old man tipped his hat and went away. Zach looked at me. "This is going to require a lot of black coffee."

The days passed by so slow you would have thought they was crippled.

I did the work Zach asked me to do, as well as kept making coffee, because once he got started on that gun he didn't sleep much, and with all that coffee, how could he?

Among the jobs I did for him was pack some powder and a specific shot inside the casings for the pistol ammunition. Those were big old bullets when they were finished. Fifty calibers, and for a pistol! But here's the odd thing, they was as light as if they was made of air and a prayer.

Zach had some metal to use for making pistols and such, but this metal he had he got out of an old trunk in the back, and the long barrel of the pistol was made of a steel so blue it made a clear spring day look dull. You could see your reflection in it. Zach looked into it with me, and I could see the baggage on his back, that horrible face. That told me there was silver in the bluing. That barrel was light in a similar way as the ammunition. The hilt was made of hawthorn wood, painted black with a paint made of ashes and drops of frog blood and glue. When the gun was finished, it looked right smart the way it gleamed in the sunlight coming through the window.

Zach let me handle it. It was the best-balanced pistol I had ever held, single-action, 'cause Zach said it was a more steady shot when cocked and aimed.

I gave Zach the holster I had been working on, made of gold-dyed leather, the dye some concoction of Zach's. He heated an iron in the fire from the woodstove and burned designs into the leather. Those designs were swirls and little figures that Zach said were spells and such. I took his word for it.

He loaded the gun, shoved it in the holster, had me put it away. When I carried it to place inside the trunk where he kept his most important stuff, that gun seemed alive in my hand. I thought I could hear it whisper.

Zach had finished his work two days early, and when he was done, he went to bed and stayed there through dark and light without waking for two whole days.

Come the morning of the day the old man was to come, Zach got up and had me heat some water and fill a number-ten tub. He stripped down and got in it and soaked in a lot of soapy suds.

When he finished bathing, he got dressed. Put on black pants and a black shirt and a black hat with linked silver conchos for a hatband. He wore a bolo tie with black strings and silver tips, and the clutch of the tie was silver and in the shape of a scorpion. He pulled on black boots fresh polished, with silver-tip toes. He had me fetch the holster and pistol. I brought it to him and he sat behind the counter on a stool and read a dime novel while waiting for the old man to come. He had me pull down the shades and lock the door and turn the sign to say CLOSED.

We sat there all day, Zach reading dime novels, and sometimes reading from the big hoodoo books he had, or from clutches of loose notes.

It was nearly dark when there was a tap on the door. I looked at Zach, and he nodded. I opened the door to the sound of the overhead bell clanging. It was the old man, dressed as he always was, like Zach, in black, except for that tall white feather. He was bent over more than before and walked like his feet was tied together. He was old the day he first came into the shop, but today he was much older.

"I have the gun," Zach said.

Zach lifted the holstered pistol up and put it on the counter. The pistol had the smell of gun oil about it, but there was something else, a tinge of something long dead; just a whiff, but it was there.

The old man spoke, sweat popping out all over his face. "I want to get Jenny off that train, but I've gotten old, and I'm not that good a gunhand anymore. I appreciate the gun, and I'm sure it's worth all the dust I paid you . . . but can I ask you to handle it? To be my surrogate?"

Zach smiled, and made a kind of gurgle that might have been a laugh, said, "I expected just this. I can tell a man that wants to do something he's afraid to do and wants someone else to do it for him the moment I talk to them."

"If I were younger—"

"When you were younger you let the Dueling Man take Jenny. You killed a woman, who though she may have had it coming, you were in the deep hoodoo before. The power, the money, the black magic. I know what kind of draw Consuela had. I was in her arms once. Does that surprise you? Her price was too high for me. But not you. Then you wanted out, and you wanted something clean and innocent to make you feel clean, so you took up with Jenny and let the doo-doo from the hoodoo rub off on her."

"I was young then."

"We all been young," Zach said. "But that's not enough of an excuse. Not for what you said you done. You got guilt on you, and shame, and that's at least a good thing. It's the only reason I'm helping you. You feel remorse for what you've done and have thought about it for years. As for Jenny, I don't know her, but she's an innocent soul, and I want to get her off that train. So, let's cut the bull and get down to brass tacks and good ammunition."

Zach looked at me. "I'm going to have to depend on you for something, son. And it's a big thing."

"Just tell me what you want," I said, and I sounded a lot braver than what I felt, having heard about the Dueling Man and the Midnight Train.

"If and when I dispatch the Dueling Man, there will be the two demons. The froglike things he's been talking about. I'll try to deal with them. Meantime, you gather up all the courage you have, because it will take it, and you get on that train and you yell, 'Miss Jenny, I'm a hoodoo man and I've come for you.'"

"But I'm not a hoodoo man," I said.

"Yes, you are. You've worked for me, and I'm going to put a spell in your pocket. It's not a strong one. There ain't much in the way of strong when it comes to the Midnight Train, 'cause you might have to face the Engineer. He gets you, all bets are off. Your ass is good and got. The good thing though is the Engineer lets the others handle the bad business most of the time, but if he should decide to handle it himself, you get off that train quick as you can.

"That little spell I'll put in your pocket, it'll make it so if someone on the train tries to grab you, they'll not be able to. But it's not a long-lasting spell. Some of those on the train will be wailing and begging for you to take them with you. You won't have the ability to take anyone off the train except the one you call out to. When you call out for Jenny, she'll come to you. She may not look just right. In fact, she will look terrible. You take her hand, and that will give her the protection you got. But that sucks on the protective spell, and you'll have even less time than before.

"Get her and you run for the door, any door that'll get you off that train. Even if it's moving, you jump, you jump as hard and far as you can, and have Jenny jump with you. She gets off the train, she'll be the Jenny that was put on that train all those many years ago.

"Course, if I can't beat the Dueling Man, then you run like your ass is on fire and don't never even think for a moment about getting on that train. I'll be done for, me and my baggage will get on that train and we'll ride and ride and ride. We succeed, then I'm free of my baggage."

"What about me," the old man said, "will I be free?"

"That remains to be seen," Zach said. "I don't like you. I got nothing for you except to help Miss Jenny. Where she is, that's on you. And just to make myself understood, if you get out there and decide to run, like you did before, I'll shoot you. That way, with the baggage you got, I can assure you of a long train ride."

"Should I actually go with you?" the old man said. "Maybe, being old like I am, decrepit, I ought to stay here until you get back. I might make things worse."

Zach laughed loud enough to tremble the rafters.

"Oh no you don't. You're going."

We had some ham and bread and Zach let the old man take a shot of whiskey, but Zach didn't have none. He had coffee instead, and when he finished with it, he said, "We'll go down early and take the lay of the land. I suggest we go to the place where you and Jenny encountered the train. Might as well make this whole thing full circle."

We played some cards as the night grew rich, and then we packed up some folding stools and a basket with more of that damn ham and bread in it. Zach went and wrapped his mirror in a black cloth and brought it out and put it with the other stuff.

"What you need that for?" the old man asked.

"I hope it'll give me an edge."

We didn't bother with horses. It wasn't that far away, and Zach said if we all got killed, or worse, taken on the train, we didn't want to leave the horses out there all alone.

That kind of talk made me nervous.

Zach had the old man carry the basket of ham and bread. I had the folding stools under my arm, and Zach carried the cloth-covered mirror, which was a really light tote. He, of course, wore the big gun on his hip.

It wasn't a long walk. You were in town one moment, and then you weren't. Before you knew it, you was traveling along a moonlit trail in the woods, on down to the river. You could hear it gurgling before you could see it.

When we got to the river, Zach said to the old man, "Where were you when the train came?"

"Almost right here. Maybe a little closer to the river."

It was a full-moon night and it was near bright as day, and the moon's reflection in the water made it look as if it was floating on the river. The water and the trees looked to be frosted.

Zach got out his big turnip watch and popped the cover on it and looked at the time in the silver moonlight.

"We are two hours ahead of time. Good."

I unfolded the stools as Zach set the mirror so that it stood upright, but with the cloth still over it. The old man placed the basket on the ground and sat down heavily on one of the stools.

I won't lie to you. I was as nervous as a long-tailed cat in a room full of rocking chairs, and the old man, well, I think he was starting to wish maybe all those years he shouldn't have been planning to come back here and set Jenny free. And maybe it wasn't so much about Jenny as it was getting rid of the baggage before he died. I figured that was what his lookout was for.

Get her off that train and lose that baggage.

Zach gave me a little bag and told me to put it in my pocket, that it was my protection. I took it and did just that, but I'll tell you, the idea that there might be anything in that little bag that would spare me from what was on that train was hard to grasp.

"What about me?" the old man said.

"You don't get a bag," Zach said. "You got to depend on me."

Zach ate some more of the ham and bread, but me, I was too nervous to eat, and so was the old man. We sat there watching the river, the woods, and the big ole moon, waiting for the tick of midnight, which came slow. The minutes weren't in any hurry that night, and seemed each of them was an hour long.

Finally, Zach got out his watch again, looked at it, said, "Won't be long now."

Short time after he said that, the air turned chill and we heard a kind of chugging, a long way off, but the sound was growing closer. There was a long, high, lonesome whistle and a series of toots. It sounded like a train, and at the same time it didn't.

Black smoke appeared above the moon-tipped trees and a rolling white mist moved between the trees and blew over the river. When the mist faded there were tracks lying right on top of the river, and running on through a gauzy silver split in the woods. Then, here come that train. You could see the cowcatcher in front, black and shiny as Cain's sin, and the one big light of the train was like a burning red eye. The whistle blew long and hard, and the air went still as an oil painting, and there was a bright cold glow around us for some distance, and outside of that glow I could see bats frozen in flight. Time had stopped out there, but we were inside the spell of the train and what it carried.

The train chugged on across the river, and the engine passed us close enough that the wind from it blew off the old man's hat. He didn't try to chase it down. He may not have even known he'd lost it, so intent was he on that strange, black train.

The train stopped with part of it on the tracks stretching across the river, but with a lot of it on the riverbank. The engine was right next to us. You could hear the train crackle as the hot engine was being cooled by the air. We was still on our stools, but now we stood up, and I could see that the old man was trembling like a naked man in a snowstorm. Zach seemed remarkably calm. He pushed his coat back so that the hilt of the hoodoo gun showed. He took a deep breath.

Then came a snapping sound, like a big bone breaking, and a door on the side of the train sprang open. Down came some steps. They just flopped right out of the train and expanded, with the bottom step lying flat out on the ground.

Something moved inside the doorway, and then it leaped out, not bothering with the steps. It was a kind of black frog, I think, and yet it looked somewhat like a man, bent low and held up by its squatty legs. Its hands were in front of it, and the thing was rubbing them together like a fat man ready for lunch. It had a mouthful of long, sharp teeth.

Another one of those things sprang into view, pale and larger than the other, more upright. It didn't have no teeth at all, just pink gums the way the old man had described them.

A boot stuck out of the doorway, rested heavy on the top step. A leg grew up from the boot, and then another boot came out of the train, and a leg grew up inside of that, and then above the legs the air darkened and took the shape of a man dressed all in white, except for black stripes on his pants. He wore a snow-white hat and had on a long white duster. He smiled. It was how the old man had described. The tops of his lips nearly touched his ears, and that mouth was like an open doorway to somewhere you didn't want to go. It was filled with teeth that made you think of murder and cannibals. The man's eyes—if it was a man—had a dead look, but in the whites of his eyes were little red shadows. They flickered and crawled. His forked tongue lashed out and whipped back inside his mouth like a snake discovering the weather was bad.

It was the Dueling Man, of course.

The Dueling Man turned his head from side to side, as if trying to figure us, and then he pushed his duster back on both sides, and you could see his guns, and they were just as the old man had described them.

Zach stepped so that he was centered with the man, and when he did he said, "Move the mirror up beside me, son. Now!"

I did just that. The mirror was so light and easy to handle I managed it in instants.

The Dueling Man's expression hadn't changed. He wiggled his long fingers and the whites of his eyes were no longer white with red shadows flicking around the edges. They had turned completely blood-red. The frog-things squatted on either side of him.

"Take the cloth off the mirror," Zach said.

I whipped it off, and when I did, the Dueling Man's head pivoted slightly to take in his reflection in that silver mirror. I looked at that reflection. It was of a handsome man in the Dueling Man's clothes, not nearly as tall, normal teeth. Squatting beside him was a sad-looking naked man on one side, and an even sadder-looking naked woman on the other side of him. Tears fat as raindrops began to run down their faces.

I glanced at them, back to the mirror. The handsome reflection of the Dueling Man drooped and he rested his hands on the hilts of his pistols like he was all worn out. He sagged inside his duster and white clothes. His unique boots looked worn and scuffed, and as I watched his white suit frayed and became covered in dust that made the cloth gray. The brim of his hat lost its snap and wilted.

The wide, ear-licking smile on the Dueling Man's face closed slowly, and he just stood there, looking at his reflection in the mirror, thinking on who he had been before he became a slave to the train and the Engineer. I felt sure that's what the reflection was. Who he had been.

In that instant, Zach drew.

It was a cheater's way to do it, but it was still the right way to do it. The Dueling Man, distracted by who he once was, hesitated, and that's when Zach's pistol cracked. A hole about the size of the tip of my thumb spotted him between the eyes and you could hear what had been in his head splattering out behind him.

His long legs wiggled and then they collapsed inside his boots and all of him, clothes and flesh, went into those boots and the white hat fell down on top.

The demons came for Zach.

The old man looked as if he might run. "Hold up," I said.

"I got him," Zach said, and even as those demons rushed forward, he whipped the gun over his shoulder and shot the old man right in the chest, without even looking.

The old man crumpled, ended up on his knees. He held his hand to his chest and fell forward, his face in the dirt.

"Consider that an extra good deed," Zach said as he shot one of the demons solid in the head, and then shot the other. It was all so fast and so calm you would have thought Zach wasn't doing nothing more than out target shooting.

The demons collapsed onto the riverbank and the next instant they were gone to dust. The train fired up and I bolted for the steps, hit them with a leap and was inside the train just as the steps clapped up behind me and the door slammed shut.

The train's corridor ran left and right. I could see all the way up to the open engine, and I could see the Engineer with his big engineer's hat on and his dirty overalls, his flesh all taut, the bones in his face breaking through in spots. I swear he had an extra set of arms that lifted up out of his overalls. He and the Fireman, who was short and stout and dark from soot, sweat-licked from the fire in the engine, were loading gut-wrapped bodies into the fire.

They stared at me, but neither moved toward me. They kept loading those bodies, working to get that train to run. If it did, and I couldn't get off before my protection went thin, then I would be trapped.

I took a deep breath and turned in the other direction, started through the cars. The seats were full and the people in them, if you could call them that, were coming out of them. They were blistered and scarred and their hair was in patches. They all reached out for me, but soon as they touched me the spell in my pocket coated them with fire.

They leapt back and the flames went away. I moved on through the boxcar, yelling, "Miss Jenny, I am a hoodoo man, and I've come for you."

A man and a woman stood up from a seat and moved into the aisle in front of me. At first, they were just two scab-covered monsters, like all the rest, and then one of them called my name and I knew immediately who they were.

My mother and father. I won't lie to you, hate them as I did, I was sad to think of where they ended up. Somewhere along the line they'd gotten in the hoodoo and when they was killed, they took the train ride. I felt my heart melt. But pretty soon it was solid again. What they wanted wasn't me, it was a way off that train. Zach was my family. Not them.

By then the train was chugging and moving and rocking, and it was hot in there. It was as if the heat was lessened by that charm in my pocket, but I could feel it pushing at the air around me. I was starting to grow weak.

I kind of closed my eyes and forced myself between my mother and father, remembering how my father had beat me with a strop and my mother had cheered him on. They reached out to touch me as I passed, and their hands flamed. They screamed and stepped back into their row.

"Miss Jenny!" I called out again and again.

Then, as I entered the next boxcar, a little figure came out of one of the seats and staggered toward me. I could see that she was female, but her boiled skin flapped off her face and her neck was broken so that her head was on her shoulder. She was naked, but it wasn't an exciting kind of naked. It was the kind that made your stomach churn and your brain deny.

She said to me in a voice that bubbled as if she was swallowing lava, "I am Jenny."

I hesitated, but finally stuck out my hand. She took it. No flames came off of me and jumped on her. It was Jenny all right. I turned and started pulling her after me as I ran back through the boxcars.

We hadn't gone far when I seen the old man that had hired Zach. He had been hoodooed onto the train, and his baggage was full grown now, weighting him down so much he was nearly bent double. He lifted an eye and looked up at me. The baggage, a filthy old woman that I knew was Consuela, grinned rotten teeth at me.

"Help me," he said.

"You earned your place," I said, and pushed by him and the thing on his back, yanked at Jenny's hand. I glanced back at her, saw her head was straight now and the flesh on her face was flapping back into place and her skin was turning to its former coffee and cream color that the old man had described.

We came to the doorway and the steps. I opened the door with my free hand, kicked the steps out.

When I looked up the Engineer was hustling from his place up front, coming along the floor like a spider, using those extra arms to launch him forward. His engineer hat tilted to one side, but it stayed on his head.

Behind him, in the engine room the Fireman's face turned soft and he yelled in a voice that coughed out in smoke, "Run. Run for all you're worth."

There wasn't really anyplace to run, but there was the open door now and the night outside, the moonlight.

I said to Jenny, "Jump."

I pushed Jenny in front of me and gave her a bit of a push, and she jumped. I stepped onto the top step, coiled my legs and leaped, just as the Engineer grabbed my boot, and it come off in his hand.

I went tumbling, and it was like I'd never stop. Down a grassy hill and into a wad of briars and brush. I hit something hard then and I was out.

When I awoke, my head was in Jenny's lap. She was put back together, so to speak. Her features were smooth and beautiful, and her skin looked like chocolate there in the moonlight. She was stroking my forehead. Tears were running down her cheeks.

"You got me off that awful train, away from that awful place."

I sat up slowly and looked around. There wasn't no train tracks and no train, and I had no idea where we was.

After I got to my feet and looked around, placed the moon, which was beginning to slide down behind the trees, I knew the direction to go. I was all cut up from the briars and such, but Jenny had pulled me out of them, and wiped me off with the folds of her dress, staining it with my blood. I had nothing worse than a missing boot and a slight limp that was going away even as we walked. Jenny had hit ahead of the briars and wasn't cut up at all. Her blue dress was ripped a little and there were pieces of weeds and cockleburs in her hair, but she looked fine.

We finally managed to get to where Zach was. He had covered the mirror and was sitting on one of the stools, eating some ham and bread.

Except for the Dueling Man's boots and his hat on top of them, there was nothing left of him. The body of the old man was there, but I knew his soul was on that train with his baggage, riding on and on for a bleak eternity. And I knew, too, from the way Zach was smiling, his baggage was gone.

"Hello there," Zach said.

Jenny stayed on with us, which suited me fine. She didn't have any connection to her old life. The café she had worked at and the people there were long gone. I found me and her kind of suited one another.

Since I didn't have no baggage on me, I felt I could have a life, a relationship, not like before when I was linked to Zach. You see, after that night I was done with the hoodoo in any shape or form.

I quit working at the gun shop too. Zach insisted. He wrapped the hoodoo gun up and put it away.

Me and Jenny was hitched by the Justice of the Peace, got a place of our own. In our little home, no demons came out after midnight, and I could get up and have a glass of water or go to the outhouse anytime I pleased.

One day, when I went to visit Zach, just to see how he was, not to get involved in anything, he and everything in the shop was gone.

A man down at the livery told me Zach bought a wagon, hitched his horses to them, and that was the last he had seen of him. But Zach had left me something, figuring I'd come to the livery to ask about him, since a wagon would have to be rented or purchased to haul off all that was in the shop.

What Zach left me was a wooden box.

"It don't have no key," said the man at the livery.

I took it home and used a chisel to pry it open. Inside was the bag of silver the old man had given Zach. In the bottom of the box was a note.

SO YOU AND JENNY DON'T HAVE TO WORRY NONE.

Well, so far, me and Jenny don't have no worries, but now and again I think about Zach and wonder where he is, and if he's still gunsmithing, or if he might be back heavy in the hoodoo business again.

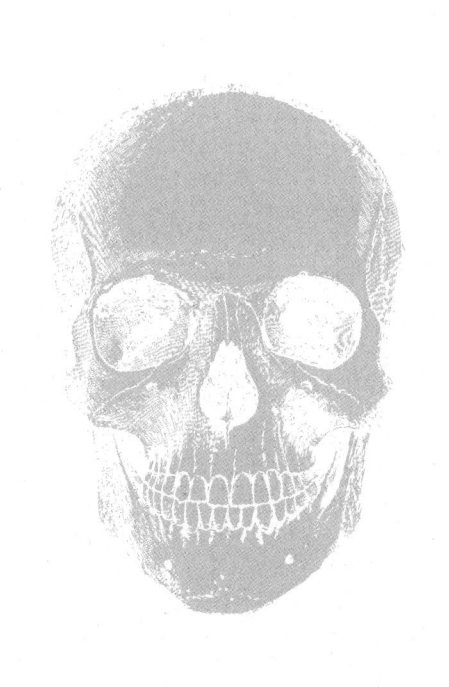

The God, or Lord, of the Razor has been with me for a very long time. There are several stories about him. This is the original short story, though the character and the ideas around the character came from my novel *The Nightrunners*.

I wrote some of the novel in 1980, right before I went full-time, and finished it in 1983, I believe. I liked it. It was as dark as spoiled fruit, but I felt it was good. It was my third novel.

Publishers were less enthused. They thought it was good, powerful, disturbing, and those last two impressions kept it from being published.

Several years later, it was published. I think it missed out on the darker horror trend by a few years, but hell, it was out there.

But while I waited for it to find a home, I borrowed from the novel. It inspired several short stories. One was directly lifted from a section of the novel, and others were inspired by scenes in the book. One of those inspired was "God of the Razor."

I took an idea from the novel that could be interpreted in different ways: a real creature or something in the warped and delusional brain of one of the novel's villains. I gave it a more solid footing. Well, I decided it was real, not a delusion. I liked that story, and still do, thus its inclusion. I also liked the God of the Razor enough to bring him back in different incarnations. I expect more will come.

It's an early story, but it still has that creep factor.

God of the Razor

RICHARDS ARRIVED AT the house about eight.

The moon was full and it was a very bright night, in spite of occasional cloud cover; bright enough that he could get a good look at the place. It was just as the owner had described it. Run-down. Old. And very ugly.

The style was sort of Gothic, sort of plantation, sort of cracker box. Like maybe the architect had been unable to decide on a game plan, or had been drunkenly in love with impossible angles.

Digging the key loaned him from his pocket, he hoped this would turn out worth the trip. More than once his search for antiques had turned into a wild goose chase. And this time, it was really a long shot. The owner, a sick old man named Klein, hadn't been inside the house in twenty years. A lot of things could happen to antiques in that time, even if the place was locked and boarded up. Theft. Insects. Rats. Leaks. Any one of those, or a combination of, could turn the finest of furniture into rubble and sawdust in no time. But it was worth the gamble. On occasion, his luck had been phenomenal.

As a thick, dark cloud rolled across the moon, Richards, guided by his flashlight, mounted the rickety porch, squeaked the screen, and groaned the door open.

Inside, he flashed the light around. Dust and darkness seemed to crawl in there until the cloud passed and the lunar light fell through the boarded windows in a speckled and slatted design akin to camouflaged netting. In places, Richards could see that the wallpaper had fallen from the wall in big sheets that dangled halfway down to the floor like the drooping branches of weeping willows.

To his left was a wide, spiraling staircase, and following its ascent with his light, he could see there were places where the railing hung brokenly askew.

Directly across from this was a door. A narrow, recessed one. As there was nothing in the present room to command his attention, he decided to begin his investigation there. It was as good a place as any.

Using his flashlight to bat his way through a skin of cobwebs, he went over to the door and opened it. Cold air embraced him, brought with it a sour smell, like a freezer full of ruined meat. It was almost enough to turn Richards's stomach, and for a moment he started to close the door and forget it. But an image of wall-to-wall antiques clustered in the shadows came to mind, and he pushed forward, determined. If he were going to go to all the trouble to get the key and drive way out here in search of old furniture to buy, then he ought to make sure he had a good look, smell or no smell.

Using his flash, and helped by the moonlight, he could tell that he had discovered a basement. The steps leading down into it looked aged and precarious, and the floor appeared oddly glasslike in the beam of his light.

So he could examine every nook and cranny of the basement, Richards decided to descend the stairs. He put one foot carefully on the first step, and slowly settled his weight on it. Nothing collapsed. He went down three more steps, cautiously, and though they moaned and squeaked, they held.

When Richards reached the sixth step, for some reason he could not define, he felt oddly uncomfortable, had a chill. It was as if someone with ice-cold water in their kidneys had taken a piss down the back of his coat collar.

Now he could see that the floor was not glassy at all. In fact, the floor was not visible. The reason it had looked glassy from above was because it was flooded with water. From the overall size of the basement, Richards determined that the water was most likely six or seven feet deep. Maybe more.

There was movement at the edge of Richards's flashlight beam, and he followed it. A huge rat was swimming away from him, pushing something before it; an old partially deflated volleyball perhaps. He could not tell for sure. Nor could he decide if the rat was trying to mount the object or bite it.

And he didn't care. Two things that gave him the willies were rats and water, and here were both. To make it worse, the rat was the biggest he'd ever seen, and the water was the dirtiest imaginable. It looked to have a lot of oil and sludge mixed in with it, as well as being stagnant.

It grew darker, and Richards realized the moon had been hazed by a cloud again. He let that be his signal. There was nothing more to see here, so he turned and started up. Stopped. The very large shape of a man filled the doorway.

Richards jerked the light up, saw that the shadows had been playing tricks on him. The man was not as large as he'd first thought. And he wasn't wearing a hat. He had been certain before that he was, but he could see now that he was mistaken. The fellow was bareheaded, and his features, though youthful, were undistinguished; any character he might have had seemed to retreat into the flesh of his face or find sanctuary within the dark folds of his shaggy hair. As he lowered the light, Richards thought he saw the wink of braces on the young man's teeth.

"Basements aren't worth a damn in this part of the country," the young man said. "Must have been some Yankees come down here and built this. Someone who didn't know about the water table, the weather and all."

"I didn't know anyone else was here," Richards said. "Klein send you?"

"Don't know a Klein."

"He owns the place. Loaned me a key."

The young man was silent a moment. "Did you know the moon is behind a cloud? A cloud across the moon can change the entire face of the night. Change it the way some people change their clothes, their moods, their expressions."

Richards shifted uncomfortably.

"You know," the young man said, "I couldn't shave this morning."

"Beg pardon?"

"When I tried to put a blade in my razor, I saw that it had an eye on it, and it was blinking at me, very fast. Like this . . . oh, you can't see from down there, can you? Well, it was very fast. I dropped it and it slid along the sink, dove off on the floor, crawled up the side of the bathtub, and got in the soap dish. It closed its eye then, but it started mewing like a kitten wanting milk. Ooooowwwwaaa, oooowwwaa, was more the way it sounded really, but it reminded me of a kitten. I knew what it wanted, of course. What it always wants. What all the sharp things want.

"Knowing what it wanted made me sick and I threw up in the toilet. Vomited up a razor blade. It was so fat it might have been pregnant. Its eye was blinking at me as I flushed it. When it was gone the blade in the soap dish started to sing high and silly-like.

"The blade I vomited, I know how it got inside of me." The young man raised his fingers to his throat. "There was a little red mark right here this morning, and it was starting to scab over. One or two of them always find a way in. Sometimes it's nails that get in me. They used to come in through the soles of my feet while I slept, but I stopped that pretty good by wearing my shoes to bed."

In spite of the cool of the basement, Richards had started to sweat. He considered the possibility of rushing the guy or just trying to push past him, but dismissed it. The stairs might be too weak for sudden movement, and maybe the fruitcake might just have his say and go on his way.

"It really doesn't matter how hard I try to trick them," the young man continued, "they always win out in the end. Always."

"I think I'll come up now," Richards said, trying very hard to sound casual.

The young man flexed his legs. The stairs shook and squealed in protest. Richards nearly toppled backward into the water.

"Hey!" Richards yelled.

"Bad shape," the young man said. "Need a lot of work. Rebuilt entirely would be the ticket."

Richards regained both his balance and his composure. He couldn't decide if he was angry or scared, but he wasn't about to move. Going up he had rotten stairs and Mr. Looney Tunes. Behind him he had the rats and water. The proverbial rock and a hard place.

"Maybe it's going to cloud up and rain," the young man said. "What do you think? Will it rain tonight?"

"I don't know," Richards managed.

"Lot of dark clouds floating about. Maybe they're rain clouds. Did I tell you about the God of the Razor? I really meant to. He rules the sharp things. He's the god of those who live by the blade. He was my friend. Donny's god. Did you know he was Jack the Ripper's god?"

The young man dipped his hand into his coat pocket, pulled it out quickly and whipped his arm across his body twice, very fast. Richards caught a glimpse of something long and metal in his hand. Even the cloud-veiled moonlight managed to give it a dull, silver spark.

Richards put the light on him again. The young man was holding the object in front of him, as if he wished it to be examined. It was an impossibly large straight razor.

"I got this from Donny," the young man said. "He got it in an old shop somewhere. Gladewater, I think. It comes from a barber kit, and the kit originally came from England. Says so in the case. You should see the handle on this baby. Ivory. With a lot of little designs and symbols carved into it. Donny looked the symbols up. They're geometric patterns used for calling up a demon. Know what else? Jack the Ripper was no surgeon. He was a barber. I know, because Donny got the razor and started having these visions where Jack the Ripper and the God of the Razor came to talk to him. They explained what the razor was for. Donny said the reason they could talk to him was because he tried to shave with the razor and cut himself. The blood on the blade, and those symbols on the handle, they opened the gate. Opened it so the God of the Razor could come and live inside Donny's head. The Ripper told him that the metal in the blade goes all the way back to a sacrificial altar the Druids used."

The young man stopped talking, dropped the blade to his side. He looked over his shoulder. "That cloud is very dark . . . slow-moving. I sort of bet on rain." He turned back to Richards. "Did I ask you if you thought it would rain tonight?"

Richards found he couldn't say a word. It was as if his tongue had turned to cork in his mouth. The young man didn't seem to notice or care.

"After Donny had the visions, he just talked and talked about this house. We used to play here when we were kids. Had the boards on the back window rigged so they'd slide like a trap door. They're still that way. . . . Donny used to say this house had angles that sharpened the dull edges of your mind. I know what he means now. It is comfortable, don't you think?"

Richards, who was anything but comfortable, said nothing. Just stood very still, sweating, fearing, listening, aiming the light.

"Donny said the angles were honed best during the full moon. I didn't know what he was talking about then. I didn't understand about the sacrifices. Maybe you know about them? Been all over the papers and on the TV. The Decapitator, they called him.

"It was Donny doing it, and from the way he started acting, talking about the God of the Razor, Jack the Ripper, this old house and its angles, I got suspicious. He got so he wouldn't even come around near or during a full moon, and when the moon started waning, he was different. Peaceful. I followed him a few times, but didn't have any luck. He drove to the Safeway, left his car there and walked. He was as quick and sneaky as a cat. He'd lose me right off. But then I got to figuring . . . him talking about this old house and all . . . and one full moon I came here and waited for him, and he showed up. You know what he was doing? He was bringing the heads here, tossing them down there in the water like those South American Indians used to toss bodies and stuff in sacrificial pools. . . . It's the angles in the house, you see."

Richards had that sensation like ice-cold piss down his collar again, and suddenly he knew what that swimming rat had been pursuing, and what it was trying to do.

"He threw all seven heads down there, I figure," the young man said. "I saw him toss one." He pointed with the razor. "He was standing about where you are now when he did it. When he turned and saw me, he ran up after me. I froze, couldn't move a muscle. Every step he took, closer he got to me, the stranger he looked. . . . He slashed me with the razor, across the chest, real deep. I fell down and he stood over me, the razor cocked." The young man cocked the razor to show Richards. "I think I screamed. But he didn't cut me again. It was like the rest of him was warring with the razor in his hand. He stood up, and walking stiff as one of those wind-up toy soldiers, he went back down the stairs, stood about where you are now, looked up at me, and drew that razor straight across his throat so hard and deep he damn near cut his head off. He fell back in the water there, sunk like an anvil. The razor landed on the last step.

"Wasn't any use; I tried to get him out of there, but he was gone, like he'd never been. I couldn't see a ripple. But the razor was lying there and I could hear it. Hear it sucking up Donny's blood like a kid sucking the sweet out of a sucker. Pretty soon there wasn't a drop of blood on it. I picked it up . . . so shiny, so damned shiny. I came upstairs, passed out on the floor from the loss of blood.

"At first I thought I was dreaming, or maybe delirious, because I was lying at the end of this dark alley between these trash cans with my back against the wall. There were legs sticking out of the trash cans, like tossed mannequins. Only they weren't mannequins. There were razor blades and nails sticking out of the soles of the feet and blood was running down the ankles and legs, swirling so that they looked like giant peppermint sticks. Then I heard a noise like someone trying to dribble a medicine ball across a hardwood floor. *Plop, plop, plop.* And then I saw the God of the Razor.

"First there's nothing in front of me but stewing shadows, and the next instant he's there. Tall and black . . . not Negro . . . but black like obsidian rock. Had eyes like smashed windshield glass and teeth like polished stickpins. Was wearing a top hat with this shiny band made out of chrome razor blades. His coat and pants looked like they were made out of human flesh, and sticking out of the pockets of his coat were gnawed fingers, like after-dinner treats. And he had this big old turnip pocket watch dangling out of his pants pocket on a strand of gut. The watch swung between his legs as he walked. And that plopping sound, know what that was? His shoes. He had these tiny, tiny feet and they were fitted right into the mouths of these human heads. One of the heads was a woman's and it dragged long black hair behind it when the God walked.

"Kept telling myself to wake up. But I couldn't. The God pulled this chair out of nowhere—it was made out of leg bones and the seat looked like scraps of flesh and hunks of hair—and he sat down, crossed his legs and dangled one of those ragged-head shoes in my face. Next thing he does is whip this ventriloquist dummy out of the air, and it looked like Donny, and was dressed like Donny had been last time I'd seen him, down there on the stairs. The God put the dummy on his knee and Donny opened his eyes and spoke. 'Hey, buddy boy,' he said, 'how goes it? What do you think of the razor's bite? You see, pal, if you don't die from it, it's like a vampire's bite. Get my drift? You got to keep passing it on. The sharp things will tell you when, and if you don't want to do it, they'll bother you until you do, or you slice yourself bad enough to come over here on the Darkside with me and Jack and the others. Well, got to go back now, join the gang. Be talking with you real soon, moving into your head.'

"Then he just sort of went limp on the God's knee, and the God took off his hat and he had this zipper running along the middle of his bald head. A goddamned zipper! He pulled it open. Smoke and fire and noises like screaming and car wrecks happening came out of there. He picked up the Donny dummy, which was real small now, and tossed him into the hole in his head way you'd toss a treat into a Great Dane's mouth. Then he zipped up again and put on his hat. Never said a word. But he leaned forward and held his turnip watch so I could see it. The watch hands were skeleton fingers, and there was a face in there, pressing its nose in little smudged circles against the glass, and though I couldn't hear it, the face had its mouth open and it was screaming, and *that face was mine.* Then the God and the alley and the legs in the trash cans were gone. And so was the cut on my chest. Healed completely. Not even a mark.

"I left out of there and didn't tell a soul. And Donny, just like he said, came to live in my head, and the razor started singing to me nights, probably a song sort of like those sirens sang for that Ulysses fellow. And come near and on the full moon, the blades act up, mew and get inside of me. Then I know what I need to do . . . I did it tonight. Maybe if it had rained I wouldn't have had to do it . . . but it was clear enough for me to be busy."

The young man stopped talking, turned, stepped inside the house, out of sight. Richards sighed, but his relief was short-lived. The young man returned and came down a couple of steps. In one hand, by the long blonde hair, he was holding a teenage girl's head. The other clutched the razor.

The cloud veil fell away from the moon, and it became quite bright.

The young man, with a flick of his wrist, tossed the head at Richards, striking him in the chest, causing him to drop the light. The head bounced between Richards's legs and into the water with a flat splash.

"Listen . . ." Richards started, but anything he might have said aged, died, and turned to dust in his mouth.

Fully outlined in the moonlight, the young man started down the steps, holding the razor before him like a battle flag.

Richards blinked. For a moment it looked as if the guy were wearing a . . . he was wearing a hat. A tall, black one with a shiny, metal band. And he was much larger now, and between his lips was a shimmer of wet, silver teeth like thirty-two polished stickpins.

Plop, plop came the sound of his feet on the steps, and in the lower and deeper shadows of the stairs, it looked as if the young man had not only grown in size and found a hat but had darkened his face and stomped his feet into pumpkins . . . but one of the pumpkins streamed long, dark hair.

Plop, plop . . . Richards screamed and the sound of it rebounded against the basement walls like a superball.

Shattered starlight eyes beneath the hat. A Cheshire smile of argentine needles in a carbon face. A big dark hand holding the razor, whipping it back and forth like a lion's talon snatching at warm, soft prey.

Swish, swish, swish.

Richards's scream was dying in his throat, if not in the echoing basement, when the razor flashed for him. He avoided it by stepping briskly backward. His foot went underwater, but found a step there. Momentarily. The rotting wood gave way, twisted his ankle, sent him plunging into the cold, foul wetness.

Just before his eyes, like portholes on a sinking ship, were covered by the liquid darkness, he saw the God of the Razor—now manifest in all his horrid form—lift a splitting head shoe and step into the water after him. Richards torqued his body, swam long, hard strokes, coasted bottom; his hand touched something cold and clammy down there and a piece of it came away in his fingers.

Flipping it from him with a fan of his hand, he fought his way to the surface and broke water as the blonde girl's head bobbed in front of him, two rat passengers aboard, gnawing viciously at the eye sockets.

Suddenly, the girl's head rose, perched on the crown of the tall hat of the God of the Razor, then it tumbled off, rats and all, into the greasy water.

Now there was the jet face of the God of the Razor and his mouth was open and the teeth blinked briefly before the lips drew tight, and the other hand, like an eggplant sprouting fingers, clutched Richards's coat collar and plucked him forward and Richards—the charnel breath of the God in his face, the sight of the lips slashing wide to once again reveal brilliant dental grill work—went limp as a pelt. And the God raised the razor to strike.

And the moon tumbled behind a thick, dark cloud.

White face, shaggy hair, no hat, a fading glint of silver teeth . . . the young man holding the razor, clutching Richards's coat collar.

The juice back in his heart, Richards knocked the man's hand free, and the guy went under. Came up thrashing. Went under again. And when he rose this time, the razor was frantically flaying the air.

"Can't swim," he bellowed, "can't—" Under he went, and this time he did not come up. But Richards felt something touch his foot from below. He kicked out savagely, dog paddling wildly all the while. Then the touch was gone and the sloshing water went immediately calm.

Richards swam toward the broken stairway, tried to ignore the blonde head that lurched by, now manned by a four-rat crew. He got hold of the loose, dangling stair rail and began to pull himself up. The old board screeched on its loosening nail, but held until Richards gained a hand on the door ledge, then it gave way with a groan and went to join the rest of the rotting lumber, the heads, the bodies, the faded stigmata of the God of the Razor.

Pulling himself up, Richards crawled into the room on his hands and knees, rolled over on his back . . . and something flashed between his legs. . . . It was the razor. It was stuck to the bottom of his shoe. . . . That had been the touch he had felt from below; the young guy still trying to cut him, or perhaps accidentally striking him during his desperate thrashings to regain the surface.

Sitting up, Richards took hold of the ivory handle and freed the blade. He got to his feet and stumbled toward the door. His ankle and foot hurt like hell where the step had given way beneath him, hurt him so badly he could hardly walk.

Then he felt the sticky, warm wetness oozing out of his foot to join the cold water in his shoe, and he knew that he had been cut by the razor.

But then he wasn't thinking anymore. He wasn't hurting anymore. The moon rolled out from behind a cloud like a colorless eye and he just stood there looking at his shadow on the lawn. The shadow of an impossibly large man wearing a top hat and balls on his feet, holding a monstrous razor in his hand.

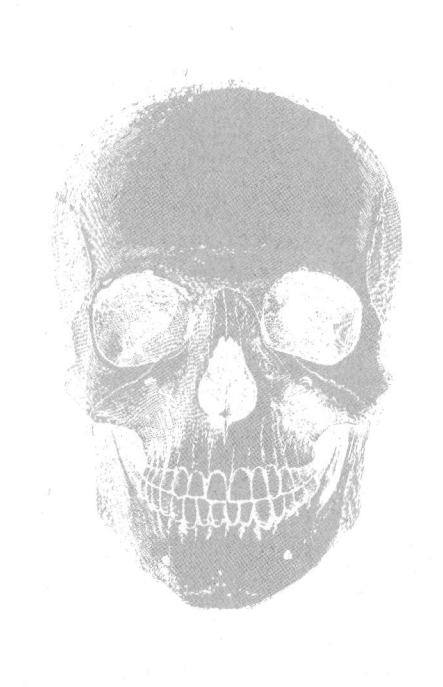

I forget where this first appeared. It's probably in the credits in the book, if you want to look it up. It's been reprinted quite a bit, and there was a "children's-style" book done of it.

It's dark, and it's funny in a disturbing way. And it's about something other than the title suggests.

That's for the reader to read and find out.

I had noticed when I was writing that there were a lot of magazines that bought short-short stories, or "flash fiction," as it called nowadays, yet there weren't many of these stories as compared to longer ones. Partly because most writers couldn't write that short effectively. And because it's an unjustly disrespected branch of story writing.

If it's short, it can't be good.

Not true.

There's a short piece often attributed to Ernest Hemingway, though there's some disagreement on that, but the story goes:

Baby shoes for sale. Never worn.

Now that's short and powerful.

This one is not that short, but I think it packs a punch beyond the obvious one.

My Dead Dog Bobby

MY DEAD DOG, Bobby, doesn't do tricks anymore. In fact, to look that sucker in the eye I either have to get down on my knees and put my head to the ground or prop him up with a stick.

I've thought of nailing his head to the shed out back, that way maybe the ants won't be so bad. But as my Old Man says, "Ants can climb." So, maybe that isn't such a good idea after all.

He was such a good dog, though, and I hate to see him rot away. But I'm also tired of carrying him around with me in a sack, lugging him into the freezer morning and night.

One thing though. Getting killed broke him from chasing cars, which is how he got mashed in the first place. Now, to get him to play with cars, I have to go out to the edge of the Interstate and throw him and his sack at them, and when he gets caught under the tires and bounced up, I have to use my foot to push on one end of him to make the other end fill up with guts again. I get so I really kind of hate to look in the sack at the end of the day, and I have to admit giving him his good-night kiss on the lips is not nearly as fun as it used to be. He has a smell and the teeth that have been smashed through his snout are sharp and stick out every which way and sometimes cut my face.

I'm going to take Bobby down to the lake again tomorrow. If you tie him to a blowed-up inner tube he floats. It's not a bad way to cool off from a hot day, and it also drowns the ants and maggots and such.

I know it does. We kept my little brother in pretty good shape for six months that way. It wasn't until we started nailing him to the shed out back that he got to looking ragged. It wasn't the ants crawling up there and getting him, it was the damn nails. We ran out of good places to drive them after his ears came off, and we had to use longer and longer nails to put through his head and neck and the like. Pulling the nails out every day with the hammer claw didn't do him any good either.

My Old Man said that if he had it do over, he wouldn't have hit my brother so hard with that chair. But he said that about my little sister, too, when he kicked her head in. She didn't keep long, by the way. We didn't know as many tricks then as we do now.

Well, I hope I can get Bobby back in this sack. He's starting to swell and come apart on me. I'm sort of ready to get him packed away so I can get home and see Mom. I always look at her for a few minutes before I put Bobby in the freezer with her.

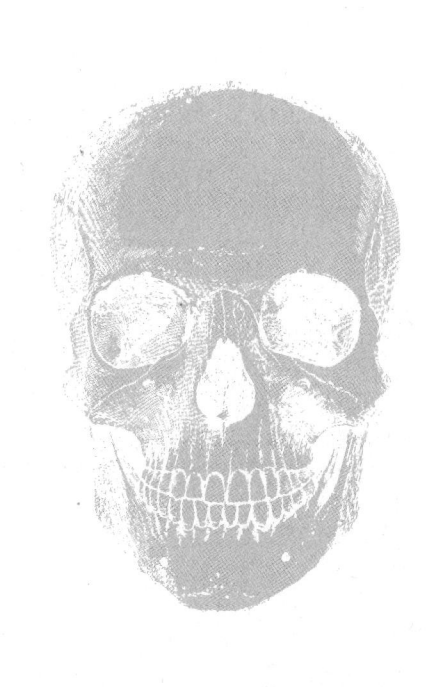

This is probably the first of my stories that really got noticed, which then led to previous stories being recognized. At the time, I was struggling to maintain having gone full-time writer. My wife had a job, and in a few years, she would be working for me, but at this moment in time I was nervous, having a young son, Keith, and a very hardworking wife, Karen, the love of my life. And here I was, fiddling with stories and hardly making enough to pay for my typewriter ribbons and carbon paper, typing paper, and mailing. Also, I wrote so much and so fast, I burned out a Montgomery Ward electric typewriter yearly. It was electric, but it still had keys, and sometimes I'd hear *PING*, and one of the keys would go flying.

Was I going to have to go back to being a janitor? Solid work that it is, it wasn't my career dream. I was selling, but not much. Bottom line, I was contributing to us making a living, but mostly I was just managing to make enough to feel that I was working. But what was I achieving? And then this story came out in John Maclay's anthology *Nukes*, edited by Jerry Williamson, the same year *Dead in the West* came out and solidified my small-press credentials and *The Magic Wagon* came out from Doubleday and put me in the publishing mainstream. The story put my short stories in demand and led to my first collection a few years later, *By Bizarre Hands*.

I didn't like the story much when I was writing it. Can't tell you why, but I had my doubts. I thought the idea was good but felt it was a little off the mark.

It was purchased, and Maclay and Williamson liked it a lot, and then it was up for the World Fantasy Award, which to

this day most people think I won for that story.

I did not. My friend David Schow won for "Red Light."

But the story has continued to be reprinted and is one of the stories often mentioned by dedicated readers of my work. Rereading sometime later, I couldn't figure what it was I was worried about. The story worked well.

It still does.

An apocalyptic world. Numerous fifties science fiction influences. Nice imagery, if I say so myself, and I do, and I truly believe that it is haunting not only during the reading but after you put the story down.

Tight Little Stitches in a Dead Man's Back

For Ardath Mayhar

FROM THE JOURNAL OF PAUL MARDER

(Boom!)

That's a little scientist joke, and the proper way to begin this. As for the purpose of my notebook, I'm uncertain. Perhaps to organize my thoughts and not to go insane.

No. Probably so I can read it and feel as if I'm being spoken to. Maybe neither of those reasons. It doesn't matter. I just want to do it, and that is enough.

What's new?

Well, Mr. Journal, after all these years I've taken up martial arts again— or at least the forms and calisthenics of Tae Kwon Do. There is no one to spar with here in the lighthouse, so the forms have to do.

There is Mary, of course, but she keeps all her sparring verbal. And as of late, there is not even that. I long for her to call me a sonofabitch. Anything. Her hatred of me has cured to 100-percent perfection and she no longer finds it necessary to speak. The tight lines around her eyes and mouth, the emotional heat that radiates from her body like a dreadful cold sore looking for a place to lie down is voice enough for her. She lives only for the moment when she (the cold sore) can attach herself to me with her needles, ink and thread. She lives only for the design on my back.

That's all I live for as well. Mary adds to it nightly and I enjoy the pain. The tattoo is of a great blue mushroom cloud, and in the cloud, etched ghost-like, is the face of our daughter, Rae. Her lips are drawn tight, eyes are closed, and there are stitches deeply pulled to simulate the lashes. When I move fast and hard they rip slightly and Rae cries bloody tears.

That's one reason for the martial arts. The hard practice of them helps me to tear the stitches so my daughter can cry. Tears are the only thing I can give her.

Each night I bare my back eagerly to Mary and her needles. She pokes deep and I moan in pain as she moans in ecstasy and hatred. She adds more color to the design, works with brutal precision to bring Rae's face out in sharper relief. After ten minutes she tires and will work no more. She puts the tools away and I go to the full-length mirror on the wall. The lantern on the shelf flickers like a jack-o'-lantern in a high wind, but there is enough light for me to look over my shoulder and examine the tattoo. And it is beautiful. Better each night as Rae's face becomes more and more defined.

Rae.

Rae. God, can you forgive me, sweetheart?

But the pain of the needles, wonderful and cleansing as they are, is not enough. So I go sliding, kicking, and punching along the walkway around the lighthouse, feeling Rae's red tears running down my spine, gathering in the waistband of my much-stained canvas pants.

Winded, unable to punch and kick anymore, I walk over to the railing and call down into the dark, "Hungry?"

In response to my voice a chorus of moans rises up to greet me. Later, I lie on my pallet, hands behind my head, examine the ceiling and try to think of something worthy to write in you, Mr. Journal. So seldom is there anything. Nothing seems truly worthwhile.

Bored of this, I roll on my side and look at the great light that once shone out to the ships, but is now forever snuffed. Then I turn the other direction and look at my wife sleeping on her bunk, her naked ass turned toward me. I try to remember what it was like to make love to her, but it is difficult. I only remember that I miss it. For a long moment I stare at my wife's ass as if it is a mean mouth about to open and reveal teeth. Then I roll on my back again, stare at the ceiling, and continue this routine until daybreak.

Mornings I greet the flowers, their bright red and yellow blooms bursting from the heads of long-dead bodies that will not rot. The flowers open wide to reveal their little black brains and their feathery feelers, and they lift their blooms upward and moan. I get a wild pleasure out of this. For one crazed moment I feel like a rock singer appearing before his starry-eyed audience.

When I tire of the game I get the binoculars, Mr. Journal, and examine the eastern plains with them, as if I expect a city to materialize there. The most interesting thing I have seen on those plains is a herd of large lizards thundering north. For a moment, I considered calling Mary to see them, but I didn't. The sound of my voice, the sight of my face, upsets her. She loves only the tattoo and is interested in nothing more.

When I finish looking at the plains, I walk to the other side. To the west, where the ocean was, there is now nothing but miles and miles of cracked, black sea bottom. Its only resemblance to a great body of water are the occasional dust storms that blow out of the west like dark tidal waves and wash the windows black at mid-day. And the creatures. Mostly mutated whales. Monstrously large, sluggish things. Abundant now where once they were near extinction. (Perhaps the whales should form some sort of Greenpeace organization for humans now. What do you think, Mr. Journal? No need to answer. Just another one of those little scientist jokes.)

These whales crawl across the sea bottom near the lighthouse from time to time, and if the mood strikes them, they rise on their tails and push their heads near the tower and examine it. I keep expecting one to flop down on us, crushing us like bugs. But no such luck. For some unknown reason the whales never leave the cracked seabed to venture onto what we formerly called the shore. It's as if they live in invisible water and are bound by it. A racial memory perhaps. Or maybe there's something in that cracked black soil they need. I don't know.

Besides the whales I suppose I should mention I saw a shark once. It was slithering along at a great distance and the tip of its fin was winking in the sunlight. I've also seen some strange, legged fish and some things I could not put a name to. I'll just call them whale food since I saw one of the whales dragging his bottom jaw along the ground one day, scooping up the creatures as they tried to beat a hasty retreat.

Exciting, huh? Well, that's how I spend my day, Mr. Journal. Roaming about the tower with my glasses, coming in to write in you, waiting anxiously for Mary to take hold of that kit and give me the signal. The mere thought of it excites me to erection. I suppose you could call that our sex act together.

And what was I doing the day they dropped The Big One?

Glad you asked that, Mr. Journal, really I am.

I was doing the usual. Up at six, did the shit, shower, and shave routine. Had breakfast. Got dressed. Tied my tie. I remember doing the latter, and not very well, in front of the bedroom mirror, and noticing that I had shaved poorly. A hunk of dark beard decorated my chin like a bruise.

Rushing to the bathroom to remedy that, I opened the door as Rae, naked as the day of her birth, was stepping from the tub.

Surprised, she turned to look at me. An arm went over her breasts, and a hand, like a dove settling into a fiery bush, covered her pubic area.

Embarrassed, I closed the door with an "excuse me" and went about my business—unshaved. It was an innocent thing. An accident. Nothing sexual. But when I think of her now, more often than not, that is the first image that comes to mind. I guess it was the moment I realized my baby had grown into a beautiful woman.

That was also the day she went off to her first day of college and got to see, ever so briefly, the end of the world.

And it was the day the triangle—Mary, Rae, and myself—shattered. If my first memory of Rae alone is that day, naked in the bathroom, my foremost memory of us as a family is when Rae was six. We used to go to the park and she would ride the merry-go-round, swing, teeter-totter, and finally my back. ("I want to piggy, Daddy.") We would gallop about until my legs were rubber, then we would stop at the bench where Mary sat waiting. I would turn my back to the bench so Mary could take Rae down, but always before she did, she would reach around from behind, caressing Rae, pushing her tight against my back, and Mary's hands would touch my chest.

God, but if I could describe those hands. She still has hands like that, after all these years. I feel them fluttering against my back when she works. They are long and sleek and artistic. Naturally soft, like the belly of a baby rabbit. And when she held Rae and me that way, I felt that no matter what happened in the world, we three could stand against it and conquer.

But now the triangle is broken and the geometry gone away.

So the day Rae went off to college and was fucked into oblivion by the dark, pelvic thrust of the bomb, Mary drove me to work. Me, Paul Marder, big shot with The Crew. One of the finest, brightest young minds in the industry. Always teaching, inventing and improving on our nuclear threat, because, as we'd often joke, "We cared enough to send only the very best."

When we arrived at the guard booth, I had out my pass, but there was no one to take it. Beyond the chain link gate there was a wild melee of people running, screaming, falling down.

I got out of the car and ran to the gate. I called out to a man I knew as he ran by. When he turned, his eyes were wild and his lips were flecked with foam. "The missiles are flying," he said, then he was gone, running madly.

I jumped in the car, pushed Mary aside and stomped the gas. The Buick leaped into the fence, knocking it asunder. The car spun, slammed into the edge of a building, and went dead. I grabbed Mary's hand, pulled her from the car and we ran toward the great elevators.

We made one just in time. There were others running for it as the door closed, and the elevator went down. I still remember the echo of their fists on the metal just as it began to drop. It was like the rapid heartbeat of something dying.

And so the elevator took us to the world of Down Under and we locked it off. There we were in a five-mile layered city designed not only as a massive office and laboratory, but as an impenetrable shelter. It was our special reward for creating the poisons of war. There was food, water, medical supplies, films, books, you name it. Enough to last two thousand people for a hundred years. Of the two thousand it was designed for, perhaps eleven hundred made it. The others didn't run fast enough from the parking lot or the other buildings, or they were late for work, or maybe they had called in sick.

Perhaps they were the lucky ones. They might have died in their sleep. Or while they were having a morning quickie with the spouse. Or perhaps as they lingered over that last cup of coffee.

Because you see, Mr. Journal, Down Under was no paradise. Before long suicides were epidemic; I considered it myself from time to time. People slashed their throats, drank acid, took pills. It was not unusual to come out of your cubicle in the morning and find people dangling from pipes and rafters like ripe fruit.

There were also the murders. Most of them performed by a crazed group who lived in the deeper recesses of the unit and called themselves the Shit Faces. From time to time they smeared dung on themselves and ran amok, clubbing men, women, and children born Down Under to death. It was rumored they ate human flesh.

We had a police force of sorts, but it didn't do much. It didn't have much sense of authority. Worse, we all viewed ourselves as deserving victims. Except for Mary, we had all helped to blow up the world.

Mary came to hate me. She came to the conclusion I had killed Rae. It was a realization that grew in her like a drip, growing and growing until it became a gushing flood of hate. She seldom talked to me. She tacked up a picture of Rae and looked at it most of the time.

Topside she had been an artist, and she took that up again. She rigged a kit of tools and inks and became a tattooist. Everyone came to her for a mark. And though each was different, they all seemed to indicate one thing: I fucked up. I blew up the world. Brand me.

Day in and day out she did her tattoos, having less and less to do with me, pushing herself more and more into this work until she was as skilled with skin and needles as she had been Topside with brush and canvas. And one night, as we lay on our separate pallets, feigning sleep, she said to me, "I just want you to know how much I hate you."

"I know," I said.

"You killed Rae."

"I know."

"You say you killed her, you bastard. Say it."

"I killed her," I said, and meant it.

Next day I asked for my tattoo. I told her of this dream that came to me nightly. There would be darkness, and out of this darkness would come a swirl of glowing clouds, and the clouds would melt into a mushroom shape, and out of that—torpedo-shaped, nose pointing skyward, striding on ridiculous cartoon legs—would step The Bomb.

There was a face painted on The Bomb, and it was my face. And suddenly the dream's point of view would change, and I would be looking out of the eyes of that painted face. Before me was my daughter. Naked. Lying on the ground. Her legs wide apart. Her sex glazed like a wet canyon.

And I/The Bomb would dive into her, pulling those silly feet after me, and she would scream. I could hear it echo as I plunged through her belly, finally driving myself out of the top of her head, then blowing to terminal orgasm. And the dream would end where it began. A mushroom cloud. Darkness.

When I told Mary the dream and asked her to interpret it in her art, she said, "Bare your back," and that's how the design began. An inch of work at a time—a painful inch. She made sure of that. Never once did I complain. She'd send the needles home as hard and deep as she could, and though I might moan or cry out, I never asked her to stop. I could feel those fine hands touching my back and I loved it. The needles. The hands. The needles. The hands.

And if that was so much fun, you ask, why did I come Topside?

You ask such probing questions, Mr. Journal. Really you do, and I'm glad you asked that. My telling will be like a laxative, I hope. Maybe if I just let the shit flow I'll wake up tomorrow and feel a lot better about myself.

Sure. And it will be the dawning of a new Pepsi generation as well. It will have all been a bad dream. The alarm clock will ring. I'll get up, have my bowl of Rice Krispies and tie my tie.

Okay, Mr. Journal. The answer. Twenty years or so after we went Down Under, a fistful of us decided it couldn't be any worse Topside than it was below. We made plans to go see. Simple as that. Mary and I even talked a little. We both entertained the crazed belief Rae might have survived. She would be thirty-eight. We might have been hiding below like vermin for no reason. It could be a brave new world up there.

I remember thinking these things, Mr. Journal, and half believing them.

We outfitted two sixty-foot crafts that were used as part of our transportation system Down Under, plugged in the half-remembered codes that opened the elevators, and drove the vehicles inside. The elevator lasers cut through the debris above them and before long we were Topside. The doors opened to sunlight muted by gray-green clouds and a desert-like landscape. Immediately I knew there was no brave new world over the horizon. It had all gone to hell in a fiery handbasket, and all that was left of man's millions of years of development were a few pathetic humans living Down Under like worms, and a few others crawling Topside like the same.

We cruised about a week and finally came to what had once been the Pacific Ocean. Only there wasn't any water now, just that cracked blackness.

We drove along the shore for another week and finally saw life. A whale. Jacobs immediately got the idea to shoot one and taste its meat.

Using a high-powered rifle he killed it, and he and seven others cut slabs off it, brought the meat back to cook. They invited all of us to eat, but the meat looked greenish and there wasn't much blood and we warned him against it. But Jacobs and the others ate it anyway. As Jacobs said, "It's something to do."

A little later on Jacobs threw up blood and his intestines boiled out of his mouth, and not long after, those who had shared the meat had the same thing happen to them. They died crawling on their bellies like gutted dogs. There wasn't a thing we could do for them. We couldn't even bury them. The ground was too hard. We stacked them like cordwood along the shoreline and moved camp down a way, tried to remember how remorse felt.

And that night, while we slept as best we could, the roses came.

Now, let me admit, Mr. Journal, I do not actually know how the roses survived, but I have an idea. And since you've agreed to hear my story—and even if you haven't, you're going to anyway—I'm going to put logic and fantasy together and hope to arrive at the truth.

These roses lived in the ocean bed, underground, and at night they came out. Up until then they had survived as parasites of reptiles and animals, but a new food had arrived from Down Under. Humans. Their creators, actually. Looking at it that way, you might say we were the god who conceived them, and their partaking of our flesh and blood was but a new version of wine and wafer.

I can imagine the pulsating brains pushing up through the sea bottom on thick stalks, extending feathery feelers and tasting the air out there beneath the light of the moon—which through those odd clouds gave the impression of a pus-filled boil—and I can imagine them uprooting and dragging their vines across the ground toward the shore where the corpses lay.

Thick vines sprouted little, thorny vines, and these moved up the bank and touched the corpses. Then, with a lashing motion, the thorns tore into the flesh, and the vines, like snakes, slithered through the wounds and inside. Secreting a dissolving fluid that turned the innards to the consistency of watery oatmeal, they slurped up the mess, and the vines grew and grew at amazing speed, moved and coiled throughout the bodies, replacing nerves and shaping into the symmetry of the muscles they had devoured, and lastly they pushed up through the necks, into the skulls, ate tongues and eyeballs and sucked up the mouse-gray brains like soggy gruel. With an explosion of skull shrapnel, the roses bloomed, their tooth-hard petals expanding into beautiful red and yellow flowers, hunks of human heads dangling from them like shattered watermelon rinds.

In the center of these blooms a fresh, black brain pulsed and feathery feelers once again tasted air for food and breeding grounds. Energy waves from the floral brains shot through the miles and miles of vines that were knotted inside the bodies, and as they had replaced nerves, muscles, and vital organs, they made the bodies stand. Then those corpses turned their flowered heads toward the tents where we slept, and the blooming corpses (another little scientist joke there if you're into English idiom, Mr. Journal) walked, eager to add the rest of us to their animated bouquet.

I saw my first rose-head while I was taking a leak.

I had left the tent and gone down by the shoreline to relieve myself when I caught sight of it out of the corner of my eye. Because of the bloom I first thought it was Susan Dyers. She wore a thick, woolly Afro that surrounded her head like a lion's mane, and the shape of the thing struck me as her silhouette. But when I zipped and turned, it wasn't an Afro. It was a flower blooming out of Jacobs. I recognized him by his clothes and the hunk of his face that hung off one of the petals like a worn-out hat on a peg.

In the center of the blood-red flower was a pulsating sack, and all around it little wormy things squirmed. Directly below the brain was a thin proboscis. It extended toward me like an erect penis. At its tip, just inside the opening, were a number of large thorns.

A sound like a moan came out of that proboscis, and I stumbled back. Jacobs's body quivered briefly, as if he had been besieged by a sudden chill, and ripping through his flesh and clothes, from neck to foot, was a mass of thorny, wagging vines that shot out to five feet in length.

With an almost invisible motion, they waved from west to east, slashed my clothes, tore my hide, knocked my feet out from beneath me. It was like being hit by a cat-o'-nine-tails.

Dazed, I rolled onto my hands and knees, bear-walked away from it. The vines whipped against my back and butt, cut deep.

Every time I got to my feet, they tripped me. The thorns not only cut, they burned like hot ice picks. I finally twisted away from a net of vines, slammed through one last shoot, and made a break for it.

Without realizing it, I was running back to the tent. My body felt as if I had been lying on a bed of nails and razor blades. My forearm hurt something terrible where I had used it to lash the thorns away from me. I glanced down at it as I ran. It was covered in blood. A strand of vine about two feet in length was coiled around it like a garter snake. A thorn had torn a deep wound in my arm, and the vine was sliding an end into the wound.

Screaming, I held my forearm in front of me like I had just discovered it. The flesh, where the vine had entered, rippled and made a bulge that looked like a junkie's favorite vein. The pain was nauseating. I snatched at the vine, ripped it free. The thorns turned against me—like fishhooks.

The pain was so much I fell to my knees, but I had the vine out of me. It squirmed in my hand, and I felt a thorn gouge my palm. I threw the vine into the dark. Then I was up and running for the tent again.

The roses must have been at work for quite some time before I saw Jacobs, because when I broke back into camp yelling, I saw Susan, Ralph, Casey, and some others, and already their heads were blooming, skulls cracking away like broken model kits.

Jane Calloway was facing a rose-possessed corpse, and the dead body had its hands on her shoulders, and the vines were jetting out of the corpse, weaving around her like a web, tearing, sliding inside her, breaking off. The proboscis poked into her mouth and extended down her throat, forced her head back. The scream she started came out a gurgle.

I tried to help her, but when I got close, the vines whipped at me and I had to jump back. I looked for something to grab, to hit the damn thing with, but there was nothing. When next I looked at Jane, vines were stabbing out of her eyes and her tongue, now nothing more than lava-thick blood, was dripping out of her mouth onto her breasts, which, like the rest of her body, were riddled with stabbing vines.

I ran away then. There was nothing I could do for Jane. I saw others embraced by corpse hands and tangles of vines, but now my only thought was Mary. Our tent was to the rear of the campsite, and I ran there as fast as I could.

She was lumbering out of our tent when I arrived. The sound of screams had awakened her. When she saw me running she froze. By the time I got to her, two vine-riddled corpses were coming up on the tent from the left side. Grabbing her hand I half pulled, half dragged her away from there. I got to one of the vehicles and pushed her inside.

I locked the doors just as Jacobs, Susan, Jane, and others appeared at the windshield, leaning over the rocket-nose hood, the feelers around the brain sacks vibrating like streamers in a high wind. Hands slid greasily down the windshield. Vines flopped and scratched and cracked against it like thin bicycle chains.

I got the vehicle started, stomped the accelerator, and the rose-heads went flying. One of them, Jacobs, bounced over the hood and splattered into a spray of flesh, ichor, and petals.

I had never driven the vehicle, so my maneuvering was rusty. But it didn't matter. There wasn't exactly a traffic rush to worry about.

After an hour or so, I turned to look at Mary. She was staring at me, her eyes like the twin barrels of a double-barreled shotgun. They seemed to say, "More of your doing," and in a way, she was right. I drove on.

Daybreak we came to the lighthouse. I don't know how it survived. One of those quirks. Even the glass was unbroken. It looked like a great stone finger shooting us the bird.

The vehicle's tank was near empty, so I assumed here was as good a place to stop as any. At least there was shelter, something we could fortify. Going on until the vehicle was empty of fuel didn't make much sense. There wouldn't be any more fill-ups, and there might not be any more shelter like this.

Mary and I (in our usual silence) unloaded the supplies from the vehicle and put them in the lighthouse. There was enough food, water, chemicals for the chemical toilet, odds and ends, extra clothes to last us a year. There were also some guns. A Colt .45 revolver, two twelve-gauge shotguns, and a .38, and enough shells to fight a small war.

When everything was unloaded, I found some old furniture downstairs and, using tools from the vehicle, tried to barricade the bottom door and the one at the top of the stairs. When I finished, I thought of a line from a story I had once read, a line that always disturbed me. It went something like, "Now we're shut in for the night."

Days. Nights. All the same. Shut in with one another, our memories, and the fine tattoo.

A few days later I spotted the roses. It was as if they had smelled us out. And maybe they had. From a distance, through the binoculars, they reminded me of old women in bright sun hats.

It took them the rest of the day to reach the lighthouse, and they immediately surrounded it, and when I appeared at the railing they would lift their heads and moan.

And that, Mr. Journal, brings us up to now.

I thought I had written myself out, Mr. Journal. Told the only part of my life story I would ever tell, but now I'm back. You can't keep a good world-destroyer down.

I saw my daughter last night and she's been dead for years. But I saw her, I did, naked, smiling at me, calling to ride piggyback.

Here's what happened.

It was cold last night. Must be getting along winter. I had rolled off my pallet onto the cold floor. Maybe that's what brought me awake. The cold. Or maybe it was just gut instinct.

It had been a particularly wonderful night with the tattoo. The face had been made so clear it seemed to stand out from my back. It had finally become more defined than the mushroom cloud. The needles went in hard and deep, but I've had them in me so much now I barely feel the pain. After looking in the mirror at the beauty of the design, I went to bed happy, or as happy as I can get.

During the night the eyes ripped open. The stitches came out and I didn't know it until I tried to rise from the cold, stone floor and my back puckered against it where the blood had dried.

I pulled myself free and got up. It was dark, but we had a good moon-spill that night and I went to the mirror to look. It was bright enough that I could see Rae's reflection clearly, the color of her face, the color of the cloud. The stitches had fallen away and now the wounds were spread wide, and inside the wounds were eyes. Oh God, Rae's blue eyes. Her mouth smiled at me and her teeth were very white.

Oh, I hear you, Mr. Journal. I hear what you're saying. And I thought of that. My first impression was that I was about six bricks shy a load, gone around the old bend. But I know better now. You see, I lit a candle and held it over my shoulder, and with the candle and the moonlight, I could see even more clearly. It was Rae all right, not just a tattoo.

I looked over at my wife on the bunk, her back to me, as always. She had not moved.

I turned back to the reflection. I could hardly see the outline of myself, just Rae's face smiling out of that cloud.

"Rae," I whispered, "is that you?"

"Come on, Daddy," said the mouth in the mirror, "that's a stupid question. Of course it's me."

"But . . . you're . . . you're. . . ."

"Dead?"

"Yes. . . . Did . . . did it hurt much?"

She cackled so loudly the mirror shook. I could feel the hairs on my neck rising. I thought for sure Mary would wake up, but she slept on.

"It was instantaneous, Daddy, and even then, it was the greatest pain imaginable. Let me show you how it hurt."

The candle blew out and I dropped it. I didn't need it anyway. The mirror grew bright and Rae's smile went from ear to ear—literally—and the flesh on her bones seemed like crepe paper before a powerful fan, and that fan blew the hair off her head, the skin off her skull and melted those beautiful blue eyes and those shiny white teeth of hers to a putrescent goo the color and consistency of fresh bird shit. Then there was only the skull, and it heaved in half and flew backwards into the dark world of the mirror and there was no reflection now, only the hurtling fragments of a life that once was and was now nothing more than swirling cosmic dust.

I closed my eyes and looked away. "Daddy?"

I opened them, looked over my shoulder into the mirror. There was Rae again, smiling out of my back. "Darling," I said, "I'm so sorry."

"So are we," she said, and there were faces floating past her in the mirror. Teenagers, children, men and women, babies, little embryos swirling around her head like planets around the sun. I closed my eyes again, but I could not keep them closed. When I opened them the multitudes of swirling dead, and those who had never had a chance to live, were gone. Only Rae was there.

"Come close to the mirror, Daddy."

I backed up to it. I backed until the hot wounds that were Rae's eyes touched the cold glass and the wounds became hotter and hotter and Rae called out, "Ride me piggy, Daddy," and then I felt her weight on my back, not the weight of a six-year-old child or a teenage girl, but a great weight, like the world was on my shoulders and bearing down.

Leaping away from the mirror I went hopping and whooping about the room, same as I used to in the park. Around and around I went, and as I did, I glanced in the mirror. Astride me was Rae, lithe and naked, her red hair fanning around her as I spun. And when I whirled by the mirror again, I saw that she was six years old. Another spin and there was a skeleton with red hair, one hand held high, the jaws open and yelling, "Ride 'em, cowboy."

"How?" I managed, still bucking and leaping, giving Rae the ride of her life. She bent to my ear and I could feel her warm breath. "You want to know how I'm here, Daddy-dear? I'm here because you created me. Once you laid between Mother's legs and thrust me into existence, the two of you, with all the love there was in you. This time you thrust me into existence with your guilt and Mother's hate. Her thrusting needles, your arching back. And now I've come back for one last ride, Daddy-o. Ride, you bastard, ride."

All the while I had been spinning, and now as I glimpsed the mirror I saw wall-to-wall faces, weaving in, weaving out, like smiling stars, and all those smiles opened wide and words came out in chorus, "Where were you when they dropped The Big One?"

Each time I spun and saw the mirror again, it was a new scene. Great flaming winds scorching across the world, babies turning to fleshy Jell-O, heaps of charred bones, brains boiling out of the heads of men and women like backed-up toilets overflowing, The Almighty, Glory Hallelujah, Ours Is Bigger Than Yours Bomb hurtling forward, the mirror going mushroom white, then clear, and me, spinning, Rae pressed tight against my back, melting like butter on a griddle, evaporating into the eye wounds on my back, and finally me alone, collapsing to the floor beneath the weight of the world.

Mary never awoke.

The vines outsmarted me.

A single strand found a crack downstairs somewhere and wound up the steps and slipped beneath the door that led into the tower. Mary's bunk was not far from the door, and in the night, while I slept and later while I spun in front of the mirror and lay on the floor before it, it made its way to Mary's bunk, up between her legs, and entered her sex effortlessly.

I suppose I should give the vine credit for doing what I had not been able to do in years, Mr. Journal, and that's enter Mary. Oh God, that's a funny one, Mr. Journal. Real funny. Another little scientist joke. Let's make that a mad scientist joke, what say? Who but a madman would play with the lives of human beings by constantly trying to build the bigger and better boom machine?

So, what of Rae, you ask?

I'll tell you. She is inside me. My back feels the weight. She twists in my guts like a corkscrew. I went to the mirror a moment ago, and the tattoo no longer looks like it did. The eyes have turned to crusty sores and the entire face looks like a scab. It's as if the bile that made up my soul, the unthinking nearsightedness, the guilt that I am, has festered from inside and spoiled the picture with pustule bumps, knots, and scabs.

To put it in layman's terms, Mr. Journal, my back is infected. Infected with what I am. A blind, senseless fool.

The wife?

Ah, the wife. God, how I loved that woman. I have not really touched her in years, merely felt those wonderful hands on my back as she jabbed the needles home, but I never stopped loving her. It was not a love that glowed anymore, but it was there, though hers for me was long gone and wasted.

This morning when I got up from the floor, the weight of Rae and the world on my back, I saw the vine coming up from beneath the door and stretching over to her. I yelled her name. She did not move. I ran to her and saw it was too late. Before I could put a hand on her, I saw her flesh ripple and bump up, like a den of mice were nesting under a quilt. The vines were at work. (Out go the old guts, in go the new vines.)

There was nothing I could do for her.

I made a torch out of a chair leg and old quilt, set fire to it, burned the vine from between her legs, watched it retreat, smoking, under the door. Then I got a board, nailed it along the bottom, hoping it would keep others out for at least a little while. I got one of the twelve-gauges and loaded it. It's on the desk beside me, Mr. Journal, but even I know I'll never use it. It was just something to do, as Jacobs said when he killed and ate the whale. Something to do.

I can hardly write anymore. My back and shoulders hurt so bad. It's the weight of Rae and the world.

I've just come back from the mirror and there is very little left of the tattoo. Some blue and black ink, a touch of red that was Rae's hair. It looks like an abstract painting now. Collapsed design, running colors. It's real swollen. I look like the hunchback of Notre Dame.

What am I going to do, Mr. Journal?

Well, as always, I'm glad you asked that. You see, I've thought this out.

I could throw Mary's body over the railing before it blooms. I could do that. Then I could doctor my back. It might even heal, though I doubt it. Rae wouldn't let that happen, I can tell you now. And I don't blame her. I'm on her side. I'm just a walking dead man and have been for years.

I could put the shotgun under my chin and work the trigger with my toes, or maybe push it with the very pen I'm using to create you, Mr. Journal. Wouldn't that be neat? Blow my brains to the ceiling and sprinkle you with my blood.

But as I said, I loaded the gun because it was something to do. I'd never use it on myself or Mary.

You see, I want Mary. I want her to hold Rae and me one last time like she used to in the park. And she can. There's a way.

I've drawn all the curtains and made curtains out of blankets for those spots where there aren't any. It'll be sunup soon and I don't want that kind of light in here. I'm writing this by candlelight and it gives the entire room a warm glow. I wish I had wine. I want the atmosphere to be just right.

Over on Mary's bunk she's starting to twitch. Her neck is swollen where the vines have congested and are writhing toward their favorite morsel, the brain. Pretty soon the rose will bloom (I hope she's one of the bright yellow ones, yellow was her favorite color and she wore it well) and Mary will come for me.

When she does, I'll stand with my naked back to her. The vines will whip out and cut me before she reaches me, but I can stand it. I'm used to pain. I'll pretend the thorns are Mary's needles. I'll stand that way until she folds her dead arms around me and her body pushes up against the wound she made in my back, the wound that is our daughter Rae. She'll hold me so the vines and the proboscis can do their work. And while she holds me, I'll grab her fine hands and push them against my chest, and it will be we three again, standing against the world, and I'll close my eyes and delight in her soft, soft hands one last time.

This was written before "Tight Little Stitches" and appeared, as I recall, in a small-press magazine. It was mostly unnoticed until the short-story collection of the same title.

It's loosely based on an encounter my mother and I had with a traveling bum, as they were once called. He came to our door looking for money and/or food.

Having lived through the Great Depression, my parents knew what it was like to be living on the edge and being hungry. My mother didn't have money to offer—we were broke, as we thought of ourselves, but that was another word for the hopeful poor. She offered to fix him some food, a fried-egg sandwich, if I remember correctly.

Mother didn't let the guy into the house, him in his black suit and black fedora, but she let him sit on our porch and eat his sandwich and drink some coffee she already had prepared.

I sat on the porch as he talked. Turned out he was a traveling preacher. That was his line of shit, anyway. Two things that always make me suspicious and put a hand on my wallet are preachers and religion.

It was then that both my mother and I—and I was young, my friends—began to feel creeped out. He was racist, disliked people with deformities or disabilities, and somehow thought it was a curse from God.

He never mentioned eliminating anyone personally, but he seemed in favor of God striking down black people and people with disabilities. It would seem he had been reading *Mein Kampf* by Hitler along with his Bible. Jesus didn't seem to be his lead in his preaching, but the Old Testament, so he could say mean things, horrible things, and feel justified.

He was as jovial about all this as a kid show host with a sock puppet, just chuckling along, talking about those horrible people who didn't deserve to be on the same Earth with the rest of us white and fit humans.

At some point, my mother inched us both into the house, telling him to leave the dishes on the porch, and she locked the door.

I only remember this event in fragments, but it was the basis for this story about a horrible person who does horrible things due to his own take on religion.

The important and scary thing about these folks is that they don't realize how crazy they are.

The woman in the story is based on a number of ignorant relatives and people I knew over the years. Combined personalities, you might say.

There was also a story that went around not long after this about murders, and that they had been committed by a traveling bum and so-called preacher.

I don't know whether that story was true or just one of those stories that got built out of something true, or marginally true, and then grew into this giant tale that was akin to folklore about the killer with a hook who terrorized young lovers in parked cars in remote spots.

If it was true, you know, I think that guy could have been the guy. If it wasn't true, and that's more likely, he still strikes me as a guy who might have been that kind of guy.

Gives me a bit of a chill thinking about it.

But a lot of my stories, different as they might be from the source material, have been built on things like this. Real people, good and bad. In this case, I'm going to go out on a limb with this guy.

He was bad.

By Bizarre Hands

WHEN THE TRAVELING preacher heard about the Widow Case and her retarded girl, he set out in his black Dodge to get over there before Halloween night.

Preacher Judd, as he called himself—though his name was really Billy Fred Williams—had this thing for retarded girls, due to the fact that his sister had been simple-headed, and his mama always said it was a shame she was probably going to burn in hell like a pan of biscuits forgot in the oven, just on account of not having a full set of brains.

This was a thing he had thought on considerable, and this considerable thinking made it so he couldn't pass up the idea of baptizing and giving some God-training to female retards. It was something he wanted to do in the worst way, though he had to admit there wasn't any burning desire in him to do the same for boys or men or women that were half-wits, but due to his sister having been one, he certainly had this thing for girl simples.

And he had this thing for Halloween, because that was the night the Lord took his sister to hell, and he might have taken her to glory had she had any Bible-learning or God-sense. But she didn't have a drop, and it was partly his own fault, because he knew about God and could sing some hymns pretty good. But he'd never turned a word of benediction or gospel music in her direction. Not one word. Nor had his mama, and his papa wasn't around to do squat.

The old man ran off with a bucktoothed laundrywoman that used to go house to house, taking in wash and bringing it back the next day, but when she took in their wash, she took in Papa too, and she never brought either of them back. And if that wasn't bad enough, the laundry contained everything they had in the way of decent clothes, including a couple of pairs of nice dress pants and some pin-striped shirts like niggers wear to funerals. This left him with one old pair of faded overalls that he used to wear to slop the hogs before the critters killed and ate Granny, and they had to get rid of them because they didn't want to eat nothing that had eaten somebody they knew. So, it wasn't bad enough Papa ran off with a beaver-toothed washwoman and his sister was a drooling retard, he now had only the one pair of ugly, old overalls to wear to school, and this gave the other kids three things to tease him about, and they never missed a chance to do it. Well, four things. He was kind of ugly too.

It got tiresome.

Preacher Judd could remember nights waking up with his sister crawled up in the bed alongside him, lying on her back, eyes wide open, her face bathed in cool moonlight, picking her nose and eating what she found, while he rested on one elbow and tried to figure out why she was that way.

He finally gave up figuring, decided that she ought to have some fun, and he could have some fun too. Come Halloween, he got him a bar of soap for marking up windows and a few rocks for knocking out some, and he made his sister and himself ghost-suits out of old sheets in which he cut mouth and eye holes.

This was her fifteenth year and she had never been trick-or-treating. He had designs that she should go this time, and they did, and later after they'd done it, he walked her back home, and later yet, they found her out back of the house in her ghost-suit, only the sheet had turned red because her head was bashed in with something and she had bled out like an ankle-hung hog. And someone had turned her trick-or-treat sack—the handle of which was still clutched in her fat grip—inside out and taken every bit of candy she'd gotten from the neighbors.

The sheriff came out, pulled up the sheet and saw that she was naked under it, and he looked her over and said that she looked raped to him, and that she had been killed by bizarre hands.

Bizarre hands never did make sense to Preacher Judd, but he loved the sound of it, and never did let it slip away, and when he would tell about his poor sister, naked under the sheets, her brains smashed out and her trick-or-treat bag turned inside out, he'd never miss ending the story with the sheriff's line about her having died by bizarre hands.

It had a kind of ring to it.

He parked his Dodge by the roadside, got out and walked up to the Widow Case's, sipping on a Frostie Root Beer. But even though it was late October, the Southern sun was as hot as Satan's ass and the root beer was anything but frosty.

Preacher Judd was decked out in his black suit, white shirt and black loafers with black and white checked socks, and he had on his black hat, which was short-brimmed and made him look, he thought, exactly like a traveling preacher ought to look.

Widow Case was out at the well, cranking a bucket of water, and nearby, running hell out of a hill of ants with a stick she was waggling, was the retarded girl, and Preacher Judd thought she looked remarkably like his sister.

He came up, took off his hat and held it over his chest as though he were pressing his heart into proper place, and smiled at the widow with all his gold-backed teeth.

Widow Case put one hand on a bony hip, used the other to prop the bucket of water on the well-curbing. She looked like a shaved weasel, Preacher Judd thought, though her ankles weren't shaved a bit and were perfectly weasel-like. The hair there was thick and black enough to be mistaken for thin socks at a distance.

"Reckon you've come far enough," she said. "You look like one of them Jehovah Witnesses or such. Or one of them kind that run around with snakes in their teeth and hop to nigger music."

"No ma'am, I don't hop to nothing, and last snake I seen I run over with my car."

"You here to take up money for missionaries to give to them starving African niggers? If you are, forget it. I don't give to the niggers around here, sure ain't giving to no hungry foreign niggers that can't even speak English."

"Ain't collecting money for nobody. Not even myself."

"Well, I ain't seen you around here before, and I don't know you from white rice. You might be one of them mash murderers for all I know."

"No ma'am, I ain't a mash murderer, and I ain't from around here. I'm from East Texas."

She gave him a hard look. "Lots of niggers there."

"Place is rotten with them. Can't throw a dog tick without you've hit a burrhead in the noggin. That's one of the reasons I'm traveling through here, so I can talk to white folks about God. Talking to niggers is like," and he lifted a hand to point, "talking to that well-curbing there, only that well-curbing is smarter and a lot less likely to sass, since it ain't expecting no civil rights or a chance to crowd up with our young'ns in schools. It knows its place and it stays there, and that's something for that well-curbing, if it ain't nothing for niggers."

"Amen."

Preacher Judd was feeling pretty good now. He could see she was starting to eat out of his hand. He put on his hat and looked at the girl. She was on her elbows now, her head down and her butt up. The dress she was wearing was way too short and had broken open in back from her having outgrown it. Her panties were dirt-stained and there was gravel, like little BBs, hanging off of them. He thought she had legs that looked strong enough to wrap around an alligator's neck and choke it to death.

"Cindereller there," the widow said, noticing he was watching, "ain't gonna have to worry about going to school with niggers. She ain't got the sense of a nigger. She ain't got no sense at all. A dead rabbit knows more than she knows. All she does is play around all day, eat bugs and such and drool. In case you haven't noticed, she's simple."

"Yes ma'am, I noticed. Had a sister the same way. She got killed on a Halloween night, was raped and murdered and had her trick-or-treat candy stolen, and it was done, the sheriff said, by bizarre hands."

"No kiddin'?"

Preacher Judd held up a hand. "No kiddin'. She went on to hell, I reckon, 'cause she didn't have any God-talk in her. And retard or not, she deserved some so she wouldn't have to cook for eternity. I mean, think on it. How hot it must be down there, her boiling in her own sweat, and she didn't do nothing, and it's mostly my fault 'cause I didn't teach her a thing about the Lord Jesus and his daddy, God."

Widow Case thought that over. "Took her Halloween candy, too, huh?"

"Whole kit and kaboodle. Rape, murder, and candy theft, one fatal swoop. That's why I hate to see a young'n like yours who might not have no Word of God in her. . . . Is she without training?"

"She ain't even toilet-trained. You couldn't perch her on the outdoor convenience if she was sick and her manage to hit the hole. She can't do nothing that don't make a mess. You can't teach her a thing. Half the time she don't even know her name." As if to prove this, Widow Case called, "Cindereller."

Cinderella had one eye against the ant hill now and was trying to look down the hole. Her butt was way up and she was rocking forward on her knees.

"See," said Widow Case, throwing up her hands. "She's worse than any little ole baby, and it ain't no easy row to hoe with her here and me not having a man around to do the heavy work."

"I can see that . . . by the way, call me Preacher Judd . . . and can I help you tote that bucket up to the house there?"

"Well now," said Widow Case, looking all the more like a weasel, "I'd appreciate that kindly."

He got the bucket and they walked up to the house. Cinderella followed, and pretty soon she was circling around him like she was a shark closing in for the kill, the circles each time getting a mite smaller. She did this by running with her back bent and her knuckles almost touching the ground. Ropes of saliva dripped out of her mouth.

Watching her, Preacher Judd got a sort of warm feeling all over. She certainly reminded him of his sister. Only she had liked to scoop up dirt, dog mess, and stuff as she ran, and toss it at him. It wasn't a thing he thought he'd missed until just that moment, but now the truth was out and he felt a little teary-eyed. He half hoped Cinderella would pick up something and throw it on him.

The house was a big, drafty thing circled by a wide flower bed that didn't look to have been worked in years. A narrow porch ran halfway around it, and the front porch had man-tall windows on either side of the door.

Inside, Preacher Judd hung his hat on one of the foil-wrapped rabbit ears perched on top of an old Sylvania TV set, and followed the widow and her child into the kitchen.

The kitchen had big iron frying pans hanging on wall pegs, and there was a framed embroidery that read GOD WATCHES OVER THIS HOUSE. It had been faded by sunlight coming through the window over the sink.

Preacher Judd sat the bucket on the icebox—the old sort that used real ice—then they all went back to the living room. Widow Case told him to sit down and asked him if he'd like some ice tea.

"Yes, this bottle of Frostie ain't so good." He took the bottle out of his coat pocket and gave it to her.

Widow Case held it up and squinted at the little line of liquid in the bottom. "You gonna want this?"

"No ma'am, just pour what's left out and you can have the deposit." He took his Bible from his other pocket and opened it. "You don't mind if I try and read a verse or two to your Cindy, do you?"

"You make an effort on that while I fix us some tea. And I'll bring some things for ham sandwiches, too."

"That would be right nice. I could use a bite."

Widow Case went to the kitchen and Preacher Judd smiled at Cinderella. "You know tonight's Halloween, Cindy?"

Cinderella pulled up her dress, picked a stray ant off her knee and ate it.

"Halloween is my favorite time of the year," he continued. "That may be strange for a preacher to say, considering it's a devil thing, but I've always loved it. It just does something to my blood. It's like a tonic for me, you know?"

She didn't know. Cinderella went over to the TV and turned it on.

Preacher Judd got up, turned it off. "Let's don't run the Sylvania right now, baby child," he said. "Let's you and me talk about God."

Cinderella squatted down in front of the set, not seeming to notice it had been cut off. She watched the dark screen like the White Rabbit considering a plunge down the rabbit hole.

Glancing out the window, Preacher Judd saw that the sun looked like a dropped cherry snow cone melting into the clay road that led out to Highway 80, and already the tumble bug of night was rolling in blue-black and heavy. A feeling of frustration went over him, because he knew he was losing time and he knew what he had to do.

Opening his Bible, he read a verse and Cinderella didn't so much as look up until he finished and said a prayer and ended it with "Amen."

"Uhman," she said suddenly.

Preacher Judd jumped with surprise, slammed the Bible shut and dunked it in his pocket. "Well, well now," he said with delight, "that does it. She's got some Bible training."

Widow Case came in with the tray of fixings. "What's that?"

"She said some of a prayer," Preacher Judd said. "That cinches it. God don't expect much from retards, and that ought to do for keeping her from burning in hell." He practically skipped over to the woman and her tray, stuck two fingers in a glass of tea, whirled and sprinkled the drops on Cinderella's head. Cinderella held out a hand as if checking for rain.

Preacher Judd bellowed out, "I pronounce you baptized. In the name of God, the Son, and the Holy Ghost. Amen."

"Well, I'll swan," the widow said. "That there tea works for baptizing?" She sat the tray on the coffee table.

"It ain't the tea water, it's what's said and who says it that makes it take. . . . Consider that gal legal baptized. . . . Now, she ought to have some fun, too, don't you think? Not having a full head of brains don't mean she shouldn't have some fun."

"She likes what she does with them ants," Widow Case said.

"I know, but I'm talking about something special. It's Halloween. Time for young folks to have fun, even if they are retards. In fact, retards like it better than anyone else. They love this stuff. . . . A thing my sister enjoyed was dressing up like a ghost."

"Ghost?" Widow Case was seated on the couch, making the sandwiches. She had a big butcher knife and she was using it to spread mustard on bread and cut ham slices.

"We took this old sheet, you see, cut some mouth and eye holes in it, then we wore them and went trick-or-treating."

"I don't know that I've got an old sheet. And there ain't a house close enough for trick-or-treatin' at."

"I could take her around in my car. That would be fun, I think. I'd like to see her have fun, wouldn't you? She'd be real scary, too, under that sheet, big as she is and liking to run stooped down with her knuckles dragging."

To make his point, he bent forward, humped his back, let his hands dangle and made a face he thought was an imitation of Cinderella.

"She would be scary, I admit that," Widow Case said. "Though that sheet over her head would take some away from it. Sometimes she scares me when I don't got my mind on her, you know? Like if I'm napping in there on the bed, and I sorta open my eyes, and there she is, looking at me like she looks at them ants. I declare, she looks like she'd like to take a stick and whirl it around on me."

"You need a sheet, a white one, for a ghost-suit."

"Now maybe it would be nice for Cindereller to go out and have some fun." She finished making the sandwiches and stood up. "I'll see what I can find."

"Good, good," Preacher Judd said, rubbing his hands together. "You can let me make the outfit. I'm real good at it."

While Widow Case went to look for a sheet, Preacher Judd ate one of the sandwiches, took one and handed it down to Cinderella. Cinderella promptly took the bread off of it, ate the meat, and laid the mustard sides down on her knees.

When the meat was chewed, she took to the mustard bread, cramming it into her mouth and smacking her lips loudly.

"Is that good, sugar?" Preacher Judd asked.

Cinderella smiled some mustard bread at him, and he couldn't help but think the mustard looked a lot like baby shit, and he had to turn his head away.

"This do?" Widow Case said, coming into the room with a slightly yellowed sheet and a pair of scissors.

"That's the thing," Preacher Judd said, taking a swig from his ice tea. He set the tea down and called to Cinderella.

"Come on, sugar, let's you and me go in the bedroom there and get you fixed up and surprise your mama."

It took a bit of coaxing, but he finally got her up and took her into the bedroom with the sheet and scissors. He half closed the bedroom door and called out to the widow, "You're going to like this."

After a moment, Widow Case heard the scissors snipping away and Cinderella grunting like a hog to trough. When the scissor sound stopped, she heard Preacher Judd talking in a low voice, trying to coach Cinderella on something, but as she wanted it to be a surprise, she quit trying to hear. She went over to the couch and fiddled with a sandwich, but she didn't eat it. As soon as she'd gotten out of eyesight of Preacher Judd, she'd upended the last of his root beer and it was as bad as he said. It sort of made her stomach sick and didn't encourage her to add any food to it.

Suddenly the bedroom door was knocked back, and Cinderella, having a big time of it, charged into the room with her arms held out in front of her yelling, "Woooo, woooo, goats."

Widow Case let out a laugh. Cinderella ran around the room yelling, "Woooo, woooo, goats," until she tripped over the coffee table and sent the sandwich makings and herself flying.

Preacher Judd, who'd followed her in after a second, went over and helped her up. The Widow Case, who had curled up on the couch in natural defense against the flying food and retarded girl, now uncurled when she saw something dangling on Preacher Judd's arm. She knew what it was, but she asked anyway. "What's that?"

"One of your piller cases. For a trick-or-treat sack."

"Oh," Widow Case said stiffly, and she went to straightening up the coffee table and picking the ham and makings off the floor.

Preacher Judd saw that the sun was no longer visible. He walked over to a window and looked out. The tumble bug of night was even more blue-black now and the moon was out, big as a dinner plate, and looking like it had gravy stains on it.

"I think we've got to go now," he said. "We'll be back in a few hours, just long enough to run the houses around here."

"Whoa, whoa," Widow Case said. "Trick-or-treatin' I can go for, but I can't let my daughter go off with no strange man."

"I ain't strange. I'm a preacher."

"You strike me as an all-right fella that wants to do things right, but I still can't let you take my daughter off without me going. People would talk."

Preacher Judd started to sweat. "I'll pay you some money to let me take her on."

Widow Case stared at him. She had moved up close now and he could smell root beer on her breath. Right then he knew what she'd done and he didn't like it any. It wasn't that he'd wanted it, but somehow it seemed dishonest to him that she swigged it without asking him. He thought she was going to pour it out. He started to say as much when she spoke up.

"I don't like the sound of that none, you offering me money."

"I just want her for the night," he said, pulling Cinderella close to him. "She'd have fun."

"I don't like the sound of that no better. Maybe you ain't as right thinking as I thought."

Widow Case took a step back and reached the butcher knife off the table and pushed it at him. "I reckon you better just let go of her and run on out to that car of yours and take your ownself trick-or-treatin'. And without my piller case."

"No ma'am, can't do that. I've come for Cindy and that's the thing God expects of me, and I'm going to do it. I got to do it. I didn't do my sister right and she's burning in hell. I'm doing Cindy right. She said some of a prayer and she's baptized. Anything happened to her, wouldn't be on my conscience."

Widow Case trembled a bit. Cinderella lifted up her ghost-suit with her free hand to look at herself, and Widow Case saw that she was naked as a jaybird underneath.

"You let go of her arm right now, you pervert. And drop that piller case . . . toss it on the couch would be better. It's clean."

He didn't do either.

Widow Case's teeth went together like a bear trap and made about as much noise, and she slashed at him with the knife.

He stepped back out of the way and let go of Cinderella, who suddenly let out a screech, broke and ran, started around the room yelling, "Wooooo, wooooo, goats."

Preacher Judd hadn't moved quick enough, and the knife had cut through the pillow case, his coat and shirt sleeve, but hadn't broke the skin.

When Widow Case saw her slashed pillow case fall to the floor, a fire went through her. The same fire that went through Preacher Judd when he realized his J. C. Penney's suit coat which had cost him, with the pants, $39.95 on sale, was ruined.

They started circling one another, arms outstretched like wrestlers ready for the run-together, and Widow Case had the advantage on account of having the knife.

But she fell for Preacher Judd holding up his left hand and wiggling two fingers like mule ears, and while she was looking at that, he hit her with a right cross and floored her. Her head hit the coffee table and the ham and fixings flew up again.

Preacher Judd jumped on top of her and held her knife hand down with one of his, while he picked up the ham with the other and hit her in the face with it, but the ham was so greasy it kept sliding off and he couldn't get a good blow in.

Finally he tossed the ham down and started wrestling the knife away from her with both hands while she chewed on one of his forearms until he screamed.

Cinderella was still running about, going, "Wooooo, wooooo, goats," and when she ran by the Sylvania, her arm hit the foil-wrapped rabbit ears and sent them flying.

Preacher Judd finally got the knife away from Widow Case, cutting his hand slightly in the process, and that made him mad. He stabbed her in the back as she rolled out from under him and tried to run off on all fours. He got on top of her again, knocking her flat, and he tried to pull the knife out. He pulled and tugged, but it wouldn't come free. She was as strong as a cow and was crawling across the floor and pulling him along as he hung tight to the thick, wooden butcher knife handle. Blood was boiling all over the place.

Out of the corner of his eye, Preacher Judd saw that his retard was going wild, flapping around in her ghost-suit like a fat dove, bouncing off walls and tumbling over furniture. She wasn't making the ghost sounds now. She knew something was up and she didn't like it.

"Now, now," he called to her as Widow Case dragged him across the floor, yelling all the while, "Bloody murder, I'm being kilt, bloody murder, bloody murder!"

"Shut up, goddamnit!" he yelled. Then, reflecting on his words, he turned his face heavenward. "Forgive me my language, God." Then he said sweetly to Cinderella, who was in complete bouncing distress, "Take it easy, honey. Ain't nothing wrong, not a thing."

"Oh Lordy mercy, I'm being kilt!" Widow Case yelled.

"Die, you stupid old cow."

But she didn't die. He couldn't believe it, but she was starting to stand. The knife he was clinging to pulled him to his feet, and when she was up, she whipped an elbow around, whacked him in the ribs and sent him flying.

About that time, Cinderella broke through a window, tumbled onto the porch, over the edge and into the empty flower bed.

Preacher Judd got up and ran at Widow Case, hitting her just above the knees and knocking her down, cracking her head a loud one on the Sylvania, but it still didn't send her out. She was strong enough to grab him by the throat with both hands and throttle him.

As she did, he turned his head slightly away from her digging fingers, and through the broken window he could see his retarded ghost. She was doing a kind of two-step, first to the left, then to the right, going, "Unhhh, unhhhh," and it reminded Preacher Judd of one of them dances sinners do in them places with lots of blinking lights and girls up on pedestals doing lashes with their hips.

He made a fist and hit the widow a couple of times, and she let go of him and rolled away. She got up, staggered a second, then started running toward the kitchen, the knife still in her back, only deeper from having fallen on it.

He ran after her and she staggered into the wall, her hands hitting out and knocking one of the big iron frying pans off its peg and down on her head. It made a loud BONG, and Widow Case went down.

Preacher Judd let out a sigh. He was glad for that. He was tired. He grabbed up the pan and whammed her a few times, then, still carrying the pan, he found his hat in the living room and went out on the porch to look for Cinderella.

She wasn't in sight.

He ran out in the front yard calling her, and saw her making the rear corner of the house, running wildly, hands close to the ground, her butt flashing in the moonlight every time the sheet popped up. She was heading for the woods out back.

He ran after her, but she made the woods well ahead of him. He followed in, but didn't see her. "Cindy," he called. "It's me. Ole Preacher Judd. I come to read you some Bible verses. You'd like that wouldn't you?" Then he commenced to coo like he was talking to a baby, but still Cinderella did not appear.

He trucked around through the woods with his frying pan for half an hour, but didn't see a sign of her. For a half-wit, she was a good hider.

Preacher Judd was covered in sweat and the night was growing slightly cool and the old Halloween moon was climbing to the stars. He felt like just giving up. He sat down on the ground and started to cry.

Nothing ever seemed to work out right. That night he'd taken his sister out hadn't gone fully right. They'd gotten the candy and he'd brought her home, but later, when he tried to get her in bed with him for a little bit of the thing animals do without sin, she wouldn't go for it, and she always had before. Now she was uppity over having a ghost-suit and going trick-or-treating. Worse yet, her wearing that sheet with nothing under it did something for him. He didn't know what it was, but the idea of it made him kind of crazy.

But he couldn't talk or bribe her into a thing. She ran out back and he ran after her and tackled her, and when he started doing to her what he wanted to do, out beneath the Halloween moon, underneath the apple tree, she started screaming. She could scream real loud, and he'd had to choke her some and beat her in the head with a rock. After that, he felt he should make like some kind of theft was at the bottom of it all, so he took all her Halloween candy.

He was sick thinking back on that night. Her dying without no God-training made him feel lousy. And he couldn't get those Tootsie Rolls out of his mind. There must have been three dozen of them. Later he got so sick from eating them all in one sitting that to this day he couldn't stand the smell of chocolate.

He was thinking on these misfortunes, when he saw through the limbs and brush a white sheet go by.

Preacher Judd poked his head up and saw Cinderella running down a little path going, "Wooooo, wooooo, goats."

She had already forgotten about him and had the ghost thing on her mind.

He got up and crept after her with his frying pan. Pretty soon she disappeared over a dip in the trail and he followed her down.

She was sitting at the bottom of the trail between two pines, and ahead of her was a clear lake with the moon shining its face in the water. Across the water the trees thinned, and he could see the glow of lights from a house. She was looking at those lights and the big moon in the water and was saying over and over, "Oh, priddy, priddy."

He walked up behind her and said, "It sure is, sugar," and he hit her in the head with the pan. It gave a real solid ring, kind of like the clap of a sweet church bell. He figured that one shot to the bean was sufficient, since it was a good overhand lick, but she was still sitting up and he didn't want to be no slacker about things, so he hit her a couple more times, and by the second time, her head didn't give a ring, just sort of a dull thump, like he was hitting a thick rubber bag full of mud.

She fell over on what was left of her head and her butt cocked up in the air, exposed as the sheet fell down her back. He took a long look at it, but found he wasn't interested in doing what animals do without sin anymore. All that hitting on the Widow Case and Cinderella had tuckered him out.

He pulled his arm way back, tossed the frying pan with all his might toward the lake. It went in with a soft splash. He turned back toward the house and his car, and when he got out to the road, he cranked up the Dodge and drove away noticing that the Halloween sky was looking blacker. It was because the moon had slipped behind some dark clouds. He thought it looked like a suffering face behind a veil, and as he drove away from the Cases', he stuck his head out the window for a better look. By the time he made the hill that dipped down toward Highway 80, the clouds had passed along, and he'd come to see it more as a happy jack-o'-lantern than a sad face, and he took that as a sign that he had done well.

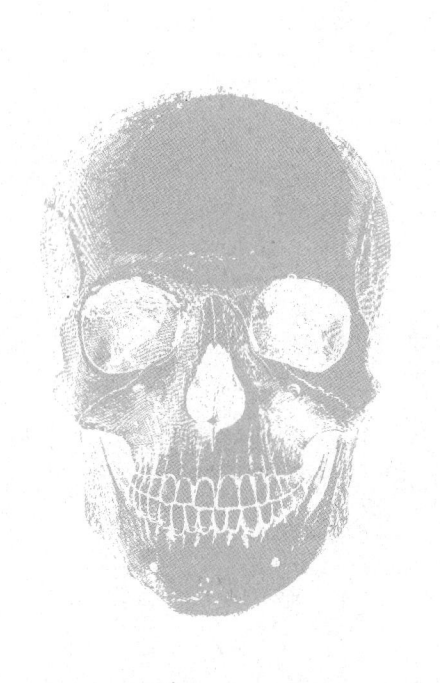

Another of my better-known early stories.

I had started a science fiction story about there having been a war between two car manufacturers, and how it was all part of a global panic. But I wasn't sure what to do with it. I had a few pages, but the idea to carry it forward wasn't working, so I put it aside.

Enter John Skipp and Craig Spector.

They were putting together a kind of George Romero tribute volume of zombie stories. I was getting some attention at this point, especially for the short stories, so they asked if I'd like to try a story.

It was then that I realized that a zombie infestation was just what I needed to make the story I had started work. I pretty much threw out what I had, except for the vibe and a few elements, and wrote this story of bad people and really bad people, and used not the sweetest people to tell it.

It's not only a love letter to Romero, it's a satirical tale that pokes fun at a number of sacred cows. It's still one of my all-time favorites, and readers loved it.

I should note, however, that satire, one of my favorite tools, is less and less appreciated these days. Readers take so much more what they read as literal than they once did.

Whatcha gonna do? You can't, and I won't, provide CliffsNotes for stories. Hell, do they even have those anymore? I read recently that so many young people these days can't finish a book because they didn't have to read them in school.

We've all been dumbed down.

You know what we have to do?

Be less dumb.

Anyway, here it is, 'On the Far Side of the Cadillac Desert with Dead Folks'.

I might also add that the long title was influenced by some of Harlan Ellison's titles. He was a troubled man but fine writer who became something of a friend over time, or at least someone I was friendly with.

My wife and I used to laugh when we'd come home and there was a message on the answering machine from him. It always started, "Lansdale. Call me."

He sounded exactly like you would think the Penguin of Batman villainy would sound.

I can still hear his voice in my head.

"Lansdale. Call me back."

On the Far Side of the Cadillac Desert with Dead Folks

AFTER A MONTH's chase, Wayne caught up with Calhoun one night at a little honky-tonk called Rosalita's. It wasn't that Calhoun had finally gotten careless, it was just that he wasn't worried. He'd killed four bounty hunters so far, and Wayne knew a fifth didn't concern him.

The last bounty hunter had been the famous Pink Lady McGuire—one mean mama—three hundred pounds of rolling, ugly meat that carried a twelve-gauge Remington pump and a bad attitude. Story was, Calhoun jumped her from behind, cut her throat, and as a joke, fucked her before she bled to death. This not only proved to Wayne that Calhoun was a dangerous sonofabitch, it also proved he had bad taste.

Wayne stepped out of his '57 Chevy reproduction, pushed his hat back on his forehead, opened the trunk, and got the sawed-off double barrel and some shells out of there. He already had a .38 revolver in the holster at his side and a bowie knife in each boot, but when you went into a place like Rosalita's it was best to have plenty of backup.

Wayne put a handful of shotgun shells in his shirt pocket, snapped the flap over them, looked up at the red-and-blue neon sign that flashed

ROSALITA'S: COLD BEER AND DEAD DANCING, found his center, as they say in Zen, and went on in.

He held the shotgun against his leg, and as it was dark in there and folks were busy with talk or drinks or dancing, no one noticed him or his artillery right off.

He spotted Calhoun's stocky, black-hatted self immediately. He was inside the dance cage with a dead buck-naked Mexican girl of about twelve. He was holding her tight around the waist with one hand and massaging her rubbery ass with the other like it was a pillow he was trying to shape. The dead girl's handless arms flailed on either side of Calhoun, and her little tits pressed to his thick chest. Her wire-muzzled face knocked repeatedly at his shoulder and drool whipped out of her mouth in thick spermy ropes, stuck to his shin, faded and left a patch of wetness.

For all Wayne knew, the girl was Calhoun's sister or daughter. It was that kind of place. The kind that had sprung up immediately after that stuff had gotten out of a lab upstate and filled the air with bacteria that brought dead humans back to life, made their basic motor functions work and made them hungry for human flesh; made it so if a man's wife, daughter, sister, or mother went belly up and he wanted to turn a few bucks, he might think: "Damn, that's tough about ole Betty Sue, but she's dead as hoot-owl shit and ain't gonna be needing nothing from here on out, and with them germs working around in her, she's just gonna pull herself out of the ground and cause me a problem. And the ground out back of the house is harder to dig than a calculus problem is to work, so I'll just toss her cold ass in the back of the pickup next to the chainsaw and the barbed-wire roll, haul her across the border to sell her to the Meat Boys to sell to the tonics for dancing.

"It's a sad thing to sell one of your own, but shit, them's the breaks. I'll just stay out of the tonics until all the meat rots off her bones and they have to throw her away. That way I won't go in some place for a drink and see her up there shaking her dead tits and end up going sentimental and dewy-eyed in front of one of my buddies or some ole two-dollar gal."

This kind of thinking supplied the dancers. In other parts of the country, the dancers might be men or children, but here it was mostly women. Men were used for hunting and target practice.

The Meat Boys took the bodies, cut off the hands so they couldn't grab, ran screws through their jaws to fasten on wire muzzles so they couldn't bite, sold them to the honky-tonks about the time the germ started stirring.

Bar owners put them inside wire enclosures up front of their joints, staffed music, and men paid five dollars to get in there and grab them and make like they were dancing when all the women wanted to do was grab and bite, which, muzzled and handless, they could not do.

If a man liked his partner enough, he could pay more money and have her tied to a cot in the back and he could get on her and at some business. Didn't have to hear no arguments or buy presents or make promises or make them come. Just fuck and hike.

As long as the establishment sprayed the dead for maggots and kept them perfumed and didn't keep them so long hunks of meat came off on a man's dick, the customers were happy as flies on shit.

Wayne looked to see who might give him trouble, and figured everyone was a potential customer. The six-foot-two, two-hundred-fifty-pound bouncer being the most immediate concern.

But, there wasn't anything to do but to get on with things and handle problems when they came up. He went into the cage where Calhoun was dancing, shouldered through the other dancers and went for him.

Calhoun had his back to Wayne, and as the music was loud, Wayne didn't worry about going quietly. But Calhoun sensed him and turned with his hand full of a little .38.

Wayne clubbed Calhoun's arm with the barrel of the shotgun. The little gun flew out of Calhoun's hand and went skidding across the floor and clanked against the metal cage.

Calhoun wasn't outdone. He spun the dead girl in front of him and pulled a big pigsticker out of his boot and held it under the girl's armpit in a threatening manner, which with a knife that big was no feat.

Wayne shot the dead girl's left kneecap out from under her and she went down. Her armpit trapped Calhoun's knife. The other men deserted their partners and went over the wire netting like squirrels.

Before Calhoun could shake the girl loose, Wayne stepped in and hit him over the head with the barrel of the shotgun. Calhoun crumpled and the girl began to crawl about on the floor as if looking for lost contacts.

The bouncer came in behind Wayne, grabbed him under the arms and tried to slip a full nelson on him.

Wayne kicked back on the bouncer's shin and raked his boot down the man's instep and stomped his foot. The bouncer let go. Wayne turned and kicked him in the balls and hit him across the face with the shotgun.

The bouncer went down and didn't even look like he wanted up.

Wayne couldn't help but note he liked the music that was playing. When he turned he had someone to dance with.

Calhoun.

Calhoun charged him, hit Wayne in the belly with his head, knocked him over the bouncer. They tumbled to the floor and the shotgun went out of Wayne's hands and scraped across the floor and hit the crawling girl in the head. She didn't even notice, just kept snaking in circles, dragging her blasted leg behind her like a skin she was trying to shed.

The other women, partnerless, wandered about the cage. The music changed. Wayne didn't like this tune as well. Too slow. He bit Calhoun's earlobe off.

Calhoun screamed and they grappled around on the floor. Calhoun got his arm around Wayne's throat and tried to choke him to death.

Wayne coughed out the earlobe, lifted his leg and took the knife out of his boot. He brought it around and back and hit Calhoun in the temple with the hilt.

Calhoun let go of Wayne and rocked on his knees, then collapsed on top of him.

Wayne got out from under him and got up and kicked him in the head a few times. When he was finished, he put the bowie in its place, got Calhoun's .38 and the shotgun. To hell with the pigsticker.

A dead woman tried to grab him, and he shoved her away with a thrust of his palm. He got Calhoun by the collar, started pulling him toward the gate.

Faces were pressed against the wire, watching. It had been quite a show. A friendly cowboy type opened the gate for Wayne and the crowd parted as he pulled Calhoun by. One man felt helpful and chased after them and said, "Here's his hat, Mister," and dropped it on Calhoun's knee and it stayed there.

Outside, a professional drunk was standing between two cars taking a leak on the ground. As Wayne pulled Calhoun past, the drunk said, "Your buddy don't look so good."

"Look worse than that when I get him to Law Town," Wayne said.

Wayne stopped by the '57, emptied Calhoun's pistol and tossed it as far as he could, then took a few minutes to kick Calhoun in the ribs and ass. Calhoun grunted and farted, but didn't come to.

When Wayne's leg got tired, he put Calhoun in the passenger seat and handcuffed him to the door.

He went over to Calhoun's '62 Impala replica with the plastic bull horns mounted on the hood—which was how he had located him in the first place, by his well-known car—and kicked the glass out of the window on the driver's side and used the shotgun to shoot the bull horns off. He took out his pistol and shot all the tires flat, pissed on the driver's door, and kicked a dent in it.

By then he was too tired to shit in the back seat, so he took some deep breaths and went back to the '57 and climbed in behind the wheel.

Reaching across Calhoun, he opened the glove box and got out one of his thin, black cigars and put it in his mouth.

He pushed the lighter in, and while he waited for it to heat up, he took the shotgun out of his lap and reloaded it.

A couple of men poked their heads outside of the tonk's door, and Wayne stuck the shotgun out the window and fired above their heads. They disappeared inside so fast they might have been an optical illusion.

Wayne put the lighter to his cigar, picked up the wanted poster he had on the seat, and set fire to it. He thought about putting it in Calhoun's lap as a joke, but didn't. He tossed the flaming poster out of the window.

He drove over close to the tonk and used the remaining shotgun load to shoot at the neon Rosalita's sign. Glass tinkled onto the tonk's roof and onto the gravel drive.

Now if he only had a dog to kick.

He drove away from there, bound for the Cadillac Desert, and finally Law Town on the other side.

2

The Cadillacs stretched for miles, providing the only shade in the desert. They were buried nose down at a slant, almost to the windshields, and Wayne could see skeletons of some of the drivers in the cars, either lodged behind the steering wheels or lying on the dashboards against the glass. The roof and hood guns had long since been removed and all the windows on the cars were rolled up, except for those that had been knocked out and vandalized by travelers, or dead folks looking for goodies.

The thought of being in one of those cars with the windows rolled up in all this heat made Wayne feel even more uncomfortable than he already was. Hot as it was, he was certain even the skeletons were sweating.

He finished pissing on the tire of the Chevy, saw the piss had almost dried. He shook the drops off, watched them fall and evaporate against the burning sand. Zipping up, he thought about Calhoun, and how when he'd pulled over earlier to let the sonofabitch take a leak, he'd seen there was a little metal ring through the head of his dick and a Texas emblem dangling from that. He could understand the Texas emblem, being from there himself, but he couldn't for the life of him imagine why a fella would do that to his general. Any idiot who would put a ring through the head of his pecker deserved to die, innocent or not.

Wayne took off his cowboy hat and rubbed the back of his neck and ran his hand over the top of his head and back again. The sweat on his fingers was thick as lube oil, and the thinning part of his hairline was tender; the heat was cooking the hell out of his scalp, even through the brown felt of his hat.

Before he put his hat on, the sweat on his fingers was dry. He broke open the shotgun, put the shells in his pocket, opened the Chevy's back door and tossed the shotgun on the floorboard.

He got in the front behind the wheel and the seat was hot as a griddle on his back and ass. The sun shone through the slightly tinted windows like a polished chrome hubcap; it forced him to squint.

Glancing over at Calhoun, he studied him. The fucker was asleep with his head thrown back and his black wilted hat hung precariously on his head—it looked jaunty almost. Sweat oozed down Calhoun's red face, flowed over his eyelids and around his neck, running in rivulets down the white seat covers, drying quickly. He had his left hand between his legs, clutching his balls, and his right was on the armrest, which was the only place it could be since he was handcuffed to the door.

Wayne thought he ought to blow the bastard's brains out and tell God he died. The shithead certainly needed shooting, but Wayne didn't want to lose a thousand dollars off his reward. He needed every penny if he was going to get that wrecking yard he wanted. The yard was the dream that went before him like a carrot before a donkey, and he didn't want any more delays. If he never made another trip across this goddamn desert, that would suit him fine.

Pop would let him buy the place with the money he had now, and he could pay the rest out later. But that wasn't what he wanted to do. The bounty business had finally gone sour, and he wanted to do different. It wasn't any goddamn fun anymore. Just met the dick cheese of the earth. And when you ran the sonofabitches to the ground and put the cuffs on them, you had to watch your ass 'til you got them turned in. Had to sleep with one eye open and a hand on your gun. It wasn't any way to live.

And he wanted a chance to do right by Pop. Pop had been like a father to him. When he was a kid and his mama was screwing the Mexicans across the border for the rent money, Pop would let him hang out in the yard and climb on the rusted cars and watch him fix the better ones, tune those babies so fine they purred like dick-whipped women.

When he was older, Pop would haul him to Galveston for the whores and out to the beach to take potshots at all the ugly, fucked-up critters swimming around in the Gulf. Sometimes he'd take him to Oklahoma for the Dead Roundup. It sure seemed to do the old fart good to whack those dead fuckers with a tire iron, smash their diseased brains so they'd lay down for good. And it was a challenge. 'Cause if one of those dead buddies bit you, you could put your head between your legs and kiss your rosy ass goodbye.

Wayne pulled out of his thoughts of Pop and the wrecking yard and turned on the stereo system. One of his favorite country-and-western tunes whispered at him. It was Billy Conteegas singing, and Wayne hummed along with the music as he drove into the welcome, if mostly ineffectual, shadows provided by the Cadillacs.

> "My baby left me,
> She left me for a cow,
> But I don't give a flying fuck,
> She's gone radioactive now,
> Yeah, my baby left me,
> Left me for a six-tittied cow."

Just when Conteegas was getting to the good part, doing the trilling sound in his throat he was famous for, Calhoun opened his eyes and spoke up.

"Ain't it bad enough I got to put up with the fucking heat and your fucking humming without having to listen to that shit? Ain't you got no Hank Williams stuff, or maybe some of that nigger music they used to make? You know, where the coons harmonize and one of 'em sings like his nuts are cut off."

"You just don't know good music when you hear it, Calhoun."

Calhoun moved his free hand to his hatband, found one of his few remaining cigarettes and a match there. He struck the match on his knee, lit the smoke and coughed a few rounds. Wayne couldn't imagine how Calhoun could smoke in all this heat.

"Well, I may not know good music when I hear it, capon, but I damn sure know bad music when I hear it. And that's some bad music."

"You ain't got any kind of culture, Calhoun. You been too busy raping kids."

"Reckon a man has to have a hobby," Calhoun said, blowing smoke at Wayne. "Young pussy is mine. Besides, she wasn't in diapers. Couldn't find one that young. She was thirteen. You know what they say. If they're old enough to bleed, they're old enough to breed."

"How old they have to be for you to kill them?"

"She got loud."

"Change channels, Calhoun."

"Just passing the time of day, capon. Better watch yourself, bounty hunter, when you least expect it, I'll bash your head."

"You're gonna run your mouth one time too many, Calhoun, and when you do, you're gonna finish this ride in the trunk with ants crawling on you. You ain't so priceless I won't blow you away."

"You lucked out at the tonk, boy. But there's always tomorrow, and every day can't be like at Rosalita's."

Wayne smiled. "Trouble is, Calhoun, you're running out of tomorrows."

3

As they drove between the Cadillacs, the sky fading like a bad bulb, Wayne looked at the cars and tried to imagine what the Chevy–Cadillac Wars had been like, and why they had been fought in this miserable desert. He had heard it was a hell of a fight, and close, but the outcome had been Chevy's and now they were the only cars Detroit made. And as far as he was concerned, that was the only thing about Detroit that was worth a damn. Cars.

He felt that way about all cities. He'd just as soon lie down and let a diseased dog shit in his face than drive through one, let alone live in one.

Law Town being an exception. He'd go there. Not to live, but to give Calhoun to the authorities and pick up his reward. People in Law Town were always glad to see a criminal brought in. The public executions were popular and varied and supplied a steady income.

Last time he'd been to Law Town he'd bought a front-row ticket to one of the executions and watched a chronic shoplifter, a redheaded rat of a man, get pulled apart by being chained between two souped-up tractors. The execution itself was pretty brief, but there had been plenty of buildup with clowns and balloons and a big-tittied stripper who could swing her tits in either direction to boom-boom music.

Wayne had been put off by the whole thing. It wasn't organized enough and the drinks and food were expensive and the front-row seats were too close to the tractors. He had gotten to see that the redhead's insides were brighter than his hair, but some of the insides got sprinkled on his new shirt, and cold water or not, the spots hadn't come out. He had suggested to one of the management that they put up a big plastic shield so the front row wouldn't get splattered, but he doubted anything had come of it.

They drove until it was solid dark. Wayne stopped and fed Calhoun a stick of jerky and some water from his canteen. Then he handcuffed him to the front bumper of the Chevy.

"See any snakes, Gila monsters, scorpions, stuff like that," Wayne said, "yell out. Maybe I can get around here in time."

"I'd let the fuckers run up my asshole before I'd call you," Calhoun said.

Leaving Calhoun with his head resting on the bumper, Wayne climbed in the back seat of the Chevy and slept with one ear cocked and one eye open.

Before dawn Wayne got Calhoun loaded in the '57 and they started out. After a few minutes of sluicing through the early morning grayness, a wind started up. One of those weird desert winds that come out of nowhere. It carried grit through the air at the speed of bullets, hit the '57 with a sound like rabid cats scratching.

The sand tires crunched on through, and Wayne turned on the windshield blower, the sand wipers, and the head-beams, and kept on keeping on.

When it was time for the sun to come up, they couldn't see it. Too much sand. It was blowing harder than ever and the blowers and wipers couldn't handle it. It was piling up. Wayne couldn't even make out the Cadillacs anymore.

He was about to stop when a shadowy, whale-like shape crossed in front of him and he slammed on the brakes, giving the sand tires a workout. But it wasn't enough.

The '57 spun around and rammed the shape on Calhoun's side. Wayne heard Calhoun yell, then felt himself thrown against the door and his head smacked metal and the outside darkness was nothing compared to the darkness into which he descended.

4

Wayne rose out of it as quickly as he had gone down. Blood was trickling into his eyes from a slight forehead wound. He used his sleeve to wipe it away.

His first clear sight was of a face at the window on his side: a sallow, moon-terrain face with bulging eyes and an expression like an idiot contemplating Sanskrit. On the man's head was a strange black hat with big round ears, and in the center of the hat, like a silver tumor, was the head of a large screw. Sand lashed at the face, imbedded in it, struck the unblinking eyes and made the round-eared hat flap. The man paid no attention. Though still dazed, Wayne knew why. The man was one of the dead folks.

Wayne looked in Calhoun's direction. Calhoun's door had been mashed in and the bending metal had pinched the handcuff attached to the armrest in two. The blow had knocked Calhoun to the center of the seat. He was holding his hand in front of him, looking at the dangling cuff and chain as if it were a silver bracelet and a line of pearls.

Leaning over the hood, cleaning the sand away from the windshield with his hands, was another of the dead folks. He, too, was wearing one of the round-eared hats. He pressed a wrecked face to the clean spot and looked in at Calhoun. A string of snot-green saliva ran out of his mouth and onto the glass.

More sand was wiped away by others. Soon all the car's glass showed the pallid and rotting faces of the dead folks. They stared at Wayne and Calhoun as if they were two rare fish in an aquarium.

Wayne cocked back the hammer of the .38.

"What about me?" Calhoun said. "What am I supposed to use?"

"Your charm," Wayne said, and at that moment, as if by signal, the dead folk faded away from the glass, leaving one man standing on the hood holding a baseball bat. He hit the glass and it went into a thousand little stars. The bat came again and the heavens fell and the stars rained down and the sand storm screamed in on Wayne and Calhoun.

The dead folks reappeared in full force. The one with the bat started though the hole in the windshield, heedless of the jags of glass that ripped his ragged clothes and tore his flesh like damp cardboard.

Wayne shot the batter through the head, and the man, finished, fell through, pinning Wayne's arm with his body.

Before Wayne could pull his gun free, a woman's hand reached through the hole and got hold of Wayne's collar. Other dead folks took to the glass and hammered it out with their feet and fist. Hands were all over Wayne; they felt dry and cool like leather seat covers. They pulled him over the steering wheel and dash and outside. The sand worked at his flesh like a cheese grater. He could hear Calhoun yelling, "Eat me, motherfuckers, eat me and choke."

They tossed Wayne on the hood of the '57. Faces leaned over him. Yellow teeth and toothless gums were very near. A roadkill odor washed through his nostrils. He thought: Now the feeding frenzy begins. His only consolation was that there were so many dead folks, there wouldn't be enough of him left to come back from the dead. They'd probably have his brain for dessert.

But no. They picked him up and carried him off. Next thing he knew was a clearer view of the whale-shape the '57 had hit, and its color. It was a yellow school bus.

The door to the bus hissed open. The dead folks dumped Wayne inside on his belly and tossed his hat after him. They stepped back and the door closed, just missing Wayne's foot.

Wayne looked up and saw a man in the driver's seat smiling at him. It wasn't a dead man. Just fat and ugly. He was probably five feet tall and bald except for a fringe of hair around his shiny bald head the color of a shit ring in a toilet bowl. He had a nose so long and dark and malignant-looking it appeared as if it might fall off his face at any moment, like an overripe banana. He was wearing what Wayne first thought was a bathrobe, but proved to be a robe like that of a monk. It was old and tattered and moth-eaten, and Wayne could see pale flesh through the holes. An odor wafted from the fat man that was somewhere between the smell of stale sweat, cheesy balls, and an unwiped asshole.

"Good to see you," the fat man said.

"Charmed," Wayne said.

From the back of the bus came a strange, unidentifiable sound. Wayne poked his head around the seats for a look.

In the middle of the aisle, about halfway back, was a nun. Or sort of a nun. Her back was to him and she wore a black-and-white nun's habit. The part that covered her head was traditional, but from there down was quite a departure from the standard attire. The outfit was cut to the middle of her thigh and she wore black fishnet stockings and thick high heels. She was slim with good legs and a high little ass that, even under the circumstances, Wayne couldn't help but appreciate. She was moving one hand above her head as if sewing the air.

Sitting on the seats on either side of the aisle were dead folks. They all wore the round-eared hats, and they were responsible for the sound.

They were trying to sing.

He had never known dead folks to make any noise outside of grunts and groans, but here they were singing. A toneless sort of singing to be sure, some of the words garbled and some of the dead folks just opening and closing their mouths soundlessly, but, by golly, he recognized the tune. It was "Jesus Loves Me."

Wayne looked back at the fat man, let his hand ease down to the bowie in his right boot. The fat man produced a little .32 automatic from inside his robe and pointed it at Wayne.

"It's small caliber," the fat man said, "but I'm a real fine shot, and it makes a nice, little hole."

Wayne quit reaching in his boot.

"Oh, that's all right," said the fat man. "Take the knife out and put it on the floor in front of you and slide it to me. And while you're at it, I think I see the hilt of one in your other boot."

Wayne looked back. The way he had been thrown inside the bus had caused his pants legs to hike up over his boots, and the hilts of both his bowies were revealed. They might as well have had blinking lights on them.

It was shaping up to be a shitty day.

He slid the bowies to the fat man, who scooped them up nimbly and dumped them on the other side of his seat.

The bus door opened and Calhoun was tossed in on top of Wayne. Calhoun's hat followed after.

Wayne shrugged Calhoun off, recovered his hat, and put it on. Calhoun found his hat and did the same. They were still on their knees.

"Would you gentlemen mind moving to the center of the bus?"

Wayne led the way. Calhoun took note of the nun now, said, "Man, look at that ass."

The fat man called back to them. "Right there will do fine."

Wayne slid into the seat the fat man was indicating with a wave of the .32, and Calhoun slid in beside him. The dead folks entered now, filled the seats up front, leaving only a few stray seats in the middle empty.

Calhoun said, "What are those fuckers back there making that noise for?"

"They're singing," Wayne said. "Ain't you got no churchin'?"

"Say they are?" Calhoun turned to the nun and the dead folks and yelled, "Y'all know any Hank Williams?"

The nun did not turn and the dead folks did not quit their toneless singing.

"Guess not," Calhoun said. "Seems like all the good music's been forgotten."

The noise in the back of the bus ceased and the nun came over to look at Wayne and Calhoun. She was nice in front too. The outfit was cut from throat to crotch, laced with a ribbon, and it showed a lot of tit and some tight, thin, black panties that couldn't quite hold in her escaping pubic hair, which grew as thick and wild as kudzu. When Wayne managed to work his eyes up from that and look at her face, he saw she was dark-complected with eyes the color of coffee and lips made to chew on.

Calhoun never made it to the face. He didn't care about faces. He sniffed, said into her crotch, "Nice snatch."

The nun's left hand came around and smacked Calhoun on the side of the head.

He grabbed her wrist, said, "Nice arm, too."

The nun did a magic act with her right hand; it went behind her back and hiked up her outfit and came back with a double-barreled derringer. She pressed it against Calhoun's head.

Wayne bent forward, hoping she wouldn't shoot. At that range the bullet might go through Calhoun's head and hit him too.

"Can't miss," the nun said.

Calhoun smiled. "No, you can't," he said, and let go of her arm.

She sat down across from them, smiled, and crossed her legs high. Wayne felt his Levi's snake swell and crawl against the inside of his thigh.

"Honey," Calhoun said, "you're almost worth taking a bullet for."

The nun didn't quit smiling. The bus cranked up. The sand blowers and wipers went to work, and the windshield turned blue, and a white dot moved on it between a series of smaller white dots.

Radar. Wayne had seen that sort of thing on desert vehicles. If he lived through this and got his car back, maybe he'd rig up something like that. And maybe not, he was sick of the desert.

Whatever, at the moment, future plans seemed a little out of place.

Then something else occurred to him. Radar. That meant these bastards had known they were coming and had pulled out in front of them on purpose.

He leaned over the seat and checked where he figured the '57 hit the bus. He didn't see a single dent. Armored, most likely. Most school buses were these days, and that's what this had been. It probably had bullet-proof glass and puncture-proof sand tires too. School buses had gone that way on account of the race riots and the sending of mutated calves to school just like they were humans. And because of the Codgers—old farts who believed kids ought to be fair game to adults for sexual purposes, or for knocking around when they wanted to let off some tension.

"How about unlocking this cuff?" Calhoun said. "It ain't for shit now anyway."

Wayne looked at the nun. "I'm going for the cuff key in my pants. Don't shoot."

Wayne fished it out, unlocked the cuff, and Calhoun let it slide to the floor. Wayne saw the nun was curious and he said, "I'm a bounty hunter.

Help me get this man to Law Town and I could see you earn a little something for your troubles."

The woman shook her head.

"That's the spirit," Calhoun said. "I like a nun that minds her own business. . . . You a real nun?"

She nodded.

"Always talk so much?"

Another nod.

Wayne said, "I've never seen a nun like you. Not dressed like that and with a gun."

"We are a small and special order," she said.

"You some kind of Sunday school teacher for these dead folks?"

"Sort of."

"But with them dead, ain't it kind of pointless? They ain't got no souls now, do they?"

"No, but their work adds to the glory of God."

"Their work?" Wayne looked at the dead folks sitting stiffly in their seats. He noted that one of them was about to lose a rotten ear. He sniffed. "They may be adding to the glory of God, but they don't do much for the air."

The nun reached into a pocket on her habit and took out two round objects. She tossed one to Calhoun, and one to Wayne. "Menthol lozenges. They help you stand the smell."

Wayne unwrapped the lozenge and sucked on it. It did help overpower the smell, but the menthol wasn't all that great either. It reminded him of being sick.

"What order are you?" Wayne asked.

"Jesus Loved Mary," the nun said.

"His mama?"

"Mary Magdalene. We think he fucked her. They were lovers. There's evidence in the scriptures. She was a harlot and we have modeled ourselves on her. She gave up that life and became a harlot for Jesus."

"Hate to break it to you, sister," Calhoun said, "but that do-gooder Jesus is as dead as a post. If you're waiting for him to slap the meat to you, that sweet thing of yours is going to dry up and blow away."

"Thanks for the news," the nun said. "But we don't fuck him in person.

We fuck him in spirit. We let the spirit enter into men so they may take us in the fashion Jesus took Mary."

"No shit?"

"No shit."

"You know, I think I feel the old boy moving around inside me now. Why don't you shuck them drawers, honey, throw back in that seat there and let ole Calhoun give you a big load of Jesus?"

Calhoun shifted in the nun's direction.

She pointed the derringer at him, said, "Stay where you are. If it were so, if you were full of Jesus, I would let you have me in a moment. But you're full of the Devil, not Jesus."

"Shit, sister, give ole Devil a break. He's a fun kind of guy. Let's you and me mount up . . . well, be like that. But if you change your mind, I can get religion at a moment's notice. I dearly love to fuck. I've fucked . . . everything I could get my hands on but a parakeet, and I'd have fucked that little bitch if I could have found the hole."

"I've never known any dead folks to be trained," Wayne said, trying to get the nun talking in a direction that might help, a direction that would let him know what was going on and what sort of trouble he had fallen into.

"As I said, we are a very special order. Brother Lazarus," she waved a hand at the bus driver, and without looking he lifted a hand in acknowledgment, "is the founder. I don't think he'll mind if I tell his story, explain about us, what we do and why. It's important that we spread the word to the heathens."

"Don't call me no fucking heathen," Calhoun said. "This is heathen, riding 'round in a fucking bus with a bunch of stinking dead folks with funny hats on. Hell, they can't even carry a tune."

The nun ignored him. "Brother Lazarus was once known by another name, but that name no longer matters. He was a research scientist, and he was one of those who worked in the laboratory where the germs escaped into the air and made it so the dead could not truly die as long as they had an undamaged brain in their heads.

"Brother Lazarus was carrying a dish of the experiment, the germs, and as a joke, one of the lab assistants pretended to trip him, and he, not knowing it was a joke, dodged the assistant's leg and dropped the dish. In a moment, the air-conditioning system had blown the germs throughout the research center. Someone opened a door, and the germs were loose on the world.

"Brother Lazarus was consumed by guilt. Not only because he dropped the dish, but because he helped create it in the first place. He quit his job at the laboratory, took to wandering the country. He came out here with nothing more than basic food, water, and books. Among these books was the Bible, and the lost books of the Bible: the Apocrypha and the many cast-out chapters of the New Testament. As he studied, it occurred to him that these cast-out books actually belonged. He was able to interpret their higher meaning, and an angel came to him in a dream and told him of another book, and Brother Lazarus took up his pen and recorded the angel's words, direct from God, and in this book, all the mysteries were explained."

"Like screwing Jesus," Calhoun said.

"Like screwing Jesus, and not being afraid of words that mean sex. Not being afraid of seeing Jesus as both God and man. Seeing that sex, if meant for Christ and the opening of the mind, can be a thrilling and religious experience, not just the rutting of two savage animals.

"Brother Lazarus roamed the desert, the mountains, thinking of the things the Lord had revealed to him, and lo and behold, the Lord revealed yet another thing to him. Brother Lazarus found a great amusement park."

"Didn't know Jesus went in for rides and such," Calhoun said.

"It was long deserted. It had once been part of a place called Disneyland. Brother Lazarus knew of it. There had been several of these Disneylands built about the country, and this one had been in the midst of the Chevy–Cadillac Wars, and had been destroyed and sand had covered most of it."

The nun held out her arms. "And in this rubble, he saw a new beginning."

"Cool off, baby," Calhoun said, "before you have a stroke."

"He gathered to him men and women of a like mind and taught the gospel to them. The Old Testament. The New Testament. The Lost Books. And his own Book of Lazarus, for he had begun to call himself Lazarus. A symbolic name signifying a new beginning, a rising from the dead and coming to life and seeing things as they really are."

The nun moved her hands rapidly, expressively as she talked. Sweat beaded on her forehead and upper lip.

"So he returned to his skills as a scientist, but applied them to a higher purpose—God's purpose. And as Brother Lazarus, he realized the use of the dead. They could be taught to work and build a great monument to the glory of God. And this monument, this coed institution of monks and nuns, would be called Jesus Land."

At the word "Jesus," the nun gave her voice an extra trill, and the dead folks, cued, said together, "Eees num be prased."

"How the hell did you train them dead folks?" Calhoun said. "Dog treats?"

"Science put to the use of our lord Jesus Christ, that's how. Brother Lazarus made a special device he could insert directly into the brains of dead folks, through the tops of their heads, and the device controls certain cravings. Makes them passive and responsive—at least to simple commands. With the regulator, as Brother Lazarus calls the device, we have been able to do much positive work with the dead."

"Where do you find these dead folks?" Wayne asked.

"We buy them from the Meat Boys. We save them from amoral purposes."

"They ought to be shot through the head and put in the goddamn ground," Wayne said.

"If our use of the regulator and the dead folks was merely to better ourselves, I would agree. But it is not. We do the Lord's work."

"Do the monks fuck the sisters?" Calhoun asked.

"When possessed by the Spirit of Christ, yes."

"And I bet they get possessed a lot. Not a bad setup. Dead folks to do the work on the amusement park—"

"It isn't an amusement park now."

"—and plenty of free pussy. Sounds cozy. I like it. Old shithead up there's smarter than he looks."

"There is nothing selfish about our motives or those of Brother Lazarus. In fact, as penance for loosing the germ on the world in the first place, Brother Lazarus injected a virus into his nose. It is rotting slowly."

"Thought that was quite a snorkel he had on him," Wayne said.

"I take it back," Calhoun said. "He *is* as dumb as he looks."

"Why do the dead folks wear those silly hats?" Wayne asked.

"Brother Lazarus found a storeroom of them at the site of the old amusement park. They are mouse ears. They represent some cartoon animal that was popular once and part of Disneyland. Mickey Mouse, he was called. This way we know which dead folks are ours, and which ones are not controlled by our regulators. From time to time, stray dead folks wander into our area. Murder victims. Children abandoned in the desert.

People crossing the desert who died of heat or illness. We've had some of the sisters and brothers attacked. The hats are a precaution."

"And what's the deal with us?" Wayne asked.

The nun smiled sweetly. "You, my children, are to add to the glory of God."

"Children?" Calhoun said. "You call an alligator a lizard, bitch?"

The nun slid back in the seat and rested the derringer in her lap. She pulled her legs into a cocked position, causing her panties to crease in the valley of her vagina; it looked like a nice place to visit, that valley.

Wayne turned from the beauty of it and put his head back and closed his eyes, pulled his hat down over them. There was nothing he could do at the moment, and since the nun was watching Calhoun for him, he'd sleep, store up and figure what to do next. If anything.

He drifted off to sleep wondering what the nun meant by, "You, my children, are to add to the glory of God."

He had a feeling that when he found out, he wasn't going to like it.

5

He awoke off and on and saw that the sunlight filtering through the storm had given everything a greenish color. Calhoun, seeing he was awake, said, "Ain't that a pretty color? I had a shirt that color once and liked it lots, but I got in a fight with this Mexican whore with a wooden leg over some money and she tore it. I punched that little bean bandit good."

"Thanks for sharing that," Wayne said, and went back to sleep.

Each time he awoke it was brighter, and finally he awoke to the sun going down and the storm having died out. But he didn't stay awake. He forced himself to close his eyes and store up more energy. To help him nod off he listened to the hum of the motor and thought about the wrecking yard and Pop and all the fun they could have, just drinking beer and playing cards and fucking the border women, and maybe some of those mutated cows they had over there for sale.

Nah. Nix the cows, or any of those genetically altered critters. A man had to draw the line somewhere, and he drew it at fucking critters, even if they had been bred so that they had human traits. You had to have some standards.

Course, those standards had a way of eroding. He remembered when he said he'd only fuck the pretty ones. His last whore had been downright scary-looking. If he didn't watch himself he'd be as bad as Calhoun, trying to find the hole in the parakeet.

He awoke to Calhoun's elbow in his ribs and the nun was standing beside their seat with the derringer. Wayne knew she hadn't slept, but she looked bright-eyed and bushy-tailed. She nodded toward their window, said, "Jesus Land."

She had put that special touch in her voice again, and the dead folks responded with, "Eees num be prased."

It was good and dark now, a crisp night with a big moon the color of hammered brass. The bus sailed across the white sand like a mystical schooner with a full wind in its sails. It went up an impossible hill toward what looked like an aurora borealis, then dove into an atomic rainbow of colors that filled the bus with fairy lights.

When Wayne's eyes became accustomed to the lights, and the bus took a right turn along a precarious curve, he glanced down into the valley. An aerial view couldn't have been any better than the view from his window.

Down there was a universe of polished metal and twisted neon. In the center of the valley was a great statue of Jesus crucified that must have been twenty-five stories high. Most of the body was made of bright metals and multicolored neon, and much of the light was coming from that. There was a crown of barbed wire wound several times around a chromium plate of a forehead and some rust-colored strands of neon hair. The savior's eyes were huge, green strobes that swung left and right with the precision of an oscillating fan. There was an ear-to-ear smile on the savior's face and the teeth were slats of sparkling metal with wide cavity-black gaps between them. The statue was equipped with a massive dick of polished, interwoven cables and coils of neon, the dick was thicker and more solid looking than the arthritic steel-tube legs on either side of it; the head of it was made of an enormous spotlight that pulsed the color of irritation.

The bus went around and around the valley, descending like a dead roach going down a slow drain, and finally the road rolled out straight and took them into Jesus Land.

They passed through the legs of Jesus, under the throbbing head of his cock, toward what looked like a small castle of polished gold bricks with an upright drawbridge inlayed with jewels.

The castle was only one of several tall structures that appeared to be made of rare metals and precious stones: gold, silver, emeralds, rubies, and sapphires. But the closer they got to the buildings, the less fine they looked and the more they looked like what they were: stucco, cardboard, phosphorescent paint, colored spotlights, and bands of neon.

Off to the left Wayne could see a long, open shed full of vehicles, most of them old school buses. And there were unlighted hovels made of tin and tar paper; homes for the dead, perhaps. Behind the shacks and the bus barn rose skeletal shapes that stretched tall and bleak against the sky and the candy-gem lights, shapes that looked like the bony remains of beached whales.

On the right, Wayne glimpsed a building with an open front that served as a stage. In front of the stage were chairs filled with monks and nuns. On the stage, six monks—one behind a drum set, one with a saxophone, the others with guitars—were blasting out a loud, rocking rhythm that made the bus shake. A nun with the front of her habit thrown open, her headpiece discarded, sang into a microphone with a voice like a suffering angel. The voice screeched out of the amplifiers and came in through the windows of the bus, crushing the sound of the engine. The nun crowed "Jesus" so long and hard it sounded like a plea from hell. Then she leapt up and came down doing the splits, the impact driving her back to her feet as if her ass had been loaded with springs.

"Bet that bitch can pick up a quarter with that thing," Calhoun said.

Brother Lazarus touched a button, the pseudo-jeweled drawbridge lowered over a narrow moat, and he drove them inside.

It wasn't as well lighted in there. The walls were bleak and gray. Brother Lazarus stopped the bus and got off, and another monk came on board. He was tall and thin and had crooked buckteeth that dented his bottom lip. He also had a twelve-gauge pump shotgun.

"This is Brother Fred," the nun said. "He'll be your tour guide."

Brother Fred forced Wayne and Calhoun off the bus, away from the dead folks in their mouse-ear hats and the nun in her tight, black panties, jabbed them along a dark corridor, up a swirl of stairs and down a longer corridor with open doors on either side and rooms filled with dark and light and spoiled meat and guts on hooks and skulls and bones lying about like discarded walnut shells and broken sticks; rooms full of dead folks (truly dead) stacked neat as firewood, and rooms full of stone shelves stuffed with beakers of fiery-red and sewer-green and sky-blue and piss-yellow liquids, as well as glass coils through which other colored fluids fled as if chased, smoked as if nervous, and ran into big flasks as if relieved; rooms with platforms and tables and boxes and stools and chairs covered with instruments or dead folks or dead-folk pieces or the asses of monks and nuns as they sat and held charts or tubes or body parts and frowned at them with concentration, lips pursed as if about to explode with some earth-shattering pronouncement; and finally they came to a little room with a tall, glassless window that looked out upon the bright, shiny mess that was Jesus Land.

The room was simple. Table, two chairs, two beds—one on either side of the room. The walls were stone and unadorned. To the right was a little bathroom without a door.

Wayne walked to the window and looked out at Jesus Land pulsing and thumping like a desperate heart. He listened to the music a moment, leaned over and stuck his head outside.

They were high up and there was nothing but a straight drop. If you jumped, you'd wind up with the heels of your boots under your tonsils.

Wayne let out a whistle in appreciation of the drop. Brother Fred thought it was a compliment for Jesus Land. He said, "It's a miracle, isn't it?"

"Miracle?" Calhoun said. "This goony light show? This ain't no miracle. This is for shit. Get that nun on the bus back there to bend over and shit a perfectly round turd through a hoop at twenty paces, and I'll call that a miracle, Mr. Fucked-Up Teeth. But this Jesus Land crap is the dumbest fucking idea since dog sweaters.

"And look at this place. You could use some knickknacks or something in here. A picture of some ole naked gal doing a donkey, couple of pigs fucking. Anything. And a door on the shitter would be nice. I hate to be straining out a big one and know someone can look in on me. It ain't decent. A man ought to have his fucking grunts in private. This place reminds me of a motel I stayed at in Waco one night, and I made the goddamn manager give me my money back. The roaches in that shithole were big enough to use the shower."

Brother Fred listened to all this without blinking an eye, as if seeing Calhoun talk was as amazing as seeing a frog sing. He said. "Sleep tight, don't let the bedbugs bite. Tomorrow you start to work."

"I don't want no fucking job," Calhoun said.

"Goodnight, children," Brother Fred said, and with that he closed the door and they heard it lock, loud and final as the clicking of the drop board on a gallows.

6

At dawn, Wayne got up and took a leak, went to the window to look out. The stage where the monks had played and the nun had jumped was empty. The skeletal shapes he had seen last night were tracks and frames from rides long abandoned. He had a sudden vision of Jesus and his disciples riding a roller coaster, their long hair and robes flapping in the wind.

The large crucified Jesus looked unimpressive without its lights and night's mystery, like a whore in harsh sunlight with makeup gone and wig askew.

"Got any ideas how we're gonna get out of here?" Calhoun asked.

Wayne looked at Calhoun. He was sitting on the bed, pulling on his boots.

Wayne shook his head.

"I could use a smoke. You know, I think we ought to work together. Then we can try to kill each other."

Unconsciously, Calhoun touched his ear where Wayne had bitten off the lobe.

"Wouldn't trust you as far as I could kick you," Wayne said.

"I hear that. But I give my word. And my word's something you can count on. I won't twist it."

Wayne studied Calhoun, thought: Well, there wasn't anything to lose. He'd just watch his ass.

"All right," Wayne said. "Give me your word you'll work with me on getting us out of this mess, and when we're good and free, and you say your word has gone far enough, we can settle up."

"Deal," Calhoun said, and offered his hand. Wayne looked at it.

"This seals it," Calhoun said.

Wayne took Calhoun's hand and they shook.

7

Moments later the door unlocked and a smiling monk with hair the color and texture of mold fuzz came in with Brother Fred, who still had his pump shotgun. There were two dead folks with them. A man and a woman. They wore torn clothes and the mouse-ear hats. Neither looked long dead or smelled particularly bad. Actually, the monks smelled worse.

Using the barrel of the shotgun, Brother Fred poked them down the hall to a room with metal tables and medical instruments.

Brother Lazarus was on the far side of one of the tables. He was smiling. His nose looked especially cancerous this morning. A white pustule the size of a thumb tip had taken up residence on the left side of his snout, and it looked like a pearl onion in a turd.

Nearby stood a nun. She was short with good, if skinny, legs, and she wore the same outfit as the nun on the bus. It looked more girlish on her, perhaps because she was thin and small-breasted. She had a nice face, and eyes that were all pupil. Wisps of blond hair crawled out around the edges of her headgear. She looked pale and weak, as if wearied to the bone. There was a birthmark on her right cheek that looked like a distant view of a small bird in flight.

"Good morning," Brother Lazarus said. "I hope you gentlemen slept well."

"What's this about work?" Wayne said.

"Work?" Brother Lazarus said.

"I described it to them that way," Brother Fred said. "Perhaps an impulsive description."

"I'll say," Brother Lazarus said. "No work here, gentlemen. You have my word on that. We do all the work. Lie on these tables and we'll take a sampling of your blood."

"Why?" Wayne said.

"Science," Brother Lazarus said. "I intend to find a cure for this germ that makes the dead come back to life, and to do that, I need living human beings to study. Sounds kind of mad scientist, doesn't it? But I assure you, you've nothing to lose but a few drops of blood. Well, maybe more than a few drops, but nothing serious."

"Use your own goddamn blood," Calhoun said.

"We do. But we're always looking for fresh specimens. Little here, little there. And if you don't do it, we'll kill you."

Calhoun spun and hit Brother Fred on the nose. It was a solid punch and Brother Fred hit the floor on his butt, but he hung onto the shotgun and pointed it up at Calhoun. "Go on," he said, his nose streaming blood. "Try that again."

Wayne flexed to help, but hesitated. He could kick Brother Fred in the head from where he was, but that might not keep him from shooting Calhoun, and there would go the extra reward money. And besides, he'd given his word to the bastard that they'd try to help each other survive until they got out of this.

The other monk clasped his hands and swung them into the side of Calhoun's head, knocking him down. Brother Fred got up, and while Calhoun was trying to rise, he hit him with the stock of the shotgun in the back of the head, hit him so hard it drove Calhoun's forehead into the floor. Calhoun rolled over on his side and lay there, his eyes fluttering like moth wings.

"Brother Fred, you must learn to turn the other cheek," Brother Lazarus said. "Now put this sack of shit on the table."

Brother Fred checked Wayne to see if he looked like trouble. Wayne put his hands in his pockets and smiled.

Brother Fred called the two dead folks over and had them put Calhoun on the table. Brother Lazarus strapped him down.

The nun brought a tray of needles, syringes, cotton, and bottles over, put it down on the table next to Calhoun's head. Brother Lazarus rolled up Calhoun's sleeve and fixed up a needle and stuck it in Calhoun's arm, drew it full of blood. He stuck the needle through the rubber top of one of the bottles and shot the blood into that.

He looked at Wayne and said, "I hope you'll be less trouble."

"Do I get some orange juice and a little cracker afterwards?" Wayne said.

"You get to walk out without a knot on your head," Brother Lazarus said.

"Guess that'll have to do."

Wayne got on the table next to Calhoun and Brother Lazarus strapped him down. The nun brought the tray over and Brother Lazarus did to him what he had done to Calhoun. The nun stood over Wayne and looked down at his face. Wayne tried to read something in her features but couldn't find a clue.

When Brother Lazarus was finished he took hold of Wayne's chin and shook it. "My, but you two boys look healthy. But you can never be sure. We'll have to run the blood through some tests. Meantime, Sister Worth will run a few additional tests on you, and," he nodded at the unconscious Calhoun, "I'll see to your friend here."

"He's no friend of mine," Wayne said.

They took Wayne off the table, and Sister Worth and Brother Fred, and his shotgun, directed him down the hall into another room.

The room was lined with shelves that were lined with instruments and bottles. The lighting was poor, most of it coming through a slatted window, though there was an anemic yellow bulb overhead. Dust motes swam in the air.

In the center of the room on its rim was a great, spoked wheel. It had two straps well spaced at the top, and two more at the bottom. Beneath the bottom straps were blocks of wood. The wheel was attached in back to an upright metal bar that had switches and buttons all over it.

Brother Fred made Wayne strip and get on the wheel with his back to the hub and his feet on the blocks. Sister Worth strapped his ankles down tight, then he was made to put his hands up, and she strapped his wrists to the upper part of the wheel.

"I hope this hurts a lot," Brother Fred said.

"Wipe the blood off your face," Wayne said. "It makes you look silly."

Brother Fred made a gesture with his middle finger that wasn't religious and left the room.

8

Sister Worth touched a switch and the wheel began to spin, slowly at first, and the bad light came through the windows and poked through the rungs and the dust swam before his eyes and the wheel and its spokes threw twisting shadows on the wall.

As he went around, Wayne closed his eyes. It kept him from feeling so dizzy, especially on the downswings.

On a turn up, he opened his eyes and caught sight of Sister Worth standing in front of the wheel staring at him. He said, "Why?" and closed his eyes as the wheel dipped.

"Because Brother Lazarus says so," came the answer after such a long time Wayne had almost forgotten the question. Actually, he hadn't expected a response. He was surprised that such a thing had come out of his mouth, and he felt a little diminished for having asked.

He opened his eyes on another swing up, and she was moving behind the wheel, out of his line of vision. He heard a snick like a switch being flipped and lightning jumped through him and he screamed in spite of himself. A little fork of electricity licked out of his mouth like a reptile tongue tasting air.

Faster spun the wheel and the jolts came more often and he screamed less loud, and finally not at all. He was too numb. He was adrift in space wearing only his cowboy hat and boots, moving away from Earth very fast. Floating all around him were wrecked cars. He looked and saw that one of them was his '57, and behind the steering wheel was Pop. Sitting beside the old man was a Mexican. Two more were in the back seat. They looked a little drunk.

One of the whores in back pulled up her dress and cocked it high up so he could see her pussy. It looked like it needed a shave.

He smiled and tried to go for it, but the '57 was moving away, swinging wide and turning its tail to him. He could see a face at the back window. Pop's face. He had crawled back there and was waving slowly and sadly. A whore pulled Pop from view.

The wrecked cars moved away, too, as if caught in the vacuum of the '57's retreat. Wayne swam with his arms, kicked with his legs, trying to pursue the '57 and the wrecks. But he dangled where he was, like a moth pinned to a board. The cars moved out of sight and left him there with his arms and legs stretched out, spinning amidst an infinity of cold, uncaring stars.

"... how the tests are run ... marks everything about you ... charts it ... EKG, brain waves, liver ... everything ... it hurts because Brother Lazarus wants it to ... thinks I don't know these things ... that I'm slow ... slow, not stupid ... smart really ... used to be scientist ... before the accident ... Brother Lazarus is not holy ... he's mad ... made the wheel because of the Holy Inquisition ... knows a lot about the Inquisition ... thinks we need it again ... for the likes of men you ... the unholy, he says ... but he just likes to hurt ... I know."

Wayne opened his eyes. The wheel had stopped. Sister Worth was talking in her monotone, explaining the wheel. He remembered asking her, "Why?" about three thousand years ago.

Sister Worth was staring at him again. She went away and he expected the wheel to start up, but when she returned, she had a long, narrow mirror under her arm. She put it against the wall across from him. She got on the wheel with him, her little feet on the wooden platforms beside his. She hiked up the bottom of her habit and pulled down her black panties. She put her face close to his, as if searching for something.

"He plans to take your body . . . piece by piece . . . blood, cells, brain, your cock . . . all of it. . . . He wants to live forever."

She had her panties in her hand, and she tossed them. Wayne watched them fly up and flutter to the floor like a dying bat.

She took hold of his dick and pulled on it. Her palm was cold and he didn't feel his best, but he began to get hard. She put him between her legs and rubbed his dick between her thighs. They were as cold as her hands, and dry.

"I know him now . . . know what he's doing . . . the dead germ virus . . . he was trying to make something that would make him live forever . . . it made the dead come back . . . didn't keep the living alive, free of old age. . . ."

His dick was throbbing now, in spite of the coolness of her body.

"He cuts up dead folks to learn . . . experiments on them . . . but the secret of eternal life is with the living . . . that's why he wants you . . . you're an outsider . . . those who live here he can . . . test . . . but he must keep them alive to do his bidding . . . not let them know how he really is . . . needs your insides and the other man's . . . he wants to be a God . . . flies high above us in a little plane and looks down . . . likes to think he is the creator, I bet. . . ."

"Plane?"

"Ultralight."

She pushed his cock inside her, and it was cold and dry in there, like liver left overnight on a drainboard. Still, he found himself ready. At this point, he would have gouged a hole in a turnip.

She kissed him on the ear and alongside the neck; cold little kisses, dry as toast.

". . . thinks I don't know . . . but I know he doesn't love Jesus . . . he loves himself, and power . . . he's sad about his nose. . . ."

"I bet."

"Did it in a moment of religious fervor . . . before he lost the belief . . . now he wants to be what he was . . . a scientist. He wants to grow a new nose . . . know how . . . saw him grow a finger in a dish once . . . grew it from the skin off a knuckle of one of the brothers . . . he can do all kinds of things."

She was moving her hips now. He could see over her shoulder into the mirror against the wall. Could see her white ass rolling, the black habit hiked up above it, threatening to drop like a curtain. He began to thrust back, slowly, firmly.

She looked over her shoulder into the mirror, watching herself fuck him. There was a look more of study than rapture on her face.

"Want to feel alive," she said. "Feel a good, hard dick . . . been too long."

"I'm doing the best I can," Wayne said. "This ain't the most romantic of spots."

"Push so I can feel it."

"Nice," Wayne said. He gave it everything he had. He was beginning to lose his erection. He felt as if he were auditioning for a job and not making the best of impressions. He felt like a knothole would be dissatisfied with him.

She got off of him and climbed down.

"Don't blame you," he said.

She went behind the wheel and touched some things on the upright. She mounted him again, hooked her ankles behind his. The wheel began to turn. Short electrical shocks leaped through him. They weren't as powerful as before. They were invigorating. When he kissed her it was like touching his tongue to a battery. It felt as if electricity was racing through his veins and flying out the head of his dick; he felt as if he might fill her with lightning instead of come.

The wheel creaked to a stop; it must have had a timer on it. They were upside down and Wayne could see their reflection in the mirror; they looked like two lizards fucking on a windowpane.

He couldn't tell if she had finished or not, so he went ahead and got it over with. Without the electricity he was losing his desire. It hadn't been an A-one piece of ass, but hell, as Pop always said, "Worst pussy I ever had was good."

"They'll be coming back," she said. "Soon . . . don't want them to find us like this . . . other tests to do yet."

"Why did you do this?"

"I want out of the order . . . want out of this desert . . . I want to live . . . and I want you to help me."

"I'm game, but the blood is rushing to my head and I'm getting dizzy. Maybe you ought to get off me."

After an eon she said, "I have a plan."

She untwined from him and went behind the wheel and hit a switch that turned Wayne upright. She touched another switch and he began to spin slowly, and while he spun and while lightning played inside him, she told him her plan.

9

"I think ole Brother Fred wants to fuck me," Calhoun said. "He keeps trying to get his finger up my asshole."

They were back in their room. Brother Fred had brought them back, making them carry their clothes, and now they were alone again, dressing.

"We're getting out of here," Wayne said. "The nun, Sister Worth, she's going to help."

"What's her angle?"

"She hates this place and wants my dick. Mostly, she hates this place."

"What's the plan?"

Wayne told him first what Brother Lazarus had planned. On the morrow he would have them brought to the room with the steel tables, and they would go on the tables, and if the tests had turned out good, they would be pronounced fit as fiddles and Brother Lazarus would strip the skin from their bodies, slowly, because according to Sister Worth he liked to do it that way, and he would drain their blood and percolate it into his formulas like coffee, cut their brains out and put them in vats and store their veins and organs in freezers.

All of this would be done in the name of God and Jesus Christ (Eees num be prased) under the guise of finding a cure for the dead folks germ. But it would all instead be for Brother Lazarus who wanted to have a new nose, fly his ultralight above Jesus Land, and live forever.

Sister Worth's plan was this:

She would be in the dissecting room. She would have guns hidden. She would make the first move, a distraction, then it was up to them.

"This time," Wayne said, "one of us has to get on top of that shotgun."

"You had your finger up your ass in there today, or we'd have had them."

"We're going to have surprise on our side this time. Real surprise. They won't be expecting Sister Worth. We can get up there on the roof and take off in that ultralight. When it runs out of gas we can walk, maybe get back to the '57 and hope it runs."

"We'll settle our score then. Whoever wins keeps the car and the split tail. As for tomorrow, I've got a little ace."

Calhoun pulled on his boots. He twisted the heel of one of them. It swung out and a little knife dropped into his hand. "It's sharp," Calhoun said. "I cut a Chinaman from gut to gill with it. It was easy as sliding a stick through fresh shit."

"Been nice if you'd had that ready today."

"I wanted to scout things out first. And to tell the truth, I thought one pop to Brother Fred's mouth and he'd be out of the picture."

"You hit him in the nose."

"Yeah, goddamn it, but I was aiming for his mouth."

10

Dawn and the room with the metal tables looked the same. No one had brought in a vase of flowers to brighten the place.

Brother Lazarus's nose had changed, however; there were two pearl onions nestled in it now.

Sister Worth, looking only a little more animated than yesterday, stood nearby. She was holding the tray with the instruments. This time the tray was full of scalpels. The light caught their edges and made them wink.

Brother Fred was standing behind Calhoun, and Brother Mold Fuzz was behind Wayne. They must have felt pretty confident today. They had dispensed with the dead folks.

Wayne looked at Sister Worth and thought maybe things were not good. Maybe she had lied to him in her slow-talking way. Only wanted a little dick and wanted to keep it quiet. To do that, she might have promised anything. She might not care what Brother Lazarus did to them.

If it looked like a double cross, Wayne was going to go for it. If he had to jump right into the mouth of Brother Fred's shotgun. That was a better way to go than having the hide peeled from your body. The idea of Brother Lazarus and his ugly nose leaning over him did not appeal at all.

"It's so nice to see you," Brother Lazarus said. "I hope we'll have none of the unpleasantness of yesterday. Now, on the tables."

Wayne looked at Sister Worth. Her expression showed nothing. The only thing about her that looked alive was the bent wings of the bird birthmark on her cheek.

All right, Wayne thought, I'll go as far as the table, then I'm going to do something. Even if it's wrong.

He took a step forward, and Sister Worth flipped the contents of the tray into Brother Lazarus's face. A scalpel went into his nose and hung there. The tray and the rest of its contents hit the floor.

Before Brother Lazarus could yelp, Calhoun dropped and wheeled. He was under Brother Fred's shotgun and he used his forearm to drive the barrel upward. The gun went off and peppered the ceiling. Plaster sprinkled down.

Calhoun had concealed the little knife in the palm of his hand and he brought it up and into Brother Fred's groin. The blade went through the robe and buried to the hilt.

The instant Calhoun made his move, Wayne brought his forearm back and around into Brother Mold Fuzz's throat, then turned and caught his head and jerked that down and kneed him a couple of times. He floored him by driving an elbow into the back of his neck.

Calhoun had the shotgun now, and Brother Fred was on the floor trying to pull the knife out of his balls. Calhoun blew Brother Fred's head off, then did the same for Brother Mold Fuzz.

Brother Lazarus, the scalpel hanging from his nose, tried to run for it, but he stepped on the tray and that sent him flying. He landed on his stomach. Calhoun took two deep steps and kicked him in the throat. Brother Lazarus made a sound like he was gargling and tried to get up.

Wayne helped him. He grabbed Brother Lazarus by the back of his robe and pulled him up, slammed him back against a table. The scalpel still dangled from the monk's nose. Wayne grabbed it and jerked, taking away a chunk of nose as he did. Brother Lazarus screamed.

Calhoun put the shotgun in Brother Lazarus's mouth and that made him stop screaming. Calhoun pumped the shotgun. He said, "Eat it," and pulled the trigger. Brother Lazarus's brains went out the back of his head riding on a chunk of skull. The brains and skull hit the table and sailed onto the floor like a plate of scrambled eggs pushed the length of a café counter.

Sister Worth had not moved. Wayne figured she had used all of her concentration to hit Brother Lazarus with the tray.

"You said you'd have guns," Wayne said to her.

She turned her back to him and lifted her habit. In a belt above her panties were two .38 revolvers. Wayne pulled them out and held one in each hand. "Two-Gun Wayne," he said.

"What about the ultralight?" Calhoun said. "We've made enough noise for a prison riot. We need to move."

Sister Worth turned to the door at the back of the room, and before she could say anything or lead, Wayne and Calhoun snapped to it and grabbed her and pushed her toward it.

There were stairs on the other side of the door and they took them two at a time. They went through a trapdoor and onto the roof and there, tied down with bungee straps to metal hoops, was the ultralight. It was blue-and-white canvas and metal rods, and strapped to either side of it was a twelve-gauge pump and a bag of food and a canteen of water.

They unsnapped the roof straps and got in the two-seater and used the straps to fasten Sister Worth between them. It wasn't comfortable, but it was a ride.

They sat there. After a moment, Calhoun said, "Well?"

"Shit," Wayne said. "I can't fly this thing."

They looked at Sister Worth. She was staring at the controls.

"Say something, damn it," Wayne said.

"That's the switch," she said. "That stick . . . forward is up, back brings the nose down . . . side to side. . . ."

"Got it."

"Well, shoot this bastard over the side," Calhoun said. Wayne cranked it, gave it the throttle. The machine rolled forward, wobbled.

"Too much weight," Wayne said.

"Throw the cunt over the side," Calhoun said.

"It's all or nothing," Wayne said. The ultralight continued to swing its tail left and right, but leveled off as they went over the edge.

They sailed for a hundred yards, made a mean curve Wayne couldn't fight, and fell straight away into the statue of Jesus, striking it in the head, right in the midst of the barbed-wire crown. Spotlights shattered, metal groaned, the wire tangled in the nylon wings of the craft and held it. The head of Jesus nodded forward, popped off, and shot out on the electric cables inside like a jack-in-the-box. The cables pulled tight a hundred feet from the ground and worked the head and the craft like a yo-yo. Then the barbed-wire crown unraveled and dropped the craft the rest of the way. It hit the ground with a crunch and a rip and a cloud of dust.

The head of Jesus bobbed above the shattered ultralight like a bird preparing to peck a worm.

11

Wayne crawled out of the wreckage and tried his legs. They worked.

Calhoun was on his feet cussing, unstrapping the shotguns and supplies.

Sister Worth lay in the midst of the wreck, the nylon and aluminum supports folded around her like butterfly wings.

Wayne started pulling the mess off of her. He saw that her leg was broken. A bone punched out of her thigh like a sharpened stick. There was no blood.

"Here comes the church social," Calhoun said.

The word was out about Brother Lazarus and the others. A horde of monks, nuns, and dead folks were rushing over the drawbridge. Some of the nuns and monks had guns. All of the dead folks had clubs. The clergy was yelling.

Wayne nodded toward the bus barn. "Let's get a bus." Wayne picked up Sister Worth, cradled her in his arms, and made a run for it. Calhoun, carrying the guns and the supplies, passed them. He jumped through the open doorway of a bus and dropped out of sight. Wayne knew he was jerking wires loose, trying to hotwire them a ride. Wayne hoped he was good at it and fast.

When Wayne got to the bus, he laid Sister Worth down beside it and pulled the .38s and stood in front of her. If he was going down he wanted to go like Wild Bill Hickok: a blazing gun in either fist and a woman to protect.

Actually, he'd prefer the bus to start.

It did.

Calhoun jerked it in gear, backed it out and around in front of Wayne and Sister Worth. The monks and nuns had started firing and their rounds bounced off the side of the armored bus.

From inside Calhoun yelled, "Get the hell on."

Wayne stuck the guns in his belt, grabbed up Sister Worth and leapt inside. Calhoun jerked the bus forward and Wayne and Sister Worth went flying over a seat and into another.

"I thought you were leaving," Wayne said.

"I wanted to. But I gave my word."

Wayne stretched Sister Worth out on the seat and looked at her leg. After that tossing Calhoun had given them, the break was sticking out even more.

Calhoun closed the bus door and checked his wing-mirror. Nuns and monks and dead folks had piled into a couple of buses, and now the buses were pursuing them. One of them moved very fast, as if souped up.

"I probably got the granny of the bunch," Calhoun said. They climbed over a ridge of sand, then they were on the narrow road that wound itself upward. Behind them, one of the buses had fallen back, maybe some kind of mechanical trouble. The other was gaining.

The road widened and Calhoun yelled, "I think this is what the fucker's been waiting for."

Even as Calhoun spoke, their pursuer put on a burst of speed and swung left and came up beside them, tried to swerve over and push them off the road, down into the deepening valley. But Calhoun fought the curves and didn't budge.

The other bus swung its door open and a nun, the very one who had been on the bus that brought them to Jesus Land, stood there with her legs spread wide, showing the black-pantied mound of her crotch. She had one arm bent around a seat post and was holding in both hands the ever-popular clergy tool, the twelve-gauge pump.

As they made a curve, the nun fired a round into the window next to Calhoun. The window made a cracking noise and thin, crooked lines spread in all directions, but the glass held.

She pumped a round into the chamber and fired again. Bulletproof or not, this time the front sheet of glass fell away. Another well-placed round and the rest of the glass would go and Calhoun could wave his head goodbye.

Wayne put his knees in a seat and got the window down. The nun saw him, whirled and fired. The shot was low and hit the bottom part of the window and starred it and pelleted the chassis.

Wayne stuck a .38 out of the window and fired as the nun was jacking another load into position. His shot hit her in the head and her right eye went big and wet, and she swung around on the pole and lost the shotgun. It went out the door. She clung there by the bend of her elbow for a moment, then her arm straightened and she fell outside. The bus ran over her and she popped red and juicy at both ends like a stomped jelly roll.

"Waste of good pussy," Calhoun said. He edged into the other bus, and it pushed back. But Calhoun pushed harder and made it hit the wall with a screech like a panther.

The bus came back and shoved Calhoun to the side of the cliff and honked twice for Jesus.

Calhoun downshifted, let off the gas, allowed the other bus to soar past by half a length. Then he jerked the wheel so that he caught the rear of it and knocked it across the road. He speared it in the side with the nose of his bus and the other started to spin. It clipped the front of Calhoun's bus and peeled the bumper back. Calhoun braked and the other bus kept spinning. It spun off the road and down into the valley amidst a chorus of cries.

Thirty minutes later they reached the top of the canyon and were in the desert. The bus began to throw up smoke from the front and make a noise like a dog strangling on a chicken bone. Calhoun pulled over.

12

"Goddamn bumper got twisted under there and it's shredded the tire some," Calhoun said. "I think if we can peel the bumper off, there's enough of that tire to run on."

Wayne and Calhoun got hold of the bumper and pulled but it wouldn't come off. Not completely. Part of it had been creased, and that part finally gave way and broke off from the rest of it.

"That ought to be enough to keep from rubbing the tire," Calhoun said.

Sister Worth called from inside the bus. Wayne went to check on her. "Take me off the bus," she said. ". . . I want to feel free air and sun."

"There doesn't feel like there's any air out there," Wayne said. "And the sun feels just like it always does. Hot."

"Please."

He picked her up and carried her outside and found a ridge of sand and laid her down so her head was propped against it.

"I . . . I need batteries," she said.

"Say what?" Wayne said.

She lay looking straight into the sun. "Brother Lazarus's greatest work . . . a dead folk that can think . . . has memory of the past . . . was a scientist too. . . ." Her hand came up in stages, finally got hold of her headgear and pushed it off.

Gleaming from the center of her tangled blonde hair was a silver knob.

"He . . . was not a good man . . . I am a good woman. I want to feel alive . . . like before . . . batteries going . . . brought others."

Her hand fumbled at a snap pocket on her habit. Wayne opened it for her and got out what was inside. Four batteries.

"Uses two . . . simple."

Calhoun was standing over them now. "That explains some things," he said.

"Don't look at me like that . . . ," Sister Worth said, and Wayne realized he had never told her his name and she had never asked. "Unscrew . . . put the batteries in . . . without them I'll be an eater . . . can't wait too long."

"All right," Wayne said. He went behind her and propped her up on the sand drift and unscrewed the metal shaft from her skull. He thought about when she had fucked him on the wheel and how desperate she had been to feel something, and how she had been cold as flint and lustless. He remembered how she had looked in the mirror hoping to see something that wasn't there.

He dropped the batteries in the sand and took out one of the revolvers and put it close to the back of her head and pulled the trigger. Her body jerked slightly and fell over, her face turning toward him.

The bullet had come out where the bird had been on her cheek and had taken it completely away, leaving a bloodless hole.

"Best thing," Calhoun said. "There's enough live pussy in the world without you pulling this broken-legged dead thing around after you on a board."

"Shut up," Wayne said.

"When a man gets sentimental over women and kids, he can count himself out."

Wayne stood up.

"Well boy," Calhoun said. "I reckon it's time."

"Reckon so," Wayne said.

"How about we do this with some class? Give me one of your pistols and we'll get back-to-back and I'll count to ten, and when I get there, we'll turn and shoot."

Wayne gave Calhoun one of the pistols. Calhoun checked the chambers, said, "I've got four loads."

Wayne took two out of his pistol and tossed them on the ground. "Even Steven," he said.

They got back-to-back and held the guns by their legs.

"Guess if you kill me you'll take me in," Calhoun said. "So that means you'll put a bullet through my head if I need it. I don't want to come back as one of the dead folks. Got your word on that?"

"Yep."

"I'll do the same for you. Give my word. You know that's worth something."

"We gonna shoot or talk?"

"You know, boy, under different circumstances, I could have liked you. We might have been friends."

"Not likely."

Calhoun started counting, and they started stepping. When he got to ten, they turned.

Calhoun's pistol barked first, and Wayne felt the bullet punch him low in the right side of his chest, spinning him slightly. He lifted his revolver and took his time and shot just as Calhoun fired again.

Calhoun's second bullet whizzed by Wayne's head. Wayne's shot hit Calhoun in the stomach.

Calhoun went to his knees and had trouble drawing a breath. He tried to lift his revolver but couldn't; it was as if it had turned into an anvil.

Wayne shot him again. Hitting him in the middle of the chest this time and knocking him back so that his legs were curled beneath him.

Wayne walked over to Calhoun, dropped to one knee and took the revolver from him.

"Shit," Calhoun said. "I wouldn't have thought that for nothing. You hit?"

"Scratched."

"Shit."

Wayne put the revolver to Calhoun's forehead and Calhoun closed his eyes and Wayne pulled the trigger.

13

The wound wasn't a scratch. Wayne knew he should leave Sister Worth where she was and load Calhoun on the bus and haul him in for bounty. But he didn't care about the bounty anymore.

He used the ragged piece of bumper to dig them a shallow side-by-side grave. When he finished, he stuck the fender fragment up between them and used the sight of one of the revolvers to scratch into it: HERE LIES SISTER WORTH AND CALHOUN WHO KEPT HIS WORD.

You couldn't really read it good and he knew the first real wind would keel it over, but it made him feel better about something, even if he couldn't put his finger on it.

His wound had opened up and the sun was very hot now, and since he had lost his hat he could feel his brain cooking in his skull like meat boiling in a pot.

He got on the bus, started it and drove through the day and the night and it was near morning when he came to the Cadillacs and turned down between them and drove until he came to the '57.

When he stopped and tried to get off the bus, he found he could hardly move. The revolvers in his belt were stuck to his shirt and stomach because of the blood from his wound.

He pulled himself up with the steering wheel, got one of the shotguns and used it for a crutch. He got the food and water and went out to inspect the '57.

It was for shit. It had not only lost its windshield, the front end was mashed way back and one of the big sand tires was twisted at such an angle he knew the axle was shot.

He leaned against the Chevy and tried to think. The bus was okay and there was still some gas in it, and he could get the hose out of the trunk of the '57 and siphon gas out of its tanks and put it in the bus. That would give him a few miles.

Miles.

He didn't feel as if he could walk twenty feet, let alone concentrate on driving.

He let go of the shotgun, the food and water. He scooted onto the hood of the Chevy and managed himself to the roof. He lay there on his back and looked at the sky.

It was a clear night and the stars were sharp with no fuzz around them. He felt cold. In a couple of hours the stars would fade and the sun would come up and the cool would give way to heat.

He turned his head and looked at one of the Cadillacs and a skeleton face pressed to its windshield, forever looking down at the sand.

That was no way to end, looking down.

He crossed his legs and stretched out his arms and studied the sky. It didn't feel so cold now, and the pain had almost stopped. He was more numb than anything else.

He pulled one of the revolvers and cocked it and put it to his temple and continued to look at the stars. Then he closed his eyes and found that he could still see them. He was once again hanging in the void between the stars wearing only his hat and cowboy boots, and floating about him were the junk cars and the '57, undamaged.

The cars were moving toward him this time, not away. The '57 was in the lead, and as it grew closer he saw Pop behind the wheel and beside him was a Mexican puta, and in the back, two more. They were all smiling and Pop honked the horn and waved.

The '57 came alongside him and the back door opened.

Sitting between the whores was Sister Worth. She had not been there a moment ago, but now she was. And he had never noticed how big the back seat of the '57 was.

Sister Worth smiled at him and the bird on her cheek lifted higher. Her hair was combed out long and straight and she looked pink-skinned and happy. On the floorboard at her feet was a chest of iced beer. Lone Star, by God.

Pop was leaning over the front seat, holding out his hand, and Sister Worth and the whores were beckoning him inside.

Wayne worked his hands and feet, found this time that he could move. He swam through the open door, touched Pop's hand, and Pop said, "It's good to see you, son," and at the moment Wayne pulled the trigger, Pop pulled him inside.

This is a feminist fable.

It's short.

I fear saying too much about it. You can read it and find out for yourself. It's simple, but it cuts deep into misogynist thinking and comes out triumphant on the other side.

Love Doll: A Fable

BUY A plastic love doll because I want something to fuck that I don't have to talk to. Right on the box it says Love Doll. I take her home and blow her up. She looks pretty and sexy and innocent.

I fuck her. I sit with her on the couch and watch TV and put an arm around her plastic shoulders and hold my dick with my other hand.

I fuck her some more. In the morning I let the air out of her and fold her up and put her in a drawer.

When I come home from work at night I give her a blowjob and she is full and stiff again. I take her into the bedroom and fuck her. I watch TV with my arm around her, one hand on my dick.

This goes on for a while.

I start to talk to the doll. I never wanted to talk to a woman, but I talk to the doll. I name her Madge. I had a dog named Madge that I liked.

I stop letting the air out of her in the mornings. I leave her in bed. I fix breakfast on a tray, enough for two. I come in and eat beside her on the bed. There's plenty of food left when I stop and get ready for work.

When I come home the tray is where it was and the doll is gone. There's no food left on the tray.

I find Madge in the shower. She smiles at me when I slide the shower door back.

"I was going to clean up for you," she said. "Be sexy. I'm sorry the house isn't clean and dinner isn't ready. It won't happen again."

I get in the shower with her. We have sex and soap each other. We dry off and go to bed and have sex again. We lie in bed and talk afterward. She talks some about girl things. She talks about me mostly. She has good things to say about my sexual prowess. We have sex again.

Next day she drives me to work, picks me up at the end of the day. All the fellas are jealous when they see her, she's such a good-looking piece.

She always looks nice. Wears frilly things, short skirts. For bop-around she wears tight sweaters and T-shirts and jeans. She smells good. She puts her hands on me a lot. The house is clean when I get home. Dinner is ready in a jiffy.

A year passes. Quite happily. Life couldn't be better. Lots of sex. A clean house. Food when I need it. Conversation. She tells me I'm a real man when I mount her, that she needs me, calls me her stallion, makes good noises beneath me and scratches at my back, she makes a la-la-la noise when she comes. She likes my muscles, the scruffiness of my beard. We watch movies on the couch, my arm around her. She holds my dick in her hand. When I tell her to, she gives me a blowjob while I watch the movie. She always swallows my load.

One night we're laying in bed and she says, "I think maybe I should go to school."

"What for?" I ask.

"To bring in more money. We could buy some things."

"I make enough money."

"I know. You're a hard-working man. But I want to help."

"You help enough. You be here for me at night, keep the house clean and the meals ready. That's a woman's place."

"Whatever you want, dear."

But she doesn't mean it. It comes up now and again, her going to school. Finally I think, so what? She goes off to school. The house isn't quite so clean. The meals aren't always ready on time. I drive myself to work. Some nights she doesn't feel like sex. I jack off in the bathroom a lot.

We sit on the couch and watch movies. She sits on one end, I sit on the other. We wear our clothes. I have a beer in one hand, the remote control in the other. We argue about little things. She doesn't like the way I spend my money.

She gets a degree. She gets a job in business. She wears suits. For bop-around, the stuff she wears is less tight. She doesn't wear makeup or perfume around the house. She keeps her hands to herself. No kissing goodbye and hello anymore. We have sex less. When we have it, she seems distracted. She doesn't call me her King, her Big Man like she used to. After sex she'll sometimes stay up late reading books by people called Sartre or Camus. She's writing something she calls a business manifesto. She sits at the typewriter for hours. She goes to business parties, and I go with her, but I can tell they think I'm boring. I don't know what they're talking about. They talk about business and books and ideas. I hear Madge say a woman has to make her own way in the world. That she shouldn't depend on a man, even if she has one. Thing to do is to be your own person. She tells a man that. Guy in a three-piece blue suit with hair spray on his hair. He agrees with her. I feel sick.

I tell her so in the car on the way home. She calls me a prick. We don't fuck that night.

I watch a lot of movies alone. She yells from the bedroom for me to turn them down, and why don't I watch something else other than car-chase movies, and why don't I read a book, even a stupid one?

I feel small these days. I go to the store and look at the love dolls. They all look so sexy and innocent. I think I might buy one, but find I can't. I don't feel man enough. I can't control the one I have. I get a new one, she might change, too. Course, a new one I could let the air out of when I finished fucking her, never let her have a day alone full-blown.

I go home. Madge is there. She's writing her book. I get angry. I tell her I've been patient long enough. I'm the man around here. I tell her to stop that typing, get her clothes off and get in bed and grab her ankles. I'm going to fuck her unconscious.

She laughs. "You skinny little stupid pencil-dick, you couldn't fuck a gnat unconscious. You're about as manly as a Kotex."

I feel as if I've been hit in the face with a fist. I go into the bedroom and close the door. I sit on the edge of the bed. I can hear her typing in there. I get up and go over to the dresser and open the bottom drawer. I take off all my clothes and find the air spigot on the head of my dick and pull it open and listen to the air go out of me. I crumple into the open drawer, and lay there like a used prophylactic.

An hour or so later the typing stops. I hear her come into the room. She looks in the drawer. No expression. I try to say something manly, but nothing will come. I have no air and no voice. She moves away.

I hear the water running while she takes a shower. She comes out naked. I can see her pubic hair above me. I note how firm and full of air her thighs are. She opens the top drawer. She takes out panties. She puts them on. She goes away. I hear her sit on the bed. She dials the phone. She tells someone to come on over, that her thing with me is finished.

Time passes. The doorbell rings. Madge gets up and goes past me. I get a glimpse of her, her hair combed out long and pretty, a robe on.

I hear her laugh in the other room. She comes back with a man. As they go by the drawer I see it's the man in the business suit from the party. I hear them sit on the bed. They laugh a lot. She says something rude about me and my sexual abilities. I can tell she has his dick out of his pants because they're laughing about something. I realize they're laughing about sex. He's making fun of his equipment. I never like being laughed at when it's about sex. I don't like being laughed at at all, especially by a woman.

The bathrobe flies across the room and lands in the drawer on top of me and everything is dark. I hear the bedsprings squeak. They squeak for hours. They talk while they screw. After a while they stop talking. He grunts like a hog. She sings like a lark. Afterward I hear them talking.

He asks her if she came. She says only a little. He says let me help you. I can't be sure, but I think he's doing something to her with his hand. I can't believe it. She doesn't seem to mind this at all.

I hear her sing again, this time louder than ever. Then they talk again. She tells him she never really came for me, that she always faked it. That I was a lousy fuck. That I didn't care if she came. That I got on and did it and got off.

A little air caught at the top of my head floats down and out of my open mouth.

They talk some more. They don't talk about him. She doesn't talk girl things. They talk about ideas. Politics. History. The office. Movies—films, they call them—and books.

In the middle of the night the robe is lifted off of me. It's Madge. She's down on her knees looking in the drawer. She smiles at me. She picks me up and folds me gently. She has a box with her. It's the box she came in. The one that says Love Doll on it. The words Love Doll have been marked through with a magic marker and Fuck Toy has been written in above it. She puts me in the box and seals the lid and puts me back in the drawer and closes it.

This story is based on a true incident. Our next-door neighbors did indeed have a blind groundskeeper, at least for a day, and he did in fact, as in the story, ask me for help when he heard my son, Keith, playing next door. He wandered across the road and into our yard, and my son, after listening to him, rushed into the house, saying, "There's a blind man wants to see you."

Irony upon irony followed.

The man had been hired to save money. Damn.

He said some of the things I have him say in the story.

But I assure you, my experience didn't end up this way. After my helping him find the yard he was supposed to be working on, seeing the damage done to the flower bed, etc., the story is fiction.

I merely had to tweak the real story a bit, change myself and my wife, Karen, and Keith about, and then I added a more problematic situation.

Another example of a story inspired by real life.

Mister Weed-Eater

Mr. Job Harold was in his living room with his feet on the couch watching *Wheel of Fortune* when his five-year-old son came inside covered with dirt. "Daddy," said the boy dripping dirt, "there's a man outside wants to see you."

Mr. Harold got up and went outside, and there standing at the back of the house next to his wife's flower bed, which was full of dead roses and a desiccated frog, was, just like his boy had said, a man.

It was over a hundred degrees out there, and the man, a skinny sucker in a white T-shirt and jeans with a face red as a baboon's ass, a waterfall of inky hair dripping over his forehead and dark glasses, stood with his head cocked like a spaniel listening for trouble. He had a bright-toothed smile that indicated everything he heard struck him as funny.

In his left hand was a new weed-eater, the cutting line coated in greasy green grass the texture of margarita vomit, the price tag dangling proudly from the handle.

In the other hand the man held a blind man's cane, the tip of which had speared an oak leaf. His white T-shirt, stained pollen yellow under the arms, stuck wetly to his chest and little potbelly tight as plastic wrap on a fish head. He had on dirty white socks with played-out elastic and they had fallen over the tops of his tennis shoes as if in need of rest.

The man was shifting his weight from one leg to the other. Mr. Harold figured he needed to pee and wanted to use the bathroom, and the idea of letting him into the house with a weed-eater and pointing him at the pot didn't appeal to Mr. Harold 'cause there wasn't any question in Mr. Harold's mind the man was blind as a peach pit, and Mr. Harold figured he got in the bathroom, he was gonna pee from one end of the place to the other trying to hit the commode, and then Mr. Harold knew he'd have to clean it up or explain to his wife when she got home from work how on his day off he let a blind man piss all over their bathroom. Just thinking about all that gave Mr. Harold a headache.

"What can I do for you?" Mr. Harold asked.

"Well, sir," said the blind man in a voice dry as Mrs. Harold's sexual equipment, "I heard your boy playin' over here, and I followed the sound. You see, I'm the groundskeeper next door, and I need a little help. I was wonderin' you could come over and show me if I've missed a few spots?"

Mr. Harold tried not to miss a beat. "You talking about the church over there?"

"Yes, sir. Just got hired. Wouldn't want to look bad on my first day."

Mr. Harold considered this. Cameras could be set in place somewhere. People in trees waiting for him to do something they could record for a TV show. He didn't want to go on record as not helping a blind man, but on the other hand, he didn't want to be caught up in no silliness either.

Finally, he decided it was better to look like a fool and a Samaritan than a cantankerous asshole who wouldn't help a poor blind man cut weeds.

"I reckon I can do that," Mr. Harold said. Then to his five-year-old who'd followed him outside and was sitting in the dirt playing with a plastic truck: "Son, you stay right here and don't go off."

"Okay, Daddy," the boy said.

The church across the street had been opened in a building about the size of an aircraft hanger. It had once been used as a liquor warehouse, and later it was called Community Storage, but items had a way of disappearing. It was a little too community for its renters, and it went out of business and Sonny Guy, who owned the place, had to pay some kind of fine and turn up with certain items deemed as missing.

This turn of events had depressed Mr. Guy, so he'd gotten religion and opened a church. God wasn't knocking them dead either, so to compensate,

Sonny Guy started a Gospel Opry, and to advertise and indicate its location, beginning on their street and on up to the highway, there was a line of huge orange Day-Glo guitars that pointed from highway to Opry.

The guitars didn't pull a lot of people in, though, bright as they were. Come Sunday the place was mostly vacant, and when the doors were open on the building back and front, you could hear wind whistling through there like it was blowing through a pipe. A special ticket you could cut out of the newspaper for five dollars off a fifteen-dollar buffet of country sausages and sliced cantaloupe hadn't rolled them in either. Sonny and God most definitely needed a more exciting game plan. Something with titties.

Taking the blind man by the elbow, Mr. Harold led him across the little street and into the yard of the church. Well, actually, it was more than a yard. About four acres. On the front acre sat Sonny Guy's house, and out to the right of it was a little music studio he'd built, and over to the left was the metal building that served as the church. The metal was aluminum and very bright and you could feel the heat bouncing off of it like it was an oven with bread baking inside.

Behind the house were three more acres, most of it weeds, and at the back of it all was a chicken-wire fence where a big black dog of undetermined breed liked to pace.

When Mr. Harold saw what the blind man had done, he let out his breath. The fella had been all over that four acres, and it wasn't just a patch of weeds now, but it wasn't manicured either. The poor bastard had tried to do the job of a lawn mower with a weed-eater, and he'd mostly succeeded in chopping down the few flowers that grew in the midst of brick-lined beds, and he'd chopped weeds and dried grass here and there, so that the whole place looked as if it were a head of hair mistreated by a drunk barber with an attitude.

At Mr. Harold's feet, he discovered a mole the blind man's shoe had dislodged from a narrow tunnel. The mole had been whipped to death by the weed-eater string. It looked like a wad of dirty hair dipped in red paint. A lasso loop of guts had been knocked out of its mouth and ants were crawling on it. The blind had slain the blind.

"How's it look?"

"Well," Mr. Harold said, "you missed some spots."

"Yeah, well they hired me 'cause they wanted to help the handicapped, but I figure it was just as much 'cause they knew I'd do the job. They had 'em a crippled nigger used to come out and do it, but they said he charged too much and kept making a mess of things."

Mr. Harold had seen the black man mow. He might have been crippled, but he'd had a riding mower and he was fast. He didn't do such a bad job either. He always wore a straw hat pushed up on the back of his head, and when he got off the mower to get on his crutches, he did it with the style of a rodeo star dismounting a show horse. There hadn't been a thing wrong with the black man's work. Mr. Harold figured Sonny Guy wanted to cut a few corners. Switch a crippled nigger for a blind honky.

"How'd you come to get this job?" Mr. Harold asked. He tried to make the question pleasant, as if he were asking him how his weekend had been.

"References," the blind man said.

"Of course," said Mr. Harold.

"Well, what do I need to touch up? I stayed me a line from the building there, tried to work straight, turn when I got to the fence and come back. I do it mostly straight?"

"You got off a mite. You've missed some pretty good-sized patches."

Mr. Harold, still holding the blind man's elbow, felt the blind man go a little limp with disappointment. "How bad is it?"

"Well. . . ."

"Go on and tell me."

"A weed-eater ain't for this much place. You need a mower."

"I'm blind. You can't turn me loose out here with a mower. I'd cut my foot off."

"I'm just saying."

"Well, come on, how bad is it? It look worse than when the nigger did it?"

"I believe so."

"By much?"

"When he did it, you could look out here and tell the place had been mowed. Way it looks now, you might do better just to poison the weeds and hope the grass dies."

The blind man really slumped now, and Mr. Harold wished he'd chosen his words more carefully. It wasn't his intention to insult a blind man on his lawn skills in hundred-degree heat. He began to wish the fella had only wanted to wet on the walls of his bathroom.

"Can't even do a nigger's job," the blind man said.

"It ain't so bad if they're not too picky."

"Shit," said the blind man. "Shit, I didn't have no references. I didn't never have a job before, really. Well, I worked out at the chicken-processing plant tossing chicken heads in a metal drum, but I kept missing and tossin' them on this lady worked by me. I just couldn't keep my mind on the drum's location. I think I might actually be more artistic than mechanical. I got one side of the brain works harder, you know?"

"You could just slip off and go home. Leave 'em a note."

"Naw, I can't do that. Besides, I ain't got no way home. They pick me up and brought me here. I come to church last week and they offered me the job, and then they come and got me and brought me here and I made a mess of it. They'll be back later and they won't like it. They ain't gonna give me my five dollars, I can see that and I can't see nothing."

"Hell, man," Mr. Harold said, "that black fella mowed this lawn, you can bet he got more than five dollars."

"You tryin' to say I ain't good as a nigger?"

"I'm not trying to say anything 'cept you're not being paid enough. A guy ought to get five dollars an hour just for standing around in this heat."

"People charge too much these days. Niggers especially will stick you when they can. It's that civil rights business. It's gone to their heads."

"It ain't got nothing to do with what color you are."

"By the hour, I reckon I'm making 'bout what I got processing chicken heads," the blind man said. "Course, they had a damn fine company picnic this time each year."

"Listen here. We'll do what we were gonna do. Check the spots you've missed. I'll lead you around to bad places, and you chop 'em."

"That sounds all right, but I don't want to share my five dollars. I was gonna get me something with that. Little check I get from the government just covers my necessities, you know?"

"You don't owe me anything."

Mr. Harold took the blind man by the elbow and led him around to where the grass was missed or whacked high, which was just about everywhere you looked. After about fifteen minutes, the blind man said he was tired. They went over to the house and leaned on a tree in the front yard. The blind man said, "You seen them shows about those crop circles, in England, I think it is?"

"No," said Mr. Harold.

"Well, they found these circles in the wheat. Just appeared out there. They think it's aliens."

"Oh yeah, I seen about those," Mr. Harold said, suddenly recalling what it was the man was talking about. "There ain't no mystery to that. It's some guys with a stick and a cord. We used to do that in tall weed patches when we were kids. There's nothing to it. Someone's just making jackasses out of folks."

The blind man took a defiant posture. "Not everything like that is a bunch of kids with a string."

"I wasn't saying that."

"For all I know, what's wrong with that patch there's got nothing to do with me and my work. It could have been alien involvement."

"Aliens with weed-eaters?"

"It could be what happened when they landed, their saucers messin' it up like that"

"If they landed, why didn't they land on you? You was out there with the weed-eater. How come nobody saw or heard them?"

"They could have messed up the yard while I was coming to get you."

"Kind of a short visit, wasn't it?"

"You don't know everything, Mister I-Got-Eyeballs. Those that talk the loudest know less than anybody."

"And them that believe every damn thing they hear are pretty stupid, Mister Weed-Eater. I know what's wrong with you now. You're lazy. It's hot out there and you don't want to be here, so you're trying to make me feel sorry for you and do the job myself, and it ain't gonna work. I don't feel sorry for you 'cause you're blind. I ain't gonna feel sorry at all. I think you're an asshole."

Mr. Harold went across the road and back to the house and called his son inside. He sat down in front of the TV. *Wheel of Fortune* wasn't on anymore. Hell, it was a rerun anyway. He changed the channel looking for something worth watching but all that was on was midget wrestling, so he watched a few minutes of that.

Those little guys were fast and entertaining and it was cool inside with the air-conditioner cranked up, so after a couple minutes Mr. Harold got comfortable watching the midgets sling each other around, tumble up together and tie themselves in knots.

However, time eroded Mr. Harold's contentment. He couldn't stop thinking about the blind man out there in the heat. He called to his son and told him to go outside and see if the blind man was still there.

The boy came back a minute later. He said, "He's out there, Daddy. He said you better come on out and help him. He said he ain't gonna talk about crop circles no more."

Mr. Harold thought a moment. You were supposed to help the blind, the hot, and the stupid. Besides, the old boy might need someone to pour gas in that weed-eater. He did it himself he was liable to pour it all over his shoes and later get around someone who smoked and wanted to toss a match. An accident might be in the making.

Mr. Harold switched the channel to cartoons and pointed them out to his son. The boy sat down immediately and started watching. Mr. Harold got the boy a glass of Kool-Aid and a stack of chocolate cookies. He went outside to find the blind man.

The blind man was in Mr. Harold's yard. He had the weed-eater on and was holding it above his head whacking at the leaves on Mr. Harold's redbud tree, his wife's favorite tree.

"Hey, now stop that," Mr. Harold said. "Ain't no call to be malicious."

The blind man cut the weed-eater and cocked his head and listened. "That you, Mister I-Know-There-Ain't-No-Aliens?"

"Now come on. I want to help you. My son said you said you wasn't gonna get into that again."

"Come on over here," said the blind man.

Mr. Harold went over, cautiously. When he was just outside of weed-eater range, he said, "What you want?"

"Do I look all right to you? Besides being blind?"

"Yeah. I guess so. I don't see nothing wrong with you. You found the leaves on that tree good enough."

"Come and look closer."

"Naw, I ain't gonna do it. You just want to get me in range. Hit me with that weed-eater. I'll stay right here. You come at me, I'll move off. You won't be able to find me."

"You saying I can't find you 'cause I'm blind?"

"Come after me, I'll put stuff in front of you so you trip." The blind man leaned the weed-eater against his leg. His cane was on a loop over his other hand, and he took hold of it and tapped it against his tennis shoe.

"Yeah, well you could do that," the blind man said, "and I bet you would too. You're like a guy would do things to the handicapped. I'll tell you now, sir, they take roll in heaven, you ain't gonna be on it."

"Listen here. You want some help over there, I'll give it, but I ain't gonna stand here in this heat and take insults. Midget wrestling's on TV and it's cool inside and I might just go back to it."

The blind man's posture straightened with interest. "Midget wrestling? Hell, that's right. It's Saturday. Was it Little Bronco Bill and Low Dozer McGuirk?"

"I think it was. They look alike to me. I don't know one midget from another, though one was a little fatter and had a haircut like he'd got out of the barber chair too soon."

"That's Dozer. He trains on beer and doughnuts. I heard him talk about it on the TV."

"You watch TV?"

"You tryin' to hurt my feelings?"

"No. I mean, it's just, well, you're blind."

"What? I am? I'll be damned! I didn't know that. Glad you was here to tell me."

"I didn't mean no harm."

"Look here, I got ears. I listen to them thumping on that floor and I listen to the announcer. I listen so good I can imagine, kinda, what's goin' on. I 'specially like them little scudders, the midgets. I think maybe on a day I've had enough to eat, I had on some pants weren't too tight, I'd like to get in a ring with one of 'em."

"You always been blind? I mean, was you born that way?"

"Naw. Got bleach in my eyes. My mama told me a nigger done it to me when I was a baby, but it was my daddy. I know that now. Mama had a bad eye herself, then the cancer got her good one. She says she sees out of her bad eye way you'd see if you seen something through a Coke bottle with dirt on the bottom."

Mr. Harold didn't really want to hear about the blind man's family history. He groped for a fresh conversation handle. Before he could get hold of one, the blind man said, "Let's go to your place and watch some of that wrestlin' and cool off, then you can come out with me and show me them places I missed."

Mr. Harold didn't like the direction this conversation was taking. "I don't know," he said. "Won't the preacher be back in a bit and want his yard cut?"

"You want to know the truth?" the blind man said. "I don't care. You're right. Five dollars ain't any wages. Them little things I wanted with that five dollars I couldn't get no how."

Mr. Harold's mind raced. "Yeah, but five dollars is five dollars, and you could put it toward something. You know, save it up 'til you got some more. They're planning on making you a permanent groundskeeper, aren't they? A little time, a raise could be in order."

"This here's kinda a trial run. They can always get the crippled nigger back."

Mr. Harold checked his watch. There probably wasn't more than twenty minutes left of the wrestling program, so he took a flyer. "Well, all right. We'll finish up the wrestling show, then come back and do the work. You ain't gonna hit me with that weed-eater if I try to guide you into the house, are you?"

"Naw, I ain't mad no more. I get like that sometimes. It's just my way."

Mr. Harold led him into the house and onto the couch and talked the boy out of the cartoons, which wasn't hard; it was some kind of stuff the boy hated. The blind man had him crank the audio on the TV up a notch and sat sideways on the couch with his weed-eater and cane, taking up all the room and leaving Mr. Harold nowhere to sit. Dirt and chopped grass dripped off of the blind man's shoes and onto the couch.

Mr. Harold finally sat on the floor beside his boy and tried to get the boy to give him a cookie, but his son didn't play that way. Mr. Harold had to get his own Kool-Aid and cookies, and he got the blind man some too.

The blind man took the Kool-Aid and cookies and didn't say thanks or kiss my ass. Just stretched out there on the couch listening, shaking from side to side, cheering the wrestlers on. He was obviously on Low Dozer McGuirk's side, and Mr. Harold figured it was primarily because he'd heard Dozer trained on beer and doughnuts. That struck Mr. Harold as a thing the blind man would latch onto and love. That and crop circles and flying saucers.

When the blind man finished up his cookies and Kool-Aid, he put Mr. Harold to work getting more, and when Mr. Harold came back with them, his son and the blind man were chatting about the wrestling match. The blind man was giving the boy some insights into the wrestling game and was trying to get the boy to try a hold on him so he could show how easily he could work out of it.

Mr. Harold nixed that plan, and the blind man ate his next plate of cookies and Kool-Aid, and somehow the wrestling show moved into an aftershow talk session on wrestling. When Mr. Harold looked at his watch nearly an hour had passed.

"We ought to get back over there and finish up," Mr. Harold said.

"Naw," said the blind man, "not just yet. This talk show stuff is good. This is where I get most of my tips."

"Well, all right, but when this is over, we're out of here."

But they weren't. The talk show wrapped up, the *Beverly Hillbillies* came on, then *Green Acres*, then *Gilligan's Island*. The blind man and Mr. Harold's son laughed their way through the first two, and damn near killed themselves with humor when *Gilligan's* was on.

Mr. Harold learned the Professor and Ginger were the blind man's favorites on *Gilligan's*, and he liked the pig, Arnold, on *Green Acres*. No one was a particular favorite on the *Beverly Hillbillies*, however.

"Ain't this stuff good?" the blind man said. "They don't make 'em like this anymore."

"I prefer educational programming myself," Mr. Harold said, though the last educational program he'd watched was a PBS special on lobsters. He'd watched it because he was sick as a dog and lying on the couch and his wife had put the remote across the room and he didn't feel good enough to get up and get hold of it.

In his feverish delirium he remembered the lobster special as pretty good 'cause it had come across a little like a science fiction movie. But that lobster special, as viewed through feverish eyes, had been the closest Mr. Harold had ever gotten to educational TV.

The sickness, the remote lying across the room, had caused him to miss what he'd really wanted to see that day, and even now, on occasion, he thought of what he had missed with a certain pang of regret: a special on how young women were chosen to wear swimsuits in special issues of sports magazines. He kept hoping it was a show that would play in reruns.

"My back's hurtin' from sitting on the floor," Mr. Harold said, but the blind man didn't move his feet so Mr. Harold could have a place on the couch. He offered a pointer, though.

"Sit on the floor, you got to hold your back straight, just like you was in a wooden chair, otherwise you'll really tighten them muscles up close to your butt."

When *Gilligan's* was wrapped up, Mr. Harold impulsively cut the television and got hold of the blind man and started pulling him up. "We got to go to work now. I'm gonna help you, it has to be now. I got plans for the rest of the day."

"Ah, Daddy, he was gonna show me a couple wrestling holds," the boy said.

"Not today," Mr. Harold said, tugging on the blind man, and suddenly the blind man moved and was behind him and had him wrestled to the floor. Mr. Harold tried to move, but couldn't. His arm was twisted behind his back and he was lying face down and the blind man was on top of him pressing a knee into his spine.

"Wow!" said the boy. "Neat!"

"Not bad for a blind fella," said the blind man. "I told you I get my tips from that show."

"All right, all right, let me go," said Mr. Harold.

"Squeal like a pig for me," said the blind man.

"Now wait just a goddamned minute," Mr. Harold said.

The blind man pressed his knee harder into Mr. Harold's spine. "Squeal like a pig for me. Come on."

Mr. Harold made a squeaking noise.

"That ain't no squeal," said the blind man. "Squeal!"

The boy got down by Mr. Harold's face. "Come on, Dad," he said. "Squeal."

"Big pig squeal," said the blind man. "Big pig! Big pig! Big pig!"

Mr. Harold squealed. The blind man didn't let go.

"Say calf rope," said the blind man.

"All right, all right. Calf rope! Calf rope! Now let me up."

The blind man eased his knee off Mr. Harold's spine and let go of the arm lock. He stood up and said to the boy, "It's mostly in the hips."

"Wow!" said the boy. "You made Dad squeal like a pig."

Mr. Harold, red-faced, got up. He said, "Come on, right now."

"I need my weed-eater," said the blind man.

The boy got both the weed-eater and the cane for the blind man. The blind man said to the boy as they went outside, "Remember, it's in the hips."

Mr. Harold and the blind man went over to the church property and started in on some spots with the weed-eater. In spite of the fact Mr. Harold found himself doing most of the weed-eating, the blind man just clinging to this elbow and being pulled around like he was a side car, it wasn't five minutes before the blind man wanted some shade and a drink of water.

Mr. Harold was trying to talk him out of it when Sonny Guy and his family drove up in a club cab Dodge pickup.

The pickup was black and shiny and looked as if it had just come off the showroom floor. Mr. Harold knew Sonny Guy's money for such things had come from Mrs. Guy's insurance before she was Mrs. Guy. Her first husband had gotten kicked to death by a maniac escaped from the nuthouse; kicked until they couldn't tell if he was a man or a jelly doughnut that had gotten run over by a truck.

When that insurance money came due, Sonny Guy, a man who had antennas for such things, showed up and began to woo her. They were married pretty quick, and the money from the insurance settlement had bought the house, the aircraft hangar church, the Day-Glo guitar signs, and the pickup. Mr. Harold wondered if there was any money left. He figured they might be pretty well run through it by now.

"Is that the Guys?" the blind man asked as the pickup engine was cut.

"Yeah," said Mr. Harold.

"Maybe we ought to look busy."

"I don't reckon it matters now."

Sonny got out of the pickup and waddled over to the edge of the property and looked at the mauled grass and weeds. He walked over to the aircraft hangar church and took it all in from that angle with his hands on his ample hips. He stuck his fingers under his overall straps and walked alongside the fence with the big black dog running behind it, barking, grabbing at the chicken wire with his teeth.

The minister's wife stood by the pickup. She had a bun of colorless hair stacked on her head. The stack had the general shape of some kind of tropical anthill that might house millions of angry ants. Way she was built, that hair and all, it looked as if the hill had been precariously built on top of a small round rock supported by an irregular-shaped one, the bottom rock wearing a print dress and a pair of black rat-heeled shoes.

The two dumpling kids, one boy and one girl, leaned against the truck's bumper as if they had just felt the effect of some relaxing drug. They both wore jeans, tennis shoes, and Disney T-shirts with the Magic Kingdom in the background. Mr. Harold couldn't help but note the whole family had upturned noses, like pigs. It wasn't something that could be ignored.

Sonny Guy shook his head and walked across the lot and over to the blind man. "You sure messed this up. It's gonna cost me more'n I'd have paid you to get it fixed. That crippled nigger never done nothing like this. He run over a sprinkler head once, but that was it. And he paid for it." Sonny turned his attention to Mr. Harold. "You have anything to do with this?"

"I was just tryin' to help," Mr. Harold said.

"I was doin' all right until he come over," said the blind man. "He started tellin' me how I was messin' up and all and got me nervous, and sure enough, I began to lose my place and my concentration. You can see the results."

"You'd have minded your own business," Sonny said to Mr. Harold, "the man woulda done all right, but you're one of those thinks a handicap can't do some jobs."

"The man's blind," said Mr. Harold. "He can't see to cut grass. Not four acres with a weed-eater. Any moron can see that."

The Reverend Sonny Guy had a pretty fast right hand for a fat man. He caught Mr. Harold a good one over the left eye and staggered him.

The blind man stepped aside so they'd have plenty of room, and Sonny set to punching Mr. Harold quite regularly. It seemed like something the two of them were made for. Sonny to throw punches and Mr. Harold to absorb them.

When Mr. Harold woke up, he was lying on his back in the grass and the shadow of the blind man lay like a slat across him.

"Where is he?" asked Mr. Harold, feeling hot and sick to his stomach.

"When he knocked you down and you didn't get up, he went in the house with his wife," said the blind man. "I think he was thirsty. He told me he wasn't giving me no five dollars. Actually, he said he wasn't giving me jackshit. And him a minister. The kids are still out here though, they're looking at their watches, I think. They had a bet on how long it'd be before you got up. I heard them talking."

Mr. Harold sat up and glanced toward the Dodge club cab. The blind man was right. The kids were still leaning against the truck. When Mr.

Harold looked at them, the boy, who was glancing at his watch, lifted one eye and raised his hand quickly and pulled it down, said, "Yesss!" The little girl looked pouty. The little boy said, "This time you blow me."

They went in the house. Mr. Harold stood up. The blind man gave him the weed-eater for support. He said, "Sonny says the crippled nigger will be back next week. I can't believe it. Scooped by a nigger. A crippled nigger."

Mr. Harold pursed his lips and tried to recall a couple of calming Bible verses. When he felt somewhat relaxed, he said, "Why'd you tell him it was my fault?"

"I figured you could handle yourself," the blind man said.

Mr. Harold rubbed one of the knots Sonny had knocked on his head. He considered homicide, but knew there wasn't any future in it. He said, "Tell you what. I'll give you a ride home."

"We could watch some more TV?"

"Nope," said Mr. Harold, probing a split in his lip. "I've got other plans."

Mr. Harold got his son and the three of them drove over to where the blind man said he lived. It was a lot on the far side of town, outside the city limits. It was bordered on either side by trees. It was a trailer lot, scraped down to the red clay. There were a few anemic grass patches here and there and it had a couple of lawn ornaments out front. A cow and a pig with tails that hooked up to hoses and spun around and around and worked as lawn sprinklers.

Behind the sprinklers a heap of wood and metal smoked pleasantly in the sunlight.

They got out of the car and Mr. Harold's son said, "Holy shit."

"Let me ask you something," said Mr. Harold to the blind man. "Your place got a cow and a pig lawn ornament? Kind that sprinkles the yard?"

The blind man appeared nervous. He sniffed the air. He said, "Is the cow one of those spotted kind?"

"A Holstein?" asked Mr. Harold. "My guess is the pig is a Yorkshire."

"That's them."

"Well, I reckon we're at your place all right, but it's burned down."

"Oh, shit," said the blind man. "I left the beans on."

"They're done now," said the boy.

The blind man sat down in the dirt and began to cry. It was a serious cry. A cat walking along the edge of the woods behind the remains of the trailer stopped to watch in amazement. The cat seemed surprised that any one thing could make such noise.

"Was they pinto beans?" the boy asked.

The blind man sputtered and sobbed and his chest heaved. Mr. Harold went and got the pig sprinkler and turned it on so that the water from its tail splattered on the pile of smoking rubble. When he felt that was going good, he got the cow working. He thought about calling the fire department, but that seemed kind of silly. About all they could do was come out and stir what was left with a stick.

"Is it all gone?" asked the blind man.

"The cow's all right," said Mr. Harold, "but the pig was a little too close to the fire, there's a little paint bubbled up on one of his legs."

Now the blind man really began to cry. "I damn near had it paid for. It wasn't no double-wide, but it was mine."

They stayed that way momentarily, the blind man crying, the water hissing onto the trailer's remains, then the blind man said, "Did the dogs get out?"

Mr. Harold gave the question some deep consideration. "My guess would be no."

"Then I don't guess there's any hope for the parakeet neither," said the blind man.

Reluctantly, Mr. Harold loaded the blind man back in the car with his son, and started home.

It wasn't the way Mr. Harold had hoped the day would turn out. He had been trying to do nothing more than a good deed, and now he couldn't get rid of the blind man. He wondered if this kind of shit ever happened to Jesus. He was always doing good stuff in the Bible. Mr. Harold wondered if he'd ever had an incident misfire on him, something that hadn't been reported in the Testaments.

Once, when Mr. Harold was about eleven, he'd experienced a similar incident, only he hadn't been trying to be a good Samaritan. Still, it was one of those times where you go in with one thing certain and it turns on you.

During recess he'd gotten in a fight with a little kid he thought would be easy to take. He punched the kid when he wasn't looking, and that little dude dropped and got hold of his knee with his arms and wrapped both his legs around him, positioned himself so that his bottom was on Mr. Harold's shoe.

Mr. Harold couldn't shake him. He dragged him across the schoolyard and even walked him into a puddle of water, but the kid stuck. Mr. Harold got a pretty good sized stick and hit the kid over the head with it, but that hadn't changed conditions. A dog tick couldn't have been fastened any tighter. He had to go back to class with the kid on his leg, pulling that little rascal after him wherever he went, like he had an anvil tied to his foot.

The teacher couldn't get the kid to let go either. They finally had to go to the principal's office and get the principal and the football coach to pry him off, and even they had to work at it. The coach said he'd once wrestled a madman with a butcher knife, and he'd rather do that again than try and get that kid off someone's leg.

The blind man was kind of like that kid. You couldn't lose the sonofabitch.

Near the house, Mr. Harold glanced at his watch and noted it was time for his wife to be home. He was overcome with deep concerns. He'd just thought the blind man pissing on his bathroom wall would be a problem, now he had greater worries. He actually had the gentleman in tow, bringing him to the house at suppertime. Mr. Harold pulled over at a station and got some gas and bought the boy and the blind man a Coke. The blind man seemed to have gotten over the loss of his trailer. Sadness for its contents, the dogs and the parakeet, failed to plague him.

While the boy and the blind man sat on the curb, Mr. Harold went around to a pay booth and called home. On the third ring his wife answered.

"Where in the world are you?" she said.

"I'm out here at a filling station. I got someone with me."

"You better have Marvin with you."

"I do, but I ain't talking about the boy. I got a blind man with me."

"You mean he can't see?"

"Not a lick. He's got a weed-eater. He's the groundskeeper next door. I tried to take him home but his trailer burned up with his dogs and bird in it, and I ain't got no place to take him but home for supper."

A moment of silence passed as Mrs. Harold considered. "Ain't there some kinda home you can put him in?"

"I can't think of any. I suppose I could tie a sign around his neck said 'Blind Man' and leave him on someone's step with his weed-eater."

"Well, that wouldn't be fair to whoever lived in that house, just pushing problems on someone else."

Mr. Harold was nervous. Mrs. Harold seemed awfully polite. Usually she got mad over the littlest thing. He was trying to figure if it was a trap when he realized that something about all this was bound to appeal to her religious nature. She went to church a lot. She read the *Baptist Standard* and watched a couple of Sunday afternoon TV shows with preaching in them. Blind people were loved by Baptists. Them and cripples. They got mentioned in the Bible a lot. Jesus had a special affection for them. Well, he liked lepers, too, but Mr. Harold figured that was where even Mrs. Harold's dedicated Baptist beliefs might falter.

A loophole presented itself to Mr. Harold. He said, "I figure it's our Christian charity to take this fella in, honey. He can't see and he's lost his job and his trailer burned down with his pets in it."

"Well, I reckon you ought to bring him on over then. We'll feed him and I'll call around and see what my ladies' charities can do. It'll be my project. Wendy Lee is goin' around gettin' folks to pick up trash on a section of the highway, but I figure helping out a blind man would be Christian. Jesus helped blind people, but I don't never remember him picking up any trash."

When Mr. Harold loaded his son and the blind man back into the car, he was a happier man. He wasn't in trouble. Mrs. Harold thought taking in the blind man was her idea. He figured he could put up with the bastard another couple hours, then he'd find him a place to stay. Some homeless shelter with a cot and some hot soup if he wanted it. Maybe some preaching and breakfast before he had to hit the road.

At the house, Mrs. Harold met them at the door. Her little round body practically bounced. She found the blind man's hand and shook it. She told him how sorry she was, and he dropped his head and looked sad and thanked her. When they were inside, he said, "Is that cornbread I smell?"

"Yes it is," Mrs. Harold said, "and it won't be no time 'til it's ready. And we're having pinto beans with it. The beans were cooked yesterday and just need heating. They taste best when they've set a night."

"That's what burned his trailer down," the boy said. "He was cooking some pinto beans and forget 'em."

"Oh my," said Mrs. Harold, "I hope the beans won't bring back sad memories."

"No ma'am, them was limas I was cookin'."

"There was dogs in there and a parakeet," said the boy. "They got burned up too. There wasn't nothing left but some burnt wood and a piece of a couch and an old birdcage."

"I have some insurance papers in a deposit box downtown," the blind man said. "I could probably get me a couple of double-wides and have enough left over for a vacation with the money I'll get. I could get me some dogs and a bird easy enough too. I could even name them the same names as the ones burned up."

They sat and visited for a while in the living room while the cornbread cooked and the beans warmed up. The blind man and Mrs. Harold talked about religion. The blind man knew her favorite gospel tunes and sang a couple of them. Not too good, Mr. Harold thought, but Mrs. Harold seemed almost swoony.

The blind man knew her Sunday preaching programs, too, and they talked about a few highlighted TV sermons. They debated the parables in the Bible and ended up discussing important and obscure points in the scripture, discovered the two of them saw things a lot alike when it came to interpretation. They had found dire warnings in Deuteronomy that scholars had overlooked.

Mrs. Harold got so lathered up with enthusiasm, she went into the kitchen and started throwing an apple pie together. Mr. Harold became nervous as soon as the pie pans began to rattle. This wasn't like her. She only cooked a pie to take to relatives after someone died or if it was Christmas or Thanksgiving and more than ten people were coming.

While she cooked, the blind man discussed wrestling holds with Mr. Harold's son. When dinner was ready, the blind man was positioned in Mr. Harold's chair, next to Mrs. Harold. They ate, and the blind man and Mrs. Harold further discussed scripture, and from time to time, the blind man would stop the religious talk long enough to give the boy a synopsis of some wrestling match or another. He had a way of cleverly turning the conversation without seeming to. He wasn't nearly as clever about passing the beans or the cornbread. The apple pie remained strategically guarded by his elbow.

After a while, the topic switched from the Bible and wrestling to the blind man's aches and miseries. He was overcome with them. There wasn't a thing that could be wrong with a person he didn't have.

Mrs. Harold used this conversational opportunity to complain about hip problems, hypoglycemia, overactive thyroids, and out-of-control sweat glands.

The blind man had a tip or two on how to make living with each of Mrs. Harold's complaints more congenial. Mrs. Harold said, "Well, sir, there's just not a thing you don't know something about. From wrestling to medicine."

The blind man nodded. "I try to keep up. I read a lot of braille and listen to the TV and the radio. They criticize the TV, but they shouldn't. I get lots of my education there. I can learn from just about anything or anyone but a nigger."

Mrs. Harold, much to Mr. Harold's chagrin, agreed. This was a side of his wife he had never known. She had opinions and he hadn't known that. Stupid opinions, but opinions.

When Mr. Harold finally left the table, pieless, to hide out in the bathroom, the blind man and Mrs. Harold were discussing a plan for getting all the black folk back to Africa. Something to do with the number of boats necessary and the amount of proper hygiene needed.

And speaking of hygiene, Mr. Harold stood up as his bottom became wet. He had been sitting on the lid of the toilet and dampness had soaked through his pants. The blind man had been in the bathroom last and he'd pissed all over the lowered lid and splattered the wall.

Mr. Harold changed clothes and cleaned up the piss and washed his hands and splashed his face and looked at himself in the mirror. It was still him in there and he was awake.

About ten p.m. Mrs. Harold and the blind man put the boy to bed and the blind man sang the kid a rockabilly song, told him a couple of nigger jokes and one kike joke, and tucked him in.

Mr. Harold went in to see the boy, but he was asleep. The blind man and Mrs. Harold sat on the couch and talked about chicken and dumpling recipes and how to clean squirrels properly for frying. Mr. Harold sat in a chair and listened, hoping for some opening in the conversation into which he could spring. None presented itself.

Finally Mrs. Harold got the blind man some bedclothes and folded out the couch and told him a pleasant good night, touching the blind man's arm as she did. Mr. Harold noted she left her hand there quite a while.

In bed, Mr. Harold, hoping to prove to himself he was still man of the house, rolled over and put his arm around Mrs. Harold's hip. She had gotten dressed and gotten into bed in record time while he was taking a leak, and now she was feigning sleep, but Mr. Harold decided he wasn't going to go for it. He rubbed her ass and tried to work his hand between her legs from behind. He touched what he wanted, but it was as dry as a ditch in the Sahara.

Mrs. Harold pretended to wake up. She was mad. She said he ought to let a woman sleep, and didn't he think about anything else? Mr. Harold admitted that sex was a foremost thought of his, but he knew now nothing he said would matter. Neither humor nor flattery would work. He would not only go pieless this night, he would go assless as well.

Mrs. Harold began to explain how one of her mysterious headaches with back pain had descended on her. Arthritis might be the culprit, she said, though sometimes she suspicioned something more mysterious and deadly. Perhaps something incurable that would eventually involve large leaking sores and a deep coma.

Mr. Harold, frustrated, closed his eyes and tried to go to sleep with a hard-on. He couldn't understand, having had so much experience now, why it was so difficult for him to just forget his boner and go to bed, but it was, as always, a trial.

Finally, after making a trip to the bathroom to work his pistol and plunk its stringy wet bullet into the toilet water, he was able to go back to bed and drift off into an unhappy sleep.

A few hours later he awoke. He heard a noise like girlish laughter. He lay in bed and listened. It was, in fact, laughter, and it was coming from the living room. The blind man must have the TV on. But then he recognized the laughter. It hadn't come to him right away, because it had been ages since he had heard it. He reached for Mrs. Harold and she was gone.

He got out of bed and opened the bedroom door and crept quietly down the hall. There was a soft light on in the living room; it was the lamp on the TV muted by a white towel.

On the couch-bed was the blind man, wearing only his underwear and dark glasses. Mrs. Harold was on the bed too. She was wearing her nightie. The blind man was on top of her and they were pressed close. Mrs. Harold's hand sneaked over the blind man's back and slid into his underwear and cupped his ass.

Mr. Harold let out his breath, and Mrs. Harold turned her head and saw him. She gave a little cry and rolled out from under the blind man. She laughed hysterically. "Why, honey, you're up."

The blind man explained immediately. They had been practicing a wrestling hold, one of the more complicated, and not entirely legal ones, that involved grabbing the back of an opponent's tights. Mrs. Harold admitted that as of tonight, she had been overcome with a passion for wrestling and was going to watch all the wrestling programs from now on. She thanked the blind man for the wrestling lesson and shook his hand and went past Mr. Harold and back to bed.

Mr. Harold stood looking at the blind man. He was on the couch on all fours looking in Mr. Harold's direction. The muted light from the towel-covered lamp hit the blind man's dark glasses and made them shine like the eyes of a wolf. His bared teeth completed the image.

Mr. Harold went back to bed. Mrs. Harold snuggled close. She wanted to be friendly. She ran her hand over his chest and down his belly and held his equipment, but he was as soft as a sock. She worked him a little and finally he got hard in spite of himself. They rolled together and did what he wanted to do earlier. For the first time in years, Mrs. Harold got off. She came with a squeak and thrust of her hips, and Mr. Harold knew that behind her closed eyes she saw a pale face and dark glasses, not him.

Later, he lay in bed and stared at the ceiling. Mrs. Harold's pussy had been as wet as a fish farm after her encounter with the blind man, wetter than he remembered it in years. What was it about the blind man that excited her? He was a racist cracker asshole who really knew nothing. He didn't have a job. He couldn't even work a weed-eater that good.

Mr. Harold felt fear. What he had here at home wasn't all that good, but he realized now he might lose it, and it was probably the best he could do. Even if his wife's conversation was as dull as the Republican convention and his son was as interesting as needlework, his home life took on a new and desperate importance. Something had to be done.

Next day, Mr. Harold got a break. The blind man made a comment about his love for snow cones. It was made while they were sitting alone in the kitchen. Mrs. Harold was in the shower and the boy was playing Nintendo in the living room. The blind man was rattling on like always. Last night rang no guilty bells for him.

"You know," said Mr. Harold, "I like a good snow cone myself. One of those blue ones."

"Oh yeah, that's coconut," said the blind man.

"What you say you and me go get one?"

"Ain't it gonna be lunch soon? I don't want to spoil my appetite."

"A cone won't spoil nothing. Come on, my treat."

The blind man was a little uncertain, but Mr. Harold could tell the idea of a free snow cone was strong within him. He let Mr. Harold lead him out to the car. Mr. Harold began to tremble with anticipation. He drove toward town, but when he got there, he drove on through.

"I thought you said the stand was close?" said the blind man. "Ain't we been driving a while?"

"Well, it's Sunday, and that one I was thinking of was closed. I know one 'cross the way stays open seven days a week during the summer."

Mr. Harold drove out into the country. He drove off the main highway and down a red clay road and pulled over to the side near a gap where irresponsibles dumped their garbage. He got out and went around to the blind man's side and took the blind man's arm and led him away from the car toward a pile of garbage. Flies hummed operative notes in the late morning air.

"We're in luck," Mr. Harold said. "Ain't no one here but us."

"Yeah, well it don't smell so good around here. Somethin' dead somewheres?"

"There's a cat hit out there on the highway."

"I'm kinda losin' my appetite for a cone."

"It'll come back soon as you put that cone in your mouth. Besides, we'll eat in the car."

Mr. Harold placed the blind man directly in front of a bag of household garbage. "You stand right here. Tell me what you want and I'll get it."

"I like a strawberry. Double on the juice."

"Strawberry it is."

Mr. Harold walked briskly back to his car, cranked it, and drove by the blind man who cocked his head as the automobile passed. Mr. Harold drove down a ways, turned around and drove back the way he had come. The blind man still stood by the garbage heap, his cane looped over his wrist, only now he was facing the road.

Mr. Harold honked the horn as he drove past.

Just before reaching the city limits, a big black pickup began to make ominous maneuvers. The pickup was behind him and was riding his bumper. Mr. Harold tried to speed up, but that didn't work. He tried slowing down, but the truck nearly ran up his ass. He decided to pull to the side, but the truck wouldn't pass.

Eventually, Mr. Harold coasted to the emergency lane and stopped, but the truck pulled up behind him and two burly men got out. They looked as if the last bath they'd had was during the last rain, probably caught out in it while pulpwooding someone's posted land.

Mr. Harold assumed it was all some dreadful mistake. He got out of the car so they could see he wasn't who they thought he must be. The biggest one walked up to him and grabbed him behind the head with one hand and hit him with the other. The smaller man, smaller because his head seemed undersized, took his turn and hit Mr. Harold. The two men began to work on him. He couldn't fall down because the car held him up, and for some reason he couldn't pass out. These guys weren't as fast as Sonny Guy, and they weren't knocking him out, but they certainly hurt more.

"What kinda fella are you that would leave a blind man beside the road?" said the bigger man just before he busted Mr. Harold a good one in the nose.

Mr. Harold finally hit the ground. The small-headed man kicked him in the balls and the bigger man kicked him in the mouth, knocking out what was left of his front teeth; the man's fist had already stolen the others. When Mr. Harold was close to passing out, the small-headed man bent down and got hold of Mr. Harold's hair and looked him in the eye and said, "We hadn't been throwing out an old stray dog down that road, that fella might have got lost or hurt."

"He's much more resourceful than you think," Mr. Harold said, realizing who they meant, and then the small-headed man hit him a short chopping blow.

"I'm glad we seen him," said the bigger man, "and I'm glad we caught up with you. You just think you've took a beating. We're just getting started."

But at that moment the blind man appeared above Mr. Harold. He had found his way from the truck to the car, directed by the sound of the beating most likely. "No, boys," said the blind man, "that's good enough. I ain't the kind holds a grudge, even 'gainst a man would do what he did. I've had some theology training and done a little Baptist ministering. Holding a grudge ain't my way."

"Well, you're a good one," said the bigger man. "I ain't like that at all. I was blind and I was told I was gonna get a snow cone and a fella put me out at a garbage dump, I'd want that fella dead, or crippled up at the least."

"I understand," said the blind man. "It's hard to believe there's people like this in the world. But if you'll just drive me home, that'll be enough. I'd like to get on the way if it's no inconvenience. I have a little Bible lesson in braille I'd like to study."

They went away and left Mr. Harold lying on the highway beside his car. As they drove by, the pickup tires tossed gravel on him and the exhaust enveloped him like a foul cotton sack.

Mr. Harold got up after five minutes and got inside his car and fell across the seat and lay there. He couldn't move. He spat out a tooth. His balls hurt. His face hurt. For that matter, his kneecaps where they'd kicked him didn't feel all that good either.

After an hour or so, Mr. Harold began to come around. An intense hatred for the blind man boiled up in his stomach. He sat up and started the car and headed home.

When he turned on his road, he was nearly sideswiped by a yellow moving van. It came at him so hard and fast he swerved into a ditch filled with sand and got his right rear tire stuck. He couldn't drive the car out. More he worked at it, the deeper the back tire spun in the sand. He got his jack out of the trunk and cranked up the rear end and put debris under the tire. Bad as he felt, it was quite a job. He finally drove out of there, and off the jack, leaving it lying in the dirt.

When he got to his house, certain in his heart the blind man was inside, he parked next to Mrs. Harold's station wagon. The station wagon was stuffed to the gills with boxes and sacks. He wondered what that was all about, but he didn't wonder too hard. He looked around the yard for a weapon. Out by the side of the house was the blind man's weed-eater. That would do. He figured he caught the blind man a couple of licks with that, he could get him down on the ground and finish him, stun him before the sonofabitch applied a wrestling hold.

He went in the house by the back door with the weed-eater cocked, and was astonished to find the room was empty. The kitchen table and chairs were gone. The cabinet doors were open and all the canned goods were missing. Where the stove had set was a greasy spot. Where the refrigerator had set was a wet spot. A couple of roaches, feeling brave and free to roam, scuttled across the kitchen floor as merry as kids on skates.

The living room was empty too. Not only of people, but furniture and roaches. The rest of the house was the same. Dust motes spun in the light. The front door was open.

Outside, Mr. Harold heard a car door slam. He limped out the front door and saw the station wagon. His wife was behind the wheel, and sitting next to her was the boy, and beside him the blind man, his arm hanging out the open window.

Mr. Harold beckoned to them by waving the weed-eater, but they ignored him. Mrs. Harold backed out of the drive quickly.

Mr. Harold could hear the blind man talking to the boy about something or another and the boy was laughing. The station wagon turned onto the road and the car picked up speed. Mr. Harold went slack and leaned on the weed-eater for support.

At the moment before the station wagon passed in front of a line of high shrubs, the blind man turned to look out the window, and Mr. Harold saw his own reflection in the blind man's glasses.

I've always loved blues music and have been equally fascinated with the legends that have grown up about certain blues performers.

Hands down, the most famous legend is that of Robert Johnson, who supposedly sold his soul to the devil to be a great guitar player and singer.

Johnson probably borrowed this story from a previous musician, or it was assigned to him at some time by others. The story was an old one, but it really stuck to Johnson more than to some other blues performers.

There's an equally interesting and influential blues musician who went by the name Henry "Ragtime Texas" Thomas. Very little is known about him. I once wrote a short article about him for the *Texas Observer*, but they kept wanting to add this or that, and finally I just said forget it. I was paid. The article is mine, and someday I'll publish it somewhere.

It was a short article because little is known about Thomas except for a story or two that may be true or may be false. There's also a short video of a man fitting Thomas's description playing guitar and mouth harp, or miniature panpipe, and though it may indeed be Thomas, it's disputed.

Johnson's story also reminded me for some reason of Lovecraft's Erich Zann, who plays strange music on a violin, and something in that music holds one of Lovecraft's creepy monsters at bay, keeps it on the other side of the veil.

I combined the two ideas, added in a lot of me, and away the story went.

The Bleeding Shadow

I WAS DOWN at the Blue Light Joint that night, finishing off some ribs and listening to some blues, when in walked Alma May. She was looking good too. Had a dress on and it fit her the way a dress ought to fit every woman in the world. She was wearing a little flat hat that leaned to one side, like an unbalanced plate on a waiter's palm. The high heels she had on made her legs look tight and way all right.

The light wasn't all that good in the joint, which is one of its appeals. It sometimes helps a man or woman get along in a way the daylight wouldn't stand, but I knew Alma May enough to know light didn't matter. She'd look good wearing a sack and a paper hat.

There was something about her face that showed me right off she was worried, that things weren't right. She was glancing left and right, like she was in some big city trying to cross a busy street and not get hit by a car.

I got my bottle of beer, left out from my table, and went over to her.

Then I knew why she'd been looking around like that. She said, "I was looking for you, Richard."

"Say you were," I said. "Well you done found me."

The way she stared at me wiped the grin off my face.

"Something wrong, Alma May?"

"Maybe. I don't know. I got to talk, though. Thought you'd be here, and I was wondering you might want to come by my place."

"When?"

"Now."

"All right."

"But don't get no business in mind," she said. "This isn't like the old days. I need your help, and I need to know I can count on you."

"Well, I kind of like the kind of business we used to do, but all right, we're friends. It's cool."

"I hoped you'd say that."

"You got a car?" I said.

She shook her head. "No. I had a friend drop me off."

I thought, *friend*? Sure.

"All right then," I said, "let's strut on out."

I guess you could say it's a shame Alma May makes her money turning tricks, but when you're the one paying for the tricks, and you are one of her satisfied customers, you feel different. Right then, anyway. Later, you feel guilty. Like maybe you done peed on the *Mona Lisa*. 'Cause that gal, she was one fine dark-skin woman who should have got better than a thousand rides and enough money to buy some eats and make some coffee in the morning. She deserved something good. Should have found and married a man with a steady job that could have done all right by her.

But that hadn't happened. Me and her had a bit of something once, and it wasn't just business, money changing hands after she got me feeling good. No, it was more than that, but we couldn't work it out. She was in the life and didn't know how to get out. And as for deserving something better, that wasn't me. What I had were a couple of nice suits, some two-tone shoes, a hat, and a gun—.45 caliber automatic, like they'd used in the war a few years back.

Alma May got a little on the dope, too, and though she shook it, it had dropped her down deep. Way I figured, she wasn't never climbing out of that hole, and it didn't have nothing to do with dope now. What it had to do with was time. You get a window open now and again, and if you don't crawl through it, it closes. I know. My window had closed some time back. It made me mad all the time.

We were in my Chevy, a six-year-old car, a forty-eight model. I'd had it reworked a bit at a time: new tires, fresh windshield, nice seat covers and so on. It was shiny and special.

We were driving along, making good time on the highway, the lights racing over the cement, making the recent rain in the ruts shine like the knees of old dress pants.

"What you need me for?" I asked.

"It's a little complicated," she said.

"Why me?"

"I don't know. . . . You've always been good to me, and once we had a thing goin'."

"We did," I said.

"What happened to it?"

I shrugged. "It quit goin'."

"It did, didn't it? Sometimes I wish it hadn't."

"Sometimes I wish a lot of things," I said.

She leaned back in the seat and opened her purse and got out a cigarette and lit it, then rolled down the window. She remembered I didn't like cigarette smoke. I never had got on the tobacco. It took your wind and it stunk and it made your breath bad too. I hated when it got in my clothes.

"You're the only one I could tell this to," she said. "The only one that would listen to me and not think I been with the needle in my arm. You know what I'm sayin'?"

"Sure, baby, I know."

"I sound to you like I been bad?"

"Naw. You sound all right. I mean, you're talkin' a little odd, but not like you're out of your head."

"Drunk?"

"Nope. Just like you had a bad dream and want to tell someone."

"That's closer," she said. "That ain't it, but that's much closer than any needle or whiskey or wine."

Alma May's place is on the outskirts of town. It's the one thing she got out of life that ain't bad. It's not a mansion. It's small, but it's tight and bright in the daylight, all painted up canary yellow color with deep blue trim. It didn't look bad in the moonlight.

Alma May didn't work with a pimp. She didn't need one. She was well known around town. She had her clientele. They were all safe, she told me once. About a third of them were white folks from on the other side of the tracks, up there in the proper part of Tyler Town. What she had besides them was a dead mother and a runaway father and a brother, Tootie, who liked to travel around, play blues and suck that bottle. He was always needing something, and Alma May, in spite of her own demons, had always managed to make sure he got it.

That was another reason me and her had to split the sheets. That brother of hers was a grown-ass man, and he lived with his mother and let her tote his water. When the mama died, he sort of went to pieces. Alma May took Mama's part over, keeping Tootie in whiskey and biscuits, even bought him a guitar. He lived off her whoring money, and it didn't bother him none. I didn't like him. But I will say this. That boy could play the blues.

When we were inside her house, she unpinned her hat from her hair and sailed it across the room and into a chair.

She said, "You want a drink?"

"I ain't gonna say no, long as it ain't too weak, and be sure to put it in a dirty glass."

She smiled. I watched from the living room doorway as she went and got a bottle out from under the kitchen sink, showing me how tight that dress fit across her bottom when she bent over. She pulled some glasses off a shelf, come back with a stiff one. We drank a little of it, still standing, leaning against the doorframe between living room and kitchen. We finally sat on the couch. She sat on the far end, just to make sure I remembered why we were there. She said, "It's Tootie."

I swigged down the drink real quick, said, "I'm gone."

As I went by the couch, she grabbed my hand. "Don't be that way, baby."

"Now I'm 'baby,'" I said.

"Hear me out, honey. Please. You don't owe me, but can you pretend you do?"

"Hell," I said and went and sat down on the couch.

She moved, said, "I want you to listen."

"All right," I said.

"First off, I can't pay you. Except maybe in trade."

"Not that way," I said. "You and me, we do this, it ain't trade. Call it a favor."

I do a little detective stuff now and then for folks I knew, folks that recommended me to others. I don't have a license. Black people couldn't get a license to shit broken glass in this town. But I was pretty good at what I did. I learned it the hard way. And not all of it was legal. I guess I'm a kind of private eye. Only I'm really private. I'm so private I might be more of a secret eye.

"Best thing to do is listen to this," she said. "It cuts back on some explanation."

There was a little record player on a table by the window, a stack of records. She went over and opened the player box and turned it on. The record she wanted was already on it. She lifted up the needle and set it right, stepped back and looked at me.

She was oh so fine. I looked at her and thought maybe I should have stuck with her, brother or no brother. She could melt butter from ten feet away, way she looked.

And then the music started to play.

It was Tootie's voice. I recognized that right away. I had heard him plenty. Like I said, he wasn't much as a person, willing to do anything so he could lay back and play that guitar, slide a pocketknife along the strings to squeal out just the right sound, but he was good at the blues, of that, there ain't no denying.

His voice was high and lonesome, and the way he played that guitar, it was hard to imagine how he could get the sounds out of it he got.

"You brought me over here to listen to records?" I said.

She shook her head. She lifted up the needle, stopped the record, and took it off. She had another in a little paper cover, and she took it out and put it on, dropped the needle down.

"Now listen to this."

First lick or two, I could tell right off it was Tootie, but then there came a kind of turn in the music, where it got so strange the hair on the back of my neck stood up. And then Tootie started to sing, and the hair on the back of my hands and arms stood up. The air in the room got thick and the lights got dim, and shadows come out of the corners and sat on the couch with me. I ain't kidding about that part. The room was suddenly full of them, and I could hear what sounded like a bird, trapped at the ceiling, fluttering fast and hard, looking for a way out.

Then the music changed again, and it was like I had been dropped down a well, and it was a long drop, and then it was like those shadows were folding around me in a wash of dirty water. The room stunk of something foul. The guitar no longer sounded like a guitar, and Tootie's voice was no longer like a voice. It was like someone dragging a razor over concrete while trying to yodel with a throat full of glass. There was something inside the music, something that squished and scuttled and honked and raved, something unsettling, like a snake in a satin glove.

"Cut it off," I said.

But Alma May had already done it.

She said, "That's as far as I've ever let it go. It's all I can do to move to cut it off. It feels like it's getting more powerful the more it plays. I don't want to hear the rest of it. I don't know I can take it. How can that be, Richard? How can that be with just sounds?"

I was actually feeling weak, like I'd just come back from a bout with the flu and someone had beat my ass. I said, "More powerful? How do you mean?"

"Ain't that what you think? Ain't that how it sounds? Like it's getting stronger?"

I nodded. "Yeah."

"And the room—"

"The shadows?" I said. "I didn't just imagine it?"

"No," she said, "only every time I've heard it, it's been a little different. The notes get darker, the guitar licks, they cut something inside me, and each time it's something different and something deeper. I don't know if it makes me feel good or it makes me feel bad, but it sure makes me feel."

"Yeah," I said, because I couldn't find anything else to say.

"Tootie sent me that record. He sent a note that said: *Play it when you have to.* That's what it said. That's all it said. What's that mean?"

"I don't know, but I got to wonder why Tootie would send it to you in the first place. Why would he want you to hear something makes you almost sick? And how in hell could he do that, make that kind of sound, I mean?"

She shook her head. "I don't know. Someday, I'm gonna play it all the way through."

"I wouldn't," I said.

"Why?"

"You heard it. I figure it only gets worse. I don't understand it, but I know I don't like it."

"Yeah," she said, putting the record back in the paper sleeve. "I know. But it's so strange. I've never heard anything like it."

"And I don't want to hear anything like it again."

"Still, you have to wonder."

"What I wonder is what I was wondering before. Why would he send this shit to you?"

"I think he's proud of it. There's nothing like it. It's . . . original."

"I'll give it that," I said. "So, what do you want with me?"

"I want you to find Tootie."

"Why?"

"Because I don't think he's right. I think he needs help. I mean, this . . . it makes me think he's somewhere he shouldn't be."

"But yet, you want to play it all the way through," I said.

"What I know is I don't like that. I don't like Tootie being associated with it, and I don't know why. Richard, I want you to find him."

"Where did the record come from?"

She got the sleeve and brought it to me. I could see through the little doughnut in the sleeve where the label on the record ought to be. Nothing but disk. The package itself was like wrapping paper you put meat in. It was stained.

"I think he paid some place to let him record," I said. "Question is, what place? You have an address where this came from?"

"I do." She went and got a large manila envelope and brought it to me. "It came in this."

I looked at the writing on the front. It had as a return address the Hotel Champion. She showed me the note. It was on a piece of really cheap stationery that said "The Hotel Champion" and had a phone number and an address in Dallas. The stationery looked old and it was sun-faded.

"I called them," she said, "but they didn't know anything about him. They had never heard of him. I could go look myself, but . . . I'm a little afraid. Besides, you know, I got clients, and I got to make the house payment."

I didn't like hearing about that, knowing what kind of clients she meant, and how she was going to make that money. I said, "All right. What you want me to do?"

"Find him."

"And then what?"

"Bring him home."

"And if he don't want to come back?"

"I've seen you work, bring him home to me. Just don't lose that temper of yours."

I turned the record around and around in my hands. I said, "I'll go take a look. I won't promise anything more than that. He wants to come, I'll bring him back. He doesn't, I might be inclined to break his leg and bring him back. You know I don't like him."

"I know. But don't hurt him."

"If he comes easy, I'll do that. If he doesn't, I'll let him stay, come back and tell you where he is and how he is. How about that?'

"That's good enough," she said. "Find out what this is all about. It's got me scared, Richard."

"It's just bad sounds," I said. "Tootie was probably high on something when he recorded it, thought it was good at the time, sent it to you because he thought he was the coolest thing since Robert Johnson."

"Who?"

"Never mind. But I figure when he got over his hop, he probably didn't even remember he mailed it."

"Don't try and tell me you've heard anything like this. That listening to it didn't make you feel like your skin was gonna pull off your bones, that some part of it made you want to dip in the dark and learn to like it. Tell me it wasn't like that? Tell me it wasn't like walking out in front of a car and the headlights in your face, and you just wanting to step out there even though it scared hell out of you and you knew it was the devil or something even worse at the wheel. Tell me you didn't feel something like that."

I couldn't. So I didn't say anything. I just sat there and sweated, the sound of that music still shaking down deep in my bones, boiling my blood.

"Here's the thing," I said. "I'll do it, but you got to give me a photograph of Tootie, if you got one, and the record so you don't play it no more."

She studied me a moment. "I hate that thing," she said, nodding at the record in my hands, "but somehow I feel attached to it. Like getting rid of it is getting rid of a piece of me."

"That's the deal."

"All right," she said, "take it, but take it now."

Motoring along by myself in the Chevy, the moon high and bright, all I could think of was that music, or whatever that sound was. It was stuck in my head like an ax. I had the record on the seat beside me, had Tootie's note and envelope, the photograph Alma May had given me.

Part of me wanted to drive back to Alma May and tell her no, and never mind. Here's the record back. But another part of me, the dumb part, wanted to know where and how and why that record had been made. Curiosity, it just about gets us all.

Where I live is a rickety third-floor walk-up. It's got the stairs on the outside, and they stop at each landing. I was at the very top.

I tried not to rest my hand too heavy on the rail as I climbed, because it was about to come off. I unlocked my door and turned on the light and watched the roaches run for cover.

I put the record down, got a cold one out of the icebox. Well, actually it was a plug-in. A refrigerator. But I'd grown up with iceboxes, so calling it that was hard to break. I picked up the record again and took a seat.

Sitting in my old armchair with the stuffings leaking out like a busted cotton sack, holding the record again, looking at the dirty brown sleeve, I noticed the grooves were dark and scabby-looking, like something had gotten poured in there and had dried tight. I tried to determine if that had something to do with that crazy sound. Could something in the grooves make that kind of noise? Didn't seem likely.

I thought about putting the record on, listening to it again, but I couldn't stomach the thought. The fact that I held it in my hand made me uncomfortable. It was like holding a bomb about to go off.

I had thought of it like a snake once. Alma May had thought of it like a hit-and-run car driven by the devil. And now I had thought of it like a bomb. That was some kind of feeling coming from a grooved-up circle of wax.

Early next morning, with the .45 in the glove box, a razor in my coat pocket, and the record up front on the seat beside me, I tooled out toward Dallas, and the Hotel Champion.

I got into Big D around noon, stopped at a café on the outskirts where there was colored, and went in where a big fat mama with a pretty face and a body that smelled real good made me a hamburger and sat and flirted with me all the while I ate it. That's all right. I like women, and I like them to flirt. They quit doing that, I might as well lay down and die.

While we was flirting, I asked her about the Hotel Champion, if she knew where it was. I had the street number, of course, but I needed tighter directions.

"Oh, yeah, honey, I know where it is, and you don't want to stay there. It's deep in the colored section, and not the good part, that's what I'm trying to tell you, and it don't matter you brown as a walnut yourself. There's folks down there will cut you and put your blood in a paper cup and mix it with whiskey and drink it. You too good-looking to get all cut up and such. There's better places to stay on the far other side."

I let her give me a few hotel names, like I might actually stay at one or the other, but I got the address for the Champion, paid up, giving her a good tip, and left out of there.

The part of town where the Hotel Champion was was just as nasty as the lady had said. There were people hanging around on the streets, and leaning into corners, and there was trash everywhere. It wasn't exactly a place that fostered a lot of pride.

I found the Hotel Champion and parked out front. There was a couple fellas on the street eyeing my car. One was skinny. One was big. They were dressed up with nice hats and shoes, just like they had jobs. But if they did, they wouldn't have been standing around in the middle of the day eyeing my Chevy.

I pulled the .45 out of the glove box and stuck it in my pants, at the small of my back. My coat would cover it just right.

I got out and gave the hotel the gander. It was nice-looking if you were blind in one eye and couldn't see out the other.

There wasn't any doorman, and the door was hanging on a hinge. Inside I saw a dusty stairway to my left, a scarred door to my right.

There was a desk in front of me. It had a glass hooked to it that went to the ceiling. There was a little hole in it low down on the counter that had a wooden stop behind it. There were flyspecks on the glass, and there was a man behind the glass, perched on a stool, like a frog on a lily pad. He was fat and colored and his hair had blue blanket wool in it. I didn't take it for decoration. He was just a nasty sonofabitch.

I could smell him when he moved the wooden stop. A stink like armpits and nasty underwear and rotting teeth. Floating in from somewhere in back, I could smell old cooking smells, boiled pigs' feet and pigs' tails that might have been good about the time the pig lost them, but now all that was left was a rancid stink. There was also a reek like cat piss.

I said, "Hey, man, I'm looking for somebody."

"You want a woman, you got to bring your own," the man said, "but I can give you a number or two. Course, I ain't guaranteeing anything about them being clean."

"Naw. I'm looking for somebody was staying here. His name is Tootie Johnson."

"I don't know no Tootie Johnson."

That was the same story Alma May had got.

"Well, all right, you know this fella?" I pulled out the photograph and pressed it against the glass.

"Well, he might look like someone got a room here. We don't sign in and we don't exchange names much."

"No? A class place like this?"

"I said he might look like someone I seen," he said. "I didn't say he definitely did."

"You fishing for money?"

"Fishing ain't very certain," he said.

I sighed and put the photograph back inside my coat and got out my wallet and took out a five-dollar bill.

Frog Man saw himself as some kind of greasy high roller. "That's it? Five dollars for prime information?"

I made a slow and careful show of putting my five back in my wallet. "Then you don't get nothing," I said.

He leaned back on his stool and put his stubby fingers together and let them lay on his round belly. "And you don't get nothing neither, jackass."

I went to the door on my right and turned the knob. Locked. I stepped back and kicked it so hard I felt the jar all the way to the top of my head. The door flew back on its hinges, slammed into the wall. It sounded like someone firing a shot.

I went on through and behind the desk, grabbed Frog Man by the shirt and slapped him hard enough he fell off the stool. I kicked him in the leg and he yelled. I picked up the stool and hit him with it across the chest, then threw the stool through a doorway that led into a kitchen. I heard something break in there and a cat made a screeching sound.

"I get mad easy," I said.

"Hell, I see that," he said, and held up a hand for protection. "Take it easy, man. You done hurt me."

"That was the plan."

The look in his eyes made me feel sorry for him. I also felt like an asshole. But that wouldn't keep me from hitting him again if he didn't answer my question. When I get perturbed, I'm not reasonable.

"Where is he?"

"Do I still get the five dollars?"

"No," I said, "now you get my best wishes. You want to lose that?"

"No. No, I don't."

"Then don't play me. Where is he, you toad?"

"He's up in room 52, on the fifth floor."

"Spare key?"

He nodded at a rack of them. The keys were on nails and they all had little wooden pegs on the rings with the keys. Numbers were painted on the pegs. I found one that said 52, took it off the rack.

I said, "You better not be messing with me."

"I ain't. He's up there. He don't never come down. He's been up there a week. He makes noise up there. I don't like it. I run a respectable place."

"Yeah, it's really nice here. And you better not be jerking me."

"I ain't. I promise."

"Good. And, let me give you a tip. Take a bath. And get that shit out of your hair. And those teeth you got ain't looking too good. Pull them. And shoot that fucking cat, or at least get him some place better than the kitchen to piss. It stinks like a toilet in there."

I walked out from behind the desk, out in the hall, and up the flight of stairs in a hurry.

I rushed along the hallway on the fifth floor. It was covered in white linoleum with a gold pattern in it; it creaked and cracked as I walked along.

The end of the hall had a window, and there was a stairwell on that end too. Room 52 was right across from it.

I heard movement on the far end of the stairs. I had an idea what that was all about. About that time, two of the boys I'd seen on the street showed themselves at the top of the stairs, all decked out in their nice hats and such, grinning.

One of them was about the size of a Cadillac, with a gold tooth that shone bright when he smiled. The guy behind him was skinny with his hand in his pocket.

I said, "Well, if it isn't the pimp squad."

"You funny, nigger," said the big man.

"Yeah, well, catch the act now. I'm going to be moving to a new locale."

"You bet you are," said the big man.

"Fat ass behind the glass down there, he ain't paying you enough to mess with me," I said.

"Sometimes, 'cause we're bored, we just like messin'."

"Say you do?"

"Uh-huh," said the skinny one.

It was then I seen the skinny guy pull a razor out of his pocket. I had one, too, but razor work, it's nasty. He kept it closed.

Big guy with the gold tooth flexed his fingers, and made a fist. That made me figure he didn't have a gun or a razor; or maybe he just liked hitting people. I know I did.

They come along toward me then, and the skinny one with the razor flicked it open. I pulled the .45 out from under my coat. "You ought to put that back in your pocket," I said, "save it for shaving."

"Oh, I'm fixing to do some shaving right now," he said.

I pointed the .45 at him.

The big man said, "That's one gun for two men."

"It is," I said, "but I'm real quick with it. And frankly, I know one of you is gonna end up dead. I just ain't sure which one right yet."

"All right then," said the big man, smiling. "That'll be enough." He looked back at the skinny man with the razor. The skinny man put the razor back in his coat pocket and they turned and started down the stairs.

I went over and stood by the stairway and listened. I could hear them walking down, but then all of a sudden, they stopped on the stairs. That's the way I had it figured.

Then I could hear the morons rushing back up. They weren't near as sneaky as they thought they was. The big one was first out of the chute, so to speak, come rushing out of the stairwell and onto the landing. I brought the butt of the .45 down on the back of his head, right where the skull slopes down. He did a kind of frog hop and bounced across the hall and hit his head on the wall, and went down and laid there like his intent all along had been a quick leap and a nap.

Then the other one was there, and he had the razor. He flicked it, and then he saw the .45 in my hand.

"Where did you think this gun was gonna go?" I said. "On vacation?"

I kicked him in the groin hard enough he dropped the razor and went to his knees. I put the .45 back where I got it. I said, "You want some, man?"

He got up, and come at me. I hit him with a right and knocked him clean through the window behind him. Glass sprinkled all over the hallway.

I went over and looked out. He was lying on the fire escape, his head against the railing. He looked right at me.

"You crazy, cocksucker. What if there hadn't been no fire escape?"

"You'd have your ass punched into the bricks. Still might."

He got up quick and clamored down the fire escape like a squirrel. I watched him 'til he got to the ground and went limping away down the alley between some overturned trash cans and a slinking dog.

I picked up his razor and put it in my pocket with the one I already had, walked over and kicked the big man in the head just because I could.

I knocked on the door. No one answered. I could hear sounds from inside. It was similar to what I had heard on that record, but not quite, and it was faint, as if coming from a distance.

No one answered my knock, so I stuck the key in the door and opened it and went straight away inside.

I almost lost my breath when I did.

The air in the room was thick and it stunk of mildew and rot and things long dead. It made those boiled pigs' feet and that shitting cat and that rotten-tooth bastard downstairs smell like perfume.

Tootie was lying on the bed, on his back. His eyes were closed. He was a guy usually dressed to the top, baby, but his shirt was wrinkled and dirty and sweaty at the neck and armpits. His pants were nasty too. He had on his shoes, but no socks. He looked like someone had set him on fire and then beat out the flames with a two-by-four. His face was like a skull, he had lost so much flesh, and he was as bony under his clothes as a skeleton.

Where his hands lay on the sheet, there were bloodstains. His guitar was next to the bed, and there were stacks and stacks of composition notebooks lying on the floor. A couple of them were open and filled with writing. Hell, I didn't even know Tootie could write.

The wall on the far side was marked up in black and red paint; there were all manner of musical notes drawn on it, along with symbols I had never seen before: swiggles and circles and stick-figure drawings. Blood was on the wall, too, most likely from Tootie's bleeding fingers. Two open paint cans, the red and the black, were on the floor with brushes stuck up in them. Paint was splattered on the floor and had dried in humped-up blisters. The guitar had bloodstains all over it.

A record player, plugged in, setting on a nightstand by the bed, was playing that strange music. I went to it right away and picked up the needle and set it aside. And let me tell you, just making my way across the room to get hold of the player was like wading through mud with my ankles tied together. It seemed to me as I got closer to the record, the louder it got, and the more ill I felt. My head throbbed. My heart pounded.

When I had the needle up and the music off, I went over and touched Tootie. He didn't move, but I could see his chest rising and falling. Except for his hands, he didn't seem hurt. He was in a deep sleep. I picked up his right hand and turned it over and looked at it. The fingers were cut deep, like someone had taken a razor to the tips. Right off, I figured that was from playing his guitar. Struck me that to get the sounds he got out of it, he really had to dig in with those fingers. And from the looks of this room, he had been at it nonstop, until recent.

I shook him. His eyes fluttered and finally opened. They were bloodshot and had dark circles around them.

When he saw me, he startled, and his eyes rolled around in his head like those little games kids get where you try to shake the marbles into holes. After a moment, they got straight, and he said, "Ricky?"

That was another reason I hated him. I didn't like being called Ricky.

I said, "Hello, shithead. Your sister's worried sick."

"The music," he said. "Put back on the music."

"You call that music?" I said.

He took a deep breath, rolled out of the bed, nearly knocking me aside. Then I saw him jerk, like he'd seen a truck coming right at him. I turned. I wished it had been a truck.

Let me try and tell you what I saw. I not only saw it, I felt it. It was in the very air we were breathing, getting inside my chest like mice wearing barbed-wire coats. The wall Tootie had painted and drawn all that crap on shook.

And then the wall wasn't a wall at all. It was a long hallway, dark as original sin. There was something moving in there, something that slithered and slid and made smacking sounds like an anxious old drunk about to take his next drink. Stars popped up, greasy stars that didn't remind me of anything I had ever seen in the night sky; a moon the color of a bleeding fish eye was in the background, and it cast a light on something moving toward us.

"Jesus Christ," I said.

"No," Tootie said. "It's not him."

Tootie jumped to the record player, picked up the needle, and put it on. There came that rotten sound I had heard with Alma May, and I knew what I had heard when I first came into the room was the tail end of that same record playing, the part I hadn't heard before.

The music screeched and howled. I bent over and threw up. I fell back against the bed, tried to get up, but my legs were like old pipe cleaners. That record had taken the juice out of me. And then I saw it.

There's no description that really fits. It was . . . a thing. All blanket-wrapped in shadow with sucker mouths and thrashing tentacles and centipede legs mounted on clicking hooves. A bulb-like head plastered all over with red and yellow eyes that seemed to creep. All around it, shadows swirled like water. It had a beak. Well, beaks.

The thing was coming right out of the wall. Tentacles thrashed toward me. One touched me across the cheek. It was like being scalded with hot grease. A shadow come loose of the thing, fell onto the floorboards of the room, turned red and raced across the floor like a gush of blood. Insects and maggots squirmed in the bleeding shadow, and the record hit a high spot so loud and so goddamn strange, I ground my teeth, felt as if my insides were being twisted up like wet wash. And then I passed out.

———

When I came to, the music was still playing. Tootie was bent over me.

"That sound," I said.

"You get used to it," Tootie said, "but the thing can't. Or maybe it can, but just not yet."

I looked at the wall. There was no alleyway. It was just a wall plastered in paint designs and spots of blood.

"And if the music stops?" I said.

"I fell asleep," Tootie said. "Record quits playing, it starts coming."

For a moment I didn't know anything to say. I finally got off the floor and sat on the bed. I felt my cheek where the tentacle hit me. It throbbed and I could feel blisters. I also had a knot on my head where I had fallen.

"Almost got you," Tootie said. "I think you can leave and it won't come after you. Me, I can't. I leave, it follows. It'll finally find me. I guess here is as good as any place."

I was looking at him, listening, but not understanding a damn thing.

The record quit. Tootie started it again. I looked at the wall. Even that blank moment without sound scared me. I didn't want to see that thing again. I didn't even want to think about it.

"I haven't slept in days, until now," Tootie said, coming to sit on the bed. "You hadn't come in, it would have got me, carried me off, taken my soul. But, you can leave. It's my lookout, not yours. . . . I'm always in some kind of shit, ain't I, Ricky?"

"That's the truth."

"This, though, it's the corker. I got to stand up and be a man for once. I got to fight this thing back, and all I got is the music. Like I told you, you can go."

I shook my head. "Alma May sent me. I said I'd bring you back."

It was Tootie's turn to shake his head. "Nope. I ain't goin'. I ain't done nothin' but mess up Sis's life. I ain't gonna do it."

"First responsible thing I ever heard you say," I said.

"Go on," Tootie said. "Leave me to it. I can take care of myself."

"If you don't die of starvation, or pass out from lack of sleep, or need of water, you'll be just fine."

Tootie smiled at me. "Yeah. That's all I got to worry about. I hope it is one of them other things kills me. 'Cause if it comes for me. . . . Well, I don't want to think about it."

"Keep the record going, I'll get something to eat and drink, some coffee. You think you can stay awake a half hour or so?"

"I can, but you're coming back?"

"I'm coming back," I said.

Out in the hallway I saw the big guy was gone. I took the stairs.

When I got back, Tootie had cleaned up the vomit, and was looking through the notebooks. He was sitting on the floor and had them stacked all around him. He was maybe six inches away from the record player. Now and again he'd reach up and start it all over.

Soon as I was in the room, and that sound from the record was snugged up around me, I felt sick. I had gone to a greasy spoon down the street, after I changed a flat tire. One of the boys I'd given a hard time had most likely knifed it. My bet was the lucky sonofabitch who had fallen on the fire escape.

Besides the tire, a half dozen long scratches had been cut into the paint on the passenger's side, and my windshield was knocked in. I got back from the café, I parked what was left of my car behind the hotel, down the street a bit, and walked a block. Car looked so bad now, maybe nobody would want to steal it.

I sat one of the open sacks on the floor by Tootie.

"Both hamburgers are yours," I said. "I got coffee for the both of us here."

I took out a tall, cardboard container of coffee and gave it to him, took the other one for myself. I sat on the bed and sipped. Nothing tasted good in that room with that smell and that sound. But Tootie, he ate like a wolf. He gulped those burgers and coffee like it was air.

When he finished with the second burger, he started up the record again, leaned his back against the bed.

"Coffee or not," he said, "I don't know how long I can stay awake."

"So what you got to do is keep the record playing?" I said.

"Yeah."

"Lay up in bed, sleep for a few hours. I'll keep the record going. You're rested, you got to explain this thing to me, and then we'll figure something out."

"There's nothing to figure," he said. "But, god, I'll take you up on that sleep."

He crawled up in the bed and was immediately out.

I started the record over.

I got up then, untied Tootie's shoes and pulled them off. Hell, like him or not, he was Alma May's brother. And another thing, I wouldn't wish that thing behind the wall on my worst enemy.

I sat on the floor where Tootie had sat and kept restarting the record as I tried to figure things out, which wasn't easy with that music going. I got up from time to time and walked around the room, and then I'd end up back on the floor by the record player, where I could reach it easy.

Between changes, I looked through the composition notebooks. They were full of musical notes mixed with scribbles like the ones on the wall. It was hard to focus with that horrid sound. It was like the air was full of snakes and razors. Got the feeling the music was pushing at something behind that wall. Got the feeling, too, there was something on the other side, pushing back.

It was dark when Tootie woke up. He had slept a good ten hours, and I was exhausted with all that record changing, that horrible sound. I had a headache from looking over those notebooks, and I didn't know any more about them than when I first started.

I went and bought more coffee, brought it back, and we sat on the bed, him changing the record from time to time, us sipping.

I said, "You sure you can't just walk away?"

I was avoiding the real question for some reason. Like, what in hell is that thing, and what is going on? Maybe I was afraid of the answer.

"You saw that thing. I can walk away, all right. And I can run. But wherever I go, it'll find me. So, at some point, I got to face it. Sometimes I make that same record sound with my guitar, give the record a rest. Thing I fear most is the record wearing out."

I gestured at the notebooks on the floor. "What is all that?"

"My notes. My writings. I come here to write some lyrics, some new blues songs."

"Those aren't lyrics, those are notes."

"I know," he said.

"You don't have a music education. You just play."

"Because of the record, I can read music, and I can write things that don't make any sense to me unless it's when I'm writing them, when I'm listening to that music. All those marks, they are musical notes, and the other marks are other kinds of notes, notes for sounds that I couldn't make until a few days back. I didn't even know those sounds were possible. But now, my head is full of the sounds and those marks and all manner of things, and the only way I can rest is to write them down. I wrote on the wall 'cause I thought the marks, the notes themselves, might hold that thing back and I could run. Didn't work."

"None of this makes any sense to me," I said.

"All right," Tootie said. "This is the best I can explain something that's got no explanation. I had some blues boys tell me they once come to this place on the South Side called Cross Road Records. It's a little record shop where the streets cross. It's got all manner of things in it, and it's got this big colored guy with a big white smile and bloodshot eyes that works the joint. They said they'd seen the place, poked their heads in, and even heard Robert Johnson's sounds coming from a player on the counter. There was a big man sitting behind the counter, and he waved them in, but the place didn't seem right, they said, so they didn't go in.

"But, you know me. That sounded like just the place I wanted to go. So, I went. It's where South Street crosses a street called Way Left.

"I go in there, and I'm the only one in the store. There's records everywhere, in boxes, lying on tables. Some got labels, some don't. I'm looking, trying to figure out how you told about anything, and this big fella with the smile comes over to me and starts to talk. He had breath like an unwiped butt, and his face didn't seem so much like black skin as it did black rock.

"He said, 'I know what you're looking for.' He reached in a box, and pulled out a record didn't have no label on it. Thing was, that whole box didn't have labels. I think he's just messing with me, trying to make a sale. I'm ready to go, 'cause he's starting to make my skin crawl. Way he moves ain't natural, you know. It's like he's got something wrong with his feet, but he's still able to move, and quick like. Like he does it between the times you blink your eyes.

"He goes over and puts that record on a player, and it starts up, and it was Robert Johnson. I swear, it was him. Wasn't no one could play like him. It was him. And here's the thing. It wasn't a song I'd ever heard by him. And I thought I'd heard all the music he'd put on wax."

Tootie sipped at his coffee. He looked at the wall a moment, and then changed the record again.

I said, "Swap out spots, and I'll change it. You sip and talk. Tell me all of it."
We did that, and Tootie continued.

"Well, one thing comes to another, and he starts talking me up good, and finally I ask him how much for the record. He looks at me, and he says, 'For you, all you got to give me is a little blue soul. And when you come back, you got to buy something with a bit more of it 'til it's all gone and I got it. 'Cause you will be back.'

"I figured he was talking about me playing my guitar for him, 'cause I'd told him I was a player, you know, while we was talking. I told him I had my guitar in a room I was renting, and I was on foot, and it would take me all day to get my guitar and get back, so I'd have to pass on that deal. Besides, I was about tapped out of money. I had a place I was supposed to play that evening, but until then, I had maybe three dollars and some change in my pocket. I had the rent on this room paid up all week, and I hadn't been there but two days. I tell him all that, and he says, 'Oh, that's all right. I know you can play. I can tell about things like that. What I mean is, you give me a drop of blood and a promise, and you can have that record.' Right then, I started to walk out, 'cause I'm thinking, this guy is nutty as fruitcake with an extra dose of nuts, but I want that record. So, I tell him, sure, I'll give him a drop of blood. I won't lie none to you, Ricky, I was thinking about nabbing that record and making a run with it. I wanted it that bad. So a drop of blood, that didn't mean nothin'.

"He pulls a record needle out from behind the counter, and he comes over and pokes my finger with it, sudden like, while I'm still trying to figure how he got over to me that fast, and he holds my hand and lets blood drip on—get this—the record. It flows into the grooves.

"He says, 'Now, you promise me your blues-playing soul is mine when you die.'

"I thought it was just talk, you know, so I told him he could have it. He says, 'When you hear it, you'll be able to play it. And when you play it, sometime when you're real good on it, it'll start to come, like a rat easing its nose into hot dead meat. It'll start to come.'

"'What will?' I said. 'What are you talking about?'

"He says, 'You'll know.'

"Next thing I know, he's over by the door, got it open and he's smiling at me, and I swear, I thought for a moment I could see right through him. Could see his skull and bones. I've got the record in my hand, and I'm walking out, and as soon as I do, he shuts the door and I hear the lock turn.

"My first thought was, I got to get this blood out of the record grooves, 'cause that crazy bastard has just given me a lost Robert Johnson song for nothing. I took out a kerchief, pulled the record out of the sleeve, and went to wiping. The blood wouldn't come out. It was in the notches, you know.

"I went back to my room here, and I tried a bit of warm water on the blood in the grooves, but it still wouldn't come out. I was mad as hell, figured the record wouldn't play, way that blood had hardened in the grooves. I put it on and thought maybe the needle would wear the stuff out, but as soon as it was on the player and the needle hit it, it started sounding just the way it had in the store. I sat on the bed and listened to it, three or four times, and then I got my guitar and tried to play what was being played, knowing I couldn't do it, 'cause though I knew that sound wasn't electrified, it sounded like it was. But, here's the thing. I could do it. I could play it. And I could see the notes in my head, and my head got filled up with them. I went out and bought those notebooks, and I wrote it all down just so my head wouldn't explode, 'cause every time I heard that record, and tried to play it, them notes would cricket-hop in my skull."

All the while we had been talking, I had been replaying the record.

"I forgot all about the gig that night," Tootie said. "I sat here until morning playing. By noon the next day, I sounded just like that record. By late afternoon, I started to get kind of sick. I can't explain it, but I was feeling that there was something trying to tear through somewhere, and it scared me and my insides knotted up.

"I don't know any better way of saying it than that. It was such a strong feeling. Then, while I was playing, the wall there, it come apart the way you seen it, and I seen that thing. It was just a wink of a look. But there it was. In all its terrible glory.

"I quit playing, and the wall wobbled back in place and closed up. I thought, damn, I need to eat or nap, or something. And I did. Then I was back on that guitar. I could play like crazy, and I started going off on that song, adding here and there. It wasn't like it was coming from me, though. It was like I was getting help from somewhere.

"Finally, with my fingers bleeding and cramped and aching, and my voice gone raspy from singing, I quit. Still, I wanted to hear it, so I put on the record. And it wasn't the same no more. It was Johnson, but the words was strange, not English. Sounded like some kind of chant, and I knew then that Johnson was in that record, as sure as I was in this room, and that that chanting and that playing was opening up a hole for that thing in the wall. It was the way that fella had said. It was like a rat working its nose through red-hot meat, and now it felt like I was the meat. Next time I played the record, the voice on it wasn't Johnson's. It was mine.

"I had had enough, so I got the record and took it back to that shop. The place was the same as before, and like before, I was the only one in there. He looked at me, and comes over, and says, 'You already want to undo the deal. I can tell. They all do. But that ain't gonna happen.'

"I gave him a look like I was gonna jump on him and beat his ass, but he gave me a look back, and I went weak as kitten.

"He smiled at me, and pulls out another record from that same box, and he takes the one I gave him and puts it back, and says, 'You done made a deal, but for a lick of your soul, I'll let you have this. See, you done opened the path, now that rat's got to work on that meat. It don't take no more record or you playing for that to happen. Rat's gotta eat now, no matter what you do.'

"When he said that, he picks up my hand and looks at my cut-up fingers from playing, and he laughs so loud everything in the store shakes, and he squeezes my fingers until they start to bleed.

"'A lick of my soul?' I asked.

"And then he pushed the record in my hand, and if I'm lying, I'm dying, he sticks out his tongue, and it's long as an old rat snake and black as a hole in the ground, and he licks me right around the neck. When he's had a taste, he smiles and shivers, like he's just had something cool to drink."

Tootie paused to unfasten his shirt and peel it down a little. There was a spot halfway around his neck like someone had worked him over with sandpaper.

"'A taste,' he says, and then he shoves this record in my hand, which is bleeding from where he squeezed my fingers. Next thing I know, I'm looking at the record, and it's thick, and I touch it, and it's two records, back to back. He says, 'I give you that extra one 'cause you tasted mighty good, and maybe it'll let you get a little more rest that way, if you got a turntable drop. Call me generous and kind in my old age.'

"Wasn't nothing for it but to take the records and come back here. I didn't have no intention of playing it. I almost threw it away. But by then, that thing in the wall, wherever it is, was starting to stick through. Each time the hole was bigger and I could see more of it, and that red shadow was falling out on the floor. I thought about running, but I didn't want to just let it loose, and I knew, deep down, no matter where I went, it would come too.

"I started playing that record in self-defense. Pretty soon, I'm playing it on the guitar. When I got scared enough, got certain enough that thing was coming through, I played hard, and that hole would close, and that thing would go back where it come from. For a while.

"I figured, though, I ought to have some insurance. You see, I played both them records, and they was the same thing, and it was my voice, and I hadn't never recorded or even heard them songs before. I knew then what was on those notes I had written, what had come to me was the counter song to the one I had been playing first. I don't know if that was just some kind of joke that record store fella had played on me, but I knew it was magic of a sort. He had give me a song to let it in and he had give me another song to hold it back. It was amusing to him, I'm sure.

"I thought I had the thing at bay, so I took that other copy, went to the post office, mailed it to Alma, case something happened to me. I guess I thought it was self-defense for her, but there was another part was proud of what I had done. What I was able to do. I could play anything now, and I didn't even need to think about it. Regular blues, it was a snap. Anything on that guitar was easy, even things you ought not to be able to play on one. Now, I realize it ain't me. It's something else out there.

"But when I come back from mailing, I bought me some paint and brushes, thought I'd write the notes and such on the wall. I did that, and I was ready to pack and go roaming some more, showing off my new skills, and all of a sudden, the thing, it's pushing through. It had gotten stronger 'cause I hadn't been playing the sounds, man. I put on the record, and I pretty much been at it ever since.

"It was all that record fella's game, you see. I got to figuring he was the devil, or something like him. He had me playing a game to keep that thing out, and to keep my soul. But it was a three-minute game, six if I'd have kept that second record and put it on the drop. If I was playing on the guitar, I could just work from the end of that record back to the front of it, playing it over and over. But it wore me down. Finally, I started playing the record nonstop. And I have for days.

"The fat man downstairs, he'd come up for the rent, but as soon as he'd use his key and crack that door, hear that music, he'd get gone. So here I am, still playing, with nothing left but to keep on playing, or get my soul sucked up by that thing and delivered to the record store man."

Tootie minded the record, and I went over to where he told me the record store was with the idea to put a boot up the guy's ass, or a .45 slug in his noggin. I found South Street, but not Way South. The other street that should have been Way South was called Back Water. There wasn't a store, either, just an empty, unlocked building. I opened the door and went inside. There was dust everywhere, and I could see where some tables had been, 'cause their leg marks was in the dust. But anyone or anything that had been there was long gone.

I went back to the hotel, and when I got there, Tootie was just about asleep. The record was turning on the turntable without any sound. I looked at the wall, and I could see the beak of that thing, chewing at it. I put the record on, and this time, when it come to the end, the thing was still chewing. I played it another time, and another, and the thing finally went away. It was getting stronger.

I woke Tootie up, said, "You know, we're gonna find out if this thing can outrun my souped-up Chevy."

"Ain't no use," Tootie said.

"Then we ain't got nothing to lose," I said.

We grabbed up the record and his guitar, and we was downstairs and out on the street faster than you can snap your fingers. As we passed where the toad was, he saw me and got up quick and went into the kitchen and closed the door. If I'd had time, I'd have beat his ass on general principles.

When we walked to where I had parked my car, it was sitting on four flats and the side windows was knocked out and the aerial was snapped off. The record Alma May had given me was still there, lying on the seat. I got it and put it against the other one in my hand. It was all I could do.

As for the car, I was gonna drive that Chevy back to East Texas like I was gonna fly back on a sheet of wet newspaper.

Now, I got to smellin' that smell. One that was in the room. I looked at the sky. The sun was kind of hazy. Green even. The air around us trembled, like it was scared of something. It was heavy, like a blanket. I grabbed Tootie by the arm, pulled him down the street. I spied a car at a curb that I thought could run, a V-8 Ford. I kicked the back side window out, reached through and got the latch.

I slid across the seat and got behind the wheel. Tootie climbed in on the passenger side. I bent down and worked some wires under the dash loose with my fingers and my razor, hot-wired the car. The motor throbbed and we was out of there.

It didn't make any kind of sense, but as we was cruising along, behind us it was getting dark. It was like chocolate pudding in a big wad rolling after us. Stars was popping up in it. They seemed more like eyes than stars. There was a bit of a moon, slightly covered over in what looked like a red fungus.

I drove that Ford fast as I could. I was hitting the needle at a hundred and ten. Didn't see a car on the highway. Not a highway cop, not an old lady on the way to the store. Where the hell was everybody? The highway looped up and down like the bottom was trying to fall out from under us.

To make it all short, I drove hard and fast, and stopped once for gas, having the man fill it quick. I gave him a bill that was more than the gas was worth, and he grinned at me as we burned rubber getting away. I don't think he could see what we could see—that dark sky with that thing in it. It was like you had to hear the music to see the thing existed, or for it to have any effect in your life. For him, it was daylight and fine and life was good.

By the time I hit East Texas, there was smoke coming from under that stolen Ford's hood. We came down a hill, and it was daylight in front of us, and behind us the dark was rolling in; it was splittin', making a kind of corridor, and there was that beaked thing, that . . . whatever it was. It was bigger than before and it was squirming its way out of the night sky like a weasel working its way under a fence. I tried to convince myself it was all in my head, but I wasn't convinced enough to stop and find out.

I made the bottom of the hill, in sight of the road that turned off to Alma May's. I don't know why I felt going there mattered, but it was something

I had in my mind. Make it to Alma May's, and deliver on my agreement, bring her brother into the house. Course, I hadn't really thought that thing would or could follow us.

It was right then the car engine blew in an explosion that made the hood bunch up from the impact of thrown pistons.

The car died and coasted onto the road that led to Alma May's house. We could see the house, standing in daylight. But even that light was fading as the night behind us eased on in.

I jerked open the car door, snatched the records off the back seat, and yelled to Tootie to start running. He nabbed his guitar, and a moment later, we were both making tracks for Alma May's.

Looking back, I saw there was a moon back there, and stars, too, but mostly there was that thing, full of eyes and covered in sores and tentacles and legs and things I can't even describe. It was like someone had thrown critters and fish and bugs and beaks and all manner of disease into a bowl and whipped it together with a whipping spoon.

When we got to Alma May's, I beat on the door. She opened it, showing a face that told me she thought I was knocking too hard, but then she looked over my shoulder, and went pale, almost as if her skin was white. She had heard the music, so she could see it too.

Slamming the door behind us, I went straight to the record player. Alma May was asking all kinds of questions, screaming them out, really. First to me, then to Tootie. I told her to shut up. I jerked one of the records out of its sleeve, put it on the turntable, lifted the needle, and—

—the electricity crackled and it went dark. There was no playing anything on that player. Outside, the world was lit by that blood-red moon.

The door blew open. Tentacles flicked in, knocked over an end table. Some knickknacks fell and busted on the floor. Big as the monster was, it was squeezing through, causing the door frame to crack, the wood breaking sounded like someone cracking whips with both hands.

Me and Alma May, without even thinking about it, backed up. The red shadow, bright as a campfire, fled away from the monster and started flowing across the floor, bugs and worms squirming in it.

But not toward us.

It was running smooth as an oil spill toward the opposite side of the room. I got it then. It didn't just want through to this side. It wanted to finish off that deal Tootie had made with the record store owner. Tootie had said it all along, but it really hit me then. It didn't want me and Alma at all.

It had come for Tootie's soul.

There was a sound so sharp I threw my hands over my ears, and Alma May went to the floor. It was Tootie's guitar. He had hit it so hard, it sounded electrified. The pulse of that one hard chord made me weak in the knees. It was a hundred times louder than the record. It was beyond belief, and beyond human ability. But, it was Tootie.

The red shadow stopped, rolled back like a tongue.

The guitar was going through its paces now. The thing at the doorway recoiled slightly, and then Tootie yelled, "Come get me. Come have me. Leave them alone."

I looked, and there in the faint glow of the red moonlight through the window, I saw Tootie's shadow lift that guitar high above his head by the neck, and down it came, smashing hard into the floor with an explosion of wood and a springing of strings.

The bleeding shadow came quickly then. Across the floor and onto Tootie. He screamed. He screamed like someone having the flesh slowly burned off. Then the beast came through the door as if shot out of a cannon.

Tentacles slashed, a million feet scuttled, and those beaks came down, ripping at Tootie like a savage dog tearing apart a rag doll. Blood flew all over the room. It was like a huge strawberry exploded.

Then another thing happened. A blue mist floated up from the floor, from what was left of Tootie, and for just the briefest of moments, I saw Tootie's face in that blue mist; the face smiled a toothless kind of smile, showing nothing but a dark hole where his mouth was. Then, like someone sniffing steam off soup, the blue mist was sucked into the beaks of that thing, and Tootie and his soul were done with.

The thing turned its head and looked at us. I started to pull my .45, but I knew there wasn't any point to it. It made a noise like a thousand rocks and broken automobiles tumbling down a cliff made of gravel and glass, and it began to suck back toward the door. It went out with a snapping sound, like a wet towel being popped. The bleeding shadow ran across the floor after it, eager to catch up, a lapdog hoping for a treat.

The door slammed as the thing and its shadow went out, and then the air got clean and the room got bright.

I looked where Tootie had been.

Nothing.

Not a bone.

Not a drop of blood.

I raised the window and looked out.

It was morning.

No clouds in the sky.

The sun looked like the sun.

Birds were singing.

The air smelled clean as a newborn's breath.

I turned back to Alma May. She was slowly getting up from where she had dropped to the floor.

"It just wanted him," I said, having a whole different kind of feeling about Tootie than I had before. "He gave himself to it. To save you, I think."

She ran into my arms and I hugged her tight. After a moment, I let go of her. I got the records and put them together. I was going to snap them across my knee. But I never got the chance. They went wet in my hands, came apart and hit the floor and ran through the floorboards like black water, and that was all she wrote.

This one was ripped from *The Nightrunners* before it sold and turned into a short story. But before that, it was taken from *The Nightrunners* and revised as a synopsis for a possible episode of *Amazing Stories*.

Richard Matheson was briefly a story editor there. He liked my synopsis and suggested a few changes, I followed his instructions, and it looked like we were off and running.

But before I could make it to contract, the series quit buying stories, and the show was canceled.

I took the synopsis and revised it into a story. It was Richard's idea to end the story with a song. I kept that idea, and I give him full credit for it.

Not from Detroit

UTSIDE IT WAS cold and wet and windy. The storm rattled the shack, slid like razor blades through the window, door and wall cracks, but it wasn't enough to make any difference to the couple. Sitting before the crumbling fireplace in their creaking rocking chairs, shawls across their knees, fingers entwined, they were warm.

A bucket behind them near the kitchen sink collected water dripping from a hole in the roof.

The drops had long since passed the noisy stage of sounding like steel bolts falling on tin, and were now gentle plops.

The old couple were husband and wife, had been for over fifty years. They were comfortable with one another and seldom spoke. Mostly they rocked and looked at the fire as it flickered shadows across the room.

Finally Margie spoke. "Alex," she said, "I hope I die before you."

Alex stopped rocking. "Did you say what I thought you did?"

"I said, I hope I die before you." She wouldn't look at him, just the fire. "It's selfish, I know, but I hope I do. I don't want to live on with you gone. It would be like cutting out my heart and making me walk around. Like one of them zombies."

"There are the children," he said. "If I died, they'd take you in."

"I'd just be in the way. I love them, but I don't want to do that. They got their own lives. I'd just as soon die before you. That would make things simple."

"Not simple for me," Alex said. "I don't want you to die before me. So how about that? We're both selfish, aren't we?"

She smiled. "Well, it ain't a thing to talk about before bedtime, but it's been on my mind, and I had to get it out."

"Been thinking on it, too, honey. Only natural we would. We ain't spring chickens anymore."

"You're healthy as a horse, Alex Brooks. Mechanic work you did all your life kept you strong. Me, I got the bursitis and the miseries and I'm tired all the time. Got the old age bad."

Alex started rocking again. They stared into the fire. "We're going to go together, hon," he said. "I feel it. That's the way it ought to be for folks like us."

"I wonder if I'll see him coming. Death, I mean."

"What?"

"My grandma used to tell me she seen him the night her daddy died."

"You've never told me this."

"Ain't a subject I like. But Grandma said this man in a black buggy slowed down out front of their house, cracked his whip three times, and her daddy was gone in instants. And she said she'd heard her grandfather tell how he had seen Death when he was a boy. Told her it was early morning and he was up, about to start his chores, and when he went outside he seen this man dressed in black walk by the house and stop out front. He was carrying a stick over his shoulder with a checkered bundle tied to it, and he looked at the house and snapped his fingers three times. A moment later they found my grandfather's brother, who had been sick with the smallpox, dead in bed."

"Stories, hon. Stories. Don't get yourself worked up over a bunch of old tall tales. Here, I'll heat us some milk."

Alex stood, laid the shawl in the chair, went over to put milk in a pan and heat it. As he did, he turned to watch Margie's back. She was still staring into the fire, only she wasn't rocking. She was just watching the blaze and, Alex knew, thinking about dying.

After the milk they went to bed, and soon Margie was asleep, snoring like a busted chainsaw. Alex found he could not rest. It was partly due to the storm; it had picked up in intensity. But it was mostly because of what Margie had said about dying. It made him feel lonesome.

Like her, he wasn't so much afraid of dying, as he was of being left alone. She had been his heartbeat for fifty years, and without her, he would only be going through motions of life, not living.

God, he prayed silently. *When we go, let us go together.* He turned to look at Margie. Her face looked unlined and strangely young. He was glad she could turn off most anything with sleep. He, on the other hand, could not.

Maybe I'm just hungry.

He slid out of bed, pulled on his pants, shirt, and house shoes—those silly things with the rabbit face and ears his granddaughter had bought him. He padded silently to the kitchen. It was not only the kitchen, it served as a den, living room, and dining room. The house was only three rooms and a closet, and one of the rooms was a small bathroom. It was times like this that Alex thought he could have done better by Margie. Gotten her a bigger house, for one thing. It was the same house where they had raised their kids, the babies sleeping in a crib here in the kitchen.

He sighed. No matter how hard he had worked, he seemed to stay in the same place. A poor place.

He went to the refrigerator and took out a half gallon of milk, drank directly from the carton.

He put the carton back and watched the water drip into the bucket. It made him mad to see it. He had let the little house turn into a shack since he retired, and there was no real excuse for it. Surely, he wasn't that tired. It was a wonder Margie didn't complain more.

Well, there was nothing to do about it tonight. But he vowed that when dry weather came, he wouldn't forget about it this time. He'd get up there and fix that damn leak.

Quietly, he rummaged a pan from under the cabinet. He'd have to empty the bucket now if he didn't want it to run over before morning. He ran a little water into the pan before substituting it for the bucket so the drops wouldn't sound so loud.

He opened the front door, went out on the porch, carrying the bucket. He looked out at his mud-pie yard and his old, red wrecker, his white logo on the side of the door faded with time: ALEX BROOKS WRECKING AND MECHANIC SERVICE.

Tonight, looking at the old war-horse, he felt sadder than ever. He missed using it the way it was meant to be used. For work. Now it was nothing more than transportation. Before he retired, his tools and hands made a living. Now nothing. Picking up a Social Security check was all that was left.

Leaning over the edge of the porch, he poured the water into the bare and empty flower bed. When he lifted his head and looked at his yard again, and beyond to Highway 59, he saw a light. Headlights, actually, looking fuzzy in the rain, like filmed-over amber eyes. They were way out there on the highway, coming from the south, winding their way toward him, moving fast.

Alex thought that whoever was driving that crate was crazy. Cruising like that on bone-dry highways with plenty of sunshine would have been dangerous, but in this weather, they were asking for a crackup.

As the car neared, he could see it was long, black, and strangely shaped. He'd never seen anything like it, and he knew cars fairly well. This didn't look like something off the assembly line from Detroit. It had to be foreign.

Miraculously, the car slowed without so much as a quiver or screech of brakes and tires. In fact, Alex could not even hear its motor, just the faint whispering sound of rubber on wet cement.

The car came even with the house just as lightning flashed, and in that instant, Alex got a good look at the driver, or at least the shape of the driver outlined in the flash, and he saw that it was a man with a cigar in his mouth and a bowler hat on his head. And the head was turning toward the house.

The lightning flash died, and now there was only the dark shape of the car and the red tip of the cigar jutting at the house. Alex felt stalactites of ice dripping down from the roof of his skull, extended through his body and out of the soles of his feet.

The driver hit down on his horn, three sharp blasts that pricked at Alex's mind.

Honk. *(visions of blooming roses, withering going black)*

Honk. *(funerals remembered, loved ones in boxes, going down)*

Honk. *(worms crawling through rotten flesh)*

Then came a silence louder than the horn blasts. The car picked up speed again. Alex watched as its taillights winked away in the blackness. The chill became less chill. The stalactites in his mind melted away.

But as he stood there, Margie's words of earlier that evening came at him in a rush: "Seen Death once . . . buggy slowed down out front . . . cracked his whip *three times* . . . man looked at the house, snapped his fingers *three times* . . . found dead a moment later. . . ."

Alex's throat felt as if a pine knot had lodged there. The bucket slipped from his fingers, clattered on the porch and rolled into the flower bed. He turned into the house and walked briskly toward the bedroom,

(can't be, just a wives' tale)

his hands vibrating with fear,

(just a crazy coincidence)

Margie wasn't snoring.

Alex grabbed her shoulder, shook her.

Nothing.

He rolled her on her back and screamed her name.

Nothing.

"Oh, baby. No."

He felt for her pulse.

None.

He put an ear to her chest, listening for a heartbeat (the other half of his life bongos), and there was none.

Quiet. Perfectly quiet.

"You can't . . . ," Alex said. "You can't . . . we're supposed to go together . . . got to be that way."

And then it came to him. He had *seen* Death drive by, had *seen* him heading on down the highway.

He came to his feet, snatched his coat from the back of the chair, raced toward the front door. "You won't have her," he said aloud. "You won't."

Grabbing the wrecker keys from the nail beside the door, he leaped to the porch and dashed out into the cold and the rain.

A moment later he was heading down the highway, driving fast and crazy in pursuit of the strange car.

The wrecker was old and not built for speed, but since he kept it well-tuned and it had new tires, it ran well over the wet highway. Alex kept pushing the pedal gradually until it met the floor. Faster and faster and faster.

After an hour, he saw Death.

Not the man himself but the license plate. Personalized and clear in his headlights. It read: DEATH/EXEMPT.

The wrecker and the strange black car were the only ones on the road. Alex closed in on him, honked his horn. Death tootled back (not the same horn sound he had given in front of Alex's house), stuck his arm out the window and waved the wrecker around.

Alex went, and when he was alongside the car, he turned his head to look at Death. He could still not see him clearly, but he could make out the shape of his bowler, and when Death turned to look at him, he could see the glowing tip of the cigar, like a bloody bullet wound.

Alex whipped hard right into the car, and Death swerved to the right, then back onto the road. Alex rammed again. The black car's tires hit roadside gravel and Alex swung closer, preventing it from returning to the highway. He rammed yet another time, and the car went into the grass alongside the road, skidded, and went sailing down an embankment and into a tree.

Alex braked carefully, backed off the road and got out of the wrecker. He reached a small pipe wrench and a big crescent wrench out from under the seat, slipped the pipe wrench into his coat pocket for insurance, then went charging down the embankment waving the crescent.

Death opened his door and stepped out. The rain had subsided and the moon was peeking through the clouds like a shy child through gossamer curtains. Its light hit Death's round pink face and made it look like a waxed pomegranate. His cigar hung from his mouth by a tobacco strand.

Glancing up the embankment, he saw an old but strong-looking Black man brandishing a wrench and wearing bunny slippers, charging down at him.

Spitting out the ruined cigar, Death stepped forward, grabbed Alex's wrist and forearm, twisted. The old man went up and over; the wrench went flying from his hand. Alex came down hard on his back, the breath bursting out of him in spurts.

Death leaned over Alex. Up close, Alex could see that the pink face was slightly pocked and that some of the pinkness was due to makeup. That was rich. Death was vain about his appearance. He was wearing a black T-shirt, pants and sneakers, and of course his derby, which had neither been stirred by the wreck nor by the jujitsu maneuver.

"What's with you, man?" Death asked.

Alex wheezed, tried to catch his breath. "You can't . . . have . . . her."

"Who? What are you talking about?"

"Don't play . . . dumb with me." Alex raised up on one elbow, his wind returning. "You're Death and you took my Margie's soul."

Death straightened. "So you know who I am. All right. But what of it? I'm only doing my job."

"It ain't her time."

"My list says it is, and my list is never wrong."

Alex felt something hard pressing against his hip, realized what it was. The pipe wrench. Even the throw Death had put on him had not hurled it from his coat pocket. It had lodged there and the pocket had shifted beneath his hip, making his old bones hurt all the worse.

Alex made as to roll over, freed the pocket beneath him, shot his hand inside and produced the pipe wrench. He hurled it at Death, struck him just below the brim of the bowler and sent him stumbling back. This time the bowler fell off. Death's forehead was bleeding.

Before Death could collect himself, Alex was up and rushing. He used his head as a battering ram and struck Death in the stomach, knocking him to the ground. He put both knees on Death's arms, pinning them, clenched his throat with his strong, old hands.

"I ain't never hurt nobody before," Alex said. "Don't want to now. I didn't want to hit you with that wrench, but you give Margie back."

Death's eyes showed no expression at first, but slowly a light seemed to go on behind them. He easily pulled his arms out from under Alex's knees, reached up, took hold of the old man's wrists, and pulled the hands away from his throat.

"You old rascal," Death said. "You outsmarted me."

Death flopped Alex over on his side, then stood up. Grinning, he turned, stooped to recover his bowler, but he never laid a hand on it.

Alex moved like a crab, scissoring his legs, and caught Death from above and behind his knees, twisted, brought him down on his face.

Death raised up on his palms and crawled from behind Alex's legs like a snake, effortlessly. This time he grabbed the hat and put it on his head and stood up. He watched Alex carefully.

"I don't frighten you much, do I?" Death asked.

Alex noted that the wound on Death's forehead had vanished. There wasn't even a drop of blood. "No," Alex said. "You don't frighten me much. I just want my Margie back."

"All right," Death said.

Alex sat bolt upright.

"What?"

"I said, all right. For a time. Not many have outsmarted me, pinned me to the ground. I give you credit, and you've got courage. I like that. I'll give her back. For a time. Come here."

Death walked over to the car that was not from Detroit. Alex got to his feet and followed. Death took the keys out of the ignition, moved to the trunk, worked the key in the lock. It popped up with a hiss.

Inside were stacks and stacks of matchboxes. Death moved his hand over them, like a careful man selecting a special vegetable at the supermarket. His fingers came to rest on a matchbox that looked to Alex no different than the others.

Death handed Alex the matchbox. "Her soul's in here, old man. You stand over her bed, open the box. Okay?"

"That's it?"

"That's it. Now get out of here before I change my mind. And remember, I'm giving her back to you. But just for a while."

Alex started away, holding the matchbox carefully. As he walked past Death's car, he saw the dents he had knocked in the side with his wrecker were popping out. He turned to look at Death, who was closing the trunk.

"Don't suppose you'll need a tow out of here?"

Death smiled thinly. "Not hardly."

Alex stood over their bed, the bed where they had loved, slept, talked and dreamed. He stood there with the matchbox in his hand, his eyes on Margie's cold face. He ever so gently eased the box open. A small flash of blue light, like Peter Pan's friend Tinkerbell, rushed out of it and hit Margie's lips. She made a sharp inhaling sound and her chest rose. Her eyes came open. She turned and looked at Alex and smiled.

"My lands, Alex. What are you doing there, and half dressed? What have you been up to . . . is that a matchbox?"

Alex tried to speak, but he found that he could not. All he could do was grin.

"Have you gone nuts?" she asked.

"Maybe a little." He sat down on the bed and took her hand. "I love you, Margie."

"And I love you . . . you been drinking?"

"No."

Then came the overwhelming sound of Death's horn. One harsh blast that shook the house, and the headbeams shone brightly through the window and the cracks lit up the shack like a cheap nightclub act.

"Who in the world?" Margie asked.

"Him. But he said . . . stay here."

Alex got his shotgun out of the closet. He went out on the porch. Death's car was pointed toward the house, and the headbeams seemed to hold Alex, like a fly in butter.

Death was standing on the bottom step, waiting.

Alex pointed the shotgun at him. "You git. You gave her back. You gave your word."

"And I kept it. But I said for a while."

"That wasn't any time at all."

"It was all I could give. My present."

"Short time like that's worse than no time at all."

"Be good about it, Alex. Let her go. I got records and they have to be kept. I'm going to take her anyway, you understand that?"

"Not tonight, you ain't." Alex pulled back the hammers on the shotgun. "Not tomorrow night neither. Not anytime soon."

"That gun won't do you any good, Alex. You know that. You can't stop Death. I can stand here and snap my fingers three times, or click my tongue, or go back to the car and honk my horn, and she's as good as mine. But I'm trying to reason with you, Alex. You're a brave man. I did you a favor because you bested me. I didn't want to just take her back without telling you. That's why I came here to talk. But she's got to go. Now."

Alex lowered the shotgun. "Can't . . . can't you take me in her place? You can do that, can't you?"

"I . . . I don't know. It's highly irregular."

"Yeah, you can do that. Take me. Leave Margie."

"Well, I suppose."

The screen door creaked open and Margie stood there in her housecoat.

"You're forgetting, Alex, I don't want to be left alone."

"Go in the house, Margie," Alex said.

"I know who this is: I heard you talking, Mr. Death. I don't want you taking my Alex. I'm the one you came for. I ought to have the right to go."

There was a pause, no one speaking. Then Alex said, "Take both of us. You can do that, can't you? I know I'm on that list of yours, and pretty high up. Man my age couldn't have too many years left. You can take me a little before my time, can't you? Well, can't you?"

Margie and Alex sat in their rocking chairs, their shawls over their knees. There was no fire in the fireplace. Behind them the bucket collected water and outside the wind whistled. They held hands. Death stood in front of them. He was holding a King Edward cigar box.

"You're sure of this?" Death asked. "You don't both have to go."

Alex looked at Margie, then back at Death.

"We're sure," he said. "Do it."

Death nodded. He opened the cigar box and held it out on one palm. He used his free hand to snap his fingers.

Once. *(the wind picked up, howled)*

Twice. *(the rain beat like drumsticks on the roof)*

Three times. *(lightning ripped and thunder roared)*

"And in you go," Death said.

The bodies of Alex and Margie slumped and their heads fell together between the rocking chairs. Their fingers were still entwined.

Death put the box under his arm and went out to the car. The rain beat on his derby hat and the wind sawed at his bare arms and T-shirt. He didn't seem to mind.

Opening the trunk, he started to put the box inside, then hesitated.

He closed the trunk.

"Damn," he said, "if I'm not getting to be a sentimental old fool."

He opened the box. Two blue lights rose out of it, elongated, touched ground. They took on the shape of Alex and Margie. They glowed against the night.

"Want to ride up front?" Death asked.

"That would be nice," Margie said.

"Yes, nice," Alex said.

Death opened the door and Alex and Margie slid inside. Death climbed in behind the wheel. He checked the clipboard dangling from the dash. There was a woman in a Tyler hospital, dying of brain damage. That would be his next stop.

He put the clipboard down and started the car that was not from Detroit.

"Sounds well-tuned," Alex said.

"I try to keep it that way," Death said.

They drove out of there then, and as they went, Death broke into song. "Row, row, row your boat, gently down the stream," and Margie and Alex chimed in with, "Merrily, merrily, merrily, merrily, life is but a dream."

Off they went down the highway, the taillights fading, the song dying, the black metal of the car melting into the fabric of night, and then there was only the whispery sound of good tires on wet cement and finally not even that. Just the blowing sound of the wind and the rain.

After "The Hoodoo Man and the Midnight Train," I was inspired to write more weird Westerns. And I did—this one. It was for a new book company that has since changed names. It was done in chapbook form and sold briskly.

I loved writing it. I used my character the Reverend Mercer. There is one book of stories about him, and now that I have renewed vigor in the weird Western department, I suspect that there will be others.

I have always been interested in the Wendigo, a Native American spirit monster. I first heard of the Wendigo in a story titled after the creature by Algernon Blackwood.

Blackwood had a brilliant, quiet, and creepy approach. I like to think that I have a loud creepy approach with this one. It was so much fun.

The Hungry Snow

In memory of Robert E. Howard,
Lord of the Pulps

reat gouts of blood on the snow. The cracking of ice.
The wind so cold.
That's what he would remember.
And IT.

In the cold, wet, blowing snow, the Reverend Jedidiah Mercer rode his horse and led his pack mule into the midst of it. It was as if God, the mean dictator for whom he worked, had taken the world in hand and filled it with slush and ice and shook it like a petulant child.

When at last the wind shifted, he could see the world again. He was high up in the Rockies. The tips of mountains were coated in snow and the trail he was on was narrow. It was easy enough to traverse when his vision was clear, but as he rounded a precarious curve, the snow dumped again, forcing him to pull his mount and lead his mule close to the side of a rock wall. Only a few feet away to his right was a deep drop-off that fell into a cluster of snow-coated trees, and between the boughs of those trees was a long, cold drop and eventually a hard bottom of solid rock.

He cinched up the lead rope on the mule and managed it around the curve of the mountain. The wind shifted again, and for a brief moment there was a part in the blowing snow. He could see where the trail rose up and near the top of it was a red haze, like a burning match seen through greasy glass. It was a large cave and there was fire inside. There were people as well, squatted together around the fire. He only glimpsed them, and then the snow blew hard and they were wiped from view.

The Reverend heard a dribbling sound, realized it was falling gravel, small rocks, slipping ice, and then he felt a tug on the mule's rope, and then the rope burned through his hands. The beast was sliding over the side of the trail and away into oblivion. Within an instant, the rope was gone and the Reverend held nothing but a clenched fist. It felt less like the mule slid away, and more like it was snatched away.

Most of his supplies for crossing the Rockies on his way farther west had been strapped on that mule's back. Now those supplies and his mule were at the bottom of a cliff. The mule had not made a sound.

The Reverend reined his mount to a stop, slipped off his horse, and led the beast. He did this by putting one hand out to his left to feel the rock wall, clutched the reins in his other. He kept as close to the rock wall as possible, aware there could still be surprises. Breaks in the trail, a narrowing of it, but to stop moving and stay where they were was sheer frozen death.

He felt he had to make it up to the cave where the fire burned, place himself among the people there. The cave might help him and his horse ride out the blizzard.

It was like a blind man threading a needle, but he managed up the trail, and soon he saw the light of the fire again, a crimson glow against the snow. The sight of it would come and go as the wind puffed and gusted, wild and white, wet and cold.

He trudged upward, and soon the fire and cave were visible again, as were those nestled around it. A couple of the men in the group stood up as he arrived. Another, a bearded man, stayed squatted close to the fire. The remaining two occupants were a woman and a boy, sitting close together, a blanket wrapped around them.

The Reverend stopped outside the entrance to the cave. The logs in the fire were popping and crackling with a sound like a man snapping peanuts free of their shell.

"Do you got food?" one of the standing men said. He was a big fellow in a thick buffalo coat that made him seem even bigger. He wore boots topped with rabbit fur, a thick leather hat. He had pushed his greatcoat open. It was lined with a checkered blanket. His hand was on the butt of his pistol, which looked to be an old converted .44. He was slightly crouched. The Reverend believed him to be a man who thought he knew what he was doing.

The other man was short and thin. He had grown so thin and pale, blue veins could be seen in his face, like colored pencil marks on a map. His coat was thinner than the other and made of leather that had turned dark and was stained from time and wear. He had on a black slouch hat with a hole in the crown. He removed his hand from the butt of his pistol and let it hang at his side.

"It'd be right nice if you did have some food," the small, thin man said. "We done boiled and ate damn near everything that's leather except what we're wearing. Horses and mules had to go, too, as did a hog and a flock of chickens we was hauling out to start a farm. We ate the goddamn seeds we had for planting. There goes the turnip crop, the beans and peas and squash as well."

"Those were our seeds," said the woman.

"Well," the skinny man said, "we all ate them."

The Reverend carefully observed the others, knowing from experience that those who did not appear threatening could be the ones to worry about. The other man was older than the rest, had a thick beard. He wore a drooping wide-brimmed hat and a weasel-hide coat. If he had a pistol it was either under his coat or in one of the wide coat pockets. His head was turned to look at the Reverend. His massive beard was flecked with snow and ice and time's gray marks.

The woman had on a hooded coat. Her hair poked out from under the hood and was dark as the bottom of a coal mine. Her face was like an animal looking out of its den. She was delicate, except for her dark eyes that appeared to contain some reservoir of strength.

The boy he thought to be twelve or thirteen. He had black, scraggly hair and was snuggled close to the woman. His mouth, like the others, was cracked and bloody from the cold. From the color of the boy's hair and eyes, the Reverend decided they were mother and child.

"About that food?" said the bearded man at the fire.

"To be exact, gentlemen, much of my chuck and supplies were on a mule that made a misstep and took flight off the mountainside and into the void, like Icarus with melting wings, but in this case, with frozen ass."

"What the hell are you talking about?" said the big man in the buffalo coat.

"He's talking metaphor," said the skinny man. "I heard a preacher talk about metaphor and how it's a lot of what the Bible is. Still, I don't know who that Icarus is."

"I'm talking truth," said the Reverend. "My mule fell off a cliff."

"Why didn't you just say that?" said the big man, the one the Reverend had come to think of as Buffalo Coat. The other standing man he decided to think of as Skinny. The man by the fire became Bearded Man, and the other two were Woman and Boy. It might be best not to know names. If things went sideways, it was best not to have names for what you might have to eat.

"Let me start with a friendly suggestion," said the Reverend. He looked right at Bearded Man. "Remove your hand from the butt of your pistol. Be assured I will not ask you twice. If you do not, I will consider you hostile, and will put a bullet, perhaps two, through your head."

The man eyed the Reverend for a moment, but any show of strength in his face faded. He straightened from his crouch and dropped his hand away. His coat fell around him and concealed the pistol.

"Who the hell are you?" Buffalo Coat said.

"Call me Reverend. This is my horse, Bill."

"A goddamn preacher," Skinny said. "I'd have preferred a gambler with a deck of cards, even if I got nothing to gamble."

"Well, you have me," the Reverend said.

Without asking permission, the Reverend led Bill around the fire and inside the cave. At the back of the cave the warmth of the fire could still be felt, even if the cave ceiling was tall and wide and pretty long. It was a relatively cozy spot.

The Reverend prepared to hobble Bill with the hobble ropes that were fastened to his saddle. He did this while keeping a cautious eye on his new companions.

He pushed his black duster coat back over his matching ivory-handled pistols in their black leather holsters. He wanted to discourage any sort of confrontation, because he sensed a tension in the air that was cold as the snow.

The Reverend was proud of his pistols. He had recently bought them from a peculiar gunsmith who said they were haunted and had belonged to Wild Bill Hickok, shortly before his demise. He said the spirit of the gunfighter's aim was in the guns. Said they should always be loaded with silver bullets.

That was something the Reverend did anyway. Went with his line of work.

As for them being the pistols of Wild Bill Hickok, the Reverend considered this a bullshit selling point to jack up the price, but he liked the pistols and didn't regret the gunsmith's subterfuge, if indeed it was. The guns did feel strange in his hands. He had yet to kill anyone with them, but shooting targets with them was a delight. He was an excellent shot, but when he fired these pistols he felt as if he were an even better one.

As he leaned down to fasten the hobbles to his horse's ankles, he noted a large pile of firewood, which was a good thing. He also saw a cache of charred bones not far from them. Some of the bones were those of a horse, and some were of a human; broken femurs and a skull that had been smashed open at the top, like a kid shattering a piggy bank to get at the loot inside.

The Reverend made no recognition of this. He removed his lantern from the saddle. It was contained in a thick, leather bag. He placed it against the cave wall. He never lit it unless he had to. He wanted to keep the coal-oil content as full as possible, in case it really became necessary to see in the night, if the moon and stars were not in sight, if a campfire was not enough. The lantern itself he had washed several times in holy water. Water that, if to do its duty, had to be blessed by someone other than himself. He was not that holy.

He removed his horse's blanket and saddle and sat them against the back wall next to the lantern. He took time to curry Bill with a brush from a bag that dangled from the saddle horn. The others watched him as if he were a bear doing human things. He pulled the saddlebags off the back of the saddle, threw them over his shoulder and headed toward the fire.

"Food?" said the woman.

This time the Reverend answered. "Some."

He rummaged in one of the bulging saddlebag pouches and pulled out a fat mound of waxed paper wrapped around strips of beef jerky. He gave a piece to everyone. They all squatted around the fire and ate. The Reverend took a piece for himself, carefully wrapped the paper around the dried meat, and put it away.

They watched him as he did this. He knew he'd have to be alert, or they would not only take the jerky, but eat him as well. From the bones in the back, he was certain they had already resorted to cannibalism, but the question was had they eaten a fellow pilgrim that had died, or had they killed to eat? One he could understand, but of the other he was less tolerant, especially if he might be on the menu.

An old sailor who had been marooned on an island told him that he and three others had been trapped in what seemed like a tropical paradise, but they couldn't catch fish. They didn't seem to be as prevalent there as expected. They lived off wild greens and fruits, an occasional crab, but nothing much edible was in abundance. When members of their group died, they ate them, raw. Cut them open and pulled out the guts and the innards, cut the flesh in strips and ate it. The old man said the strips of flesh were chewy, but tasty, and he developed quite an appreciation for it.

In the end, he said it was only him and another, and that they watched each other like hawks, hoping one or the other would die. He admitted he occasionally considered helping the other to do just that. Said he was so hungry he could see cornbread walking on the ground.

Fortunately, a ship found them, and he and his island companion were rescued. He never saw his companion after their return to civilization, but for a short time they were both famous as Robinson Crusoe. He never went to sea again. Worked the docks. Never mentioned what happened to the others until he was an old man and read that his surviving companion had died. Somehow that set him free to tell his tale.

"You know," the old marooned sailor said. "I still have me a hankering for a strip of that raw people meat. In fact, I don't think I've ever had anything as tasty. Of course, maybe I was just hungry."

The Reverend had never forgotten the story. There was also the fact eventually he had to kill the old man, but that was for righteous reasons and had nothing to do with cannibalism.

"How long have you been trapped here?" the Reverend asked.

"No idea, exactly," said the woman. "But a long time."

The older man said, "We were crossing the mountains, trying to get out West. We took a wrong cutoff."

"As did I," the Reverend said.

"We were trapped in the pass for maybe a month or more," said the woman. "We had plenty of supplies at first. Plenty of feed for the horses. And then we didn't. We ate what we could find. The men hunted. We scrounged for anything edible, even the bark off trees."

"That bark was better than I would have thought," said the boy.

"Hell," said Buffalo Coat, "we picked grain out of our horse's shit to eat. Even that tasted pretty good. What I want to know is how come you look so good, and you got that sleek horse?"

"I got trapped in a valley, and it wasn't terrible there. There was plenty of game and the snow wasn't so bad, but I couldn't get out until the other day, and when I did, I soon wished I'd stayed. The storm that had gone away came back with a vengeance. I believe I'd have been all right had I stayed on the original trail, but I'd heard of this cutoff, that it took days off the trip. It might in fact do that if the weather is perfect and you hold your mouth just right. Left the valley too early, decided on the wrong trail, and here I am."

"We studied the trail you was on," Buffalo Coat said. "Decided it might be worse than here. Cave is at least a sight better than being out in the bad weather. Thing is, though, we ain't got no supplies."

"You probably made a better choice," the Reverend said. "If the snow were to blow over and out, the ice melt some, then I'd try and go back the way I came. But not otherwise. That trail takes the brunt of the North Wind. And it is narrow as the edge of a butcher's knife."

"Up here, there hasn't been a break in the snow in weeks, maybe it's been months," said Buffalo Coat. "Oh, there was that one day when we could see the sun. I remember. I had gone out of the cave to shit, was squatted doing my business, and the sun hit me like a bullet. It was so warm for a couple of minutes, I thought I'd cry. Instead, I looked through my shit for something edible. I think I found a seed. The sun got covered in clouds and the wind blew snow, and that moment was gone."

"Don't talk like that in front of a lady," said Bearded Man.

"She ain't no lady no more," Buffalo Coat said. "Ain't none of us nothing more than survivors."

No one challenged this. Night slithered out of the sky and began to choke out the sun. The Reverend noted that as it did all the pilgrims looked at the gathering darkness as if watching themselves bleed out.

"At least it's nice and warm in here," the Reverend said.

"We chopped some trees growing alongside the cave," Bearded Man said. "There's no more to chop. This wood runs out, then it's just us and the cold and that won't play out so well. And then there's the real reason we've stayed here close to the fire."

"And what would that be?" the Reverend said.

"IT," said the woman.

There was a loud cracking of ice out in the night. Everyone looked out into the darkness.

"It's out there, and it's coming closer," she said. "But it doesn't like fire. We have to seal the entrance with it. We do it every night. Why the wood goes quick."

The Reverend helped them spread the fire-licked wood about so that the front of the cave had a barrier of flame in front of it. Bearded Man and Skinny went to the back of the cave and pulled some firewood forward, stacked it on the fire.

When that was done, Bearded Man squatted back down by the fire, looked out of the cave at the night. "It don't come in daylight, but just night. It always does. It's hungry, like us."

The wind sighed. All that could be seen from the mouth of the cave was the swirling of the snow. The Reverend sniffed. There was a stench of evil the Reverend knew so well. It had a stink not common to human experience. Even with all that he had faced—vampires, werewolves, walking dead, and monsters from the edges of time—he felt his skin crawl.

Bearded Man said, "We have another day or two of firewood. Like Jane said, it doesn't like fire, though it's gotten bolder of late. Comes closer."

"Jane," the Reverend said, now having a name to call her. "Can you tell me more about this IT?"

"You'll think we're crazy, but you'll know soon enough what I say is true," she said.

"I've seen strange things in my time," the Reverend said. "You might say strange things are my business."

"Very well," Jane said. "We started out in fine weather, and there was a much larger number of us, twenty or so. We had horses and mules and were well stocked. The trip was fine. Then Mr. Meeker thought we might do better to take a shortcut he'd been told about. It would cut days, even weeks off our travels, he said. But it was only a good way to go when the weather was good, and it wasn't good. We were trapped by bad weather, and after some time we begin to run out of food. We were eating bark off trees and eating all our leather. Of course, the horses and mules were killed and eaten, and then it was just us."

"You don't have to say," Bearded Man said.

"It's all right," Jane said. "I'm not happy about it, but I'm not ashamed either. We began to eat the dead, Reverend. Meeker was the first. I know how that must sound to a man of God."

"I'm not judging you."

"Then it went from worse to worst. Someone among us began to kill. They would strike in the night, drag their victim off in the woods. Next morning, we'd see bloody drag marks in the snow. Whoever killed their pick for the night ate all of them, save for a few bones. Can you imagine? One person eating a whole human body in one night, leaving only crushed skulls where the brains were taken out. Leg and arm bones cracked and the marrow sucked. Of course, when one of us died, it was understood they would be eaten by the rest of us. It was a matter of who was to be last. That was letting nature take its course, but this was someone outside of nature. And he wasn't sharing. We quickly realized the killer was Gabriel Johnson. He was a terrible man to begin with, before he became what he became. Greedy and lustful, a thief and other things worse that were rumored."

The Reverend said, "It is known there are mountain spirits, spirits of the cold and snow and the cutting wind. Starving spirits that seek a host. They prefer the malicious, the desperate and the greedy. We all have those components, but they float at a higher level in some."

"Gabriel Johnson was all those things," Jane said. "Always eating more than his fair share and talking about how he planned to open up a mining-camp store when we got out West, jack up the prices for goods, water the whiskey. He asked me if I wanted a job serving miners, and he wasn't referring to me waiting tables. He was proud of that kind of thinking. As we traveled, he kept apart from us more and more. Would wander into the forest alone.

"He was stealing flour and salt and smoked meats from our stock. A little at a time at first, and then a lot. By the time we found out it was too late. He had stashed it away. We went to confront him, but he disappeared into the dark. Didn't come out during the day. At night he would call to us. Taunt us. But over time he sounded strange. Like himself, but not exactly. I know how this will sound, but he became immune to the cold. He was never around the fire. And when we did catch a glimpse of him, moving between the trees, in spite of having our supplies and having killed and eaten folks in our group, he was thin. Skeletal."

"His eyes were odd," Bearded Man said. "They glowed in the night, but could turn dead black in a moment."

"Got so we didn't see Johnson," Jane said. "Merely saw his shadow. It would fall down on the snow just before complete dark. But he wasn't to be seen. Just that shadow. Then the night would come in solid and the shadow would blend with it. It was unnerving.

"Then one night a man lit a torch, stepped outside the heat and light of the campfire. In the torchlight we could see the shadow rise on hands and knees, then scuttle off like a lizard. Then it rose up and ran, like a human, but it was growing in size as it went. And the snow was flying to it. Almost immediately the shadow was turned into a creature made of snow. It ran off into the woods. It sure didn't like that torch, the light and the heat from it.

"From then on it would come in the night. It would call in Johnson's voice, and there was a smell about it. I noticed you wrinkle your nose. That is the smell, right there. Right now. And then we'd see it coming closer. Not right up to the fire, but close enough for us to see there was no more Mr. Johnson. It was a kind of snowman. And it was hungry. It would whistle and stomp and frighten the few mules we had left. They tugged their halters loose. And then they were gone. Johnson would get to them some way or another.

"We built bigger fires. And we kept the mules close to it. It helped. But we had to eat the last of the mules ourselves. Then this thing followed us as we moved along. Oh, maybe not during the daylight, but it would catch up come night. Nightfall, it made promises in Johnson's voice. Some of our group couldn't keep from leaving the fire and going off in the woods. Starving, exhausted, not thinking straight, they lost their will. They walked out into the dark and never came back."

"And then we came to this cave," Bearded Man said. "We only have the front of it to guard. The fire takes care of that. We're down to nothing to eat, and my belly is full of empty. Perhaps giving Johnson what it wants is better than starving to death."

"No," the Reverend said. "It isn't. Your soul will continue to be pained after your death. What's out there isn't Johnson. He's its catalyst and host, but now he's something other than what he was. Johnson has become that mountain spirit I mentioned. It's called the Wendigo."

"Wendigo," the boy said.

"The Indians know of it. The Cree, Ojibwe. The tribes that live in cold places and have known starvation and darkness. The Wendigo goes by many names. It kills and cannibalizes. It entices others to do the same. It's a taboo that breaks a soul down. Untethers it so that it may more easily fly away. But it's not a flight to escape. It's a flight into darkness and eternal pain. Johnson was chosen to become its host because of who he is, or was. The Wendigo exists without a host, but its powers are limited. Cold wind. Hunger. That's all it has until it occupies a soul. Then it lives off other souls and becomes stronger. It's never satisfied. It is always hungry for meat and for human essence."

"None among us are innocent of ravenous hunger. Starvation," Bearded Man said.

"But we didn't murder for it," Buffalo Coat said. "Though I admit it has crossed my mind. Just as a thought, you see. Those that died. That was different. We were starving, and it was the only thing to do. Not let the meat go to waste when we could eat and live and not die out here with ice on our bones. But the other, you know, sometimes I think about it."

"That's the Wendigo," the Reverend said. "It gives those urges to you."

"It calls out for us to break apart the circle of fire and let it in," the boy said.

"And sometimes we want to," Skinny said. "There is something about that voice. It promised we could eat. That we would have all the food we wanted. Way that thing talked, you almost believed what it was saying. Then you would see it standing outside the fire, bigger each time. In the morning we would find the bones of bears and elk and all manner of beasts. Now and again, someone would make the mistake of listening to that thing, and would go mad, go outside the fire. Next morning, their bones and blood were on the snow. Sometimes there was a bit of meat still on the bones."

"We took some of those bones," Jane said. "God forgive us all."

"God is a soulless terror," the Reverend said. "His will is my business, and His will is one of suffering and pain. It's hard to know what His plan is, or if there is one. There's no end to His punishments. I deserve them. But He doles them out to the good and the bad, the sinners and those without sin in equal amounts. He is both God and Satan. He's unreliable in his intentions."

"Blasphemy," said Buffalo Coat.

"Perhaps, but you don't know Him as well as I do," the Reverend said.

"Still, we ate human flesh," Jane said. "And if someone died, I would do it again. I would feed it to my boy by my own hand. What does that say about me?"

"It says you are hungry," the Reverend said.

"Bones in the back, ones I saw you eyeing," Bearded Man said. "They belong to Old Man Carruthers. He was a good man. He knew his fate. He was dying, and he knew we were eyeing his flesh as if we were in a meat market. We had already killed and eaten his horse. He told us to think of him as a gift."

"You did what you had to do," the Reverend said. "Johnson did what he wanted to do. I can assure you of that. Had he not, there would be no Wendigo following you. Johnson fit the bill for what the Wendigo needed. No doubt about that. He was a Wendigo's dream. If indeed they dream. The Wendigo is the opposite of warmth. That's why the fire holds it back. But even so, in time, it can become bolder. You want to survive, then you will have to leave this cave. Take your chances traveling. Possibly find game. Building fires as you go. We can find fallen wood as we travel, and I have plenty of lucifers to strike up a fire with me. They are well wrapped in wax paper and made waterproof inside an oiled water-shedding pouch. I also have flint and steel. You can stay here and die, or you can take a chance and leave. I'll be leaving soon. Stay if you like, but if you go with me, from that moment on I will make the choices for all of us."

"What gives you the right?" Buffalo Coat said.

"I take the right and do not ask your permission," the Reverend said. "If you have a different point of view, you may express it, but it will do you no good. I can leave you and be fine. And if you come with me, I can offer you no guarantees. Just the sum of my knowledge, which, to be immodest, in these matters is considerable."

There was a cracking sound like a limb burdened by too much snow, and then a more terrible stench than before. A stench like a pit full of rotting meat and vegetables, overlayed by a too-sweet smell of fermenting fruit. The fire wavered as if pushed by the wind. But there was no wind. The Reverend's horse nickered. Then came a voice, strangely close and simultaneously distant. The mere sound of it chilled the bones.

The voice said, "Pull back the fire. Let a cold man in."

"It's Johnson," Skinny said.

"It's the Wendigo," the Reverend said.

There was a laugh more like a cackle, and now the wind was back. It twirled the snow and danced the flames. The cackle seemed to tumble downhill and away, crashing along like dropped dishes shattering on the rocks below.

The Reverend stood from his squat and rested his hands on his revolvers, tried to see through the high-burning fire. And he did see something. Something that had a near-human shape, but larger. It shifted, and then it was nothing more than the twirling of the driven snow and a lingering reek that made the stomach shift.

"When we run out of wood, it'll get in," said the boy.

"It's all right," the woman said, but the boy was not reassured. He looked out at the dark as if he were about to mount the gallows.

Some time passed. The odor dissolved. There were no more voices. Buffalo Coat, who had been squatting, stood up, took off his hat and held it politely in front of him as he spoke to the Reverend.

"May we eat your horse?"

"No," said the Reverend. "And if you try to harm that horse, it will be you who is eaten."

"All right, then," Buffalo Coat said, and put his hat back on.

They built up the fire, and though there was still wood, the Reverend could see that one more night, and that would be it. A small fire would not contain it. Bother it, perhaps, but not contain it. Over time no fire would hold it. There were other methods, but even they had their limits. He would consider those later.

The Reverend curried his horse and put oats in a feed bag and fed him. He fastened a cloth over Bill's face and eyes to soothe him, then unrolled his blankets and sat with his back against the cave wall and drew his blankets over him. Back there, away from the fire, it was cooler, but not exactly cold. Comfortable enough, all things considered.

He pulled his revolvers and clutched them by his sides under the blankets. Kept a loose eye on Buffalo Coat. The big man was sitting near the fire with his back against the side of the cave. He was watching the Reverend, waiting for him to drift off, he figured. Skinny was doing the same, eyeing him like a greasy pork chop soon to be dipped in blood gravy. Their own weaknesses and the power of the Wendigo were having an effect.

The Reverend pulled his hat down so that it partially covered his eyes, but he could still see. He was exhausted and feared he would drift off. If he did, if they moved toward him, his horse, Bill, would hear them and snort and stamp. It wasn't exactly like having a watchdog, but it was some comfort.

The Reverend catnapped. But when Bill snorted and stamped, he came wide awake. Buffalo Coat and Skinny stood close by, awkwardly looking at him. The others were asleep near the fire.

"Howdy there," Buffalo Coat said.

"I will warn you but once, gentlemen. If you make your move, you'll never make another. Go to the fire and stay there. I see your hand on your gun, or you come close again while I'm resting, I will shoot you without investigation or guilt."

Buffalo Coat pushed his coat open to reveal his pistol. "You talk a good game, Reverend, but I think you're all blow."

That was when the Reverend moved. Flipping the blanket aside and bringing up his revolver in his left hand, he fired. A hole appeared in the middle of Buffalo Coat's head and there was a spray of blood and brains flying toward the fire like a clutch of insects. Buffalo Coat fell backward and hit with his ankles crossed.

Jane, the boy, and Bearded Man were suddenly awake, sitting up. They looked at the Reverend and the body with open mouths.

The Reverend waved the gun at Skinny. "You take out your pistol and you lay it at my feet, so I don't have to get up and take it from you or give you a third eye like loudmouth there. You have another gun, let me assure you, you had best divest yourself of it. I find you are carrying after this moment, then I'll kill you."

"Yes sir," Skinny said and gently pulled his pistol with his thumb and forefinger and laid it on the ground. "Is it okay if we eat him?"

"That is your prerogative."

"We'll save you a piece."

"No. I will maintain. Jane, boy, I'm sorry you had to see that."

"It's all right," said the boy. "I didn't like him, and I'm hungry. And I done seen worse."

All of them had left the fire and were creeping toward Buffalo Coat's body. "I claim the coat," said Skinny.

"No," the Reverend said. "That belongs to the lady."

"Who says it belongs to her?" Skinny said.

"Who did you hear?" the Reverend said.

Skinny nodded.

"Boy," the Reverend said. "Bring me that pistol. And bring me the one underneath the buffalo coat."

The boy brought both pistols to him, then hurriedly returned to Buffalo Coat's body.

The others had begun to pull off the dead man's coat and were removing the dead man's clothes. The coat was given to Jane as instructed.

"Take him closer to the fire," the Reverend said. "I don't want that going on near me."

"You'll grow hungry yourself," Bearded Man said.

"I am not there yet. Do as you do, but not close to me."

By morning most of Buffalo Coat's corpse had been cooked and devoured by the hungry travelers. The entire middle of the man had been cut open and his innards ripped out, blood and fecal matter from his body was all over the front of the cave, and the eaters were covered in blood. A blood-stained rib cage lay nearby.

Having slept very little, the Reverend was surprised at how refreshed he felt by the sunlight and the cessation of the blowing snow.

He fed Bill and tried not to step in horseshit. When finished, he walked over and kicked the rib cage through the fire and out into the snow. Then he edged the fire aside on one end with a stick of firewood and went outside the cave and looked at the snow. There were no tracks. That didn't surprise him. A creature like the Wendigo wouldn't leave any.

The snowy trail below had been replaced by ice. Trying to skirt down to it would be impossible. Even if they could make it, the trail was so precarious they would be trapped on it before nightfall, and there might not be a place as protective from the Wendigo as the cave. He had to find another route.

He stepped back inside the cave. "I'm going to take a look around. I will leave my horse where he is. If the horse is harmed, I will kill every last one of you without consideration. Understood?"

They all agreed it was understood.

"Sir," said the boy, "may I go with you?"

"You may if your mother approves."

The boy looked at her.

"I believe you may be safer with him than us," she said.

The Reverend picked his saddlebags off the ground where he had used them as a pillow, threw them over his shoulders, thinking the jerky in his bags might be too much of a temptation for the group. There were other things in them as well. Silver bullets. A spare revolver. A few odds and ends of string and leather strips. He left the lantern.

The boy stood nearby, as if waiting for the school bell to ring. The Reverend said, "Do you have an ax?"

"We do," said the boy. "We got a hatchet too."

"Get them both."

A moment later, the Reverend and the boy stepped outside the cave. The boy was holding the ax and had the hatchet handle tucked through his belt. The air was as sharp as a razor and cold as a polar bear's nuts.

There was a little trail that went up and around the back of the cave, then led farther up into the mountains. The Reverend started in that direction.

"Why go up there?" the boy said. "That leads back to the trail that brought us here. It's just more of the same."

"You did ask to come with me. If you are going to spend your time giving me pointers, perhaps you should stay in the cave."

"Sorry."

"We need to go higher to have a vigil where we may peek out at the land. Perhaps we can find fuel, as well as another path."

Climbing, they ended up in a cluster of cedar trees, both short and tall. From that angle they could see down a five-acre-wide, three-acre-deep slope covered by a sheet of ivory-colored ice. At the bottom of it was a mountain lake, also covered by ice. The water beneath it made the ice look sky-blue.

The Reverend considered the terrain. Beyond the lake was a trail that was considerably clearer of snow than the trail the Reverend had used to arrive at the cave. It split through the mountains. Boulders and trees bordered it on both sides. If one could get past the acres of slanting ice, cross the frozen lake, the trail looked to be a better way out. But the ice slope looked deadly. And how thick was the ice over the lake? Was it thick enough to walk on?

Unanswered questions.

"You thinking about that clearer trail down there, ain't you?" the boy said.

"I am."

"It might not be any better once you get down it a piece."

"I was thinking the same, but unless we can chop an immense amount of wood daily, haul it to the cave, soon there will be no fire. Even if we can keep the fire going, there is no food, except one another. And, of course, there's the Wendigo."

"I have kind of gotten used to eating people," the boy said.

"There is your mother. Should you eat her or she you?"

"I done told her she can eat me if I die."

"Eventually, we will run out of people. There is only one choice, and I intend to make it. Leave. You and the others will do as you will. Give me the ax. We spend our time chattering, the day will run away from us."

They set about finding suitable trees or dead wood. After a few hours, the Reverend had a considerable pile of wood chopped and shortened. There was plenty of dead wood as well. The boy had used the hatchet to clear the chopped wood of limbs.

The Reverend used some of the evergreen limbs the boy had chopped, and lashed them together with leather strips from his saddlebag. He added some green poles they had cut, and turned them into runners.

The Reverend studied the boy. He seemed strong for all he had been through. Then again, on this very morning he had eaten a hardy meal of Buffalo Coat's remains. That was bound to brace him a bit. Buffalo Coat's blood was still on his face and stained the front of his coat.

"Now, saddle and bring my horse. By the way, what's your name?"

"Evan," the boy said.

"Evan, you may ride him back. But be careful of the trail."

After a while, Evan came back riding Bill, the hobbles fastened to the saddle horn. As Evan climbed down, the Reverend removed one of the two coils of rope he carried on his saddle. He cut pieces off of it and used them to fasten together a travois made from the wood runners and limbs he had salvaged.

It was a simple device, the evergreen limbs fastened between the runners to make a bed for the wood. The Reverend then fastened the long runners to the sides of the saddle.

They loaded up the chopped logs, but there was still wood they had to leave due to lack of space and the device's inability to carry huge loads. The Reverend let the boy lead the horse down the trail and back to the cave. It was slow work.

When they were inside the cave, they removed and stored the travois in back, stacked up the wood at the sides of the cave.

"We going back for more?" Evan asked the Reverend. "We left some."

"The day is darkening. We would do all right going, but coming back we might find ourselves in the dark with IT. We have plenty for the night, so let's lay low and keep the fire high."

The Reverend went to the back of the cave and leaned his back against the rock wall. He took jerky from the saddlebags, chewed on a piece. Sitting by the fire, the others watched him, licked their cracked lips.

"You ate a whole man, just about," the Reverend said. "Had some of him for lunch while me and Evan were occupied. If you are still hungry, I spied some toes and a hand you missed over there. But I warn you. Share. Me, I have not had any nourishment but this, so you can turn your gaze away."

In short time the hand and toes were found, cooked and eaten. The Reverend enjoyed the smell of the meat cooking.

It came in the night and called in Johnson's voice, but it made other noises as well, and the noises were enticing, like the flute-playing of the Pied Piper. No one succumbed.

It prowled and called and darted in front of the cave, cackled, and was gone before daylight. When the first rays of morning came, the Reverend used his coffee grounds and the small pot he had wrapped in his bedroll to make coffee. He offered some to the others. Poured it in bowls and cups they provided. Skinny drank his from Buffalo Coat's skull, from which all the flesh had been stripped. He gave them all a chunk of jerky from his saddlebags, then he and Evan went back up the hill with the horse and travois, loaded the wood that was left from the day before, and brought it back to the cave.

There was still plenty of daylight, so he and Evan returned with Bill to cut more wood, but this time the Reverend had the boy help him cut a large pine. When it fell it shook the snow and ice and caused birds to fly up and squirrels to scamper from the fallen top of the tree.

The Reverend took the ax and cut the tree in sections. The top section extended over the slope of ice. He cut the limbs off of it, and he and the boy chopped them up for kindling. Finished, they looked back at the icy slope, the blue lake sheeted by ice, the trail beyond. It seemed so close and yet so dangerously far away.

Evan stood on the front end of the fallen tree and wobbled it.

"Do that, and you will soon take a trip down the slope. Broken bones might well be in the offing."

Evan stepped off the section. He said, "Should I care?"

"You get to choose."

They hauled the firewood back to the cave. The Reverend and Evan began to build the fire up with the help of Jane and the Bearded Man. Skinny threw a few sticks onto it. Skinny had begun to take on an attitude that reminded the Reverend of Buffalo Coat.

Just before night, Jane began to cough a lot. She had been coughing before, but not consistently, but now the cough was more frequent and deeper within her chest.

"She ain't been doing good all day," Bearded Man said. "Cough has gotten considerable worse." He spoke like a man hopeful she might soon die.

The Reverend took some horse liniment from his saddlebags, had Jane came to the back of the cave, told Evan to remain up front by the fire.

The Reverend held up the liniment bottle. "You can do this yourself if you're modest, or you can let me do it. I'll need your coat wide open, your blouse open to expose your chest."

"Sounds like to me you're just having fun."

"You can do it, then."

She shook her head. "You do it."

She unbuttoned her blouse and the Reverend rubbed the liniment across her chest and breasts. There was nothing erotic about it. She was as thin as a bird and due to malnutrition, her breasts were small like fried eggs. But even with the bones in her face poking tight against her flesh, he could see she was a pretty woman. Regular meals for a month, hot water and a bath, nice clothes, and she'd be a standout.

The male mind, he thought.

"It's going to burn a bit, but it'll get into your chest, maybe help clear up that cough."

"We're not going to make it, or are we?"

"I am," the Reverend said.

Nighttime came and there was a revival of blowing snow and howling wind. This encouraged the travelers to build the fire higher, to push it from one edge of the cave mouth to the other.

The fire roared five feet high. The wood crackled and oozed sap. Beyond it, through wafts of flames, rises of snow could be seen. The mounds were growing higher. Tomorrow they might need to find a way to move some of the snow, so as not to be trapped by it.

The Reverend noticed that the corners of the fire were being gently nudged. He strained to see if it was the wind. Finally, he saw that it was a stick poking out of the dark, gently pushing a log.

The Wendigo was investigating.

No one else had noticed.

"It's getting braver," the Reverend said. "I suggest we move to the back of the cave. I have a few tricks that might hold it off."

"What you mean?" Skinny said. "Best fire we've had. I actually feel warm for a change."

"Best fire because we cut enough wood to build it," Evan said. "Not like you did anything."

"You shush, boy, or I'll be eating dinner out of your belly."

Skinny produced a knife.

"Whoa," Bearded Man said. "We can't lose our heads like this."

The Reverend, without anyone realizing it, had drawn one of his pistols. "Put the knife up, or you will end up like your partner, who you've eaten and shat out into the early morning snow."

Skinny put the knife away. His eyes glowed in the firelight.

"I just ain't got no time for insults from a child," Skinny said.

"Yes, you do," the Reverend said.

They moved to the back of the cave near the Reverend's horse. Bill had been groomed, fed, and hobbled, and a mask had been put over his eyes.

While Jane coughed and spat flecks of blood into an already stained handkerchief, the Reverend began to draw a large circle on the cave floor with the tip of his knife. He drew it so that they were within it. The Reverend didn't quite complete it. He stopped at the wall at the back of the cave. He then drew an extension of the circle on the wall, five feet high. Used his knife to carve symbols into the cave rock along the sides of the extended circle on the wall. Then he drew the same symbols on the floor, just outside the loop. The markings were crude and strange. They looked like stick men and dancing creatures.

Bearded Man said, "What is that?"

"Symbols of power. Cree used similar drawings, though I've added in a bit of this and that from other beliefs."

"Are you saying it makes us safe?" Bearded Man said.

"I have used similar before. But no guarantees. It might be more like a picket fence that will hold out the less determined."

"The fire has held just fine," Skinny said. "Why do we need these silly marks in the dirt? I don't see that working, preacher man."

"I think you don't see a lot of things, fellow. We need the circle and the spell because it has grown stronger and bolder. Fire or no fire, it will come through. It has been trying the fire, a little at a time. Evil is like that. It nudges, then it pushes, then it shoves. In time, it can break down barriers."

"I don't plan to sit inside some damn circle, or stand in one neither," Skinny said.

"Suit yourself," the Reverend said.

"I want to stay inside," Evan said.

Jane and Bearded Man agreed.

"To hell with your circle. I'll take my chances up close to the fire," Skinny said.

"Fine. But do not smear my line or drawings."

Skinny stepped out of the circle, making big steps, as if stepping over a snake. He moved close to the fire, rubbed his hands together, basked in its warmth.

"What do you think now?" Skinny said.

"That you should come back," the Reverend said.

Skinny, feeling bolder, cocked his head as if to say something, then stopped. A chilly wind blew into the cave. The fire's flames ruffled like red feathers. The Reverend and those in the circle could see a shape on the opposite side of the roaring blaze. It was the first time the Reverend had seen the Wendigo clearly.

It was tall and broad and made of snow and sticks and chunks of ice wadded together in a rough facsimile of human form. Its face had a long line of a mouth set tight in its round head of snow. The sticks and debris poked from its body like hair and warts. There was a faint definition of a nose and two deep dark holes for eyes. It reached a long arm over the fire and an enormous hand made of snow and sticks flexed. Water dripped from it, hissed in the flames. The cave filled with its stench. Skinny, aware now that something was behind him, wheeled toward it, knife in hand. The Wendigo grabbed him by the head and lifted him up. Skinny's legs dangled momentarily in the fire. Skinny screamed. It was the kind of high-pitched dying-rat scream that made buttholes pucker and skin slither over a person's bones.

Skinny was lifted out of the cave.

The beast roared. The roar was even more terrifying than Skinny's scream. The sound of it filled the cave and made the Reverend's horse try to shuffle away in his hobbles. The Reverend grabbed the rope that he had fastened around Bill's nose, and pulled him back.

The Wendigo had switched to holding Skinny by one of his feet. He slung Skinny about, popping him like a whip. The third time he was popped, Skinny's head snapped off and landed in the snow. Blood gushed. A boot fell off Skinny's foot.

The creature split open its long mouth and poked Skinny into it. The creature began to chomp with teeth that were jagged like cracked ice. Gouts of blood sprayed into the fire, coated the rises of snow beside the creature like strawberry topping on mounds of fresh-churned vanilla ice cream. The face of the Wendigo was reddened with gore, spattered with chunks of flesh.

It took one long stride and picked up Skinny's head where it had fallen, began to eat it like an apple.

"Jesus, help us," Bearded Man said.

"He won't," the Reverend said.

The monster peered over the fire at them. The dark holes that served as its eyes had something in them that moved and flickered. The crackling flames caused those things to be better seen. They were miniature shapes of humans, small and fluttering about like moths in a jar.

"It's all them that came with us," Bearded Man said. "Only they're little."

The Reverend could see Skinny in there with them. Pushing against an invisible wall, trying to get out.

The behemoth parted its blood-stained lips and a cascade of voices fell out, all of them so kneaded together they were impossible to understand one from the other; they were an avalanche of sound.

Jane put her hands over her ears and screamed. The boy yelled. Bill stamped his feet and whinnied, tugged at the rope around his nose.

The Reverend said, "Evan, hold this rope," and he passed it to him.

Evan took it without thinking.

The Reverend drew his pistols and fired.

The bullets whistled and the silver-coated loads hit the Wendigo in the face and sizzled. The holes they punched exhaled smoke. The creature let out with a fresh roar. It was different this time. It was a cry of pain. The silver bullets had hurt it. It dropped what was left of Skinny's partially eaten head and went away so quickly it was hard to believe it was gone or had even been there.

Moments later, it returned. It carried a small sapling in one hand. The sapling's roots dripped dark earth. It had pulled it from the ground.

Poking the sapling into the fire, the monster lifted away logs. The fire sparked and sizzled. The beast continued to push with the sapling until the fire was parted and a wide path was made.

"It's coming through," Evan said.

"Evan, saddle and bridle Bill. Make sure the saddlebags and the lantern are fastened in place. But stay in the circle."

The boy didn't move.

"Son. Do as I say."

Evan slowly began to do as he was told, boosting the blanket off the ground, tossing it over the horse's back, preparing to lift the saddle into place. Bearded Man and Jane stood staring at the Wendigo, mesmerized.

The monster hadn't stirred from its spot. It held the sapling and stared at them. The movement inside its eyes was gone; they had turned dark. The voices were silent. There was only the wind. The thing looked at the path it had made, as if considering its chances. It used the sapling to cautiously push the fire even wider apart. As it did, it breathed out flakes of snow and flecks of ice.

Evan pulled the bridle on, cinched the saddle into place, removed the rope from Bill's nose. A scarf was over the horse's eyes, put there when they had returned from their wood chopping. Evan left that in place. He held the reins tight as Bill chomped at the bit and stamped his feet.

"No matter what the Wendigo does," the Reverend said, "stay inside the circle until I say otherwise. Evan, here's my knife. If I say 'Cut,' you cut the hobbles off Bill, cut them close to the hooves. No dangles."

"A circle in the dirt don't seem like much," Bearded Man said. He was shivering, and not from the cold.

"We'll soon find out," the Reverend said.

The Wendigo's thin, long line of a mouth twisted, and it started through the gap in the fire, its snowy skin hissing from the heat, birthing a thin mist that filled the cave.

Bearded Man pulled a small pistol from his coat pocket. He had been armed all along.

"Unless those bullets are coated with silver, they will not cause it injury," the Reverend said.

"This bullet ain't for it," Bearded Man said.

Bearded Man put the gun to his head and pulled the trigger. The bullet passed through his head and whizzed near the Reverend's nose as it exited. Hot blood splattered against the side of the Reverend's face. Bearded Man fell to his knees and onto his face.

Jane picked up the gun.

"Do not dare," the Reverend said, and twisted it out of her hand, dropped it in his coat pocket.

"It wasn't for me," she said.

"No thanks," Evan said. "I trust the Reverend."

The Wendigo moved swiftly to the circle. It lifted the sapling and swung it down. When the tree hit the realm of the circle, it burst into golden flame and would not pass through. Sparks of gold flared about the cave.

The Wendigo swung the flaming sapling again, but this time it came apart in its hands, shedding gold ash, none of it passing into the circle.

The Wendigo slammed its fists down against the invisible barrier. They too flamed with golden fire. The howl from the beast was loud enough it dislodged dust that dribbled from the roof of the cave and fell into the circle.

Wheeling away, the Wendigo charged through the split in the fire and out into the dark and the snow.

"It worked," Evan said.

"The dust from the ceiling," Jane said. "How can that be? That thing couldn't swing a tree through, but dust fell inside?"

"What the beast touches is tainted with the beast," the Reverend said. "Otherwise, the natural order is unaffected."

Stepping outside the circle, the Reverend hastened toward the fire. He grabbed the unburned end of a flaming log and dragged it into the circle, then used his knife to reinstate the part of the circle that had been damaged by his efforts. He chanted a combination prayer and spell.

"Evan," the Reverend said. "Get some of that kindling and firewood from the back, but stay inside the circle."

"Yes, sir," Evan said.

The Reverend studied the fire at the mouth of the cave. It roared in two sections now. He considered pulling the sections together again by using a stick of firewood, then decided against it.

He tugged the body of Bearded Man out of the circle and close to one side of the cave. For a starving man, the sonofabitch had some weight on him.

The Reverend repaired the circle again, repeated his spell and prayer. Evan had brought up firewood and kindling. The Reverend carefully stacked it onto the burning log. Soon there was a solid blaze.

"Will the circle hold?" the woman said.

"No guarantee. That thing has moved past the fire, which it fears, so its determination is growing stronger. According to legend, the more the Wendigo eats the hungrier they get. Those it eats become part of IT, part of its power."

"Then why give it more to eat?" She nodded at Bearded Man.

"Distraction. Rest while you may. Come morning we must depart. It's no longer safe here."

Jane and Evan cuddled together close to the fire, and fell quickly asleep. Even with the fear of the Wendigo, slumber had claimed them. The Reverend could not and would not sleep. He sat down in front of the fire and held his pistols in his lap.

It was only an hour or so until daylight cracked the blackness. Would it come back before the sun came up? Or was it through for the night?

The Reverend noted in the firelight that the circle he had marked was beginning to thin, the markings to fade. That was a signal that evil was gaining strength. The protection he had created was beginning to fade.

There would be no redrawing it. The magic was done. From this point on it was assholes and elbows.

The wind groaned like an old man dying. Snow drifted into the mouth of the cave and fell into the remains of the fire.

Seeing that made the Reverend more mindful of the fire inside the circle. He placed more firewood on it. When the spell was gone there would only be the fire, and the Wendigo was less fearful of it than before.

The Reverend was considering options when he felt the hairs on the back of his neck lift up. The air thickened with a stench. He saw the shadows outside the cave twist, saw flakes of snow fly to them, cling to the shadows like cotton to tar. Sticks were picked up by the wind and tossed at the shape, spearing it. It was like watching an invisible sculptor build a statue from available materials. The shape was now the color of snow.

The Wendigo was larger than before. It bent at the waist, looked inside the cave. Its eyes were greater than before, deeper and black as original sin. A light came on inside of them, as if an early riser had lit a lamp. The light was the color of shit in amber. Once again, the Reverend could see the miniature souls of those it had consumed inside its eyes. They writhed, reached out, imploring rescue. Again, a thin dark line formed for the mouth. The wind blew two dents into its face. The dents became its nostrils.

The Reverend glanced at the circle. It was withdrawing. Growing closer to the fire. The symbols outside the ring were barely identifiable. They moved like crippled insects to keep up with the receding circle.

Glancing back at the Wendigo, the Reverend saw the thin line of its mouth had split open to show those horrid cracked-ice teeth. Was that a smile?

The Reverend placed his pistols in their holsters, said, "Jane."

He said her name twice. Jane sat up. She saw what he saw.

"Wake the boy," the Reverend said.

The Wendigo sniffed loudly. It smelled, then spied the body of Bearded Man lying against the cave wall. It eased itself through the split in the dying embers and moved toward the body.

Jane and Evan were both up, watching the thing as it entered the cave. It tossed a quick look at them, and then at the body. A tongue like a wet, red rope licked out of its mouth and slathered its cracked-ice teeth with bloody saliva the texture of gruel.

"I'm going to climb on Bill," the Reverend said. "Evan, cut the hobble ropes close to the hooves. Jane, climb up here behind me. Evan, you in front of me. Stretch out over Bill's neck."

The Reverend mounted, pulled Jane up and behind him. Evan cut the hobbles, was about to climb on board Bill.

"Give me a torch," the Reverend said.

Evan picked out a flaming stick of firewood by the unburned end. He handed it to the Reverend, who held it high above his head, used his other hand to help boost Evan in front of him.

The Reverend knew that carrying three was more than Bill could do comfortably, but there was nothing for it.

The Wendigo picked up Bearded Man. Just as it tilted its head back to drop its meal into its now widely spread mouth, the Reverend jerked the covering away from Bill's eyes and yelled to him, and out of the circle they bolted.

The mouth of the cave was close, but so was the Wendigo. The Reverend flung the torch in the monster's face. It caused the Wendigo to step back, Bearded Man's legs dangling from its mouth.

Out of the cave they rode, into the cold night air. Bill's hooves slipped and the Reverend was certain they were about to go down. But Bill gained purchase on the rocks beneath the snow, and up the trail they went, riding hard toward the woodyard the Reverend and Evan had made.

The Reverend glanced back.

Behind them the Wendigo came, seeming to glide on the wind, its legs and feet blending with the white of the snow. It was gaining.

The Reverend pulled a pistol with his left hand, leaned out and shot back. The silver bullet struck the Wendigo and sizzled like bacon in a hot frying pan. The Wendigo howled and fell back a pace. But it was like a bear stung by a bee. It was an annoyance, nothing more.

Bill slipped on the ice. They were almost to the peak of the hill when it happened. Jane flew off and tumbled backwards. Bill rolled, nickered, and then made a noise seldom heard from a horse—a scream. The Reverend and Evan were tossed into the snow.

The Reverend and Evan stood up. They saw Jane rolling down hill, right to the Wendigo. The Reverend drew one of his revolvers, fired rapidly, and accurately. The bullets tore the air and impacted the monster, but it was less annoyed by them than before.

The Reverend's last shot wasn't meant for the Wendigo, but it found its mark as well—Jane. It was a better death than what might have been.

Jane's body was lifted limply into the Wendigo's mouth like a cheap sweet, and devoured in a mist of blood and a crunch of bone.

Evan charged past the Reverend, having grabbed a stick. The Reverend leapt after him, grabbed his coat collar, pulled him back.

"Nothing you can do, boy."

The Reverend hurried them upward, pushing at Evan's back, pausing only long enough to stop where Bill was panting in pain. He pulled his second revolver as he replaced the first. He shot Bill in the head, finishing him off. He pulled the leather lantern pouch off of Bill, grabbed the saddlebags. Then up the last bit of the hill they went.

The Reverend glanced down. The Wendigo had stopped. It turned its great round head and looked east. The sunrise, the Reverend thought. It needs to be tucked away somewhere dark before the sun comes up.

It looked up at the Reverend, and he knew it had decided to take its chances. It rose up the hill. The Reverend pulled the lantern from the leather case, lit it with a match from the saddlebags, flung it just as the Wendigo was almost on them. The lantern burst. The oil in the lantern exploded into flames and the holy water flared with holy fire and spread over the Wendigo's head and turned it into what looked like a giant blazing match.

Tugging the boy along, the Reverend ran to the edge of the ice where the trimmed top section of the pine tree rested. He pulled the boy in front of him, lifted him with one hand onto the log.

"Straddle it," he said. "Don't let your feet touch the ground. Hang on with everything you got."

The Reverend pushed the large log slightly. It tilted over the slope of ice. He jumped on as it dipped down, glancing back once to see the flame-head Wendigo gliding after them, the blaze wafting in the breeze. The Wendigo howled.

The log shot down the slope, scratching up ice in a stinging spray. The front of the Reverend's hat brim lifted in the breeze. Evan was almost flat on the log, clutching it with all his strength. He was whimpering.

The log slid like a sled for some goodly distance, then it started to wobble, threatening to tip and roll over. It stayed upright until it finished the slope and launched out onto the icy lake, tossing them loose and onto the frozen surface.

Out of habit, the Reverend drew his pistols as he rose. He yelled to Evan as the boy wobbled to his feet. "Run like a deer."

He then took his own advice. They ran as fast as their tired bodies would carry them. The Reverend felt as if his heart would burst. He wondered if the lake might crack beneath them.

The flames on the Wendigo's head had burnt out. It paused at the enormous log of pine that had been used as a sled. It picked it up as if it were nothing more than a switch. The Wendigo glided over the ice toward them, slamming the log in anger against the frozen lake.

As it neared them, it slammed the log down again, close enough the Reverend felt the wind from the blow on the back of his neck, felt a slight pressure against the heel of his boot.

Then there was a noise akin to a bullwhip cracking, but the sound didn't end right away. A line in the ice formed beside the Reverend and then the line split and he could see cold blue water in the rip. The line expanded more.

The Reverend forced himself to look back. The Wendigo looked down with its hollow eyes as the crack broadened beneath it and it plunged into it, sending up a slosh like an ocean wave. The Wendigo was about to float above it. But then the night was striped with the color of a fresh egg yolk. The light moved like a bully into the blue-black strands of night, consuming it.

The Wendigo was climbing out of the water. It was being blown apart by the wind. It was less like a wraith now, and more like a man. Small. An animated skeleton, flesh dangling from it like rags.

Johnson.

Crawling out of the icy split, Johnson turned its bare skull to look at the Reverend. From the eyes little naked bodies, souls, were leaping out and away. They scrambled like insects on the ice, then quickly melted in the sunlight, dissolved into buttery puddles.

Johnson managed to rise on bony legs and feet, and staggered over the ice. The Reverend raised a pistol and fired. A bullet nested in Johnson's skull, causing it to burst into pieces. The skeleton collapsed and rattled apart. A shadow in the shape of Johnson lay on the ice like an oil spill, then soaked into the ice and became clear.

The sun was golden. The sky was blue. The wind was gentle. The spirit of the Wendigo was gone.

The Reverend caught up with the boy.

"Is it dead?" Evan asked.

"For now. That's what greed did for it. It wanted us so badly it neglected the rising of the light. Consider this some kind of goddamn Bible lesson."

They walked carefully across the ice to where the other trail began. It was clear enough to travel. They found an indentation in the rocks just before night and made a fire with dead wood and matches from the Reverend's saddlebags. They ate the last of the Reverend's jerky. The Wendigo was no longer a threat.

Come morning they moved on. Late afternoon of the next day, the Reverend shot an elk with his pistol, three fast shots to the heart. They made a camp in a copse of trees for two days, finding a gap in the midst of them where they could build a fire from dead wood and roast and eat elk until they were full. The Reverend cut strips of meat from the elk and placed them in the snow until they started out again come morning.

Two days later, still living off the remains of the elk, the trail broke wide and slanted down and out of the mountains. The earth below was touched with ice and snow, but much clearer. Bits of grass could be seen poking up from the frost. The Reverend and Evan descended and walked the flatter trail for two more days. Then a band of noisy pilgrims with oxen, wagons, horses, and mules showed up.

They were given a ride in one of the wagons. Fed beans and cornbread. Evan told a story of harrowing survival, but he left out the Wendigo, which the Reverend considered wise. Evan turned the Wendigo into a bear. He also left out the cannibalism. Also a wise decision.

The travelers reached civilization a week and a half later. Evan found a home with a family that had lost their son while crossing the mountains, dying of some unknown disease. Evan seemed happy enough. He and the Reverend never spoke again.

When the Reverend regained his strength, he took a job at the stables. He earned enough to pay for the room and board he had taken, enough to buy a horse and saddle, riding gear, as well as a few supplies.

The horse he had bought was no Bill, but it was a strong Paint and it was enough. The Reverend rode the Paint toward California.

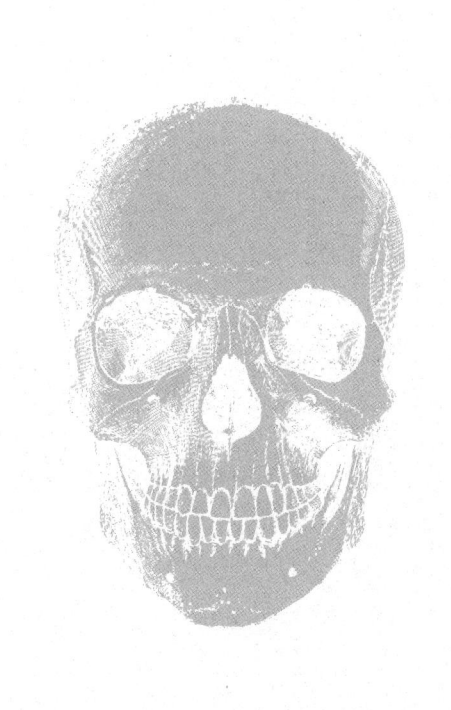

When my wife and I had our first child, we were worried that our Siberian Husky, Avatar, might not take to the screaming little creature.

Therefore, we practiced caution to keep child and dog separated.

We need not have worried—the dog dealt with baby Keith by ignoring him.

We didn't have a cat at the time, but the idea of being concerned about animal jealousy came to me, and I thought, what if there were a dog *and* a cat, along with a baby?

This popped out.

Another story inspired by real-life situations.

Dog, Cat, and Baby

For John Maclay

DOG DID NOT like Baby. For that matter, Dog did not like Cat. But Cat had claws—sharp claws.

Dog had always gotten attention. Pat on head. "Here, boy, here's a treat. Nice dog. Good dog. Shake hands. Speak! Sit. Nice dog."

Now there was Baby.

Cat had not been problem, really.

Cat was liked, not loved, by family. They petted Cat sometimes. Fed her. Did not mistreat her. But they not love her. Not way they loved Dog—before Baby.

Damn little pink thing that cried.

Baby got "Oooohs" and "Ahhs." When Dog tried to get close to Masters, they say, "Get back, boy. Not *now*."

When would be *now*?

Dog never see now. Always Baby get now. Dog get nothing. Sometimes they so busy with Baby it be all day before Dog get fed. Dog never get treats anymore. Could not remember last pat on head or "Good Dog!"

Bad business. Dog not like it.

Dog decide to do something about it.

Kill Baby. Then there be Dog, Cat again. They not love Cat, so things be okay.

Dog thought that over. Wouldn't take much to rip little Baby apart. Baby soft, pink. Would bleed easy.

Baby often put in Jumper which hung between doorway when Master Lady hung wash. Baby be easy to get then.

So Dog waited.

One day Baby put in Jumper and Master Lady go outside to hang wash. Dog looks at pink thing jumping, thinks about ripping to pieces. Thinks on it long and hard. Thought makes him so happy his mouth drips water. Dog starts toward Baby, making fine moment last.

Baby looks up, sees Dog coming toward it slowly, almost creeping. Baby starts to cry.

But before Dog can reach Baby, Cat jumps.

Cat been hiding behind couch.

Cat goes after Dog, tears Dog's face with teeth, with claws. Dog bleeds, tries to run. Cat goes after him.

Dog turns to bite.

Cat hangs claw in Dog's eye.

Dog yelps, runs.

Cat jumps on Dog's back, biting on top of head.

Dog tries to turn corner into bedroom. Cat, tearing at him with claws, biting with teeth, makes Dog lose balance. Dog running very fast, fast as he can go, hits the edge of doorway, stumbles back, falls over.

Cat gets off Dog.

Dog lies still.

Dog not breathing.

Cat knows Dog is dead. Cat licks blood from claws, from teeth with rough tongue.

Cat has gotten rid of Dog.

Cat turns to look down hall where Baby is screaming.

Now for *other* one.

Cat begins to creep down hall.

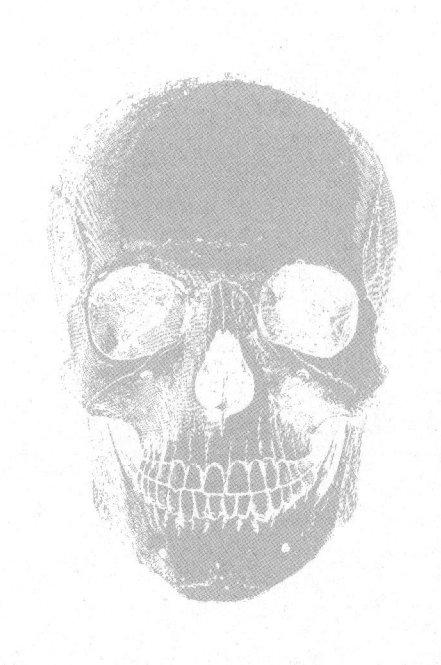

Possibly my most famous story, though I think it's safe to say that more people have seen the film than read the story. Don Coscarelli, who directed it, did a marvelous job, and it is the best of all the adaptations of my work. It doesn't try to reinvent me or show how clever the screenwriter (Coscarelli) is. It is a close adaptation, and that's far more difficult. Don won the Bram Stoker Award for the screenplay. Well deserved.

This story has to do with Elvis not dying but trading places with an impersonator and going on to live a simpler life. Or is it someone who thinks he's Elvis and is, in fact, the impersonator?

Either way, due to a hip injury, he's ended up in a rest home, and no one believes that he's Elvis. And again, maybe he isn't.

In the film, he's played by the incredible Bruce Campbell, and I tell you true, his is an Oscar performance, if only the Oscars had been looking his way.

John F. Kennedy is the secondary character, but only slightly so, and he's Black and thinks that he was painted that color, and that his brain is in a jar in the White House, and that in its place he has a bag of sand in his head. He is, of course, in the rest home with Elvis.

He is played by the great Ossie Davis. Meeting him was a highlight for me, as I have admired him for years, not only for acting but for producing, directing, and his civil rights activities. A kind of hero of mine.

There is also Kemosabe, who thinks that he's a former TV cowboy. There are other real-life characters in the story who don't make it into the film. Still, what a close and loving adaptation.

I should also mention that there's a mummy who is stealing the souls of those in the rest home and that Elvis and JFK team up to stop him in a climatic showdown right out of the story.

Years later, in Italy, at a literary and music concert where my wife and I were watching our daughter perform music, we also got to see Guy Davis perform. He was marvelous.

When he came off the stage, he saw that I was wearing a Bubba Ho-Tep T-shirt. He said that he loved his dad in that film and got a picture with me for Mama.

What an incredible coincidence.

Don also adapted another story of mine, "Incident on and off a Mountain Road," for Showtime's *Masters of Horror*. I liked it a lot as well. I think that we kind of had each other's number.

ELVIS DREAMED HE had his dick out, checking to see if the bump on the head of it had filled with pus again. If it had, he was going to name the bump Priscilla, after his ex-wife, and bust it by jacking off. Or he liked to think that's what he'd do. Dreams let you think like that. The truth was, he hadn't had a hard-on in years.

That bitch, Priscilla. Gets a new hairdo and she's gone, just because she caught him fucking a big-tittied gospel singer. It wasn't like the singer had mattered. Priscilla ought to have understood that, so what was with her making a big deal out of it?

Was it because she couldn't hit a high note the same and as good as the singer when she came?

When had that happened anyway, Priscilla leaving?

Yesterday? Last year? Ten years ago?

Oh God, it came to him instantly as he slipped out of sleep like a soft turd squeezed free of a loose asshole, for he could hardly think of himself or life in any context other than sewage, since so often he was too tired to do anything other than let it all fly in his sleep, wake up in an ocean of piss or shit, waiting for the nurses or the aides to come in and wipe his ass. But now it came to him. Suddenly he realized it had been years ago that he had supposedly died, and longer years than that since Priscilla left, and how old was she anyway? Sixty-five? Seventy?

And how old was he?

Christ! He was almost convinced he was too old to be alive, and had to be dead, but he wasn't convinced enough, unfortunately. He knew where he was now, and in that moment of realization, he sincerely wished he was dead. This was worse than death.

From across the room, his roommate, Bull Thomas, bellowed and coughed and moaned and fell back into painful sleep, the cancer gnawing at his insides like a rat plugged up inside a watermelon.

Bull's bellow of pain and anger and indignation at growing old and diseased was the only thing bullish about him now, though Elvis had seen photographs of him when he was younger, and Bull had been very bullish indeed. Thick-chested, slab-faced, and tall. Probably thought he'd live forever, and happily. A boozing, pill-popping, swinging dick until the end of time.

Now Bull was shrunk down, was little more than a wrinkled sheet-white husk that throbbed with occasional pulses of blood while the carcinoma fed.

Elvis took hold of the bed's lift button, eased himself upright. He glanced at Bull. Bull was breathing heavily and his bony knees rose up and down like he was peddling a bicycle; his kneecaps punched feebly at the sheet, making pup tents that rose up and collapsed, rose up and collapsed.

Elvis looked down at the sheet stretched over his own bony knees. He thought: *My God, how long have I been here? Am I really awake now, or am I dreaming I'm awake? How could my plans have gone so wrong? When are they going to serve lunch, and considering what they serve, why do I care? And if Priscilla discovered I was alive, would she come see me, would she want to see me, and would we still want to fuck, or would we have to merely talk about it? Is there finally, and really, anything to life other than food and shit and sex?*

Elvis pushed the sheet down to do what he had done in the dream. He pulled up his gown, leaned forward, and examined his dick. It was wrinkled and small. It didn't look like something that had dive-bombed movie starlet pussies or filled their mouths like a big zucchini or pumped forth a load of sperm frothy as cake icing. The healthiest thing about his pecker was the big red bump with the black ring around it and the pus-filled white center.

Fact was, that bump kept growing, he was going to have to pull a chair up beside his bed and put a pillow in it so the bump would have some place to sleep at night. There was more pus in that damn bump than there was cum in his loins. The old diddlebopper was no longer a flesh cannon loaded for bare ass. It was a peanut too small to harvest; wasting away on the vine. His nuts were a couple of darkening, about-to-rot grapes, too limp to produce juice for life's wine. His legs were stick-and-paper things with over-large, vein-swollen feet on the ends. His belly was such a bloat, it was a pain for him to lean forward and scrutinize his dick and balls.

Pulling his gown down and the sheet back over himself, Elvis leaned back and wished he had a peanut butter and banana sandwich fried in butter. There had been a time when he and his crew would board his private jet and fly clean across country just to have a special-made fried peanut butter and 'nanner sandwich. He could still taste the damn things.

Elvis closed his eyes and thought he would awake from a bad dream, but didn't. He opened his eyes again, slowly, and saw that he was still where he had been, and things were no better. He reached over and opened his dresser drawer and got out a little round mirror and looked at himself.

He was horrified. His hair was white as salt and had receded dramatically. He had wrinkles deep enough to conceal outstretched earthworms, the big ones, the night crawlers. His pouty mouth no longer appeared pouty. It looked like the drooping waddles of a bulldog, seeming more that way because he was slobbering a mite. He dragged his tired tongue across his lips to daub the slobber, revealed to himself in the mirror that he was missing a lot of teeth.

Goddamn it! How had he gone from King of Rock and Roll to this? Old guy in a rest home in East Texas with a growth on his dick?

And what was that growth? Cancer? No one was talking. No one seemed to know. Perhaps the bump was a manifestation of the mistakes of his life, so many of them made with his dick.

He considered on that. Did he ask himself this question every day, or just now and then? Time sort of ran together when the last moment and the immediate moment and the moment forthcoming were all alike.

Shit, when was lunchtime? Had he slept through it?

Was it about time for his main nurse again? The good-looking one with the smooth chocolate skin and tits like grapefruits? The one who came in and sponge bathed him and held his pitiful little pecker in her gloved hands and put salve on his canker with all the enthusiasm of a mechanic oiling a defective part?

He hoped not. That was the worst of it. A doll like that handling him without warmth or emotion. Twenty years ago, just twenty, he could have made with the curled-lip smile and had her eating out of his asshole. Where had his youth gone? Why hadn't fame denied old age and death, and why had he left his fame in the first place, and did he want it back, and could he have it back, and if he could, would it make any difference?

And finally, when he was evacuated from the bowels of life into the toilet bowl of the beyond and was flushed, would the great sewer pipe flow him to the other side where God would—in the guise of a great all-seeing turd with corn-kernel eyes—be waiting with open turd arms, and would there be amongst the sewage his mother (bless her fat little heart) and father and friends, waiting with fried peanut butter and 'nanner sandwiches and ice cream cones, predigested, of course?

He was reflecting on this, pondering the afterlife, when Bull gave out with a hell of a scream, pooched his eyes damn near out of his head, arched his back, grease-farted like a blast from Gabriel's trumpet, and checked his tired old soul out of the Mud Creek Shady Grove Convalescence Home, flushed it on out and across the great shitty beyond.

Later that day, Elvis lay sleeping, his lips fluttering the bad taste of lunch—steamed zucchini and boiled peas—out of his belly. He awoke to a noise, rolled over to see a young attractive woman cleaning out Bull's dresser drawer. The curtains over the window next to Bull's bed were pulled wide open, and the sunlight was cutting through it and showing her to great advantage. She was blonde and Nordic-featured and her long hair was tied back with a big red bow and she wore big gold hoop earrings that shimmered in the sunlight. She was dressed in a white blouse and a short black skirt and dark hose and high heels. The heels made her ass ride up beneath her skirt like soft bald baby heads under a thin blanket.

She had a big yellow plastic trash can and she had one of Bull's dresser drawers pulled out, and she was picking through it, like a magpie looking for bright things. She found a few coins, a pocketknife, a cheap watch. These were plucked free and laid on the dresser top, then the remaining contents of the drawer—Bull's photographs of himself when young, a rotten pack of rubbers (wishful thinking never deserted Bull), a Bronze Star and a Purple Heart from his performance in the Vietnam War—were dumped into the trash can with a bang and a flutter.

Elvis got hold of his bed's lift button and raised himself for a better look. The woman had her back to him now, and didn't notice. She was replacing the dresser drawer and pulling out another. It was full of clothes. She took out the few shirts and pants and socks and underwear, and laid them on Bull's bed remade now, and minus Bull, who had been toted off to be taxidermied, embalmed, burned up, whatever.

"You're gonna toss that stuff," Elvis said. "Could I have one of them pictures of Bull? Maybe that Purple Heart? He was proud of it."

The young woman turned and looked at him, "I suppose," she said. She went to the trash can and bent over it and showed her black panties to Elvis as she rummaged. He knew the revealing of her panties was neither intentional or unintentional. She just didn't give a damn. She saw him as so physically and sexually nonthreatening, she didn't mind if he got a bird's-eye view of her; it was the same to her as a house cat sneaking a peek.

Elvis observed the thin panties straining and slipping into the caverns of her ass cheeks and felt his pecker flutter once, like a bird having a heart attack, then it laid down and remained limp and still.

Well, these days, even a flutter was kind of reassuring.

The woman surfaced from the trash can with a photo and the Purple Heart, went over to Elvis's bed and handed them to him.

Elvis dangled the ribbon that held the Purple Heart between his fingers, said, "Bull your kin?"

"My daddy," she said.

"I haven't seen you here before."

"Only been here once before," she said. "When I checked him in."

"Oh," Elvis said. "That was three years ago, wasn't it?"

"Yeah. Were you and him friends?"

Elvis considered the question. He didn't know the real answer. All he knew was Bull listened to him when he said he was Elvis Presley and seemed to believe him. If he didn't believe him, he at least had the courtesy not to patronize. Bull always called him Elvis, and before Bull grew too ill, he always played cards and checkers with him.

"Just roommates," Elvis said. "He didn't feel good enough to say much. I just sort of hated to see what was left of him go away so easy. He was an all right guy. He mentioned you a lot. You're Callie, right?"

"Yeah," she said. "Well, he was all right."

"Not enough you came and saw him though."

"Don't try to put some guilt trip on me, Mister. I did what I could. Hadn't been for Medicaid, Medicare, whatever that stuff was, he'd have been in a ditch somewhere. I didn't have the money to take care of him."

Elvis thought of his own daughter, lost long ago to him. If she knew he lived, would she come to see him? Would she care? He feared knowing the answer.

"You could have come and seen him," Elvis said.

"I was busy. Mind your own business. Hear?"

The chocolate-skin nurse with the grapefruit tits came in. Her white uniform crackled like cards being shuffled. Her little white nurse hat was tilted on her head in a way that said she loved mankind and made good money and was getting regular dick. She smiled at Callie and then at Elvis. "How are you this morning, Mr. Haff?"

"All right," Elvis said. "But I prefer Mr. Presley. Or Elvis. I keep telling you that. I don't go by Sebastian Haff anymore. I don't try to hide anymore."

"Why, of course," said the pretty nurse. "I knew that. I forgot. Good morning, Elvis."

Her voice dripped with sorghum syrup. Elvis wanted to hit her with his bedpan.

The nurse said to Callie, "Did you know we have a celebrity here, Miss Jones? Elvis Presley. You know, the rock and roll singer?"

"I've heard of him," Callie said. "I thought he was dead."

Callie went back to the dresser and squatted and set to work on the bottom drawer. The nurse looked at Elvis and smiled again, only she spoke to Callie. "Well, actually, Elvis is dead, and Mr. Haff knows that, don't you, Mr. Haff?"

"Hell no," said Elvis. "I'm right here. I ain't dead, yet."

"Now, Mr. Haff, I don't mind calling you Elvis, but you're a little confused, or like to play sometimes. You were an Elvis impersonator. Remember? You fell off a stage and broke your hip. What was it . . . twenty years ago? It got infected and you went into a coma for a few years. You came out with a few problems."

"I was impersonating myself," Elvis said. "I couldn't do nothing else. I haven't got any problems. You're trying to say my brain is messed up, aren't you?"

Callie quit cleaning out the bottom drawer of the dresser. She was interested now, and though it was no use, Elvis couldn't help but try and explain who he was, just one more time. The explaining had become a habit, like wanting to smoke a cigar long after the enjoyment of it was gone.

"I got tired of it all," he said. "I got on drugs, you know. I wanted out. Fella named Sebastian Haff, an Elvis imitator, the best of them. He took my place. He had a bad heart and he liked drugs, too. It was him died, not me. I took his place."

"Why would you want to leave all that fame," Callie said, "all that money?" And she looked at the nurse, like *Let's humor the old fart for a lark.*

"'Cause it got old. Woman I loved, Priscilla, she was gone. Rest of the women . . . were just women. The music wasn't mine anymore. I wasn't even me anymore. I was this thing they made up. Friends were sucking me dry. I got away and liked it, left all the money with Sebastian, except for enough to sustain me if things got bad. We had a deal, me and Sebastian. When I wanted to come back, he'd let me. It was all written up in a contract in case he wanted to give me a hard time, got to liking my life too good. Thing was, copy of the contract I had got lost in a trailer fire. I was living simple. Way Haff had been. Going from town to town doing the Elvis act. Only I felt like I was really me again. Can you dig that?"

"We're digging it, Mr. Haff . . . Mr. Presley," said the pretty nurse.

"I was singing the old way. Doing some new songs. Stuff I wrote. I was getting attention on a small but good scale. Women throwing themselves at me, 'cause they could imagine I was Elvis—only I *was* Elvis, playing Sebastian Haff playing Elvis. . . . It was all pretty good. I didn't mind the contract being burned up. I didn't even try to go back and convince anybody. Then I had the accident. Like I was saying, I'd laid up a little money in case of illness, stuff like that. That's what's paying for here. These nice facilities. Ha!"

"Now, Elvis," the nurse said. "Don't carry it too far. You may just get way out there and not come back."

"Oh fuck you," Elvis said.

The nurse giggled.

Shit, Elvis thought. *Get old, you can't even cuss somebody and have it bother them. Everything you do is either worthless or sadly amusing.*

"You know, Elvis," said the pretty nurse, "we have a Mr. Dillinger here too. And a President Kennedy. He says the bullet only wounded him and his brain is in a fruit jar at the White House, hooked up to some wires and a battery, and as long as the battery works, he can walk around without it. His brain, that is. You know, he says everyone was in on trying to assassinate him. Even Elvis Presley."

"You're an asshole," Elvis said.

"I'm not trying to hurt your feelings, Mr. Haff," the nurse said. "I'm merely trying to give you a reality check."

"You can shove that reality check right up your pretty black ass," Elvis said.

The nurse made a sad little snicking sound. "Mr. Haff, Mr. Haff. Such language."

"What happened to get you here?" said Callie. "Say you fell off a stage?"

"I was gyrating," Elvis said. "Doing 'Blue Moon,' but my hip went out. I'd been having trouble with it." Which was quite true. He'd sprained it making love to a blue-haired old lady with ELVIS tattooed on her fat ass. He couldn't help himself from wanting to fuck her. She looked like his mother, Gladys.

"You swiveled right off the stage?" Callie said. "Now that's sexy."

Elvis looked at her. She was smiling. This was great fun for her, listening to some nut tell a tale. She hadn't had this much fun since she put her old man in the rest home.

"Oh, leave me the hell alone," Elvis said.

The women smiled at one another, passing a private joke. Callie said to the nurse, "I've got what I want." She scraped the bright things off the top of Bull's dresser into her purse. "The clothes can go to Goodwill or the Salvation Army."

The pretty nurse nodded to Callie. "Very well. And I'm very sorry about your father. He was a nice man."

"Yeah," said Callie, and she started out of there. She paused at the foot of Elvis's bed. "Nice to meet you, Mr. Presley."

"Get the hell out," Elvis said.

"Now, now," said the pretty nurse, patting his foot through the covers, as if it were a little cantankerous dog. "I'll be back later to do that . . . little thing that has to be done. You know?"

"I know," Elvis said, not liking the words "little thing."

Callie and the nurse started away then, punishing him with the clean lines of their faces and the sheen of their hair, the jiggle of their asses and tits. When they were out of sight, Elvis heard them laugh about something in the hall, then they were gone, and Elvis felt as if he were on the far side of Pluto without a jacket. He picked up the ribbon with the Purple Heart and looked at it.

Poor Bull. In the end, did anything really matter?

Meanwhile . . .

The Earth swirled around the sun like a spinning turd in the toilet bowl (to keep up with Elvis's metaphors) and the good old abused Earth clicked about on its axis and the hole in the ozone spread slightly wider, like a shy lady fingering open her vagina, and the South American trees that had stood for centuries were visited by the dozer, the chainsaw, and the match, and they rose up in burned black puffs that expanded and dissipated into minuscule wisps, and while the puffs of smoke dissolved, there were IRA bombings in London, and there was more war in the Mideast. Blacks died in Africa of famine, the HIV virus infected a million more, the Dallas Cowboys lost again, and that Ole Blue Moon that Elvis and Patsy Cline sang so well about swung around the Earth and came in close and rose over the Shady Grove Convalescent Home, shone its bittersweet, silver-blue rays down on the joint like a flashlight beam shining through a blue-haired lady's do, and inside the rest home, evil waddled about like a duck looking for a spot to squat, and Elvis rolled over in his sleep and awoke with the intense desire to pee.

All right, thought Elvis. *This time I make it. No more piss or crap in the bed.* (Famous last words.)

Elvis sat up and hung his feet over the side of the bed and the bed swung far to the left and around the ceiling and back, and then it wasn't moving at all. The dizziness passed.

Elvis looked at his walker and sighed, leaned forward, took hold of the grips and eased himself off the bed and clumped the rubber-padded tips forward, and made for the toilet.

He was in the process of milking his bump-swollen weasel when he heard something in the hallway—a kind of scrambling, like a big spider scuttling about in a box of gravel.

There was always some sound in the hallway, people coming and going, yelling in pain or confusion, but this time of night, three a.m., was normally quite dead.

It shouldn't have concerned him, but the truth of the matter was, now that he was up and had successfully pissed in the pot, he was no longer sleepy; he was still thinking about that bimbo, Callie, and the nurse (what the hell was her name?) with the tits like grapefruits, and all they had said.

Elvis stumped his walker backwards out of the bathroom, turned it, made his way forward into the hall. The hall was semi-dark, with every other light out, and the lights that were on were dimmed to a watery egg-yolk yellow. The black and white tile floor looked like a great chessboard, waxed and buffed for the next game of life, and here he was, a semi-crippled pawn, ready to go.

Off in the far wing of the home, Old Lady McGee, better known in the home as the Blue Yodeler, broke into one of her famous yodels (she claimed to have sung with a country and western band in her youth), then ceased abruptly. Elvis swung the walker forward and moved on. He hadn't been out of his room in ages, and he hadn't been out of his bed much either. Tonight, he felt invigorated because he hadn't pissed his bed, and he'd heard the sound again, the spider in the box of gravel. (Big spider. Big box. Lots of gravel.) And following the sound gave him something to do.

Elvis rounded the corner, beads of sweat popping out on his forehead like heat blisters. Jesus. He wasn't invigorated now. Thinking about how invigorated he was had bushed him. Still, going back to his room to lie on his bed and wait for morning so he could wait for noon, then afternoon and night, didn't appeal to him.

He went by Jack McLaughlin's room, the fellow who was convinced he was John F. Kennedy, and that his brain was in the White House running on batteries. The door to Jack's room was open. Elvis peeked in as he moved by, knowing full well that Jack might not want to see him. Sometimes he accepted Elvis as the real Elvis, and when he did, he got scared, saying it was Elvis who had been behind the assassination.

Actually, Elvis hoped he felt that way tonight. It would at least be some acknowledgment that he was who he was, even if the acknowledgment was a fearful shriek from a nut.

Course, Elvis thought, *maybe I'm nuts too. Maybe I am Sebastian Haff and I fell off the stage and broke more than my hip, cracked some part of my brain that lost my old self and made me think I'm Elvis.*

No. He couldn't believe that. That's the way they wanted him to think. They wanted him to believe he was nuts and he wasn't Elvis, just some sad old fart who had once lived out part of another man's life because he had none of his own.

He wouldn't accept that. He wasn't Sebastian Haff. He was Elvis Goddamn Aaron Fucking Presley with a boil on his dick.

Course, he believed that, maybe he ought to believe Jack was John F. Kennedy, and Mums Delay, another patient here at Shady Grove, was Dillinger. Then again, maybe not. They were kind of scanty on evidence. He at least looked like Elvis gone old and sick. Jack was black—he claimed The Powers That Be had dyed him that color to keep him hidden—and Mums was a woman who claimed she'd had a sex change operation.

Jesus, was this a rest home or a nuthouse?

Jack's room was one of the special kind. He didn't have to share. He had money from somewhere. The room was packed with books and little luxuries. And though Jack could walk well, he even had a fancy electric wheelchair that he rode about in sometimes. Once, Elvis had seen him riding it around the outside circular drive, popping wheelies and spinning doughnuts.

When Elvis looked into Jack's room, he saw him lying on the floor. Jack's gown was pulled up around his neck, and his bony black ass appeared to be made of licorice in the dim light. Elvis figured Jack had been on his way to the shitter, or was coming back from it, and had collapsed. His heart, maybe.

"Jack," Elvis said.

Elvis clumped into the room, positioned his walker next to Jack, took a deep breath and stepped out of it, supporting himself with one side of it. He got down on his knees beside Jack, hoping he'd be able to get up again. God, but his knees and back hurt.

Jack was breathing hard. Elvis noted the scar at Jack's hairline, a long scar that made Jack's skin lighter there, almost gray. ("That's where they took the brain out," Jack always explained, "put it in that fucking jar. I got a little bag of sand up there now.")

Elvis touched the old man's shoulder. "Jack. Man, you okay?"

No response.

Elvis tried again. "Mr. Kennedy."

"Uh," said Jack (Mr. Kennedy).

"Hey, man. You're on the floor," Elvis said.

"No shit? Who are you?"

Elvis hesitated. This wasn't the time to get Jack worked up.

"Sebastian," he said. "Sebastian Haff."

Elvis took hold of Jack's shoulder and rolled him over. It was about as difficult as rolling a jelly roll. Jack lay on his back now. He strayed an eyeball at Elvis. He started to speak, hesitated. Elvis took hold of Jack's nightgown and managed to work it down around Jack's knees, trying to give the old fart some dignity.

Jack finally got his breath. "Did you see him go by in the hall? He scuttled like."

"Who?"

"Someone they sent."

"Who's they?"

"You know. Lyndon Johnson. Castro. They've sent someone to finish me. I think maybe it was Johnson himself. Real ugly. Real goddamn ugly."

"Johnson's dead," Elvis said.

"That won't stop him," Jack said.

Later that morning, sunlight shooting into Elvis's room through venetian blinds, Elvis put his hands behind his head and considered the night before while the pretty black nurse with the grapefruit tits salved his dick. He had reported Jack's fall and the aides had come to help Jack back in bed, and him back on his walker. He had clumped back to his room (after being scolded for being out there that time of night) feeling that an air of strangeness had blown into the rest home, an air that wasn't there the day before. It was at low ebb now, but certainly still present, humming in the background like some kind of generator ready to buzz up to a higher notch at a moment's notice.

And he was certain it wasn't just his imagination. The scuttling sound he'd heard last night, Jack had heard it, too. What was that all about? It wasn't the sound of a walker, or a crip dragging their foot, or a wheelchair creeping along, it was something else, and now that he thought about it, it wasn't exactly spider legs in gravel, more like a roll of barbed wire tumbling across tile.

Elvis was so wrapped up in these considerations, he lost awareness of the nurse until she said, "Mr. Haff!"

"What . . . ?" He saw that she was smiling and looking down at her hands. He looked too. There, nestled in one of her gloved palms, was a massive, blue-veined hooter with a pus-filled bump on it the size of a pecan. It was *his* hooter and *his* pus-filled bump.

"You ole rascal," she said, and gently lowered his dick between his legs. "I think you better take a cold shower, Mr. Haff."

Elvis was amazed. That was the first time in years he'd had a boner like that. What gave here?

Then he realized what gave. He wasn't thinking about not being able to do it. He was thinking about something that interested him, and now, with something clicking around inside his head besides old memories and confusions, concerns about his next meal and going to the crapper, he had been given a dose of life again. He grinned his gums and what teeth were in them at the nurse.

"You get in there with me," he said, "and I'll take that shower."

"You silly thing," she said, and pulled his nightgown down and stood and removed her plastic gloves and dropped them in the trash can beside his bed.

"Why don't you pull on it a little," Elvis said.

"You ought to be ashamed," the nurse said, but she smiled when she said it.

She left the room door open after she left. This concerned Elvis a little, but he felt his bed was at such an angle no one could look in, and if they did, tough luck. He wasn't going to look a gift hard-on in the pee-hole. He pulled the sheet over him and pushed his hands beneath the sheets and got his gown pulled up over his belly. He took hold of his snake and began to choke it with one hand, running his thumb over the pus-filled bump. With his other hand, he fondled his balls. He thought of Priscilla and the pretty black nurse and Bull's daughter and even the blue-haired fat lady with ELVIS tattooed on her butt, and he stroked harder and faster, and goddamn but he got stiffer and stiffer, and the bump on his cock gave up its load first, exploded hot pus down his thighs, and then his balls, which he thought forever empty, filled up with juice and electricity, and finally he threw the switch. The dam broke and the juice flew. He heard himself scream happily and felt hot wetness jetting down his legs, splattering as far as his big toes.

"Oh God," he said softly. "I like that. I like that."

He closed his eyes and slept. And for the first time in a long time, not fitfully.

Lunchtime. The Shady Grove lunchroom.

Elvis sat with a plate of steamed carrots and broccoli and flaky roast beef in front of him. A dry roll, a pat of butter and a short glass of milk soldiered on the side. It was not inspiring.

Next to him, the Blue Yodeler was stuffing a carrot up her nose while she expounded on the sins of God, the Heavenly Father, for knocking up that nice Mary in her sleep, slipping up her ungreased poontang while she snored, and—bless her little heart—not even knowing it, or getting a clit throb from it, but waking up with a belly full of baby and no memory of action.

Elvis had heard it all before. It used to offend him, this talk of God as rapist, but he'd heard it so much now he didn't care. She rattled on.

Across the way, an old man who wore a black mask and sometimes a white Stetson, known to residents and staff alike as Kemosabe, snapped one of his two capless cap pistols at the floor and called for an invisible Tonto to bend over so he could drive him home.

At the far end of the table, Dillinger was talking about how much whiskey he used to drink, and how many cigars he used to smoke before he got his dick cut off at the stump and split so he could become a she and hide out as a woman. Now she said she no longer thought of banks and machine guns, women and fine cigars. She now thought about spots on dishes, the colors of curtains and drapes as coordinated with carpets and walls.

Even as the depression of his surroundings settled over him again, Elvis deliberated last night, and glanced down the length of the table at Jack (Mr. Kennedy), who headed its far end. He saw the old man was looking at him, as if they shared a secret. Elvis's ill mood dropped a notch; a real mystery was at work here, and come nightfall, he was going to investigate.

Swing the Shady Grove Convalescent Home's side of the Earth away from the sun again, and swing the moon in close and blue again. Blow some gauzy clouds across the nasty black sky. Now ease on into three a.m.

Elvis awoke with a start and turned his head toward the intrusion. Jack stood next to the bed looking down at him. Jack was wearing a suit coat over his nightgown and he had on thick glasses. He said, "Sebastian. It's loose."

Elvis collected his thoughts, pasted them together into a not-too-scattered collage. "What's loose?"

"It," said Jack. "Listen."

Elvis listened. Out in the hall he heard the scuttling sound of the night before. Tonight, it reminded him of great locust wings beating frantically inside a small cardboard box, the tips of them scratching at the cardboard, cutting it, ripping it apart.

"Jesus Christ, what is it?" Elvis said.

"I thought it was Lyndon Johnson, but it isn't. I've come across new evidence that suggests another assassin."

"Assassin?"

Jack cocked an ear. The sound had gone away, moved distant, then ceased.

"It's got another target tonight," said Jack. "Come on. I want to show you something. I don't think it's safe if you go back to sleep."

"For Christ's sake," Elvis said. "Tell the administrators."

"The suits and the white starches," Jack said. "No thanks. I trusted them back when I was in Dallas, and look where that got my brain and me. I'm thinking with sand here, maybe picking up a few waves from my brain. Someday, who's to say they won't just disconnect the battery at the White House?"

"That's something to worry about, all right," Elvis said.

"Listen here," Jack said. "I know you're Elvis, and there were rumors, you know . . . about how you hated me, but I've thought it over. You hated me, you could have finished me the other night. All I want from you is to look me in the eye and assure me you had nothing to do with that day in Dallas, and that you never knew Lee Harvey Oswald or Jack Ruby."

Elvis stared at him as sincerely as possible. "I had nothing to do with Dallas, and I knew neither Lee Harvey Oswald nor Jack Ruby."

"Good," said Jack. "May I call you Elvis instead of Sebastian?"

"You may."

"Excellent. You wear glasses to read?"

"I wear glasses when I really want to see," Elvis said.

"Get 'em and come on."

Elvis swung his walker along easily, not feeling as if he needed it too much tonight. He was excited. Jack was a nut, and maybe he himself was nuts, but there was an adventure going on.

They came to the hall restroom. The one reserved for male visitors. "In here," Jack said.

"Now wait a minute," Elvis said. "You're not going to get me in there and try and play with my pecker, are you?"

Jack stared at him. "Man, I made love to Jackie and Marilyn and a ton of others, and you think I want to play with your nasty ole dick?"

"Good point," said Elvis.

They went into the restroom. It was large, with several stalls and urinals.

"Over here," said Jack. He went over to one of the stalls and pushed open the door and stood back by the commode to make room for Elvis's walker. Elvis eased inside and looked at what Jack was now pointing to.

Graffiti.

"That's it?" Elvis said. "We're investigating a scuttling in the hall, trying to discover who attacked you last night, and you bring me in here to show me stick pictures on the shithouse wall?"

"Look close," Jack said.

Elvis leaned forward. His eyes weren't what they used to be, and his glasses probably needed to be upgraded, but he could see that instead of writing, the graffiti was a series of simple pictorials.

A thrill, like a shot of good booze, ran through Elvis. He had once been a fanatic reader of ancient and esoteric lore, like *The Egyptian Book of the Dead* and *The Complete Works of H. P. Lovecraft*, and straight away he recognized what he was staring at. "Egyptian hieroglyphics," he said.

"Right-a-reen-o," Jack said. "Hey, you're not as stupid as some folks made you out."

"Thanks," Elvis said.

Jack reached into his suit coat pocket and took out a folded piece of paper and unfolded it. He pressed it to the wall. Elvis saw that it was covered with the same sort of figures that were on the wall of the stall.

"I copied this down yesterday. I came in here to shit because they hadn't cleaned up my bathroom. I saw this on the wall, went back to my room and looked it up in my books and wrote it all down. The top line translates something like *Pharaoh gobbles donkey goober*. And the bottom line is *Cleopatra does the dirty*."

"What?"

"Well, pretty much," Jack said.

Elvis was mystified. "All right," he said. "One of the nuts here, present company excluded, thinks he's Tutankhamun or something, and he writes on the wall in hieroglyphics. So what? I mean, what's the connection? Why are we hanging out in a toilet?"

"I don't know how they connect exactly," Jack said. "Not yet. But this . . . thing, it caught me asleep last night, and I came awake just in time to . . . well, he had me on the floor and had his mouth over my asshole."

"A shit eater?" Elvis said.

"I don't think so," Jack said. "He was after my soul. You can get that out of any of the major orifices in a person's body. I've read about it."

"Where?" Elvis asked. "*Hustler*?"

"*The Everyday Man or Woman's Book of the Soul* by David Webb. It has some pretty good movie reviews about stolen soul movies in the back, too."

"Oh, that sounds trustworthy," Elvis said.

They went back to Jack's room and sat on his bed and looked through his many books on astrology, the Kennedy assassination, and a number of esoteric tomes, including the philosophy book, *The Everyday Man or Woman's Book of the Soul*.

Elvis found that book fascinating in particular; it indicated that not only did humans have a soul, but that the soul could be stolen, and there was a section concerning vampires and ghouls and incubi and succubi, as well as related soul suckers. Bottom line was, one of those dudes was around, you had to watch your holes. Mouth hole. Nose hole. Asshole. If you were a woman, you needed to watch a different hole. Dick pee-holes and ear holes—male or female—didn't matter. The soul didn't hang out there.

They weren't considered major orifices for some reason.

In the back of the book was a list of items, related and not related to the book, that you could buy. Little plastic pyramids. Hats you could wear while channeling. Subliminal tapes that would help you learn Arabic. Postage was paid.

"Every kind of soul eater is in that book except politicians and science fiction fans," Jack said. "And I think that's what we got here in Shady Grove. A soul eater. Turn to the Egyptian section."

Elvis did. The chapter was prefaced by a movie still from *The Ten Commandments* with Yul Brynner playing Pharaoh. He was standing up in his chariot looking serious, which seemed a fair enough expression, considering the Red Sea, which had been parted by Moses, was about to come back together and drown him and his army.

Elvis read the article slowly while Jack heated water with his plug-in heater and made cups of instant coffee. "I get my niece to smuggle this stuff in," said Jack. "Or she claims to be my niece. She's a black woman. I never saw her before I was shot that day in Dallas and they took my brain out. She's part of the new identity they've given me. She's got a great ass."

"Damn," said Elvis. "What it says here is that you can bury some dude, and if he gets the right tana leaves and spells said over him and such bullshit, he can come back to life some thousands of years later, and to stay alive, he has to suck on the souls of the living, and that if the souls are small, his life force doesn't last long. Small. What's that mean?"

"Read on . . . no, never mind, I'll tell you." Jack handed Elvis his cup of coffee and sat down on the bed next to him. "Before I do, want a Ding Dong? Not mine. The chocolate kind. Well, I guess mine is chocolate, now that I've been dyed."

"You got Ding Dongs?" Elvis asked.

"Couple of PAYDAYS and Baby Ruth too," Jack said. "Which will it be? Let's get decadent."

Elvis licked his lips. "I'll have a Ding Dong."

While Elvis savored the Ding Dong, gumming it sloppily, sipping his coffee between bites, Jack, coffee cup balanced on his knee, a Baby Ruth in one mitt, expounded.

"Small souls means those without much fire for life," Jack said. "You know a place like that?"

"If souls were fires," Elvis said, "they couldn't burn much lower without being out than here. Only thing we got going in this joint is the pilot light."

"Exactamundo," Jack said. "What we got here in Shady Grove is an Egyptian soul sucker of some sort. A mummy hiding out, coming in here to feed on the sleeping. It's perfect, you see. The souls are little, and don't provide him with much. If this thing comes back two or three times in a row to wrap his lips around some elder's asshole, that elder is going to die pretty soon, and who's the wiser? Our mummy may not be getting much energy out of this, way he would with big souls, but the prey is easy. A mummy couldn't be too strong, really. Mostly just husk. But we're pretty much that way ourselves. We're not too far off being mummies."

"And with new people coming in all the time," Elvis said, "he can keep this up forever, this soul robbing."

"That's right. Because that's what we're brought here for. To get us out of the way until we die. And the ones don't die first of disease, or just plain old age, he gets."

Elvis considered all that. "That's why he doesn't bother the nurses and aides and administrators? He can go unsuspected."

"That, and they're not asleep. He has to get you when you're sleeping or unconscious."

"All right, but the thing throws me, Jack, is how does an ancient Egyptian end up in an East Texas rest home, and why is he writing on shithouse walls?"

"He went to take a crap, got bored, and wrote on the wall. He probably wrote on pyramid walls, centuries ago."

"What would he crap?" Elvis said. "It's not like he'd eat, is it?"

"He eats souls," Jack said, "so I assume, he craps soul residue. And what that means to me is, you die by his mouth, you don't go to the other side, or wherever souls go. He digests the souls 'til they don't exist anymore—"

"And you're just so much toilet water decoration," Elvis said.

"That's the way I've got it worked out," Jack said. "He's just like anyone else when he wants to take a dump. He likes a nice clean place with a flush. They didn't have that in his time, and I'm sure he finds it handy. The writing on the walls is just habit. Maybe, to him, Pharaoh and Cleopatra were just yesterday."

Elvis finished off the Ding Dong and sipped his coffee. He felt a rush from the sugar and he loved it. He wanted to ask Jack for the PAYDAY he had mentioned, but restrained himself. Sweets, fried foods, late nights, and drugs had been the beginning of his original downhill spiral. He had to keep himself collected this time. He had to be ready to battle the Egyptian soul-sucking menace.

Soul-sucking menace?

God. He was really bored. It was time for him to go back to his room and to bed so he could shit on himself, get back to normal.

But Jesus and Ra, this was different from what had been going on up until now! It might all be bullshit, but considering what was going on in his life right now, it was absorbing bullshit. It might be worth playing the game to the hilt, even if he was playing it with a black guy who thought he was John F. Kennedy and believed an Egyptian mummy was stalking the corridors of Shady Grove Convalescent Home, writing graffiti on toilet stalls, sucking people's souls out through their assholes, digesting them, and crapping them down the visitors' toilet.

Suddenly, Elvis was pulled out of his considerations. There came from the hall the noise again. The sound that each time he heard it reminded him of something different. This time it was dried corn husks being rattled in a high wind. He felt goose bumps travel up his spine and the hairs on the back of his neck and arms stood up. He leaned forward and put his hands on his walker and pulled himself upright.

"Don't go in the hall," Jack said.

"I'm not asleep."

"That doesn't mean it won't hurt you."

"'It' my ass, there isn't any mummy from Egypt."

"Nice knowing you, Elvis."

Elvis inched the walker forward. He was halfway to the open door when he spied the figure in the hallway.

As the thing came even with the doorway, the hall lights went dim and sputtered. Twisting about the apparition, like pet crows, were flutters of shadows. The thing walked and stumbled, shuffled and flowed. Its legs moved like Elvis's own, meaning not too good, and yet there was something about its locomotion that was impossible to identify. Stiff, but ghostly smooth. It was dressed in nasty-looking jeans, a black shirt and a black cowboy hat that came down so low it covered where the thing's eyebrows should be. It wore large cowboy boots with the toes curled up, and there came from the thing a kind of mixed stench: a compost pile of mud, rotting leaves, resin, spoiled fruit, dry dust, and gassy sewage.

Elvis found that he couldn't scoot ahead another inch. He froze. The thing stopped and cautiously turned its head on its apple-stem neck and looked at Elvis with empty eye sockets, revealing that it was, in fact, uglier than Lyndon Johnson.

Surprisingly, Elvis found he was surging forward as if on a zooming camera dolly, and that he was plunging into the thing's right eye socket, which swelled speedily to the dimensions of a vast canyon bottomed by blackness.

Down Elvis went, spinning and spinning, and out of the emptiness rushed resin-scented memories of pyramids and boats on a river, hot blue skies, and a great silver bus lashed hard by black rain, a crumbling bridge and a charge of dusky water and a gleam of silver. Then there was a darkness so caliginous it was beyond being called dark, and Elvis could feel and taste mud in his mouth and a sensation of claustrophobia beyond expression. And he could perceive the thing's hunger, a hunger that prodded him like hot pins, and then—

—there came *popping* sounds in rapid succession, and Elvis felt himself whirling even faster, spinning backwards out of that deep memory canyon of the dusty head, and now he stood once again within the framework of his walker, and the mummy—for Elvis no longer denied to himself that it was such—turned its head away and began to move again, to shuffle, to flow, to stumble, to glide, down the hall, its pet shadows screeching with rusty throats around its head. *Pop! Pop! Pop!*

As the thing moved on, Elvis compelled himself to lift his walker and advance into the hall. Jack slipped up beside him, and they saw the mummy in cowboy clothes traveling toward the exit door at the back of the home. When it came to the locked door, it leaned against where the door met the jam and twisted and writhed, squeezed through the invisible crack where the two connected. Its shadows pursued it, as if sucked through by a vacuum cleaner.

The popping sound went on, and Elvis turned his head in that direction, and there, in his mask, his double concho-studded holster belted around his waist, was Kemosabe, a silver Fanner Fifty in either hand. He was popping caps rapidly at where the mummy had departed, the black-spotted red rolls flowing out from behind the hammers of his revolvers in smoky relay.

"Asshole!" Kemosabe said. "Asshole!"

And then Kemosabe quivered, dropped both hands, popped a cap from each gun toward the ground, stiffened, collapsed.

Elvis knew he was dead of a ruptured heart before he hit the black and white tile, gone down and out with both guns blazing, soul intact.

The hall lights trembled back to normal.

The administrators, the nurses, and the aides came then. They rolled Kemosabe over and drove their palms against his chest, but he didn't breathe again. No more Hi-Yo Silver. They sighed over him and clucked their tongues, and finally an aide reached over and lifted Kemosabe's mask, pulled it off his head and dropped it on the floor, nonchalantly, and without respect, revealed his identity.

It was no one anyone really knew.

Once again, Elvis got scolded, and this time he got quizzed about what had happened to Kemosabe, and so did Jack, but neither told the truth. Who was going to believe a couple of nuts? Elvis and Jack Kennedy explaining that Kemosabe was gunning for a mummy in cowboy duds, a Bubba Ho-Tep with a flock of shadows roiling about his cowboy-hatted head?

So, what they did was lie.

"He came snapping caps and then he fell," Elvis said, and Jack corroborated his story and when Kemosabe had been carried off, Elvis, with some difficulty, using his walker for support, got down on his knee and picked up the discarded mask and carried it away with him. He had wanted the guns, but an aide had taken those for her four-year-old son.

Later, he and Jack learned through the grapevine that Kemosabe's roommate, an eighty-year-old man who had been in a semi-comatose condition for several years, had been found dead on the floor of his room. It was assumed Kemosabe had lost it and dragged him off his bed and onto the floor and the eighty-year-old man had kicked the bucket during the fall. As for Kemosabe, they figured he had then gone nuts when he realized what he had done, and had wandered out in the hall firing, and had a heart attack.

Elvis knew different. The mummy had come and Kemosabe had tried to protect his roommate in the only way he knew how. But instead of silver bullets, his gun smoked sulfur. Elvis felt a rush of pride in the old fart.

He and Jack got together later, talked about what they had seen, and then there was nothing left to say.

Night went away and the sun came up, and Elvis, who had slept not a wink, came up with it and put on khaki pants and a khaki shirt and used his walker to go outside. It had been ages since he had been out, and it seemed strange out there, all that sunlight and the smells of flowers and the Texas sky so high and the clouds so white.

It was hard to believe he had spent so much time in his bed. Just the use of his legs with the walker these last few days had tightened the muscles, and he found he could get around better.

The pretty nurse with the grapefruit tits came outside and said, "Mr. Presley, you look so much stronger. But you shouldn't stay out too long. It's almost time for a nap and for us, to, you know. . . ."

"Fuck off, you patronizing bitch," said Elvis. "I'm tired of your shit. I'll lube my own transmission. You treat me like a baby again, I'll wrap this goddamn walker around your head."

The pretty nurse stood stunned, then went away quietly.

Elvis inched his way with the walker around the great circular drive that surrounded the home. It was a half hour later when he reached the back of the home and the door through which the mummy had departed. It was still locked, and he stood and looked at it amazed. How in hell had the mummy done that, slipping through an indiscernible chink between door and frame?

Elvis looked down at the concrete that lay at the back of the door. No clues there. He used the walker to travel toward the growth of trees out back, a growth of pin oaks and sweet gums and hickory nut trees that shouldered on either side of the large creek that flowed behind the home.

The ground tipped sharply there, and for a moment he hesitated, then reconsidered. *Well, what the fuck?* he thought.

He planted the walker and started going forward, the ground sloping ever more dramatically. By the time he reached the bank of the creek and came to a gap in the trees, he was exhausted. He had the urge to start yelling for help, but didn't want to belittle himself, not after his performance with the nurse. He knew that he had regained some of his former confidence. His cursing and abuse had not seemed cute to her that time. The words had bitten her, if only slightly. Truth was, he was going to miss her greasing his pecker.

He looked over the bank of the creek. It was quite a drop there. The creek itself was narrow, and on either side of it was a gravel-littered six feet of shore. To his left, where the creek ran beneath a bridge, he could see where a mass of weeds and mud had gathered over time, and he could see something shiny in their midst.

Elvis eased to the ground inside his walker and sat there and looked at the water churning along. A huge woodpecker laughed in a tree nearby and a jay yelled at a smaller bird to leave his territory.

Where had ole Bubba Ho-Tep gone? Where did he come from? How in hell did he get here?

He recalled what he had seen inside the mummy's mind. The silver bus, the rain, the shattered bridge, the wash of water and mud.

Well, now wait a minute, he thought. *Here we have water and mud and a bridge, though it's not broken, and there's something shiny in the midst of all those leaves and limbs and collected debris.* All these items were elements of what he had seen in Bubba Ho-Tep's head. Obviously there was a connection.

But what was it?

When he got his strength back, Elvis pulled himself up and got the walker turned, and worked his way back to the home. He was covered in sweat and stiff as wire by the time he reached his room and tugged himself into bed. The blister on his dick throbbed and he unfastened his pants and eased down his underwear. The blister had refilled with pus, and it looked nastier than usual.

It's a cancer, he determined. He made the conclusion in a certain final rush. *They're keeping it from me because I'm old and to them it doesn't matter. They think age will kill me first, and they are probably right.*

Well, fuck them. I know what it is, and if it isn't, it might as well be.

He got the salve and doctored the pus-filled lesion, and put the salve away, and pulled up his underwear and pants, and fastened his belt.

Elvis got his TV remote off the dresser and clicked it on while he waited for lunch. As he ran the channels, he hit upon an advertisement for Elvis Presley week. It startled him. It wasn't the first time it had happened, but at the moment it struck him hard. It showed clips from his movies, *Clambake*, *Roustabout*, several others. All shit movies. Here he was complaining about loss of pride and how life had treated him, and now he realized he'd never had any pride and much of how life had treated him had been quite good, and the bulk of the bad had been his own fault. He wished now he'd fired his manager, Colonel Parker, about the time he got into films. The old fart had been a fool, and he had been a bigger fool for following him. He wished, too, he had treated Priscilla right. He wished he could tell his daughter he loved her.

Always the questions. Never the answers. Always the hopes. Never the fulfillments.

Elvis clicked off the set and dropped the remote on the dresser just as Jack came into the room. He had a folder under his arm. He looked like he was ready for a briefing at the White House.

"I had the woman who calls herself my niece come get me," he said. "She took me downtown to the newspaper morgue. She's been helping me do some research."

"On what?" Elvis said.

"On our mummy."

"You know something about him?" Elvis asked.

"I know plenty."

Jack pulled a chair up next to the bed, and Elvis used the bed's lift button to raise his back and head so he could see what was in Jack's folder.

Jack opened the folder, took out some clippings, and laid them on the bed. Elvis looked at them as Jack talked.

"One of the lesser mummies, on loan from the Egyptian government, was being circulated across the United States. You know, museums, that kind of stuff. It wasn't a major exhibit, like the King Tut exhibit some years back, but it was of interest. The mummy was flown or carried by train from state to state. When it got to Texas, it was stolen.

"Evidence points to the fact that it was stolen at night by a couple of guys in a silver bus. There was a witness. Some guy walking his dog or something. Anyway, the thieves broke in the museum and stole it, hoping to get a ransom probably. But in came the worst storm in East Texas history. Tornadoes. Rain. Hail. You name it. Creeks and rivers overflowed. Mobile homes were washed away. Livestock drowned. Maybe you remember it. . . . No matter. It was one hell of a flood.

"These guys got away, and nothing was ever heard from them. After you told me what you saw inside the mummy's head—the silver bus, the storm, the bridge, all that—I came up with a more interesting and, I believe, considerably more accurate scenario."

"Let me guess. The bus got washed away. I think I saw it today. Right out back in the creek. It must have washed up there years ago."

"That confirms it. The bridge you saw breaking, that's how the bus got in the water, which would have been as deep then as a raging river. The bus was carried downstream. It lodged somewhere nearby, and the mummy was imprisoned by debris, and recently it worked its way loose."

"But how did it come alive?" Elvis asked. "And how did I end up inside its memories?"

"The speculation is broader here, but from what I've read, sometimes mummies were buried without their names, a curse put on their sarcophagus, or coffin, if you will. My guess is our guy was one of those. While he was in the coffin, he was a drying corpse. But when the bus was washed off the road, the coffin was overturned, or broken open, and our boy was freed of coffin and curse. Or more likely, it rotted open in time, and the holding spell was broken. And think about him down there all that time, waiting for freedom, alive, but not alive. Hungry, and no way to feed. I said he was free of his curse, but that's not entirely true. He's free of his imprisonment, but he still needs souls.

"And now, he's free to have them, and he'll keep feeding unless he's finally destroyed. . . . You know, I think there's a part of him, oddly enough, that wants to fit in. To be human again. He doesn't entirely know what he's become. He responds to some old desires and the new desires of his condition. That's why he's taken on the illusion of clothes, probably copying the dress of one of his victims.

"The souls give him strength. Increase his spectral powers. One of which was to hypnotize you, kinda, draw you inside his head. He couldn't steal your soul that way, you have to be unconscious to have that done to you, but he could weaken you, distract you."

"And those shadows around him?"

"His guardians. They warn him. They have some limited powers of their own. I've read about them in *The Everyday Man or Woman's Book of the Soul*."

"What do we do?" Elvis asked.

"I think changing rest homes would be a good idea," Jack said. "I can't think of much else. I will say this. Our mummy is a nighttime kind of guy. Three a.m. actually. So, I'm going to sleep now, and again after lunch. Set my alarm for before dark so I can fix myself a couple cups of coffee. He comes tonight, I don't want him slapping his lips over my asshole again. I think he heard you coming down the hall about the time he got started on me the other night, and he ran. Not because he was scared, but because he didn't want anyone to find out he's around. Consider it. He has the proverbial bird's nest on the ground here."

After Jack left, Elvis decided he should follow Jack's lead and nap. Of course, at his age, he napped a lot anyway, and could fall asleep at any time, or toss restlessly for hours. There was no rhyme or reason to it.

He nestled his head into his pillow and tried to sleep, but sleep wouldn't come. Instead, he thought about things. Like, what did he really have left in life but this place? It wasn't much of a home, but it was all he had, and he'd be damned if he'd let a foreign, graffiti-writing, soul-sucking sonofabitch in an oversized hat and cowboy boots (with elf toes) take away his family members' souls and shit them down the visitors' toilet.

In the movies he had always played heroic types. But when the stage lights went out, it was time for drugs and stupidity and the coveting of women. Now it was time to be a little of what he had always fantasized being.

A hero.

Elvis leaned over and got hold of his telephone and dialed Jack's room. "Mr. Kennedy," Elvis said when Jack answered. "Ask not what your rest home can do for you. Ask what you can do for your rest home."

"Hey, you're copping my best lines," Jack said.

"Well then, to paraphrase one of my own, 'Let's take care of business.'"

"What are you getting at?"

"You know what I'm getting at. We're gonna kill a mummy."

The sun, like a boil on the bright blue ass of day, rolled gradually forward and spread its legs wide to reveal the pubic thatch of night, a hairy darkness in which stars crawled like lice, and the moon crabbed slowly upward like an albino dog tick striving for the anal gulch.

During this slow-rolling transition, Elvis and Jack discussed their plans, then they slept a little, ate their lunch of boiled cabbage and meat loaf, slept some more, ate a supper of white bread and asparagus and a helping of shit on a shingle without the shingle, slept again, awoke about the time the pubic thatch appeared and those starry lice began to crawl.

And even then, with night about them, they had to wait until midnight to do what they had to do.

Jack squinted through his glasses and examined his list. "Two bottles of rubbing alcohol?" Jack said.

"Check," said Elvis. "And we won't have to toss it. Look here." Elvis held up a paint sprayer. "I found this in the storage room."

"I thought they kept it locked." Jack said.

"They do. But I stole a hairpin from Dillinger and picked the lock."

"Great!" Jack said. "Matches?"

"Check. I also scrounged a cigarette lighter."

"Good. Uniforms?"

Elvis held up his white suit, slightly grayed in spots with a chili stain on the front. A white silk scarf and the big gold and silver and ruby-studded belt that went with the outfit lay on the bed. There were zippered boots from Kmart. "Check."

Jack held up a gray business suit on a hanger. "I've got some nice shoes and a tie to go with it in my room."

"Check," Elvis said.

"Scissors?"

"Check."

"I've got my motorized wheelchair oiled and ready to roll," Jack said, "and I've looked up a few words of power in one of my magic books. I don't know if they'll stop a mummy, but they're supposed to ward off evil. I wrote them down on a piece of paper."

"We use what we got," Elvis said. "Well then. 2:45 out back of the place."

"Considering our rate of travel, better start moving about 2:30," Jack said.

"Jack," Elvis asked, "do we know what we're doing?"

"No, but they say fire cleanses evil. Let's hope they, whoever they are, are right."

"Check on that, too," said Elvis. "Synchronize watches."

They did, and Elvis added, "Remember. The key words for tonight are *Caution* and *Flammable*. And *Watch Your Ass*."

The front door had an alarm system, but it was easily manipulated from the inside. Once Elvis had the wires cut with the scissors, they pushed the compression lever on the door, and Jack shoved his wheelchair outside and held the door while Elvis worked his walker through. Elvis tossed the scissors into the shrubbery, and Jack jammed a paperback book between the doors to allow them reentry, should reentry be an option at a later date.

Elvis was wearing a large pair of glasses with multicolored gem-studded chocolate frames and his stained white jumpsuit with scarf and belt and zippered boots. The suit was open at the front and hung loose on him, except at the belly. To make it even tighter there, Elvis had made up an Indian medicine bag of sorts, and stuffed it inside his jumpsuit. The bag contained Kemosabe's mask, Bull's Purple Heart, and the newspaper clipping where he had first read of his alleged death.

Jack had on his gray business suit with a black-and-red-striped tie knotted carefully at the throat, sensible black shoes, and black nylon socks. The suit fit him well. He looked like a former president.

In the seat of the wheelchair was the paint sprayer, filled with rubbing alcohol, and beside it, a cigarette lighter and a paper folder of matches. Jack handed Elvis the paint sprayer. A strap made of a strip of torn sheet had been added to the device. Elvis hung the sprayer over his shoulder, reached inside his belt and got out a flattened, half-smoked stogie he had been saving for a special occasion. An occasion he had begun to think would never arrive. He clenched the cigar between his teeth, picked the matches from the seat of the wheelchair, and lit his cigar. It tasted like a dog turd, but he puffed it anyway. He tossed the folder of matches back on the chair and looked at Jack, said, "Let's do it, amigo."

Jack put the matches and the lighter in his suit pocket. He sat down in the wheelchair, kicked the foot stanchions into place and rested his feet on them. He leaned back slightly and flicked a switch on the armrest. The electric motor hummed, the chair eased forward.

"Meet you there," said Jack. He rolled down the concrete ramp, on out to the circular drive, and disappeared around the edge of the building.

Elvis looked at his watch. It was nearly 2:45. He had to hump it. He clenched both hands on the walker and started truckin'.

Fifteen exhausting minutes later, out back, Elvis settled in against the door, the place where Bubba Ho-Tep had been entering and exiting. The shadows fell over him like an umbrella. He propped the paint gun across the walker and used his scarf to wipe the sweat off his forehead.

In the old days, after a performance, he'd wipe his face with it and toss it to some woman in the crowd, watch as she creamed on herself. Panties and hotel keys would fly onto the stage at that point, bouquets of roses.

Tonight, he hoped Bubba Ho-Tep didn't use the scarf to wipe his ass after shitting him down the crapper.

Elvis looked where the circular concrete drive rose up slightly to the right, and there, seated in the wheelchair, very patient and still, was Jack. The moonlight spread over Jack and made him look like a concrete yard gnome.

Apprehension spread over Elvis like a dose of the measles. He thought, *Bubba Ho-Tep comes out of that creek bed, he's going to come out hungry and pissed, and when I try to stop him, he's going to jam this paint gun up my ass, then jam me and that wheelchair up Jack's ass.*

He puffed his cigar so fast it made him dizzy. He looked out at the creek bank, and where the trees gaped wide, a figure rose up like a cloud of termites, scrabbled like a crab, flowed like water, chunked and chinked like a mass of oil field tools tumbling downhill.

Its eyeless sockets trapped the moonlight and held it momentarily before permitting it to pass through and out the back of its head in irregular gold beams. The figure simultaneously gave the impression of shambling and gliding, appeared one moment as nothing more than a shadow surrounded by more active shadows, then it was a heap of twisted brown sticks and dried mud molded into the shape of a human being, and in another moment, it was a cowboy-hatted, booted thing taking each step as if it were its last.

Halfway to the rest home it spotted Elvis, standing in the dark framework of the door. Elvis felt his bowels go loose, but he was determined not to shit his only good stage suit. His knees clacked together like stalks of ribbon cane rattling in a high wind. The dog turd cigar fell from his lips.

He picked up the paint gun and made sure it was ready to spray. He pushed the butt of it into his hip and waited.

Bubba Ho-Tep didn't move. He had ceased to come forward. Elvis began to sweat more than before. His face and chest and balls were soaked. If Bubba Ho-Tep didn't come forward, their plan was fucked. They had to get him in range of the paint sprayer. The idea was he'd soak him with the alcohol, and Jack would come wheeling down from behind, flipping matches or the lighter at Bubba, catching him on fire.

Elvis said softly, "Come and get it, you dead piece of shit."

Jack had nodded off for a moment, but now he came awake. His flesh was tingling. It felt as if tiny ball bearings were being rolled beneath his skin. He looked up and saw Bubba Ho-Tep paused between the creek bank, himself, and Elvis at the door.

Jack took a deep breath. This was not the way they had planned it. The mummy was supposed to go for Elvis because he was blocking the door. But, no soap.

Jack got the matches and the cigarette lighter out of his coat pocket and put them between his legs on the seat of the chair. He put his hand on the gearbox of the wheelchair, gunned it forward. He had to make things happen, had to get Bubba Ho-Tep to follow him, come within range of Elvis's spray gun.

Bubba Ho-Tep stuck out his arm and clotheslined Jack Kennedy. There was a sound like a rifle crack (no question, Warren Commission, this blow was from the front), and over went the chair, and out went Jack, flipping and sliding across the driveway, the cement tearing his suit knees open, gnawing into his hide. The chair, minus its rider, tumbled over and came upright, and, still rolling, veered downhill toward Elvis in the doorway, leaning on his walker, spray gun in hand.

The wheelchair hit Elvis's walker. Elvis bounced against the door, popped forward, grabbed the walker just in time, but dropped his spray gun.

He glanced up to see Bubba Ho-Tep leaning over the unconscious Jack. Bubba Ho-Tep's mouth went wide, and wider yet, and became a black toothless vacuum that throbbed pink as a raw wound in the moonlight; then Bubba Ho-Tep turned his head and the pink was not visible. Bubba Ho-Tep's mouth went down over Jack's face, and as Bubba Ho-Tep sucked, the shadows about it thrashed and gobbled like turkeys.

Elvis used the walker to allow him to bend down and get hold of the paint gun. When he came up with it, he tossed the walker aside, eased himself around, and into the wheelchair. He found the matches and the lighter there. Jack had done what he had done to distract Bubba Ho-Tep, to try and bring him down closer to the door. But he had failed. Yet by accident, he had provided Elvis with the instruments of mummy destruction, and now it was up to him to do what he and Jack had hoped to do together. Elvis put the matches inside his open-chested outfit, pushed the lighter tight under his ass.

Elvis let his hand play over the wheelchair switches, as nimbly as he had once played with studio keyboards. He roared the wheelchair up the incline toward Bubba Ho-Tep, terrified, but determined, and as he rolled, in a voice cracking, but certainly reminiscent of him at his best, he began to sing "Don't Be Cruel," and within instants, he was on Bubba Ho-Tep and his busy shadows.

Bubba Ho-Tep looked up as Elvis roared into range, singing. Bubba Ho-Tep's open mouth irised to normal size, and teeth, formerly nonexistent, rose up in his gums like little black stumps. Electric locusts crackled and hopped in his empty sockets. He yelled something in Egyptian. Elvis saw the words jump out of Bubba Ho-Tep's mouth in visible hieroglyphics like dark beetles and sticks.

 *

Elvis bore down on Bubba Ho-Tep. When he was in range, he ceased singing, and gave the paint sprayer trigger a squeeze. Rubbing alcohol squirted from the sprayer and struck Bubba Ho-Tep in the face.

Elvis swerved, screeched around Bubba Ho-Tep in a sweeping circle, came back, the lighter in his hand. As he neared Bubba, the shadows swarming around the mummy's head separated and flew high up above him like startled bats.

The black hat Bubba wore wobbled and sprouted wings and flapped away from his head, becoming what it had always been, a living shadow. The shadows came down in a rush, screeching like harpies. They swarmed over Elvis's face, giving him the sensation of skinned animal pelts—blood-side in—being dragged over his flesh.

Bubba bent forward at the waist like a collapsed puppet, bopped his head against the cement drive. His black bat hat came down out of the dark in a

---

* *"By the unwinking red eye of Ra!"*

swoop, expanding rapidly and falling over Bubba's body, splattering it like spilled ink. Bubba blob-flowed rapidly under the wheels of Elvis's mount and rose up in a dark swell beneath the chair and through the spokes of the wheels and billowed over the front of the chair and loomed upward, jabbing his ravaged, ever-changing face through the flittering shadows, poking it right at Elvis.

Elvis, through gaps in the shadows, saw a face like an old jack-o'-lantern gone black and to rot, with jagged eyes, nose, and mouth. And that mouth spread tunnel-wide, and down that tunnel-mouth Elvis could see the dark and awful forever that was Bubba's lot, and Elvis clicked the lighter to flame, and the flame jumped, and the alcohol lit Bubba's face, and Bubba's head turned baby-eye blue, flowed jet-quick away, splashed upward like a black wave carrying a blazing oil slick. Then Bubba came down in a shuffle of blazing sticks and dark mud, a tar baby on fire, fleeing across the concrete drive toward the creek. The guardian shadows flapped after it, fearful of being abandoned.

Elvis wheeled over to Jack, leaned forward and whispered, "Mr. Kennedy."

Jack's eyelids fluttered. He could barely move his head, and something grated in his neck when he did. "The president is soon dead," he said, and his clenched fist throbbed and opened, and out fell a wad of paper. "You got to get him."

Jack's body went loose and his head rolled back on his damaged neck and the moon showed double in his eyes. Elvis swallowed and saluted Jack. "Mr. President," he said.

Well, at least he had kept Bubba Ho-Tep from taking Jack's soul. Elvis leaned forward, picked up the paper Jack had dropped. He read it aloud to himself in the moonlight: "You nasty thing from beyond the dead. No matter what you think and do, good things will never come to you. If evil is your black design, you can bet the goodness of the Light Ones will kick your bad behind."

That's it? thought Elvis. *That's the chant against evil from the* Book of the Soul? *Yeah, right, boss. And what kind of decoder ring does that come with? Shit, it doesn't even rhyme well.*

Elvis looked up. Bubba Ho-Tep had fallen down in a blue blaze, but he was rising up again, preparing to go over the lip of the creek, down to wherever his sanctuary was.

Elvis pulled around Jack and gave the wheelchair full throttle. He gave out with a rebel cry. His white scarf fluttered in the wind as he thundered forward.

Bubba Ho-Tep's flames had gone out. He was on his feet. His head was hissing gray smoke into the crisp night air. He turned completely to face Elvis, stood defiant, raised an arm and shook a fist. He yelled, and once again Elvis saw the hieroglyphics leap out of his mouth. The characters danced in a row, briefly—

—and vanished.

Elvis let go of the protective paper. It was dogshit. What was needed here was action.

When Bubba Ho-Tep saw Elvis was coming, chair geared to high, holding the paint sprayer in one hand, he turned to bolt, but Elvis was on him.

Elvis stuck out a foot and hit Bubba Ho-Tep in the back, and his foot went right through Bubba. The mummy squirmed, spitted on Elvis's leg. Elvis fired the paint sprayer, as Bubba Ho-Tep, himself, and chair went over the creek bank in a flash of moonlight and a tumble of shadows.

Elvis screamed as the hard ground and sharp stones snapped his body like a piñata. He made the trip with Bubba Ho-Tep still on his leg, and when he quit sliding, he ended up close to the creek.

Bubba Ho-Tep, as if made of rubber, twisted around on Elvis's leg, and looked at him.

Elvis still had the paint sprayer. He had clung to it as if it were a life preserver. He gave Bubba another dose. Bubba's right arm flopped way out and ran along the ground and found a hunk of wood that had washed up on the edge of the creek, gripped it, and swung the long arm back. The arm came around and hit Elvis on the side of the head with the wood.

Elvis fell backwards. The paint sprayer flew from his hands. Bubba Ho-Tep was leaning over him. He hit Elvis again with the wood. Elvis felt himself

---

* *"Eat the dog dick of Anubis, you ass wipe!"*

going out. He knew if he did, not only was he a dead sonofabitch, but so was his soul. He would be just so much crap; no afterlife for him; no reincarnation; no angels with harps. Whatever lay beyond would not be known to him. It would all end right here for Elvis Presley. Nothing left but a quick flush.

Bubba Ho-Tep's mouth loomed over Elvis's face. It looked like an open manhole. Sewage fumes came out of it.

Elvis reached inside his open jumpsuit and got hold of the folder of matches. Laying back, pretending to nod out so as to bring Bubba Ho-Tep's ripe mouth closer, he thumbed back the flap on the matches, thumbed down one of the paper sticks, and pushed the sulfurous head of the match across the black strip.

Just as Elvis felt the cloying mouth of Bubba Ho-Tep falling down on his kisser like a Venus flytrap, the entire folder of matches ignited in Elvis's hand, burned him and made him yell.

The alcohol on Bubba's body called the flames to it, and Bubba burst into a stalk of blue flame, singeing the hair off Elvis's head, scorching his eyebrows down to nubs, blinding him until he could see nothing more than a scalding white light.

Elvis realized that Bubba Ho-Tep was no longer on or over him, and the white light became a stained white light, then a gray light, and eventually, the world, like a Polaroid negative developing, came into view, greenish at first, then full of the night's colors.

Elvis rolled on his side and saw the moon floating in the water. He saw, too, a scarecrow floating in the water, the straw separating from it, the current carrying it away.

No, not a scarecrow. Bubba Ho-Tep. For all his dark magic and ability to shift, or to appear to shift, fire had done him in, or had it been the stupid words from Jack's book on souls? Or both?

It didn't matter. Elvis got up on one elbow and looked at the corpse. The water was dissolving it more rapidly and the current was carrying it away.

Elvis fell over on his back. He felt something inside him grate against something soft. He felt like a water balloon with a hole poked in it.

He was going down for the last count, and he knew it.

But I've still got my soul, he thought. *Still mine. All mine. And the folks in Shady Grove, Dillinger, the Blue Yodeler, all of them, they have theirs, and they'll keep 'em.*

Elvis stared up at the stars between the forked and twisted boughs of an oak. He could see a lot of those beautiful stars, and he realized now that the constellations looked a little like the outlines of great hieroglyphics. He turned away from where he was looking, and to his right, seeming to sit on the edge of the bank, were more stars, more hieroglyphics.

He rolled his head back to the figures above him, rolled to the right and looked at those. Put them together in his mind.

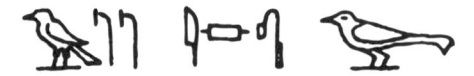

He smiled. Suddenly, he thought he could read hieroglyphics after all, and what they spelled out against the dark beautiful night was simple, and yet profound.

ALL IS WELL.

Elvis closed his eyes and did not open them again.

THE END

Thanks to

Mark Nelson for translating East Texas "Egyptian" hieroglyphics.

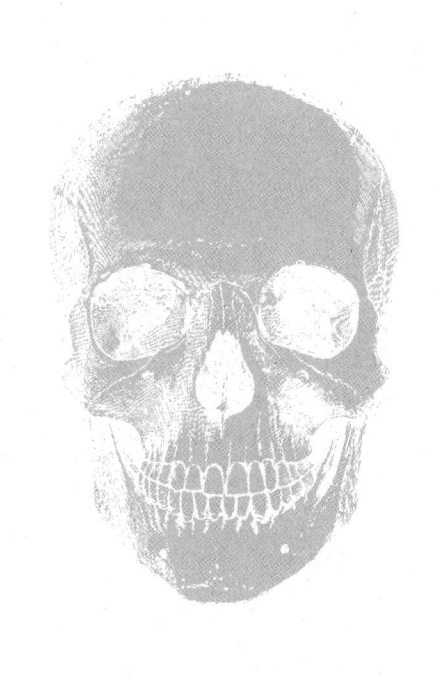

This is possibly my first truly good short story, though "White Rabbit" certainly showed that I was moving in my own direction and opened the door for this one, different as they might be.

Nostalgia can hide some ugly facts. Wishful thinking isn't always what you think it might be if your wish were granted.

I was inspired to write this story by a silver fish mobile my wife bought for us. I was lying on the couch looking at it when I drifted off, and the general idea of this story appeared.

Stories, they come from anywhere and everywhere.

Fish Night

IT WAS A bleached-bone afternoon with a cloudless sky and a monstrous sun.

The air trembled like a mass of gelatinous ectoplasm. No wind blew.

Through the swelter came a worn black Plymouth, coughing and belching white smoke from beneath its hood. It wheezed twice, backfired loudly, died by the side of the road.

The driver got out and went around to the hood. He was a man in the hard winter years of life, with dead brown hair and a heavy belly riding his hips. His shirt was open to the navel, the sleeves rolled up past his elbows. The hair on his chest and arms was gray.

A younger man climbed out on the passenger side, went around front too. Yellow sweat explosions stained the pits of his white shirt. An unfastened, striped tie was draped over his neck like a pet snake that had died in its sleep.

"Well?" the younger man asked.

The old man said nothing. He opened the hood. A calliope note of steam blew out from the radiator in a white puff, rose to the sky, turned clear.

"Damn," the old man said, and he kicked the bumper of the Plymouth as if he were kicking a foe in the teeth. He got little satisfaction out of the action, just a nasty scuff on his brown wingtip and a jar to his ankle that hurt like hell.

"Well?" the young man repeated.

"Well what? What do you think? Dead as the can-opener trade this week. Deader. The radiator's chickenpocked with holes."

"Maybe someone will come by and give us a hand."

"Sure."

"A ride anyway."

"Keep thinking that, college boy."

"Someone is bound to come along," the young man said.

"Maybe. Maybe not. Who else takes these cutoffs? The main highway, that's where everyone is. Not this little no-account shortcut." He finished by glaring at the young man.

"I didn't make you take it," the young man snapped. "It was on the map. I told you about it, that's all. You chose it. You're the one that decided to take it. It's not my fault. Besides, who'd have expected the car to die?"

"I did tell you to check the water in the radiator, didn't I? Wasn't that back as far as El Paso?"

"I checked. It had water then. I tell you, it's not my fault. You're the one that's done all the Arizona driving."

"Yeah, yeah," the old man said, as if this were something he didn't want to hear. He turned to look up the highway.

No cars. No trucks. Just heat waves and miles of empty concrete in sight.

They seated themselves on the hot ground with their backs to the car. That way it provided some shade—but not much. They sipped on a jug of lukewarm water from the Plymouth and spoke little until the sun fell down. By then they had both mellowed a bit. The heat had vacated the sands and the desert chill had settled in. Where the warmth had made the pair snappy, the cold drew them together.

The old man buttoned his shirt and rolled down his sleeves while the young man rummaged a sweater out of the back seat. He put the sweater on, sat back down. "I'm sorry about this," he said suddenly.

"Wasn't your fault. Wasn't anyone's fault. I just get to yelling sometime, taking out the can-opener trade on everything but the can openers and myself. The days of the door-to-door salesman are gone, son."

"And I thought I was going to have an easy summer job," the young man said.

The old man laughed. "Bet you did. They talk a good line, don't they?"

"I'll say!"

"Make it sound like found money, but there ain't no found money, boy. Ain't nothing simple in this world. The company is the only one ever makes any money. We just get tireder and older with more holes in our shoes. If I had any sense I'd have quit years ago. All you got to make is this summer—"

"Maybe not that long."

"Well, this is all I know. Just town after town, motel after motel, house after house, looking at people through screen wire while they shake their heads 'no.' Even the cockroaches at the sleazy motels begin to look like little fellows you've seen before, like maybe they're door-to-door peddlers that have to rent rooms too."

The young man chuckled. "You might have something there."

They sat quietly for a moment, welded in silence. Night had full grip on the desert now. A mammoth gold moon and billions of stars cast a whitish glow from eons away.

The wind picked up. The sand shifted, found new places to lie down. The undulations of it, slow and easy, were reminiscent of the midnight sea. The young man, who had crossed the Atlantic by ship once, said as much.

"The sea?" the old man replied. "Yes, yes, exactly like that. I was thinking the same. That's part of the reason it bothers me. Part of why I was stirred up this afternoon. Wasn't just the heat doing it. There are memories of mine out here," he nodded at the desert, "and they're visiting me again."

The young man made a face. "I don't understand."

"You wouldn't. You shouldn't. You'd think I'm crazy."

"I already think you're crazy. So tell me."

The old man smiled. "All right, but don't you laugh."

"I won't."

A moment of silence moved in between them. Finally the old man said, "It's fish night, boy. Tonight's the full moon and this is the right part of the desert if memory serves me, and the feel is right—I mean, doesn't the night feel like it's made up of some soft fabric, that it's different from other nights, that it's like being inside a big, dark bag, the sides sprinkled with glitter, a spotlight at the top, at the open mouth, to serve as a moon?"

"You lost me."

The old man sighed. "But it feels different. Right? You can feel it, too, can't you?"

"I suppose. Sort of thought it was just the desert air. I've never camped out in the desert before, and I guess it is different."

"Different, all right. You see, this is the road I got stranded on twenty years back. I didn't know it at first, least not consciously. But down deep in my gut I must have known all along I was taking this road, tempting fate, offering it, as the football people say, an instant replay."

"I still don't understand about fish night. What do you mean, you were here before?"

"Not this exact spot, somewhere along in here. This was even less of a road back then than it is now. The Navajos were about the only ones who traveled it. My car conked out, like this one today, and I started walking instead of waiting. As I walked the fish came out. Swimming along in the starlight pretty as you please. Lots of them. All the colors of the rainbow. Small ones, big ones, thick ones, thin ones. Swam right up to me . . . *right through me!* Fish just as far as you could see. High up and low down to the ground.

"Hold on, boy. Don't start looking at me like that. Listen: You're a college boy, you know something about these things. I mean, about what was here before we were, before we crawled out of the sea and changed enough to call ourselves men. Weren't we once just slimy things, brothers to the things that swim?"

"I guess, but—"

"Millions and millions of years ago this desert was a sea bottom. Maybe even the birthplace of man. Who knows? I read that in some science books. And I got to thinking this: If the ghosts of people who have lived can haunt houses, why can't the ghosts of creatures long dead haunt where they once lived, float about in a ghostly sea?"

"Fish with a soul?"

"Don't go small-mind on me, boy. Look here: Some of the Indians I've talked to up north tell me about a thing they call the manitou. That's a spirit. They believe everything has one. Rocks, trees, you name it. Even if the rock wears to dust or the tree gets cut to lumber, the manitou of it is still around."

"Then why can't you see these fish all the time?"

"Why can't we see ghosts all the time? Why do some of us never see them? Time's not right, that's why. It's a precious situation, and I figure it's like some fancy time lock—like the banks use. The lock clicks open at the bank, and there's the money. Here it ticks open and we get the fish of a world long gone."

"Well, it's something to think about," the young man managed.

The old man grinned at him. "I don't blame you for thinking what you're thinking. But this happened to me twenty years ago and I've never forgotten it. I saw those fish for a good hour before they disappeared. A Navajo came along in an old pickup right after and I bummed a ride into town with him. I told him what I'd seen. He just looked at me and grunted. But I could tell he knew what I was talking about. He'd seen it, too, and probably not for the first time.

"I've heard that Navajos don't eat fish for some reason or another, and I bet it's the fish in the desert that keep them from it. Maybe they hold them sacred. And why not? It was like being in the presence of the Creator; like crawling back inside your mother and being unborn again, just kicking around in the liquids with no cares in the world."

"I don't know. That sounds sort of . . ."

"Fishy?" The old man laughed. "It does, it does. So this Navajo drove me to town. Next day I got my car fixed and went on. I've never taken that cutoff again—until today, and I think that was more than accident. My subconscious was driving me. That night scared me, boy, and I don't mind admitting it. But it was wonderful, too, and I've never been able to get it out of my mind."

The young man didn't know what to say.

The old man looked at him and smiled. "I don't blame you," he said. "Not even a little bit. Maybe I am crazy."

They sat awhile longer with the desert night, and the old man took his false teeth out and poured some of the warm water on them to clean them of coffee and cigarette residue.

"I hope we don't need that water," the young man said.

"You're right. Stupid of me! We'll sleep awhile, start walking before daylight. It's not too far to the next town. Ten miles at best." He put his teeth back in. "We'll be just fine."

The young man nodded.

No fish came. They did not discuss it. They crawled inside the car, the young man in the front seat, the old man in the back. They used their spare clothes to bundle under, to pad out the cold fingers of the night.

Near midnight the old man came awake suddenly and lay with his hands behind his head and looked up and out the window opposite him, studied the crisp desert sky.

And a fish swam by.

Long and lean and speckled with all the colors of the world, flicking its tail as if in goodbye. Then it was gone.

The old man sat up. Outside, all about, were the fish—all sizes, colors, and shapes.

"Hey, boy, wake up!"

The younger man moaned.

"Wake up!"

The young man, who had been resting face down on his arms, rolled over. "What's the matter? Time to go?"

"The fish."

"Not again."

"Look!"

The young man sat up. His mouth fell open. His eyes bloated. Around and around the car, faster and faster in whirls of dark color, swam all manner of fish.

"Well, I'll be. . . . *How?*"

"I told you, I told you."

The old man reached for the door handle, but before he could pull it a fish swam lazily through the back window glass, swirled about the car, once, twice, passed through the old man's chest, whipped up and went out through the roof.

The old man cackled, jerked open the door. He bounced around beside the road. Leaped up to swat his hands through the spectral fish. "Like soap bubbles," he said. "No. Like smoke!"

The young man, his mouth still agape, opened his door and got out. Even high up he could see the fish. Strange fish, like nothing he'd ever seen pictures of or imagined. They flitted and skirted about like flashes of light.

As he looked up, he saw, nearing the moon, a big dark cloud. The only cloud in the sky. That cloud tied him to reality suddenly, and he thanked the heavens for it. Normal things still happened. The whole world had not gone insane.

After a moment the old man quit hopping among the fish and came out to lean on the car and hold his hand to his fluttering chest.

"Feel it, boy? Feel the presence of the sea? Doesn't it feel like the beating of your own mother's heart while you float inside the womb?"

And the younger man had to admit that he felt it, that inner rolling rhythm that is the tide of life and the pulsating heart of the sea.

"How?" the young man said. "Why?"

"The time lock, boy. The locks clicked open and the fish are free. Fish from a time before man was man. Before civilization started weighing us down. I know it's true. The truth's been in me all the time. It's in us all."

"It's like time travel," the young man said. "From the past to the future, they've come all that way."

"Yes, yes, that's it. . . . Why, if they can come to our world, why can't we go to theirs? Release that spirit inside of us, tune into their time?"

"Now, wait a minute. . . ."

"My God, that's it! They're pure, boy, pure. Clean and free of civilization's trappings. That must be it! They're pure and we're not. We're weighted down with technology. These clothes. That car."

The old man started removing his clothes.

"Hey!" the young man said. "You'll freeze."

"If you're pure, if you're completely pure," the old man mumbled, "that's it . . . yeah, that's the key."

"You've gone crazy."

"I won't look at the car," the old man yelled, running across the sand, trailing the last of his clothes behind him. He bounced about the desert like a jackrabbit. "God, God, nothing is happening, nothing," he moaned. "This isn't my world. I'm of that world. I want to float free in the belly of the sea, away from can openers and cars and—"

The young man called the old man's name. The old man did not seem to hear.

"I want to leave here!" the old man yelled. Suddenly he was springing about again. "The teeth!" he yelled. "It's the teeth. Dentist, science, foo!" He punched a hand into his mouth, plucked the teeth free, tossed them over his shoulder.

Even as the teeth fell the old man rose. He began to stroke. To swim up and up and up, moving like a pale pink seal among the fish.

In the light of the moon the young man could see the pooched jaws of the old man, holding the last of the future's air. Up went the old man, up, up, up, swimming strong in the long lost waters of a time gone by.

The young man began to strip off his own clothes. Maybe he could nab him, pull him down, put the clothes on him. Something . . . God, something. . . . But, what if *he* couldn't come back? And there were the fillings in his teeth, the metal rod in his back from a motorcycle accident. No, unlike the old man, this was his world and he was tied to it. There was nothing he could do.

A great shadow weaved in front of the moon, made a wriggling slat of darkness that caused the young man to let go of his shirt buttons and look up.

A black rocket of a shape moved through the invisible sea: a shark, the granddaddy of all sharks, the seed for all of man's fears of the deeps.

And it caught the old man in its mouth, began swimming upward toward the golden light of the moon. The old man dangled from the creature's mouth like a ragged rat from a house cat's jaws. Blood blossomed out of him, coiled darkly in the invisible sea.

The young man trembled. "Oh God," he said once.

Then along came that thick dark cloud, rolling across the face of the moon. Momentary darkness.

And when the cloud passed there was light once again, and an empty sky. No fish.

No shark.

And no old man.

Just the night, the moon, and the stars.

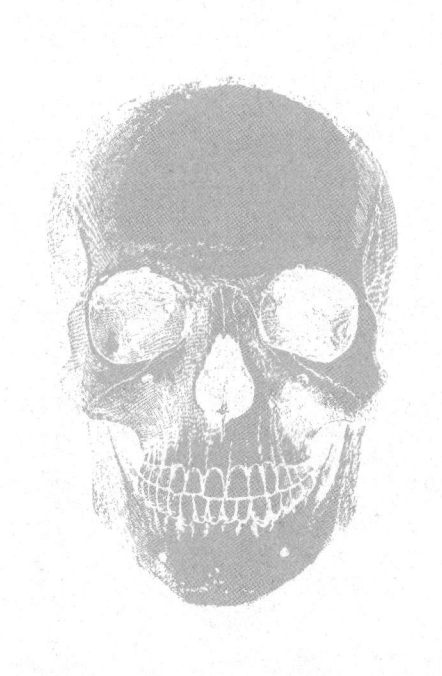

If 'Bubba Ho-Tep' is my best-known story, this is the second best known and is one of my many attacks on racism. It goes at it face-to-face, not sugarcoating or avoiding the ugly aspects of it.

When I wrote this story, I had been out of high school for fifteen years, and I had grown up in a racist society. I remember how mad some folks were when they saw *Night of the Living Dead* and found out it has a Black lead character.

Some of the stuff I heard made me wince. I think that *Night* doesn't get enough good press for having a Black lead, Duane Jones, at the time it did. Jones is a fantastic hero.

Anyway, those memories, and wanting to make a statement about racism, while using humor that would turn so dark it wasn't funny anymore, led me to write this.

It won a Bram Stoker Award. I consider it the best of all my stories. Some readers see words that offend them, but they are supposed to.

It's a story about racism that shows the ugly side. For me, that is far more impactful than trying to avoid the obvious. The less obvious approach is also valid, but for me, this shows exactly what I heard and how people thought.

But even then, there were those who thought even more badly than the main characters. It's a story of the bad guys meeting some *really* bad guys.

I should also note that though this isn't a true story, it's based on some real people, and some of them I knew. I have also taken some bad people and made them worse, but they come from living inspiration—well, living then.

I knew the folks who dragged the dead dog around. That happened. The rest, thankfully not. Most of these people are dead and gone now, one quite recently.

Again, a story, but based in the tone of the time, and with true characters twisted here and there to make my statement and to tell this grim story.

Night They Missed the Horror Show

F THEY'D GONE to the drive-in like they'd planned, none of this would have happened. But Leonard didn't like drive-ins when he didn't have a date, and he'd heard about *Night of the Living Dead*, and he knew a nigger starred in it. He didn't want to see no movie with a nigger star. Niggers chopped cotton, fixed flats, and pimped nigger girls, but he'd never heard of one that killed zombies. And he'd heard, too, that there was a white girl in the movie that let the nigger touch her, and that peeved him. Any white gal that would let a nigger touch her must be the lowest trash in the world. Probably from Hollywood, New York, or Waco, some godforsaken place like that.

Now Steve McQueen would have been all right for zombie killing and girl handling. He would have been the ticket. But a nigger? No sir.

Boy, that Steve McQueen was one cool head. Way he said stuff in them pictures was so good you couldn't help but think someone had written it down for him. He could sure think fast on his feet to come up with the things he said, and he had that real cool, mean look.

Leonard wished he could be Steve McQueen, or Paul Newman even. Someone like that always knew what to say, and he figured they got plenty of bush too. Certainly they didn't get as bored as he did. He was so bored he felt as if he were going to die from it before the night was out. Bored, bored,

bored. Just wasn't nothing exciting about being in the Dairy Queen parking lot leaning on the front of his '64 Impala looking out at the highway. He figured maybe old crazy Harry who janitored at the high school might be right about them flying saucers. Harry was always seeing something. Bigfoot, six-legged weasels, all manner of things. But maybe he was right about the saucers. He'd said he'd seen one a couple nights back hovering over Mud Creek and it was shooting down these rays that looked like wet peppermint sticks. Leonard figured if Harry really had seen the saucers and the rays, then those rays were boredom rays. It would be a way for space critters to get at Earth folks, boring them to death. Getting melted down by heat rays would have been better. That was at least quick, but being bored to death was sort of like being nibbled to death by ducks.

Leonard continued looking at the highway, trying to imagine flying saucers and boredom rays, but he couldn't keep his mind on it. He finally focused on something in the highway. A dead dog.

Not just a dead dog. But a DEAD DOG. The mutt had been hit by a semi at least, maybe several. It looked as if it had rained dog. There were pieces of that pooch all over the concrete and one leg was lying on the curbing on the opposite side, stuck up in such a way that it seemed to be waving hello. Doctor Frankenstein with a grant from Johns Hopkins and assistance from NASA couldn't have put that sucker together again.

Leonard leaned over to his faithful, drunk companion, Billy—known among the gang as Farto, because he was fart-lighting champion of Mud Creek—and said, "See that dog there?"

Farto looked where Leonard was pointing. He hadn't noticed the dog before, and he wasn't nearly as casual about it as Leonard. The puzzle-piece hound brought back memories. It reminded him of a dog he'd had when he was thirteen. A big, fine German shepherd that loved him better than his mama.

Sonofabitch dog tangled its chain through and over a barbed-wire fence somehow and hung itself. When Farto found the dog its tongue looked like a stuffed black sock and he could see where its claws had just been able to scrape the ground, but not quite enough to get a toehold.

It looked as if the dog had been scratching out some sort of a coded message in the dirt. When Farto told his old man about it later, crying as he did, his old man laughed and said, "Probably a goddamn suicide note."

Now, as he looked out at the highway, and his whiskey-laced Coke collected warmly in his gut, he felt a tear form in his eyes. Last time he'd felt that sappy was when he'd won the fart-lighting championship with a four-inch burner that singed the hairs of his ass and the gang awarded him with a pair of colored boxing shorts. Brown and yellow ones so he could wear them without having to change them too often.

So there they were, Leonard and Farto, parked outside the DQ, leaning on the hood of Leonard's Impala, sipping Coke and whiskey, feeling bored and blue and horny, looking at a dead dog and having nothing to do but go to a show with a nigger starring in it. Which, to be up front, wouldn't have been so bad if they'd had dates. Dates could make up for a lot of sins, or help make a few good ones, depending on one's outlook.

But the night was criminal. Dates they didn't have. Worse yet, wasn't a girl in the entire high school would date them. Not even Marylou Flowers, and she had some kind of disease.

All this nagged Leonard something awful. He could see what the problem was with Farto. He was ugly. Had the kind of face that attracted flies. And though being fart-lighting champion of Mud Creek had a certain prestige among the gang, it lacked a certain something when it came to charming the gals.

But for the life of him, Leonard couldn't figure his own problem. He was handsome, had some good clothes, and his car ran good when he didn't buy that old cheap gas. He even had a few bucks in his jeans from breaking into washaterias. Yet his right arm had damn near grown to the size of his thigh from all the whacking off he did. Last time he'd been out with a girl had been a month ago, and as he'd been out with her along with nine other guys, he wasn't rightly sure he could call that a date. He wondered about it so much, he'd asked Farto if he thought it qualified as a date. Farto, who had been fifth in line, said he didn't think so, but if Leonard wanted to call it one, wasn't no skin off his back.

But Leonard didn't want to call it a date. It just didn't have the feel of one, lacked that something special. There was no romance to it.

True, Big Red had called him Honey when he put the mule in the barn, but she called everyone Honey—except Stoney. Stoney was Possum Sweets, and he was the one who talked her into wearing the grocery bag with the mouth and eye holes. Stoney was like that. He could sweet-talk the camel out from under a sand nigger. When he got through chatting Big Red down, she was plumb proud to wear that bag.

When finally it came his turn to do Big Red, Leonard had let her take the bag off as a gesture of goodwill. That was a mistake. He just hadn't known a good thing when he had it. Stoney had had the right idea. The bag coming off spoiled everything. With it on, it was sort of like balling the Lone Hippo or some such thing, but with the bag off, you were absolutely certain what you were getting, and it wasn't pretty.

Even closing his eyes hadn't helped. He found that the ugliness of that face had branded itself on the back of his eyeballs. He couldn't even imagine the sack back over her head. All he could think about was that puffy, too-painted face with the sort of bad complexion that began at the bone.

He'd gotten so disappointed, he'd had to fake an orgasm and get off before his hooter shriveled up and his Trojan fell off and was lost in the vacuum.

Thinking back on it, Leonard sighed. It would certainly be nice for a change to go with a girl that didn't pull the train or have a hole between her legs that looked like a manhole cover ought to be on it. Sometimes he wished he could be like Farto, who was as happy as if he had good sense. Anything thrilled him. Give him a can of Wolf Brand Chili, a big moon pie, Coke and whiskey and he could spend the rest of his life fucking Big Red and lighting the gas out of his asshole.

God, but this was no way to live. No women and no fun. Bored, bored, bored. Leonard found himself looking overhead for spaceships and peppermint-colored boredom rays, but he saw only a few moths fluttering drunkenly through the beams of the DQ's lights.

Lowering his eyes back to the highway and the dog, Leonard had a sudden flash. "Why don't we get the chain out of the back and hook it up to Rex there? Take him for a ride?"

"You mean drag his dead ass around?" Farto asked.

Leonard nodded.

"Beats stepping on a tack," Farto said.

They drove the Impala into the middle of the highway at a safe moment and got out for a look. Up close the mutt was a lot worse. Its innards had been mashed out of its mouth and asshole and it stunk something awful. The dog was wearing a thick, metal-studded collar and they fastened one end of their fifteen-foot chain to that and the other to the rear bumper.

Bob, the Dairy Queen manager, noticed them through the window, came outside and yelled, "What are you fucking morons doing?"

"Taking this doggie to the vet," Leonard said. "We think this sumbitch looks a might peaked. He may have been hit by a car."

"That's so fucking funny I'm about to piss myself," Bob said.

"Old folks have that problem," Leonard said.

Leonard got behind the wheel and Farto climbed in on the passenger side. They maneuvered the car and dog around and out of the path of a tractor-trailer truck just in time. As they drove off, Bob screamed after them, "I hope you two no-dicks wrap that Chevy piece of shit around a goddamn pole."

As they roared along, parts of the dog, like crumbs from a flaky loaf of bread, came off. A tooth here. Some hair there. A string of guts. A dewclaw. And some unidentifiable pink stuff. The metal-studded collar and chain threw up sparks now and then like fiery crickets. Finally they hit seventy-five and the dog was swinging wider and wider on the chain, like it was looking for an opportunity to pass.

Farto poured him and Leonard Cokes and whiskey as they drove along. He handed Leonard his paper cup and Leonard knocked it back, a lot happier now than he had been a moment ago. Maybe this night wasn't going to turn out so bad after all.

They drove by a crowd at the side of the road, a tan station wagon and a wreck of a Ford up on a jack. At a glance they could see that there was a nigger in the middle of the crowd and he wasn't witnessing to the white boys. He was hopping around like a pig with a hotshot up his ass, trying to find a break in the white boys so he could make a run for it. But there wasn't any break to be found and there were too many to fight. Nine white boys were knocking him around like he was a pinball and they were a malicious machine.

"Ain't that one of our niggers?" Farto asked. "And ain't that some of the White Tree football players that's trying to kill him?"

"Scott," Leonard said, and the name was dogshit in his mouth. It had been Scott who had outdone him for the position of quarterback on the team. That damn jig could put together a play more tangled than a can of fishing worms, but it damn near always worked. And he could run like a spotted-ass ape.

As they passed, Farto said, "We'll read about him tomorrow in the papers."

But Leonard drove only a short way before slamming on the brakes and whipping the Impala around. Rex swung way out and clipped off some tall, dried sunflowers at the edge of the road like a scythe.

"We gonna go back and watch?" Farto asked. "I don't think them White Tree boys would bother us none if that's all we was gonna do, watch."

"He may be a nigger," Leonard said, not liking himself, "but he's our nigger and we can't let them do that. They kill him, they'll beat us in football."

Farto saw the truth of this immediately. "Damn right. They can't do that to our nigger."

Leonard crossed the road again and went straight for the White Tree boys, hit down hard on the horn. The White Tree boys abandoned beating their prey and jumped in all directions. Bullfrogs couldn't have done any better.

Scott stood startled and weak where he was, his knees bent in and touching one another, his eyes as big as pizza pans. He had never noticed how big grillwork was. It looked like teeth there in the night and the headlights looked like eyes. He felt like a stupid fish about to be eaten by a shark.

Leonard braked hard, but off the highway in the dirt it wasn't enough to keep from bumping Scott, sending him flying over the hood and against the glass where his face mashed to it then rolled away, his shirt snagging one of the windshield wipers and pulling it off.

Leonard opened the car door and called to Scott who lay on the ground, "It's now or never."

A White Tree boy made for the car, and Leonard pulled the taped hammer handle out from beneath the seat and stepped out of the car and hit him with it. The White Tree boy went down to his knees and said something that sounded like French but wasn't. Leonard grabbed Scott by the back of the shirt and pulled him up and guided him around and threw him into the open door. Scott scrambled over the front seat and into the back. Leonard threw the hammer handle at one of the White Tree boys and stepped back, whirled into the car behind the wheel. He put the car in gear again and stepped on the gas. The Impala lurched forward, and with one hand on the door Leonard flipped it wider and clipped a White Tree boy with it as if he were flexing a wing. The car bumped back on the highway and the chain swung out and Rex cut the feet out from under two White Tree boys as neatly as he had taken down the dried sunflowers.

Leonard looked in his rear-view mirror and saw two White Tree boys carrying the one he had clubbed with the hammer handle to the station wagon. The others he and the dog had knocked down were getting up. One had kicked the jack out from under Scott's car and was using it to smash the headlights and windshield.

"Hope you got insurance on that thing," Leonard said.

"I borrowed it," Scott said, peeling the windshield wiper out of his T-shirt. "Here, you might want this." He dropped the wiper over the seat and between Leonard and Farto.

"That's a borrowed car?" Farto said. "That's worse."

"Nah," Scott said. "Owner don't know I borrowed it. I'd have had that flat changed if that sucker had had him a spare tire, but I got back there and wasn't nothing but the rim, man. Say, thanks for not letting me get killed, else we couldn't have run that ole pig together no more. Course, you almost run over me. My chest hurts."

Leonard checked the rear-view again. The White Tree boys were coming fast. "You complaining?" Leonard said.

"Nah," Scott said, and turned to look through the back glass. He could see the dog swinging in short arcs and pieces of it going wide and far. "Hope you didn't go off and forget your dog tied to the bumper."

"Goddamn," said Farto, "and him registered too."

"This ain't so funny," Leonard said. "Them White Tree boys are gaining."

"Well speed it up," Scott said.

Leonard gnashed his teeth. "I could always get rid of some excess baggage, you know."

"Throwing that windshield wiper out ain't gonna help," Scott said.

Leonard looked in his mirror and saw the grinning nigger in the back seat. Nothing worse than a comic coon. He didn't even look grateful. Leonard had a sudden horrid vision of being overtaken by the White Tree boys. What if he were killed with the nigger? Getting killed was bad enough, but what if tomorrow they found him in a ditch with Farto and the nigger? Or maybe them White Tree boys would make him do something awful with the nigger before they killed them. Like making him suck the nigger's dick or some such thing. Leonard held his foot all the way to the floor; as they passed the Dairy Queen he took a hard left and the car just made it and Rex swung out and slammed a light pole then popped back in line behind them.

The White Tree boys couldn't make the corner in the station wagon and they didn't even try. They screeched into a car lot down a piece, turned around and came back. By that time the taillights of the Impala were moving away from them rapidly, looking like two inflamed hemorrhoids in a dark asshole.

"Take the next right coming up," Scott said, "then you'll see a little road off to the left. Kill your lights and take that."

Leonard hated taking orders from Scott on the field, but this was worse. Insulting. Still, Scott called good plays on the field, and the habit of following instructions from the quarterback died hard. Leonard made the right and Rex made it with them after taking a dip in a water-filled bar ditch.

Leonard saw the little road and killed his lights and took it. It carried them down between several rows of large tin storage buildings, and Leonard pulled between two of them and drove down a little alley lined with more. He stopped the car and they waited and listened. After about five minutes, Farto said, "I think we skunked those father rapers."

"Ain't we a team?" Scott said.

In spite of himself, Leonard felt good. It was like when the nigger called a play that worked and they were all patting each other on the ass and not minding what color the other was because they were just creatures in football suits.

"Let's have a drink," Leonard said.

Farto got a paper cup off the floorboard for Scott and poured him up some warm Coke and whiskey. Last time they had gone to Longview, he had peed in that paper cup so they wouldn't have to stop, but that had long since been poured out, and besides, it was for a nigger. He poured Leonard and himself drinks in their same cups.

Scott took a sip and said, "Shit, man, that tastes kind of rank."

"Like piss," Farto said.

Leonard held up his cup. "To the Mud Creek Wildcats and fuck them White Tree boys."

"You fuck 'em," Scott said. They touched their cups, and at that moment the car filled with light.

Cups upraised, the Three Musketeers turned blinking toward it. The light was coming from an open storage-building door and there was a fat man standing in the center of the glow like a bloated fly on a lemon wedge.

Behind him was a big screen made of a sheet and there was some kind of movie playing on it. And though the light was bright and fading out the movie, Leonard, who was in the best position to see, got a look at it. What he could make out looked like a gal down on her knees sucking this fat guy's dick (the man was visible only from the belly down) and the guy had a short, black revolver pressed to her forehead. She pulled her mouth off of him for an instant and the man came in her face then fired the revolver. The woman's head snapped out of frame and the sheet seemed to drip blood, like dark condensation on a window pane. Then Leonard couldn't see anymore because another man had appeared in the doorway, and like the first he was fat. Both looked like huge bowling balls that had been set on top of shoes. More men appeared behind these two, but one of the fat men turned and held up his hand and the others moved out of sight. The two fat guys stepped outside and one pulled the door almost shut, except for a thin band of light that fell across the front seat of the Impala.

Fat Man Number One went over to the car and opened Farto's door and said, "You fucks and the nigger get out." It was the voice of doom. They had only thought the White Tree boys were dangerous. They realized now they had been kidding themselves. This was the real article. This guy would have eaten the hammer handle and shit a two-by-four.

They got out of the car and the fat man waved them around and lined them up on Farto's side and looked at them. The boys still had their drinks in their hands, and sparing that, they looked like cons in a lineup.

Fat Man Number Two came over and looked at the trio and smiled. It was obvious the fatties were twins. They had the same bad features in the same fat faces. They wore Hawaiian shirts that varied only in profiles and color of parrots and had on white socks and too-short black slacks and black, shiny Italian shoes with toes sharp enough to thread needles.

Fat Man Number One took the cup away from Scott and sniffed it. "A nigger with liquor," he said. "That's like a cunt with brains. It don't go together. Guess you was getting tanked up so you could put the old black snake to some chocolate pudding after a while. Or maybe you was wantin' some vanilla and these boys were gonna set it up."

"I'm not wanting anything but to go home," Scott said.

Fat Man Number Two looked at Fat Man Number One and said, "So he can fuck his mother."

The fatties looked at Scott to see what he'd say but he didn't say anything. They could say he screwed dogs and that was all right with him. Hell, bring one on and he'd fuck it now if they'd let him go afterwards.

Fat Man Number One said, "You boys running around with a jungle bunny makes me sick."

"He's just a nigger from school," Farto said. "We don't like him none. We just picked him up because some White Tree boys were beating on him and we didn't want him to get wrecked on account of he's our quarterback."

"Ah," Fat Man Number One said, "I see. Personally, me and Vinnie don't cotton to niggers in sports. They start taking showers with white boys the next thing they want is to take white girls to bed. It's just one step from one to the other."

"We don't have nothing to do with him playing," Leonard said. "We didn't integrate the schools."

"No," Fat Man Number One said, "that was ole Big Ears Johnson, but you're running around with him and drinking with him."

"His cup's been peed in," Farto said. "That was kind of a joke on him, you see. He ain't our friend, I swear it. He's just a nigger that plays football."

"Peed in his cup, huh?" said the one called Vinnie. "I like that, Pork, don't you? Peed in his fucking cup."

Pork dropped Scott's cup on the ground and smiled at him. "Come here, nigger. I got something to tell you."

Scott looked at Farto and Leonard. No help there. They had suddenly become interested in the toes of their shoes; they examined them as if they were true marvels of the world.

Scott moved toward Pork, and Pork, still smiling, put his arm around Scott's shoulders and walked him toward the big storage building. Scott said, "What are we doing?"

Pork turned Scott around so they were facing Leonard and Farto who still stood holding their drinks and contemplating their shoes. "I didn't want to get it on the new gravel drive," Pork said and pulled Scott's head in close to his own and with his free hand reached back and under his Hawaiian shirt and brought out a short black revolver and put it to Scott's temple and pulled the trigger. There was a snap like a bad knee going out and Scott's feet lifted in unison and went to the side and something dark squirted from his head and his feet swung back toward Pork and his shoes shuffled, snapped, and twisted on the concrete in front of the building.

"Ain't that somethin'," Pork said as Scott went limp and dangled from the thick crook of his arm. "The rhythm is the last thing to go."

Leonard couldn't make a sound. His guts were in his throat. He wanted to melt and run under the car. Scott was dead and the brains that had made plays twisted as fishing worms and commanded his feet on down the football field were scrambled like breakfast eggs.

Farto said, "Holy shit."

Pork let go of Scott and Scott's legs split and he sat down and his head went forward and clapped on the cement between his knees. A dark pool formed under his face.

"He's better off, boys," Vinnie said. "Nigger was begat by Cain and the ape and he ain't quite monkey and he ain't quite man. He's got no place in this world 'cept as a beast of burden. You start trying to train them to do things like drive cars and run with footballs, it ain't nothing but grief to them and the whites too. Get any on your shirt, Pork?"

"Nary a drop."

Vinnie went inside the building and said something to the men there that could be heard but not understood, then he came back with some crumpled newspapers. He went over to Scott and wrapped them around the bloody head and let it drop back on the cement. "You try hosing down that shit when it's dried, Pork, and you wouldn't worry none about that gravel. The gravel ain't nothing."

Then Vinnie said to Farto, "Open the back door of that car." Farto nearly twisted an ankle doing it. Vinnie picked Scott up by the back of the neck and the seat of his pants and threw him onto the floorboard of the Impala.

Pork used the short barrel of his revolver to scratch his nuts, then put the gun behind him, under his Hawaiian shirt. "You boys are gonna go to the river bottoms with us and help us get shed of this nigger."

"Yes, sir," Farto said. "We'll toss his ass in the Sabine for you."

"How about you?" Pork asked Leonard. "You trying to go weak, sister?"

"No," Leonard croaked, "I'm with you."

"That's good," Pork said. "Vinnie, you take the truck and lead the way."

Vinnie took a key from his pocket and unlocked the building door next to the one with the light, went inside, and backed out a sharp-looking gold

Dodge pickup. He backed it in front of the Impala and sat there with the motor running.

"You boys keep your place," Pork said. He went inside the lighted building for a moment. They heard him say to the men inside, "Go on and watch the movies. And save some of them beers for us. We'll be back." Then the light went out and Pork came out, shutting the door. He looked at Leonard and Farto and said, "Drink up, boys."

Leonard and Farto tossed off their warm Coke and whiskey and dropped the cups on the ground.

"Now," Pork said, "you get in the back with the nigger, I'll ride with the driver."

Farto got in the back and put his feet on Scott's knees. He tried not to look at the head wrapped in newspaper, but he couldn't help it. When Pork opened the front door and the overhead light came on Farto saw there was a split in the paper and Scott's eye was visible behind it. Across the forehead the wrapping had turned dark. Down by the mouth and chin was an ad for a fish sale.

Leonard got behind the wheel and started the car. Pork reached over and honked the horn. Vinnie rolled the pickup forward and Leonard followed him to the river bottoms. No one spoke. Leonard found himself wishing with all his heart that he had gone to the outdoor picture show to see the movie with the nigger starring in it.

The river bottoms were steamy and hot from the closeness of the trees and the under- and overgrowth. As Leonard wound the Impala down the narrow red clay roads amidst the dense foliage, he felt as if his car were a crab crawling about in a pubic thatch. He could feel from the way the steering wheel handled that the dog and the chain were catching brush and limbs here and there. He had forgotten all about the dog and now being reminded of it worried him. What if the dog got tangled and he had to stop? He didn't think Pork would take kindly to stopping, not with the dead burrhead on the floorboards and him wanting to get rid of the body.

Finally they came to where the woods cleared out a spell and they drove along the edge of the Sabine River. Leonard hated water and always had. In the moonlight the river looked like poisoned coffee flowing there. Leonard knew there were alligators and gars big as little alligators and water moccasins by the thousands swimming underneath the water, and just the thought of all those slick, darting bodies made him queasy.

They came to what was known as Broken Bridge. It was an old worn-out bridge that had fallen apart in the middle and it was connected to the land on this side only. People sometimes fished off of it. There was no one fishing tonight.

Vinnie stopped the pickup and Leonard pulled up beside it, the nose of the Chevy pointing at the mouth of the bridge. They all got out and Pork made Farto pull Scott out by the feet. Some of the newspapers came loose from Scott's head, exposing an ear and part of the face. Farto patted the newspaper back into place.

"Fuck that," Vinnie said. "It don't hurt if he stains the fucking ground. You two idgits find some stuff to weight this coon down so we can sink him."

Farto and Leonard started scurrying about like squirrels, looking for rocks or big, heavy logs. Suddenly they heard Vinnie cry out. "Godamighty, fucking A. Pork. Come look at this."

Leonard looked over and saw that Vinnie had discovered Rex. He was standing looking down with his hands on his hips. Pork went over to stand by him, then Pork turned around and looked at them. "Hey, you fucks, come here."

Leonard and Farto joined them in looking at the dog. There was mostly just a head now, with a little bit of meat and fur hanging off a spine and some broken ribs.

"That's the sickest fucking thing I've ever fucking seen," Pork said.

"Godamighty," Vinnie said.

"Doing a dog like that. Shit, don't you got no heart? A dog. Man's best fucking goddamn friend and you two killed him like this."

"We didn't kill him," Farto said.

"You trying to fucking tell me he done this to himself? Had a bad fucking day and done this."

"Godamighty," Vinnie said.

"No, sir," Leonard said. "We chained him on there after he was dead."

"I believe that," Vinnie said. "That's some rich shit. You guys murdered this dog. Godamighty."

"Just thinking about him trying to keep up and you fucks driving faster and faster makes me mad as a wasp," Pork said.

"No," Farto said. "It wasn't like that. He was dead and we were drunk and we didn't have anything to do, so we—"

"Shut the fuck up," Pork said, sticking a finger hard against Farto's forehead. "You just shut the fuck up. We can see what the fuck you fucks did. You drug this here dog around until all his goddamn hide came off. . . . What kind of mothers you boys got anyhow that they didn't tell you better about animals?"

"Godamighty," Vinnie said.

Everyone grew silent, stood looking at the dog. Finally Farto said, "You want us to go back to getting some stuff to hold the nigger down?"

Pork looked at Farto as if he had just grown up whole from the ground. "You fucks are worse than niggers, doing a dog like that. Get on back over to the car."

Leonard and Farto went over to the Impala and stood looking down at Scott's body in much the same way they had stared at the dog. There, in the dim moonlight shadowed by trees, the paper wrapped around Scott's head made him look like a giant papier-mâché doll. Pork came up and kicked Scott in the face with a swift motion that sent newspapers flying and sent a thonking sound across the water that made frogs jump.

"Forget the nigger," Pork said. "Give me your car keys, ball sweat." Leonard took out his keys and gave them to Pork and Pork went around to the trunk and opened it. "Drag the nigger over here."

Leonard took one of Scott's arms and Farto took the other and they pulled him over to the back of the car.

"Put him in the trunk," Pork said.

"What for?" Leonard asked.

"'Cause I fucking said so," Pork said.

Leonard and Farto heaved Scott into the trunk. He looked pathetic lying there next to the spare tire, his face partially covered with newspaper. Leonard thought, if only the nigger had stolen a car with a spare he might not be here tonight. He could have gotten that flat changed and driven on before the White Tree boys even came along.

"All right, you get in there with him," Pork said, gesturing to Farto.

"Me?" Farto said.

"Nah, not fucking you, the fucking elephant on your fucking shoulder. Yeah, you, get in the trunk. I ain't got all night."

"Jesus, we didn't do anything to that dog, mister. We told you that. I swear. Me and Leonard hooked him up after he was dead. . . . It was Leonard's idea."

Pork didn't say a word. He just stood there with one hand on the trunk lid looking at Farto. Farto looked at Pork, then the trunk, then back to Pork. Lastly he looked at Leonard, then climbed into the trunk, his back to Scott.

"Like spoons," Pork said, and closed the lid. "Now you, whatsit, Leonard? You come over here." But Pork didn't wait for Leonard to move. He scooped the back of Leonard's neck with a chubby hand and pushed him over to where Rex lay at the end of the chain with Vinnie still looking down at him.

"What you think, Vinnie?" Pork asked. "You got what I got in mind?"

Vinnie nodded. He bent down and took the collar off the dog. He fastened it on Leonard. Leonard could smell the odor of the dead dog in his nostrils. He bent his head and puked.

"There goes my shoeshine," Vinnie said, and he hit Leonard a short one in the stomach. Leonard went to his knees and puked some more of the hot Coke and whiskey.

"You fucks are the lowest pieces of shit on this earth, doing a dog like that," Vinnie said. "A nigger ain't no lower."

Vinnie got some strong fishing line out of the back of the truck and they tied Leonard's hands behind his back. Leonard began to cry.

"Oh shut up," Pork said. "It ain't that bad. Ain't nothing that bad."

But Leonard couldn't shut up. He was caterwauling now and it was echoing through the trees. He closed his eyes and tried to pretend he had gone to the show with the nigger starring in it and had fallen asleep in his car and was having a bad dream, but he couldn't imagine that. He thought about Harry the janitor's flying saucers with the peppermint rays, and he knew if there were any saucers shooting rays down, they weren't boredom rays after all. He wasn't a bit bored.

Pork pulled off Leonard's shoes and pushed him back flat on the ground and pulled off the socks and stuck them in Leonard's mouth so tight he couldn't spit them out. It wasn't that Pork thought anyone was going to hear Leonard, he just didn't like the noise. It hurt his ears.

Leonard lay on the ground in the vomit next to the dog and cried silently. Pork and Vinnie went over to the Impala and opened the doors and stood so they could get a grip on the car to push. Vinnie reached in and moved the gear from park to neutral and he and Pork began to shove the car forward. It moved slowly at first, but as it made the slight incline that led down to the old bridge, it picked up speed. From inside the trunk, Farto hammered lightly at the lid as if he didn't really mean it. The chain took up slack and Leonard felt it jerk and pop his neck. He began to slide along the ground like a snake.

Vinnie and Pork jumped out of the way and watched the car make the bridge and go over the edge and disappear into the water with amazing quietness. Leonard, pulled by the weight of the car, rustled past them. When he hit the bridge, splinters tugged at his clothes so hard they ripped his pants and underwear down almost to his knees.

The chain swung out once toward the edge of the bridge and the rotten railing, and Leonard tried to hook a leg around an upright board there, but that proved wasted. The weight of the car just pulled his knee out of joint and jerked the board out of place with a screech of nails and lumber.

Leonard picked up speed and the chain rattled over the edge of the bridge, into the water and out of sight, pulling its connection after it like a pull toy. The last sight of Leonard was the soles of his bare feet, white as the bellies of fish.

"It's deep there," Vinnie said. "I caught an old channel cat there once, remember? Big sucker. I bet it's over fifty feet deep down there."

They got in the truck and Vinnie cranked it.

"I think we did them boys a favor," Pork said. "Them running around with niggers and what they did to that dog and all. They weren't worth a thing."

"I know it," Vinnie said. "We should have filmed this, Pork, it would have been good. Where the car and that nigger lover went off in the water was choice."

"Nah, there wasn't any women."

"Point," Vinnie said, and he backed around and drove onto the trail that wound its way out of the bottoms.

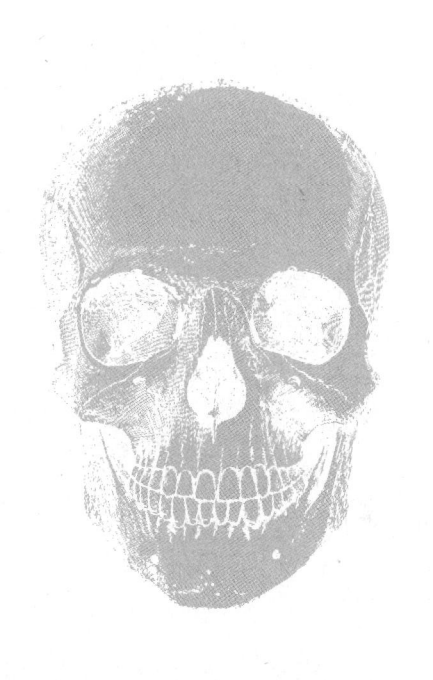

About JOE R. LANSDALE

OE R. LANSDALE is probably the only person in the International Martial Arts Hall of Fame who has received the Edgar, ten Bram Stokers, the Raymond Chandler, the British Fantasy, the Spur, the Golden Lion, the Grinzane Cavour Prize, the Herodotus, and the Inkpot Awards. Lansdale has also been designated as a Grandmaster of Horror by the World Horror Association. His acclaimed works have landed him in the Texas Literary Hall of Fame and the Texas Institute of Letters.

Lansdale's extraordinary output includes mysteries, Westerns, horror, pulp fiction, science fiction, and thrillers. He has written more than 40 novels, 400 shorter works, numerous comic books, and a handful of screenplays as well as creating the Shen Chuan Martial Science. His novels include *Dead in the West* (1986), *The Magic Wagon* (1986), *The Nightrunners* (1987), *The Drive-In* (1988), *Cold in July* (1989), the Edgar Award–winning *The Bottoms* (2000), *A Fine Dark Line* (2002), *Flaming Zeppelins* (2010), *The Thicket* (2013), the Spur Award–winning *Paradise Sky* (2015), *More Better Deals* (2020), *Moon Lake* (2021), and *The Donut Legion* (2023). Beginning with *By Bizarre Hands* (1989), Lansdale's short stories have been collected in several volumes, including *The Best of Joe R. Lansdale* (2010), *Terror Is Our Business* (2018, with Kasey Lansdale), *Things Get Ugly* (2023), and *The*

Senior Girls Bayonet Drill Team and Other Stories (2024). He has edited fifteen anthologies, including *Dark at Heart* (1992, with Karen Lansdale), *Weird Business* (1995, with Richard Klaw), *Retro Pulp Tales* (2006), *Crucified Dreams* (2011), and *The Urban Fantasy Anthology* (2011, with Peter S. Beagle).

Lansdale's most famous creation is the unlikely duo of Hap and Leonard. Hap Collins is white, liberal, and even-tempered. Leonard Pine, who is quick to anger, is Black, conservative, and gay. In a series of 15 novels, spanning *Savage Season* (1990) through *Hatchet Girls* (2025), and several novellas and short stories, the best friends encounter violence, racism, and adventure in their East Texas haunts. The often-humorous tales have garnered much praise and a legion of devoted fans. Many of the Hap and Leonard novellas and shorter tales are collected in *Veil's Visit* (1999), *Hap and Leonard* (2016), *Hap and Leonard: Blood and Lemonade* (2018), *Of Mice and Minestrone* (2020), and *Born for Trouble* (2021). For three seasons, the pair were featured on the television series *Hap and Leonard* (2016–18), starring James Purefoy and Michael K. Williams.

Lansdale's works that have been adapted for film treatments include *Bubba Ho-Tep, Cold in July.* and *The Thicket*; "Incident on and off a Mountain Road" for *Masters of Horror*; "The Dump," "Fish Night," and "The Tall Grass," for the Netflix series *Love, Death & Robots*; "The Companion" for *Creepshow*; and *Christmas with the Dead*, which Lansdale produced with a screenplay by his son, Keith. He has written many screenplays and teleplays, including episodes of *Batman: The Animated Series*. He has also written graphic novels for DC, Marvel, Dark Horse, IDW, and others. The documentary *All Hail the Popcorn King* explores the enduring legacy of Lansdale and his creations.

Lansdale also possesses multiple black belts, and he is the founder of the Shen Chuan Martial Science system and its affiliate, the Shen Chuan Family System.

Joe R. Lansdale lives with his wife, Karen, in Nacogdoches, Texas.

About JOE HILL

JOE HILL IS the #1 *New York Times* bestselling author of *The Fireman*, *Horns*, and *King Sorrow*. He won the Eisner Award for Best Writer, the comic book industry's top award, for his work scripting *Locke & Key*, a seven-volume series cocreated with artist Gabriel Rodriguez. Much of his work has been adapted for film and television, including his novel *NOS4A2*, which became a cult two-season sensation for AMC, and his story "The Black Phone," which was a smash hit for Blumhouse in 2021. He lives in New Hampshire.

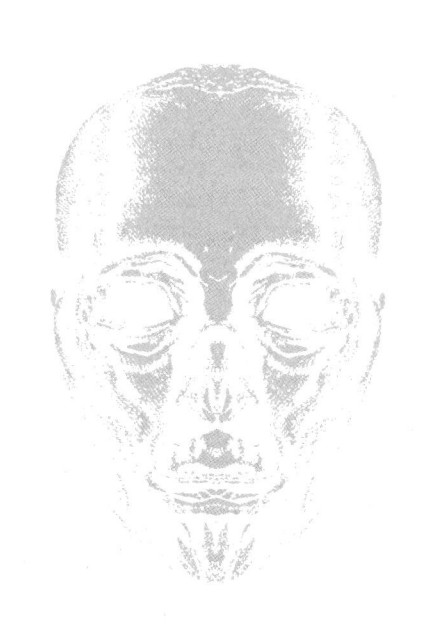